THE LIFE
SHE WAS
GIVEN

Center Point
Large Print

Also by Ellen Marie Wiseman and
available from Center Point Large Print:

Coal River

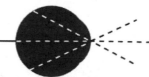

THE LIFE SHE WAS GIVEN

Ellen Marie Wiseman

CENTER POINT LARGE PRINT
THORNDIKE, MAINE

This Center Point Large Print edition is published in the year 2017 by arrangement with Kensington Publishing Corp.

Copyright © 2017 by Ellen Marie Wiseman

The text of this Large Print edition is unabridged. In other aspects, this book may vary from the original edition. Printed in the United States of America on permanent paper. Set in 16-point Times New Roman type.

ISBN: 978-1-68324-503-2

Library of Congress Cataloging-in-Publication Data
Names: Wiseman, Ellen Marie, author.
Title: The life she was given / Ellen Marie Wiseman.
Description: Large print edition. | Thorndike, Maine : Center Point Large Print, [2017]
Identifiers: LCCN 2017026496 | ISBN 9781683245032 (hardcover : alk. paper)
Subjects: LCSH: Large type books. | GSAFD: Mystery fiction.
Classification: LCC PS3623.I833 L54 2017 | DDC 813/.6—dc23
LC record available at https://lccn.loc.gov/2017026496

For Benjamin and Jessica—
You are my greatest accomplishment
and
I love you beyond words.

ACKNOWLEDGMENTS

Once again, it is with great joy and true amazement that I express my appreciation for the people who helped, supported, and believed in me during the writing of this, my fourth novel. To my readers far and wide, my online supporters and friends, and the people who live in and around my community, thank you for your continued enthusiasm and warm encouragement. Thank you for the cards and letters and e-mails, and for the many invitations to visit and speak at your book clubs, libraries, and meetings. Thank you also to everyone who took time out of their busy schedules, and in some cases drove through winter storms, to attend my events. Seeing your smiling faces and hearing your kind words means more than you know.

To my friends and family, thank you for understanding that writing a novel takes considerable time and effort, for cheering me on, for believing in me every time I lost faith in myself, for celebrating my victories, and for always being there when I needed a break.

To my mentor, William Kowalski, thank you for giving me the tools to make a career out of writing. This book, along with the others, would not exist if it weren't for your brilliant advice, gentle guidance, and confidence in me. When we were working together a hundred years ago, I never dreamed it would turn into this!

Thank you to my BP author family for keeping me sane. I'm not sure I would have made it this far without you.

A thousand thanks and heaps of love to Debra Battista, Beth Massey, and Barbara Titterington for reading the first three chapters of the manuscript and for reassuring me that I was on the right track. You have no idea what your uplifting words mean to me.

Again my sincere appreciation goes out to my wonderful editor, John Scognamiglio, for your continued faith in me, for your enthusiasm about my work, and for coming up with the title of this book. Thank you also to Kristine Mills for another amazing cover, and to the rest of the Kensington team for your dedication and hard work behind the scenes. You rock!

I will never find adequate words to thank my trusted friend and brilliant agent, Michael Carr, for everything you do for me. From your always-reliable advice about my career to your spot-on feedback on every manuscript, you continue to be everything I could ask for in an agent. To say I appreciate your wisdom, guidance, and friendship would be an understatement.

As always, I can never thank my beloved family

enough for always supporting and believing in me. To my parents, my brother and his wife, your unconditional love is the foundation on which I've built my life. To my wonderful mother, Sigrid, there are no words to express how much I love, appreciate, and cherish you. Thank you for being my biggest fan, and for helping me believe in myself. The best part of this journey has been making you proud. If I'm half the wife, mother, grandmother, and Oma you are, I will consider my life a success. To my husband, Bill, thank you for riding this roller coaster with me, for being my biggest champion and best friend, and for always, always being there when I need you. I can't imagine sharing this crazy ride with anyone else.

Last but certainly not least, I want to express my endless love and gratitude to my children, Ben, Jessica, Shanae, and Andrew, and my precious grandchildren, Rylee, Harper, and Lincoln. Thank you for loving and believing in me, and for making me the proudest mother and grandmother on earth. You are my reason for living, and my greatest accomplishment. I love you with everything that I am.

CHAPTER 1
Lilly

July 1931
Blackwood Manor Horse Farm
Dobbin's Corner, New York

Nine-year-old Lilly Blackwood stood in the attic dormer of Blackwood Manor for what felt like the thousandth time, wishing the window would open so she could smell the outdoors. Tomorrow was her birthday and she couldn't think of a better present. Sure, Daddy would bring her a new dress and another book when he came home from Pennsylvania, but it had rained earlier and she wanted to know if the outside air felt different than the inside air. She wondered if raindrops made everything feel soft and cool, the way water did when she took a sponge bath. Or did the outside feel warm and sticky, like the air inside her room? She had asked Momma a hundred times to change the window so it would open, and to take the swirly metal off the outside so it would be easier to see out, but as usual, Momma wouldn't listen. If Momma knew Daddy let her play in another part of the attic when she was at church, Daddy would be in big trouble. Even bigger trouble than for teaching her how to read and for giving her a cat on her third birthday. Lilly sighed, picked up her telescope off the sill, and put it to her eye. At least it was summertime and she didn't have to scrape ice off the glass.

Daddy called this time of day twilight, and the outside looked painted in only two colors— green and blue. The row of pine trees on the other side of the barn, past the fields where the horses played, looked like the felt Lilly used for doll blankets. Shadows were everywhere, growing darker by the minute.

Lilly skimmed the edge of the woods, looking for the deer she saw yesterday. There was the crooked willow tree. There was the rock next to the bush that turned red in the winter. There was the broken log next to the stone fence. There was the—She stopped and swung the telescope back to the fence. Something looked different on the other side of the woods, near the train tracks that cut through the faraway meadow. She took the telescope away from her eye, blinked, then looked through it again and gasped. Air squeaked in her chest, like it always did when she got excited or upset.

A string of blue, red, yellow, and green lights— like the ones Daddy put above her bed at Christmastime—hung above a giant glowing house made out of something that looked like cloth. More lights surrounded other houses that looked like fat, little ghosts. Lilly couldn't make out the words, but there were signs too, with letters lit up by colored bulbs. Flags hung from tall poles, and a line of square yellow lights floated above the railroad tracks. It looked like the windows of a stopped train. A really long one.

Lilly put down the telescope, waited for her lungs to stop whistling, then went over to her bookcase and pulled out her favorite picture book. She flipped through the pages until she found what she was looking for—a colorful drawing of a striped tent surrounded by wagons, horses, elephants, and clowns. She hurried back to the window to compare the shape of the tent in the book to the glowing house on the other side of the trees.

She was right.

It was a circus.

And she could see it.

Normally, the only things outside her window were horses and fields, and Daddy and his helper working on the white fences or yellow horse barn. Sometimes, Momma walked across the grass to the barn, her long blond hair trailing behind her like a veil. Other times, trucks pulled into the barn driveway and Daddy's helper put horses in and out of trailers or unloaded bags and hay bales. Once, two men in baggy clothes— Daddy called them *bums*—walked up the drive- way and Daddy's helper came out of the barn with a shotgun. If Lilly was lucky, deer came out of the woods, or raccoons scurried along the fence toward the feed shed, or a train zoomed along the tracks. And if she put her ear to the window, the chug of the train's engine or the shriek of the whistle came through the glass.

But now there was a circus outside her window. A real, live circus! For the first time in her life, she was seeing something different that wasn't in a picture book. It made her happy, but a little bit mad at herself too. If she hadn't been reading all afternoon, she might have seen the train stop to unload. She could have watched the tents go up and caught sight of the elephants and zebras and clowns. Now it was too dark to see anything but lights.

She put down the book and counted the boards around the window. Sometimes counting made her feel better. *One, two, three, four, five.* It didn't help. She couldn't stop thinking about what she'd missed. She pressed her ear against the glass. Maybe she could hear the ringleader's cries or the circus music. The only thing she heard was air squeaking in her chest and her heartbeat going fast.

On the windowsill, her cat, Abby, woke up and blinked. Lilly wrapped an arm around the orange tabby and pulled her close, burying her nose in the animal's soft fur. Abby was her best friend and the smartest cat in the world. She could stand on her hind legs to give kisses and lift her front paw to shake. She even jumped up on Lilly's bed and got down when told.

"I bet Momma will go to the circus," Lilly said. "She doesn't have to worry about people being afraid of her."

The cat purred.

What would it be like to see an elephant in person? Lilly wondered. *What would it feel like to touch its wrinkly skin and look into its big brown eyes? What about riding a pink and white horse on a carousel? Or walking among other people, eating peanuts and cotton candy? What about watching a real, live lion perform?*

As far back as Lilly could remember, there had been times at night after her light was out when she snuggled in her bed, her mind racing with thoughts of leaving her room and going downstairs. She'd read enough books to know there was more than one floor in a house, and she imagined sneaking across the attic, finding a staircase, making her way through the bottom floors of Blackwood Manor, and walking out the front door. She imagined standing with her feet on the earth, taking a deep breath, and for the first time in her life, smelling something besides old wood, cobwebs, and warm dust.

One of her favorite games during Daddy's weekly visits was guessing the different smells on his clothes. Sometimes he smelled like horses and hay, sometimes shoe polish or smoke, sometimes baking bread or—what did he call that stuff that was supposed to be a mix of lemons and cedar trees? Cologne? Whatever it was, it smelled good.

Daddy had told her about the outside world and she had read about it in books, but she had no idea how grass felt between her toes, or how tree bark felt in her hand. She knew what flowers smelled like because Daddy brought her a bouquet every spring, but she wanted to walk through a field of dandelions and daisies, to feel dirt and dew on her bare feet. She wanted to hear birds singing and the sound of the wind. She wanted to feel a breeze and the sun on her skin. She'd read everything she could on plants and animals, and could name them all if given the chance. But besides Abby and the mice she saw running along the baseboard in the winter, she'd never seen a real animal up close.

Her other favorite game was picking a place in her book of maps and reading everything she could about it, then planning a trip while she fell asleep, deciding what she would do and see when she got there. Her favorite place was Africa, where she pictured herself running with the lions and elephants and giraffes. Sometimes she imagined breaking the dormer window, crawling out on the roof, climbing down the side of the house, and sneaking over to the barn to see the horses. Because from everything she had seen and read, they were her favorite animals. Besides cats, of course. Not only were horses strong and beautiful, but they pulled wagons and sleighs and plows. They let people ride on their backs and could find their way home if they got lost. Daddy said Blackwood Manor's horses were too far away from the attic window to tell who was who, so Lilly made up her own names for them—*Gypsy, Eagle, Cinnamon, Magic, Chester, Samantha, Molly,* and *Candy.* How she would have loved to get close to them, to touch their manes and ride through the fields on their backs. If only it weren't for those stupid swirly bars outside her window that Momma said were there for her own good. Then she remembered Momma's warning, and as quickly as they started, her dreams turned to nightmares.

"The bars are there to protect you," Momma said. "If someone got in, they'd be afraid of you and they'd try to hurt you."

When Lilly asked why anyone would be afraid of her, Momma said it was because she was a monster, an abomination. Lilly didn't know what an abomination was, but it sounded bad. Her shoulders dropped and she sighed in the stillness of her room. There would be no circus for her. Not now, not ever. There would be no getting out of the attic either. The only way she would see the world was through her books. Daddy said the outside world was not as wonderful as she thought, and Lilly should be happy she had a warm bed and food to eat. A lot of people didn't have a house or a job, and they had to stand in line for bread and soup. He told her a story about banks and money and some kind of crash, but she didn't understand it. And it didn't make her feel better anyway.

She gathered Abby in her arms and sat on her iron bed tucked beneath a wallpapered nook with a rounded ceiling. Her bedside lamp cast long shadows across the plank floor, meaning it would be dark soon and it was time to turn off the light. She didn't want to forget again and have Momma teach her another lesson. Momma had warned her a hundred times if anyone saw her light and found her up there they would take her away and she'd never see her or Daddy or Abby again. But one night last week, Lilly started a new book and forgot.

She put the cat on the bed and examined the scars on her fingers. Daddy was right, the lotion made them feel better. But oh, how the flame of Momma's lantern had burned!

"Spare the rod and spoil the child," Momma said.

Lilly wanted to ask if the Bible said anything about sparing the fire, but didn't dare. She was supposed to know what the Bible said.

"I wonder what Momma would do if she found

out I read the books from Daddy instead of that boring old Bible?" she asked Abby. The cat rubbed its face on Lilly's arm, then curled into a ball and went back to sleep.

Lilly took the Bible from the nightstand—she didn't dare put it anywhere else—moved the bookmark in a few pages, and set it back down. Momma would check to see how much reading she had done this week and if the bookmark hadn't moved, Lilly would be in big trouble. According to Momma, the Holy Bible and the crucifix on the wall above her bed were the only things she needed to live a happy life.

Everything else in the room came from Daddy—the wicker table set up for a tea party, complete with a lace doily, silver serving tray, and china cups. The matching rocking chair and the teddy bear sitting on the blue padded stool next to her wardrobe. The dollhouse filled with miniature furniture and straight-backed dolls. The model farm animals lined up on a shelf above her bookcase, all facing the same way, as if about to break into song. Three porcelain dolls with lace dresses in a wicker baby pram, one with eyes that opened and closed. And, of course, her bookcase full of books. It seemed, for a while, like Daddy would give her everything — until she read *Snow White* and asked for a mirror.

Sometimes, in the middle of the night, when she was certain everyone was asleep and there was nothing but blackness outside her window, she turned on her light and studied her reflection in the glass. All she saw was a blurry, ghost-like mask looking back at her, the swirly metal outside coiling across her skin like snakes. She stared at her white reflection and touched her forehead and nose and cheeks, trying to find a growth or a missing part, but nothing stuck out or caved in. When she asked Daddy what was wrong with her, he said she was beautiful to him and that was all that mattered. But his eyes looked funny when he said it, and she didn't think he was telling the truth. He'd be in big trouble if Momma found out because Momma said lying was a sin.

Good thing Lilly would never tell on Daddy. He was the one who taught her how to read and write, and how to add and subtract numbers. He was the one who decorated the walls of her room with rose-covered wallpaper and brought her new dresses and shoes when she got too big for the old ones. He was the one who brought Abby food and let Lilly in the other part of the attic so she could walk and stretch. One time, he even brought up a wind-up record player and tried to teach her the Charleston and tango, but she got too tired and they had to stop. She loved the music and begged him to leave the record player in her room. But he took it back downstairs because Momma would be mad if she found it.

Momma brought food and necessities, not presents. She came into Lilly's room every morning—except for the times she forgot—with a tray of toast, milk, eggs, sandwiches, apples, and cookies, to be eaten over the rest of the day. She brought Lilly soap and clean towels, and reminded her to pray before every meal. She stood by the door every night with a ring of keys in her hands and waited for Lilly to kneel by her bed to ask the Lord to forgive her sins, and to thank Him for giving her a mother who took such good care of her. Other than that, Momma never came in her room just to talk or have fun. She never said "I love you" like Daddy did. Lilly would never forget her seventh birthday, when her parents argued outside her door.

"You're spoiling her with all those presents," Momma said. "It's sinful how much you give her."

"It's not hurting anyone," Daddy said.

"Nevertheless, we need to stop spending money."

"Books aren't that expensive."

"Maybe not, but what if she starts asking questions? What if she wants to come downstairs or go outside? Are you going to say no?"

At first, Daddy didn't say anything and Lilly's heart lifted. Maybe he would take her outside after all. Then he cleared his throat and said, "What else is she supposed to do in there? The least we can do is try to give her a normal birthday. It's not her fault she "

Momma gasped. "It's not her fault? Then whose is it? Mine?"

"That's not what I was going to say," Daddy said. "It's not anyone's fault. Sometimes these things just happen."

"Well, if you had listened to me from the beginning, we wouldn't . . ." She made a funny noise, like her words got stuck in her throat.

"She's still our daughter, Cora. Other than that one thing, she's perfectly normal."

"There's nothing normal about what's on the other side of that door," Momma said, her voice cracking.

"That's not true," Daddy said. "I talked to Dr. Hillman and he said—"

"Oh, dear Lord . . . tell me you didn't! How could you betray me like that?" Momma was crying now.

"There, there, my darling. I didn't tell anyone. I was just asking Dr. Hillman if he had ever seen . . ."

Momma's sobs drowned out his words and her footsteps hurried across the attic.

"Darling, wait!" Daddy said.

The next day, Lilly quit praying before every meal, but she had not told Momma that. Since then, she had disobeyed her mother in a hundred little ways. Momma said it was wicked to look at her naked body and made Lilly close her eyes during her weekly sponge bath until she was old enough to wash herself. Now Lilly looked down at her milk-colored arms and legs when she bathed, examining her thin white torso and pink nipples. She felt ashamed afterward, but she wasn't being bad on purpose. She just wanted to know what made her a monster. The only thing she knew for sure was that her parents looked different than she did. Momma had curly blond hair and rosy skin; Daddy had a black mustache, black hair, and tan skin; but her skin was powder-white, her long, straight hair the color and texture of spider webs. It was like God forgot to give her a color. Is that what made her a monster? Or was it something else?

Now, hoping she'd be able to see more of the circus tomorrow, she changed into her night-clothes, climbed into bed, and switched off the light. Then she realized Momma hadn't come up to make sure she said her prayers.

Lilly curled up next to Abby and pulled her close. "She's probably at the circus," she said, closing her eyes.

The next night, after Lilly first saw the circus outside her window, the rattle of a key in her door startled her awake. She sat up and reached for her bedside lamp, then stopped, her fingers on the switch. It was the middle of the night and if Momma saw the light, it would mean big trouble. Maybe Momma had found out she'd spent the entire day watching the circus through her telescope instead of straightening her room and reading the Bible. The circus looked tiny through the end of her telescope and she couldn't make out every detail, but no matter what Momma did to her, it was worth seeing the elephants and giraffes being taken into the big top. It was worth seeing the crowds of people outside the tents and the parade of wagons and clowns and costumed performers. It had been the most exciting day of her life, and nothing was going to ruin it. She took her hand away from the lamp and, one at a time, touched her fingers with her thumbs. *One, two, three, four.* The door opened and Momma slipped inside carrying an oil lantern. Lilly watched her enter and her belly trembled. Momma never came into her room this late. At the end of the bed, Abby lifted her furry head, surprised to see Momma too.

Momma—Daddy said her real name was Coralline—was a tall, pretty woman, and she always wore her long blond hair pinned back on the sides. Her only jewelry was the wedding band on her left hand, and she dressed in simple skirts and sensible shoes in the name of modesty and for the glory of God. Daddy said Momma put on her best dresses and furs when she went out to important dinners and parties, but only because that was what everyone in the outside world expected. Lilly didn't understand why

Momma changed what she looked like, but Daddy said that was okay. One time, Daddy showed her a picture of Momma all dressed up and Lilly thought it was someone else.

Daddy liked to tell the story of how he had first spotted Momma between the barn and the round pen, sitting on a barrel watching the horses play in the field. Momma's father, a retired Pentecostal minister who always dreamed of raising horses, had come to Blackwood Manor Horse farm to buy a stallion. Daddy thought Momma was the prettiest girl he had ever seen. But it was six months before she would talk to him, and another six before she agreed to have dinner. For some reason, Momma's parents didn't trust Daddy. But eventually Momma and Daddy were walking hand in hand through the apple orchards; then they got married. When Daddy got to that part of the story, his face always changed to sad and he said Momma had a hard time growing up.

Now, Momma came into Lilly's room in a flowery dress and pink heels. Her lips were painted red and she was wearing a yellow hat. Lilly couldn't stop staring. She had never seen Momma dressed like that, not in person anyway. Momma's cheeks were flushed and she was breathing hard, as if she had run up the stairs.

Lilly's stomach turned over. Daddy was supposed to come back from Pennsylvania tomorrow. He promised birthday presents first thing. But he had told her a long time ago that she didn't need to worry about being left alone when he and Momma went out because his helper was always downstairs in case someone called about a horse. If "something" happened to Daddy and Momma, the helper would read a letter in Daddy's desk. He would find Lilly in the attic, and he would know what to do. Lilly wasn't sure what "something" was, but she knew it was bad. What if Momma was here to tell her "something" had happened to Daddy and he wasn't coming back?

Lilly touched her tongue to each tooth and counted, waiting for Momma to speak. *One, two, three, four . . .*

Then Momma smiled.

Momma never smiled.

"I've got a surprise for you," Momma said.

Lilly blinked. She didn't know what to say. Daddy brought surprises, not Momma. "Where's Daddy?" she managed.

"Get dressed," Momma said. "And hurry up, we don't have much time."

Lilly pushed back her covers and got out of bed. Abby sat up and stretched her front legs, treading the blanket with her claws. "Is someone coming to see me?" Lilly asked Momma.

Besides her parents, no one had ever been inside her room. One winter she got sick and

Daddy wanted to call a doctor, but Momma refused because the doctor would take her away and put her "some place." Instead Daddy spent three days wiping Lilly's forehead and applying mustard powder and warm dressings to her chest. She would never forget the sad look on his face when she woke up and said, "Daddy? What's 'some place'?"

"It's a hospital for sick people," Daddy said. "But don't worry, you're staying right here with us."

Now, Momma watched Lilly take her dress from the back of the rocking chair. Lilly's legs felt wobbly. What if someone was coming to take her "some place"?

Momma chuckled. "No, Lilly, no one is coming to see you."

Lilly glanced at Momma, her stomach getting wobbly too. Momma never laughed. Maybe she had been drinking the strange liquid Daddy sometimes brought up to her room in a silver container. Lilly didn't know what the drink was, but it made his eyes glassy and gave his breath a funny smell. Sometimes it made him laugh more than usual. What did he call it? Whiskey? No, that was impossible. Momma would never drink whiskey. Drinking alcohol was a sin.

"Why do I have to get dressed, Momma?"

"Because today's your birthday, remember?"

Lilly frowned. Momma didn't care about birthdays. "Yes," she managed.

"And I'm sure you saw the circus outside."

Lilly nodded.

"Well, that's where we're going."

Lilly stared at Momma, her mouth open. Her legs shook harder, and her arms too. "But . . . what . . . what if someone sees me?"

Momma smiled again. "Don't worry, circus performers are used to seeing people like you. And no one else will be there but us. Because against my better judgment, your father insisted on paying the circus owner to put on a special show for you."

Goose bumps popped up on Lilly's arms. Something felt bad, but she didn't know what. She glanced at Abby, as if the cat would know the answer. Abby looked back at her with curious eyes. "Daddy said he wasn't coming back until tomorrow," Lilly said.

Momma kept smiling, but her eyes changed. The top half of her face looked like it did when Lilly was in big trouble. The bottom half looked like someone Lilly had never seen before. "He came home early," Momma said.

"Then where is he?" Lilly said. "He always comes to see me first when he gets home."

"He's waiting for us over at the circus. Now hurry up!"

"Why didn't he come get me instead of you?" As soon as the words were out of her mouth, Lilly wished she hadn't said them.

Momma walked toward her and her hand rose with a sudden speed. It struck Lilly across the jaw and she fell to the floor. Abby leapt sideways on the bed and crouched next to the wall, her ears back.

"You ungrateful spawn of the devil!" Momma yelled. "How many times have I told you not to question me?"

"I'm sorry, Momma," Lilly cried.

Momma thumped her with the side of her foot. "What did I do to deserve this curse?" she hissed. "Now get on your knees and pray."

"But, Momma . . ." Lilly's sobs were too strong. She couldn't get up and she could barely breathe. She crawled to her bed with her hair hanging in her face and pulled herself up, air squeaking in her chest.

"Bow your head and ask for forgiveness," Momma said.

Lilly put her hands together beneath her chin and counted her fingers by pressing them against each other. *One, two, three, four.* "Oh Lord," she said, pushing the words out between wheezes. *Five, six, seven, eight.* "Please forgive me for questioning my momma, and for all the other ways I have made her life so difficult." *Nine, ten.* "I promise to walk the straight and narrow from here on out. Amen."

"Now get dressed," Momma said. "We don't have much time."

Lilly got off her knees and put on her undergarments with shaky hands, then took off her nightgown and pulled her play dress on over her head. Her side hurt where Momma kicked her and snot ran from her nose.

"Not that one," Momma said. "Find something better."

Lilly took off the play dress and half-walked, half-stumbled over to the wardrobe. She pulled out her favorite outfit, a yellow satin dress with a lace collar and ruffled sleeves. "Is this one all right?" she said, holding up the dress.

"That will do. Find your best shoes too. And brush your hair."

Lilly put on the dress and tied the belt behind her back. She brushed her hair—*one, two, three, four, five, six* strokes—then sat on the bed to put on her patent leather shoes. Abby edged across the covers and rubbed against Lilly's arm. Lilly gave her a quick pet, then got up and stood in the middle of the room, her ribs aching and her heart thumping. Momma opened the door and stood back, waiting for Lilly to go through it.

Lilly had waited for this moment her entire life. But now, more than anything, she wanted to stay in the attic. She didn't want to go outside. She didn't want to go to the circus. Her chest grew tighter and tighter. She could barely breathe.

"Let's go," Momma said, her voice hard. "We don't have all night."

Lilly wrapped her arms around herself and started toward the door, gulping air into her lungs. Then she stopped and looked back at Abby, who was watching from the foot of her bed.

"That cat will be here when you get back," Momma said. "Now move it."

CHAPTER 2
Julia

November 1956
Hatfield, Long Island

Eighteen-year-old Julia Blackwood glanced up and down the supermarket aisle to make sure no one was watching. The store was small, maybe thirty feet wide by forty feet long, and she could see over the shelves and into each corner. A pimple-faced teenager sat on a stool behind the counter, chewing gum and staring at a black and white television above the cash register. A radio on a shelf played "Why Do Fools Fall in Love" while a gray-haired lady checked eggs for cracks next to the open dairy cooler door.

Julia took a deep breath, went down on one knee, and pretended to tie her grease-spotted Keds. She glanced both ways down the aisle to make sure no one was watching, grabbed a can of Spam off the middle shelf, slipped it into her coat pocket, then straightened and pushed her hair behind her ears. The boy at the counter absently picked at a pimple on his chin, his eyes still glued to the television. Julia let out her breath and made her way to the next aisle, walking slowly and pretending to examine the groceries. She plucked a small apple from a produce bin, put it in her pocket, and made her way toward the counter.

"Can I get the key to the restroom?" she asked the pimple-faced boy.

Still watching television, the boy reached beneath the cash register and handed her a key on a brown rabbit foot. Then he snapped his gum and grinned at her. "Just replaced the soap this morning."

Heat rose in Julia's cheeks and she had to fight the urge to leave. The boy knew why she wanted to use the bathroom. It was the fourth time in as many months that there was no water in her room above the liquor store—this time due to frozen pipes instead of an unpaid bill—and she hadn't washed her hair or taken a shower in three days. Sure, no one at work would know whether or not she'd had a bath, but who wanted an oily-haired waitress serving them fried eggs and onion-covered burgers? Big Al's Diner was already a greasy spoon; it didn't need any more help in that department. Instead of leaving, she swallowed her pride, took the key from the boy, and trudged to the back of the store.

The cold, green-enameled restroom smelled like rotten food and old socks. Grime and black mold colored the grout between the broken, mismatched floor tiles, and a jagged yellow crack ran across the toilet seat. Julia washed her hands in the silver-legged sink, dried them with brown paper towels, then ate the apple as fast as she could, trying to ignore the stench of old urine. When she was finished, she stripped down to her underwear and bra, folded her cranberry-colored waitress uniform on top of her coat, and put them on the toilet tank lid—the only place that looked halfway clean. Shivering, she scrubbed her face and armpits with paper towels and Lava soap, then washed her hair in the sink, trying not to get soaked. The water was ice cold and the gritty lather made her hair feel like straw, but at least it would be clean. When the last of the soap was out of her hair, she used paper towels to squeeze out the excess water, then got dressed again, combed the tangles out of her hair, put it in a bun, and studied her reflection in the tarnished mirror.

The stealthy progress of time since she ran away from home three years ago showed in her pronounced cheekbones and the rings under her eyes. Her tanned, smooth skin had turned pale and chalky from too little sleep and too little sun. Even her blond hair, which was once the white-blond of angel wings, seemed darker and thinner. Her fingernails were chewed to the quick, and her shoulders pointed sharply through the fabric of her uniform. She leaned closer to the mirror to examine the yellow remnants of a bruise around her left eye. Thankfully it was almost gone. *How did you end up in a place like this, stealing food from an express mart and washing your hair in a public bathroom? You could have waited another year and gone to college, far away from Blackwood Manor. Mother would have paid for everything. Instead, you traded nine o'clock curfews and Sunday confessions for double shifts and a controlling boyfriend who hits you and spends money faster than either of you can make it. Maybe Mother was right. You aren't going to amount to anything. So what's the point of trying?*

Mother—with her spite and bony fists—was a rule maker and a rule follower. And she expected the same from everyone around her. Among the countless rules of Blackwood Manor—where certain rooms were kept locked and entire floors were off limits—Julia was to pray three times a day, keep her room spotless, do her chores, get perfect grades, and follow the guidelines at school. She could watch her parents' horses from a distance but wasn't allowed in the barn because it was a business, not a playground. Makeup, poodle skirts, pedal pushers, and tight sweaters were forbidden, and dresses had to be a modest length. Most importantly of all, she had to remember that bad things would happen if she didn't behave.

After spending the majority of her life wondering why her parents had her, running away seemed like the solution to everything. Yes, she had been clothed, fed, and had everything of monetary value she needed. But Mother was too busy praying, cleaning, cooking, and making rules to give her any guidance or affection. And her father, who she considered the demonstrative one, only hugged her on Christmas and birthdays. Most of the time he was in the barn with the horses, or drinking behind the locked doors of his den with the same scratchy gramophone record—"Little White Lies"—playing over and over and over.

For years, she wondered what it meant when her father went on vacation "to recover" or "get help." It was a strained time, more than usual, a time of keeping going and pretending, of being "normal" and not fussing. The Blackwoods never bared their souls, or poured out their hearts. Then, when Julia turned twelve, Mother explained her husband's alcoholism and said it was Julia's fault for being such a difficult child.

Julia thought back to the day her father was killed. The sky was clear and blue. The breeze was gentle and scented with pine. Who would have expected someone to die on a beautiful day like that?

She had skipped church to go to the lake. It was the last day of summer, a hot, humid day, perfect for swimming, and one of the popular girls had *finally* invited her to hang out with her and her friends at the isthmus. When it came time to leave for church, Julia locked the door to the bathroom and pretended to be sick. As long as she made it back before Mother returned, everything would be fine.

But when Julia came home, there was a police car in the driveway, the early-afternoon sun glinting off the chrome and the windshield. Then she saw Mother on the front steps, one hand gripping the balustrade, and her heart sank. Had Julia gotten the time wrong? Had Mother come home early and called the police because she wasn't in her room? Either way, she was in deep trouble. When Mother saw her coming up the driveway, she rushed down the steps and marched toward her, her face contorted in anger, her long skirt twisting around her legs.

"Where have you been?" Mother shrieked.

"I . . . I . . ." Julia said.

"Speak up, girl!"

"I went swimming with some friends. It's the last day before school starts and they never invited me before. I knew you wouldn't let me go so—"

Mother slapped her, hard across the face. Julia's head whipped to the side and her damp hair flew in her eyes and stuck to her skin.

"I told you something bad would happen if you didn't follow the rules!" Mother cried.

Julia put a hand over her cheek, her eyes burning. "What are you talking about? What happened?"

Mother reached blindly for the porch railing, her face suddenly gray. "Your father was . . ."

Julia started trembling. She had never seen Mother like this. "My father was what?" she said. "Tell me."

"He was in a car crash."

Julia's breath caught. "Is he okay?"

Mother gaped at her, shaking her head, as if she couldn't believe what she was about to say. "No, he's not okay. He's dead."

The ground tilted beneath Julia's feet and her knees nearly buckled. It seemed, for an instant, that she was falling. But then she realized, somehow, she had remained upright. In what sounded like slow motion, she heard herself say again, "What happened?"

"He was looking for you," Mother said. Then her face contorted and changed. The grief in her eyes turned to anger and hate, and her mouth twisted into a sneer. She raised her arms and pounded on Julia's head and shoulders with bony fists. "It's your fault!" she screamed. "It's your fault! It's your fault!"

Julia put her arms up to protect herself, but Mother's blows slammed into her head and chest and face, even after she knocked her to the ground. The police pulled Mother off, but not before she split Julia's lip and bruised her cheek and shoulders.

That night, Julia stole the tithe money from the canister inside the spice cupboard, ignoring the gaze of Jesus on the decorative tin, then packed a bag and left Blackwood Manor, vowing never to return. There would be no more early curfews and strict rules, no more nightly prayers and weekly confessions, no more locked rooms, no more blame for her father's drinking. From that day on, she'd be free to do as she pleased. She'd take her future into her own hands. And she'd never let anyone blame her for anything again.

Except things hadn't turned out the way she planned. Sure, freedom was fun at first, taking the bus to Long Island and making friends on the boardwalk, pawning her jewelry and moving into an apartment a mile from the beach with Kelly, a cocktail waitress, and Tom, a veteran from the Korean War. The first few months were lost in a haze of music, parties, beer, and marijuana. Then Kelly moved back home, winter came, the boardwalk closed, and the money ran out. Julia wasn't exactly sure how it happened, but she and Tom moved to a cheap room in the city, and things stopped being fun a long time ago. Tom had trouble keeping a job, and he warned her over and over that something bad would happen if she didn't keep hers.

Now she came out of the supermarket bathroom, gave the key on the rabbit foot back to the pimple-faced kid at the cash register, and left the store. Earlier, when she went in, it was snowing, but now it had stopped.

The new snow brightened the street. The neighborhood was still seedy, grimy, and litter-strewn, but it didn't look half as bad as it did yesterday, without the snow. Big Al's Diner sat near the corner, flanked by a liquor store with bars over the windows and a pawnshop with a soggy, ripped carpet in front of the door.

Julia buttoned her coat, hunched her shoulders against the cold and, trying to ignore the slush seeping through her Keds, made her way toward the diner. She touched the can of Spam in her pocket to make sure it was still there, wishing she'd grabbed something else to go with it. When she got out of work ten hours from now, Spam on white bread would be her and Tom's supper, like it had been every night for the past four days. Today was payday, but her entire check had to go toward rent. Otherwise, they'd be out on the street by the end of the week.

When she reached Big Al's diner, she passed the front entrance, went around the corner, and entered the alley behind it. For some reason, Big

Al had a thing about the help coming and going through the front door, as if the diner were a fine restaurant instead of a greasy spoon. The smell of bacon and fried potatoes filled the cold air in the alley and, despite the apple she'd eaten earlier, Julia's stomach growled with hunger. A boy in ripped jeans and a white T-shirt dug through the Dumpster next to the diner's back steps. Beside him, a thin brown dog sniffed the air, waiting patiently for his owner to find something good. When the dog saw Julia, it wagged its tail and ambled toward her, all feet and ears and fur. Julia bent down to scratch the dog's scruffy head.

"Hey, buddy," she said to the dog. Then she straightened and called out to the boy. "You know what Big Al will do if he catches you out here again, Danny?"

The boy spun around, his eyes wide. "Oh," he breathed. "It's you."

He was nine years old, with hazel eyes and shaggy hair the color of coffee. Julia met him last year when he and his dog were begging for change in front of the pawnshop.

"Where's your coat?" she said.

Danny shrugged. "My brother needed it."

"Your dad out of work again?"

Danny nodded. "And Mom's sick."

Julia took the Spam out of her pocket. "Here, take this. After my shift, I'll try to stop by with something else."

Danny took the Spam, immediately pried off the lid, shook the pressed meat into his hand, and took a big bite. "Thanks." He broke off a hunk and gave it to the dog, who swallowed it whole.

"You're welcome," Julia said. "Now get out of here."

Danny smiled and ran down the alley, the thin dog at his heels.

Julia went up the back steps of the diner, knocked on the entrance, and stepped back to wait. On the other side of the door, footsteps tramped across a tile floor. Someone fumbled with the doorknob and the door swung open. It was Sheila, one of the other waitresses.

"Where have you been?" she whispered. "Your shift started two hours ago. Big Al is about ready to fire you!"

Julia frowned. "What do you mean? I don't work until ten on Wednesdays." She entered the diner, already taking off her coat.

"It's Tuesday!" Sheila said.

"Shit," Julia said. She hung her coat on a hook, took an apron from the basket outside the walk-in cooler, slipped it over her head, and hurried into the kitchen, tying the apron strings behind her back. Sheila followed.

Big Al came through the swinging doors between the kitchen and dining area, his forehead covered in sweat, his greasy salt and pepper hair hanging in his eyes. As his name

41

implied, he was a big man, over six feet tall with wide shoulders and thick legs. But it was his enormous belly that earned him the nickname Big Al. Covered in a greasy white apron, it hung over his pants like a beluga whale.

"Look who decided to show up for work today," he snarled.

"Sorry," Julia said. "I thought it was Wednesday."

"And I thought it was my birthday," Big Al said. "That's why I got to wait tables and cook at the same time."

"I'm sorry," Julia said. "I made a mistake. It won't happen again."

Big Al grunted. "Damn right it won't. I'm holding your paycheck until next week. Maybe by then you'll figure out if you want this job or not."

"But I . . ." Julia said. "Please, Al. I need it for rent."

"Maybe you should have thought about that before coming in late," Big Al said. "Now shut up and get your ass to work."

Julia gritted her teeth and pushed through the swinging doors into the dining area. The counter and nearly every booth were packed. Sheila came out of the kitchen behind her, two plates of eggs and a plate of pancakes balanced in one hand, a plate of French toast in the other.

"Can you cover the counter, hon?" she said

to Julia. "Just 'til the breakfast rush is over."

"Sure," Julia said. She grabbed a pad and pen and scanned the counter for the next customer. A man in a black jacket and fedora sat at the far end, the menu closed in front of him. She started toward him.

"Can I get a refill on my coffee," someone said as she went by.

"Yes, sir," she said. She put her pen and pad in her apron, grabbed the coffee urn, refilled the man's coffee, then went to wait on the man in the fedora. She turned over a white mug in front of him.

"Coffee?" she said.

"Yup," the man said.

Julia filled his cup, set the urn on the counter, and dug her pen and pad out of her apron.

"Miss?" someone shouted from the other end of the counter. "Where's my pancakes?"

Julia forced a smile. "I'll be right with you."

Just then, the bell over the entrance jingled and a man in a pin-striped suit and shiny shoes held the door for a woman and a young girl in matching blue coats. The little girl held the woman's hand and they both smiled as they took a seat in one of the booths. Cold air reddened the identical tips of their noses and the round apples of their cheeks. Julia stared at them, her pen poised above the pad in her hand. *Mother and daughter,* she thought. The mother took off

43

her gloves, then smiled and reached across the table to help the girl take off her mittens. The daughter laughed when the mother rubbed her hands between hers to warm them. *I wonder if it's the little girl's birthday,* Julia wondered. *Or maybe they're on a shopping trip.* Then the mother kissed the little girl's fingertips and Julia's eyes grew moist. She looked for the man in the pin-striped suit, assuming he was the little girl's father. But he stood in the center of the room, skimming the diner as if looking for someone. Maybe he was lost. He didn't look like he belonged in this neighborhood.

"I'll have two eggs over easy," the man at the counter in front of her said. "With toast and butter."

Julia blinked and looked down at him, as if she'd forgotten where she was. She shook her head to clear it. "Um, okay. Sorry. Coming right up."

She headed toward the kitchen to place the order, berating herself for getting distracted. She had to stop daydreaming. If Big Al caught her staring off into the distance, she'd be fired for sure. But sometimes she just couldn't help it. She was drawn to watching people who clearly loved each other, especially parents and their children. She loved seeing their faces light up with affection and recognition of their unconditional love, and the fact that they knew how important they were to each other without ever saying a word. She wondered what it felt like.

"I asked for ketchup ten minutes ago," a woman said to Julia as she hurried by.

Julia grabbed a squeeze bottle of ketchup and put it in front of her.

"Where's my bill?" another woman said.

"I'll find it," Julia said. She placed the order on the kitchen turnstile, rang the bell, and asked about the missing pancakes. Big Al pushed a pile of pancakes through the window and wiped his forehead on the back of his arm, glowering at her. Julia took the hot plate and delivered it to the customer. When she went back to the other end of counter, the man in the pin-striped suit was there, standing behind the stools. She dropped off the woman's bill and went over to see what he wanted.

"Can I help you?" she said.

"I'm looking for Julia Coralline Blackwood," he said.

Julia's mouth went dry. *Is this guy a cop? Is he here to arrest me for stealing from the super-market?* With a knot in her chest, she smiled. "She's not working today. Can I can give her a message for you?"

The man reached into the breast pocket inside his suit, pulled out a photograph, and turned it around so she could see it. Julia felt the blood drain from her face. It was her high school picture, taken the year she left home. How did he get it? And what did he want?

"I'm a private investigator, Miss Blackwood," the man said. "Hired by your parents' attorney." He reached into his pocket again and pulled out an envelope. "I've been searching for you for nearly a year. This is for you." He handed her the envelope. "Have a good day." He tipped his hat and left the diner.

Julia stared at the envelope in her shaking hands. Mother had found her.

CHAPTER 3

Lilly

Lilly stepped out of her attic bedroom, her teeth chattering and her breath wheezing in her chest. She didn't want to go to the circus, especially without Daddy, but she had to do what she was told. Momma followed her out the door, then closed it behind them and started across the room. The light from Momma's oil lamp flickered off an empty bookcase, three broken chairs, and the high walls of the other part of the attic, where Daddy sometimes let Lilly play when Momma went to church.

Lilly wrapped her arms around herself and followed Momma, counting every step, then waited while Momma unlocked another door.

Momma opened the door and held it, frowning and glaring at her as if to say "move it along." Lilly stepped into a part of the attic she had never seen before and hunched her shoulders to make herself smaller. The room felt gigantic—at least four times bigger than the other side—but too close at the same time, as if she were inside a whale with a belly full of fish and boats and rocks, waiting to be crushed and swallowed. She stood trembling in a walkway between piles of dusty boxes and books and trunks. Momma locked the door behind her, then led the way through a rug-lined maze of cobweb-covered dressers, wooden chests, empty picture frames, and broken lamps. A set of rusty bicycles leaned up against a crooked wardrobe, and dirty dishes and books lined grimy stands and shelves. The rugs felt crumbly beneath Lilly's shoes.

At the far end of the room, a long, narrow hole in the floor opened to a staircase. Momma went down the wooden steps, her lantern light disappearing into the tight space. At the bottom, she stopped in front of a short door and looked up at Lilly.

Lilly couldn't move. She felt like she was going to throw up.

"Hang on to the railing and take one step at a time," Momma said.

With shaky hands, Lilly gripped the railing and lowered her foot over the edge to the first step. She had never walked down a staircase before and her head felt light and woozy. It was a little bit like stepping down from the stool she used when she was younger to see out the dormer window, but this was a whole row of stools. She felt like was about to fall forward and tumble down the stairs. She swallowed and glanced down at Momma, who was watching with a scowl. It was either move down the steps, or make Momma madder.

"Let's go," Momma said. "We don't have all night."

Lilly put both feet on the first step. *One.* Then she took another, putting both feet on that step before taking the next. *Two. Three.* Slowly but surely, she made her way to the bottom. When Lilly reached the last stair, Momma ducked and went out a short door. Lilly followed her into a narrow space about twice the size of her water closet. On the other end, another door led into another room. Momma told Lilly to wait, then locked the door to the staircase and reached up to pull a red string. A shiny cloth decorated with a house and flower gardens fell over the top half of the door. Then Momma moved a small table with feet that looked like claws beneath the shiny cloth, and, like magic, the door disappeared. Momma put her ring of keys in the table drawer and led Lilly out into another room with an enormous bed and odd, sheet-draped figures.

What is beneath those sheets? Lilly wondered. She stayed close to Momma, fighting the urge to hold on to her arm. But Momma didn't like to be touched, so Lilly didn't do it. She wanted to close her eyes, but then she'd trip and Momma wouldn't like that either.

After the bedroom, they went into a long, thin space with shiny floors and walls lined with pictures and decorations. What was it called? Lilly tried to remember but couldn't. One side of the space had a swirly metal railing instead of a wall, like the swirly metal bars outside her window. She stayed close to the wall and away from the railing, feeling mixed up and dizzy, like she was going to fall. Everything felt too big, too wide, too long. Her breath rattled in her chest. She touched her thumbs to her fingers and tried to count, but kept losing track of her numbers. She coughed and Momma gave her a stern look.

If she had known the bottom part of the house was going to feel like a giant pit waiting to swallow her whole, she never would have wished to leave her room. She wanted to run back up there now, but that would make Momma really mad. As they made their way toward a staircase with more swirly railings, Momma's lantern reflected off the high ceiling and cast marching shadows above her head, making the walls seem like they were moving. Lilly gripped the railing tight in her fists and made her way down the steps, certain she was going to cartwheel and tumble, end over end, to the bottom. On one hand, she wanted to see everything, to explore and inspect every part of Blackwood Manor. On the other, she wanted to close her eyes and make it all go away.

At the bottom of the staircase, she followed Momma across an open area with a fireplace, bookshelves that went up to the ceiling, and chairs that looked soft as pillows. The air smelled like soap and wood and metal and dead flowers. Pictures of mountains, people, and horses filled the walls, and a sparkly light made of shiny beads hung from the ceiling. The rug beneath Lilly's feet felt as thick as the mattress on her bed.

She could hardly believe what she was feeling and seeing and smelling. How could the ceilings be so high, the walls so far apart? What kept such a giant house from falling in on itself? And what did her parents do with all this space? This one room alone could house twenty people. She felt weak and wobbly, like she did when Momma forgot to feed her. More than anything, she wanted to go back upstairs. The world was almost too much.

Then she pictured Momma reading a book next to the fancy windows while Daddy smoked by the fireplace, his feet on the footstool. She pictured Momma and Daddy comfortable and warm, drinking hot tea and enjoying each other's company. And for the first time ever, anger at Daddy knotted in her stomach. *How could he leave me upstairs? Why didn't he let me come down here when no one else was around? Maybe then I wouldn't be so scared right now. Didn't he care that I was all alone?*

Tears blurred her vision, but she kept going. There was no other choice. After the fireplace room, she followed Momma down another shadowy walkway with doors on both sides. The light from Momma's lantern filled each open doorway, and Lilly craned her neck to see inside the rooms. High shelves and books filled one room, and a long table surrounded by cloth-covered chairs filled another. At the end of the hall, they entered what looked like a kitchen, their footsteps clacking on the black and white tile floor. Copper pots and pans hung over a center counter, and a black stove sat beneath a stone archway. White cupboards with glass doors lined the blue walls. Above the double sink, a flowered curtain hung over a window made of little squares, with potted plants lining the sill. What Lilly imagined were the leftover aromas of cooking and cleaning filled the kitchen—fried onions and baking bread, water boiling in a kettle and strong soap. For reasons she didn't under-stand, she wanted to stay there, to open the cupboards and see what was inside, to soak in

51

the warmth from the stove and eat a meal. It reminded her of the kitchens she had read about in books, where mothers and daughters peeled potatoes and frosted cakes, where entire families sat at tables eating and talking. What was it like to stand at a sink and wash dishes in soapy water, to bake cookies in the oven and make soup on the stove? What was it like to eat with other people?

Momma said Lilly couldn't eat with her and Daddy because seeing her across the dinner table would make them lose their appetites.

Remembering what Momma said made Lilly's lungs squeeze shut. All of a sudden, she couldn't breathe. She stopped and gripped the edge of the counter, air squeaking in her chest.

Momma glanced back at her. "What are you doing?"

"I don't want to . . ." Lilly said between struggling breaths. "Everyone will think . . . I'm a monster! They're going to . . . to . . ."

Momma scowled. "I told you, circus performers are used to people like you. Now stop being bad and do what I say. Your father went to a lot of time and expense to surprise you, and I won't have you ruining it."

Before Lilly could say another word, Momma grabbed her wrist and dragged her into a small room off the kitchen. Coats hung from hooks on the walls, shoes and boots lined the floor, and a door looked like it led outside. Lilly counted the boots and shoes, trying to calm down. *One, two, three, four, five, six*. Little by little, her chest loosened and she could breathe better. Momma set the lantern on the floor and took a sweater from a hook. She put it on, picked up the lantern, and grabbed the door handle. Then she paused, lifted a jacket from a hook, and handed it to Lilly.

"Put this on. You might need it later."

"Later?" Lilly said.

Momma shook her head. "I mean, when we come back."

Lilly took the jacket and put it on. It felt heavy on her shoulders and the sleeves hung past her hands.

"Roll them up," Momma said. "And hurry. We've got to get over there before it's too late."

Lilly did as she was told, shivering and sweating at the same time. She wanted to ask what they might be too late for, but couldn't find the right words.

Momma pulled open the door and slipped out into the night.

Lilly stood in the open doorway, holding the jacket tight around herself. This was the moment she had imagined a thousand times, the moment she had dreamed about nearly every night, the moment she thought would be the happiest of her life. But now, the idea that she was about to walk out of the house shocked her so badly she felt like she was about to float out of her body into the dark outside. It seemed, for an instant, that she did, and she could look back and see herself standing in the doorway.

"Come on," Momma called over her shoulder. "Hurry up." She kept walking, unaware that Lilly had stopped on the threshold.

Lilly thought about turning around and running back up to her room, but Momma would just come after her. And she would hit her again. That would be worse than going to the circus. Besides, what if she never had this chance again? She took a deep breath, ignored the rattle in her chest, and stepped out of Blackwood Manor. The outdoors felt enormous, bigger than she ever could have imagined, vaster than she ever could have dreamed. She stood shaking, surprised and scared and happy all at the same time.

She was outside.

A half-moon slid down the side of a cloudless sky filled with a million stars, casting a wintery glow over the summer night. And the smells, oh, the smells! She wasn't sure what wonderful aromas filled the air, but she imagined grass and dirt and trees and water and mud and insects and leaves. She imagined horses and hay and flowers and rain. The thousands of pictures she had pored over in books flashed in her mind, and now she was about to see them in real life. A warm breeze caressed her face. Night felt warm and soft, like breathing under a blanket. She pushed up her sleeves to feel the air on her skin, and moonlight reflected off her white hands and arms. They looked like they belonged to a ghost.

Momma kept going, walking fast, and the yellow circle of lantern light moved farther and farther away, bouncing across the grass. On one hand, Lilly wanted to know what it felt like to be surrounded by night. On the other, she was terrified by the massive, empty space. Who knew what lay beyond the darkness, just feet from where she stood? Who knew if she would be swallowed by blackness, or snatched up by a wild animal?

She hurried after Momma, counting her steps until she caught up. *One, two, three, four, five, six, seven* . . . The feeling of walking and walking and not hitting a wall felt strange and exciting and scary at the same time. Together they crossed the shadowy yard, past the long silhouettes of trees and the towering shape of the barn. Horses whinnied and nickered inside the dark building, thumping against the walls of their stalls. A sweet, dry grass smell filled Lilly's nostrils, along with a musty, warm tang she imagined was manure.

Momma opened the gate to one of the pastures, let Lilly through, then closed it again. Side by side they moved across the field. Insects chirped and clicked all around them. Lilly wanted to walk slower, but Momma was in a hurry. On the other side of the field, they ducked beneath a white plank fence and made their way toward a line of trees. The ground was rutted and uneven and Lilly kept tripping on clumps of dirt and grass. She was wheezing again, but didn't dare stop to catch her breath. She thought about asking why they didn't take the road, then remembered they couldn't chance being seen. Who knew what would happen if someone saw a white monster on the side of the highway?

Following Momma into a stand of evergreen trees, she did her best to keep up. Her shoes, which she only wore when Daddy asked her to, pinched her toes. Sweat broke out on her forehead and her nose started to run. Inside the trees, Momma led the way along a narrow dirt path padded with pine needles. A clean smell filled the air, like soap and Daddy's cologne. Lilly wondered if it was the trees. She thought about asking Momma, but it was all she could do to stay behind her. An owl hooted above her head and she jumped, then craned her neck to see it and nearly tripped over a rock.

When they finally made their way out of the woods, through thinning trees and low bushes, they came out at the grassy edge of another field. From there, Lilly could see the dark shapes of circus tents and wagons. The colored lights had been turned off, and the midway was deserted. Momma led her across the grass into a sawdust-carpeted lot, beneath a huge banner that read: THE BARLOW BROTHERS' CIRCUS. Overhead, triangle flags hung limp in the warm air. Closed lemonade and hot-dog stands lined the lot next to stands with signs that read: COTTON CANDY, ICE CREAM, and ROASTED PEANUTS. A giant painting of clown faces filled the sky above one tent. The silent clowns stared back at Lilly, frozen mid-laugh. Traces of moonlight glinted off flagpoles, making them look silver and cold. Purple-black shadows and gray light criss-crossed the grounds, and a strange mixture of hot grease and animal dung filled the air. There was so much to see and smell, it made Lilly dizzy.

"Where's Daddy?" she whispered.

Momma shushed her and kept going.

Lilly scanned the lot, waiting for someone to come running at them through the maze of tents, popcorn, and candy apple stands to ask what they were doing there. If the circus owner had agreed to put on a show for her, where was everyone? Where were the animals and performers? Why was everything so dark and quiet?

When Momma's lantern light swept over a row of giant banners in front of a parade of tents, Lilly wanted to close her eyes again. She shrank away from the paintings of scary-looking people below words that read: ALDO THE ALLIGATOR MAN, LUCIFER THE DEVIL BABY, VIDAL THE THREE-LEGGED BOY, and DINA THE LIVING

HALF GIRL. The people in the pictures looked like something out of a nightmare, each one more upsetting than the next. *Where are the clowns and the elephants and the horses?* she wondered. *And where is Daddy?*

She stopped next to a ticket stand, gasping for air. "I want to go home," she said.

Momma came back to where she stood, grabbed her wrist, and dragged her forward. Lilly tripped and stumbled, but Momma didn't care.

Then they came to a big tent with poles and beams and wires sticking out in all different directions, like the bones of a giant beast. It was the big top Lilly had seen from her attic window. The front flap read: TO THE CIRCUS MAIN ENTRANCE. But the entrance was dark. When Momma passed it and kept going, Lilly dug in her heels.

"Where are we going?" she said.

Momma ignored her and yanked her forward.

On the other side of the big top, a train sat parked on the railroad tracks, a long row of passenger cars and boxcars behind a massive black engine. It was bigger than Lilly could have imagined. From her window, trains looked the same size as her model farm animals. Yellow lights shone here and there behind square windows, and circus wagons with animal cages sat on the ground beside the engine and first few cars. Lilly couldn't see inside the cages because it was too dark, but to the left of the wagons, a group of bulky mounds lay on the grass.

Elephants, she thought. *Real, live elephants. One, two, three, four.* Number four stood on its thick legs, its trunk hanging down like a giant worm.

Lilly started toward them, but Momma pulled her in the other direction, toward the back of the big tent into a cluster of covered trailers, trucks, and wagons painted with horses and winged lions. Lilly tried to get Momma to let go because she was hurting her arm and pulling too hard. But she was no match for Momma.

"Where are we going?" she said again. "Where's Daddy?"

Finally, Momma slowed, and a gloom-shrouded figure moved out from behind one of the trucks and walked toward them. It was a man, quite big, with a thick neck and broad shoulders.

"Daddy?" Lilly said. Then the man moved into Momma's lantern light and Lilly screamed.

It wasn't Daddy.

It was a giant monster with a bony forehead, eyebrows grown together over a wide nose, an ape-like jaw, and a mouth that looked like a steam shovel. The monster had massive shoulders and huge arms, and his boat-sized feet kicked up clouds of dust from the earth. A jagged slit ran up the middle of his face, separating his top lip and splitting his nose into two mangled pieces.

In the middle of his forehead a mass of dark red tissue looked like a third eye. Big gray teeth filled his mouth, crowding one another for space and overlapping at several points. A checkered shirt stretched over his muscled chest, and the bottom of his worn trousers stopped just below his tree-trunk-sized knees.

Lilly tried to look away but couldn't. She stood frozen in terror and amazement. Maybe he was an ogre, like the one in *Puss in Boots*. She didn't know those things were real. Momma gasped and shrank back, but held tight to Lilly's wrist. Lilly moved behind her, her limbs heavy as stone.

"Please, Momma," she cried in a weak voice. "I want to go home."

Then a normal-looking man appeared behind the monster, dressed in black trousers and a long jacket. He took a drag from a fat cigar and moved toward them, smoke wafting from the corners of his mouth.

"No need to be afraid," the man said. "Viktor won't hurt you." His oily dark hair was pulled into a ponytail, and his face reminded Lilly of pictures she'd seen of the moon, with craters and dents and rocky parts.

"What . . . who is he?" Momma said.

"Viktor is my star attraction," the moon-faced man said. "But that's not what you're here for, is it? Where's the girl?"

Momma dragged Lilly out from behind her, her

mouth twisting with the effort. The moon-faced man turned on a flashlight and shined it at Lilly. She blinked and squinted, blinded by the light, then dropped her chin to her chest, breathing hard. Air squeaked and rattled in her lungs. What did the man want? And what would he do when he saw her face? Would he run away in fear, or would he try to hurt her? If she really was the devil's spawn, maybe he'd try to kill her. Momma had told her over and over that she was only trying to protect her. Maybe she brought her here to prove why.

"Take off her coat," the man said.

Momma yanked the coat off Lilly and let it fall to the ground.

The man shined the flashlight from the top of Lilly's head to her feet.

"How do I know she's really your daughter?" he said to Momma. Then he put his hand—it was fleshy and damp—beneath Lilly's chin and lifted her face. She held her breath, unable to pull her eyes away from his, waiting to see his reaction. For what seemed like forever, she stared at him. What was he going to do? Why wasn't he afraid? At the same time, she couldn't help examining the face of the only person, besides Momma and Daddy, she'd ever seen up close. To her surprise, his expression remained calm. No shock or fear showed in his eyes. Maybe he was used to monsters.

"How dare you question me," Momma said. "I signed the papers, didn't I?"

"That doesn't mean anything," the man said.

"If you're accusing me of lying," Momma said, "I'll leave this instant and take her with me."

The man shut off the flashlight. "It wouldn't be the first time someone tried passing a kid off as their own."

"Well, I can assure you," Momma said. "I'm telling the truth. I'm a God-fearing Christian and I—"

The moon-faced man laughed and Viktor the monster laughed with him.

"Is there something funny about that?" Momma said.

The moon-faced man waved a hand in the air, still grinning. "No, not at all. I'm sure God is happy to know you're not lying about this girl being your daughter." He glanced at Viktor and rolled his eyes. "I just need to know one more thing. Is your husband aware of our agreement?"

Momma nodded. "My husband is not long for this world. And Lilly has been nothing but a cross to bear since the day she was born."

Lilly frowned at Momma. What did "not long for this world" mean? Whatever it was, it sounded bad.

The man leaned forward and fixed his eyes on Lilly's. "Tell me the truth, little girl, or you'll be sorry. Is this woman your mother?"

Lilly thought about saying no, but she wasn't sure who would be more mad, the moon-faced man or Momma. She nodded once and stepped back.

"Good," he said. "We wouldn't want anyone accusing me of stealing you."

Lilly's chin quivered and she turned toward Momma, who still held her wrist in an iron grip. "Where's my daddy?"

Momma ignored her. "Do we have a deal, then?" she said to the man.

Lilly's chest grew tighter and she grabbed at her throat. She couldn't get air. "Please, Momma," she gasped between breaths. "I promise to be good . . . from now on. I'll read the Bible and . . ."

The man grabbed Lilly's chin and shined the flashlight in her eyes again. He squinted and turned her head from side to side, blowing his hot, sour breath over her face. Lilly tried to pull away, but couldn't. "What's wrong with her?" the man said. "Is she sick?"

Momma shook her head. "No, she has trouble breathing when she's upset, that's all. It'll pass."

"If she turns up dead in the next few months," the man said, "I'll come back for my money. And it won't be pretty."

"If you're not interested," Momma said, "the Ringling Brothers are coming to Albany next week. I'm sure they can pay more anyway."

With that, the man scowled and let go of Lilly's

chin. He gestured once and the monster moved forward, grabbed her by the arms, and dragged her away from Momma. Lilly screamed and twisted and kicked, trying to break free.

"Momma . . . please . . . !"

Momma acted like she didn't hear her.

"Don't . . . touch . . . me . . . !" Lilly said. She kicked the monster's legs as hard as she could.

He grunted, spun her around, clamped a giant hand over her mouth, and held her against his stomach, one sweaty arm across her chest. Lilly dug at his skin, trying to get him to let go. It was no use. She stared at Momma, struggling to breathe, her wide eyes filled with terror and tears.

The moon-faced man took a shiny clip from his pocket, pulled a stack of money from it, and held the money out to Momma. "It's all there," he said. "Count it if you want."

"One more thing," Momma said. "Don't ever come back here. I'm not leasing land to any more circuses."

"Understood."

Momma took the money and counted it.

Lilly tried to yell and scream, to beg her mother not to leave her there, but the only noise she could make was a strangled, high-pitched wail.

Momma stood for a moment, her eyes locked on Lilly, the money in her fist. "It's for the best," she said, and walked away.

CHAPTER 4
Julia

After the breakfast rush at Big Al's Diner was over, Julia went into the restroom and locked the door. She sat on the closed toilet lid and, with trembling fingers, opened the envelope from the private investigator hired by her mother's lawyer. The letter read:

FROM THE OFFICE OF
SCOGNAMIGLIO & CARR
ATTORNEYS AT LAW

Dear Miss Blackwood,
It is with sincere sympathy that I regret to inform you of the passing of your mother, Coralline Livingston Blackwood, on September 21, 1955. As your parents' attorney, it is my duty to notify you that your mother's last will and testament has been read and, as the only living child of Coralline and Howard Blackwood, you are the sole heir of their entire estate.
Blackwood Manor Horse Farm has continued to function under the careful supervision of your parents' barn manager,

Claude Miller, and a local veterinarian, Fletcher Reid. Although a number of horses were sold before your mother's passing, it was your mother's express wish that these men continue to be paid until you were found and could take over, or until the estate ran out of money. Fortunately, due to your father's astute business sense and careful financial planning, your parents' estate should be monetarily viable for many, many years. With that being said, Blackwood Manor Horse Farm is rightfully yours should you choose to claim it. However, there is one condition. To become the rightful owner of Blackwood Manor and the financial benefits included herein, you must return home and reside on the property. Please contact my office immediately so we can see to it that the proper paperwork is signed.

Thank you for your time. I hope to hear from you soon.

Sincerely,

Wallace Carr

Julia stared at the letter for what seemed like forever, trying to let the words sink in. Mother had been dead for a year. And she was the sole heir to Blackwood Manor. She started to shake, shocked and slightly saddened that her mother was gone—had died nearly a year ago in fact—and she had no idea. Weren't family members supposed to *know* when a relative died? Weren't they supposed to feel a sudden, tremendous loss when a loved one passed from this earth? Then she remembered she had been swimming with friends when her father died. She had felt happy and carefree, ignorant of the fact that the one person who seemed to love her had been killed in a car crash. Maybe family members only sensed one another's passing when they shared genuine love and true affection.

Her eyes flooded. She was officially an orphan now. Her mother and father were gone. And yet, she grieved something else even more—a loving family. But how could you miss something you never had?

Someone knocked on the restroom door. "You in there?" It was Sheila.

"Be right out," Julia said.

She wiped her cheeks, put the letter back in the envelope, and stood on rubbery legs. She stuffed the envelope in her apron pocket and looked at herself in the cracked mirror above the sink. How could she return to Blackwood Manor, with its bad memories and closely guarded secrets? Then again, how could she stay here?

CHAPTER 5
Lilly

Following the moon-faced man, Viktor the monster held Lilly to his chest, his sweaty hand clamped over her mouth, and carried her toward the train. Lilly kicked and twisted and tried to scream, but she could hardly breathe and she was starting to grow weak. The monster held her tighter. When they reached the train, he hauled her up a set of steps between two boxcars and waited. An oil lamp hung from a hook outside the boxcar door. The moon-faced man took the lamp from the hook, slid open the entrance, and led them inside. Goats and llamas filled the pens on one side of the car, and bales of hay and stacks of burlap bags lined the other.

Viktor followed the moon-faced man to the end of the aisle and waited for him to open a metal cage. When he loosened his hand over her mouth and bent over to push her inside, she bit down on his palm as hard as she could. He yelled and let go. She twisted in his arms and almost got away, but the moon-faced man grabbed her by the scruff of the neck and shoved her into the cage. She stumbled, fell, and landed on her hands and knees. Viktor slammed the door shut and the moon-faced man locked it with a padlock, swearing under his breath.

Filthy straw lined the bottom of the cage, and a horrible smell filled her nostrils. She scrambled on her knees over to the door and hooked her fingers through the bars, wheezing and gasping for air.

"Let me out!" she screamed.

"Sorry, sugar," the moon-faced man said. "I just paid hard-earned money for you. And in case you haven't figured it out yet, you belong to me now."

"Please!" she cried. "I want to go home!"

He laughed. "You are home, and I'm your legal guardian now."

Lilly gagged and tried to catch her breath. This had to be a nightmare. It had to be. Why would Momma do this to her? Why? "No . . . my daddy . . . my daddy will come get me."

"I'm afraid not, little one. Your daddy is dying and your mother signed the papers. It's all legal."

"That's not true!" she said. "My father is in Pennsylvania. He's coming back tomorrow . . . and when he does, he'll be looking for me!"

"Believe what you want if it makes you feel better, but that's not what your mother said."

Lilly let go of the bars and slumped in the cage, too weak to sit up. "What are you . . . What are you going to do to me?"

"When I decide, you'll be the first to know."

He picked up the oil lamp, started to walk away, and signaled Viktor to follow.

"Please," Lilly cried. "I'm begging you. Please. Let me out."

"Want me to stay here and keep an eye on her, boss?" Viktor said. His voice was low and gravelly, as if his throat were full of rocks.

"No," the moon-faced man said. "She's not going anywhere." He made his way toward the other end of the boxcar.

Lilly screamed until she ran out of breath and her throat felt like it was on fire. The goats and llamas bleated and pawed at the insides of their stalls.

The moon-faced man came back and glared at her. "Scream all you want," he said. "No one will hear you. And if they do, no one cares."

He kicked the cage and disappeared down the aisle. Viktor went with him. The boxcar door opened and slammed shut, and the inside of the car was plunged into blackness. Lilly pulled in a shaky breath and screamed again, rattling the cage with her hands. She reached through the bars and yanked on the padlock with every ounce of strength she had left. It was no use. The lock was too strong. She screamed until her throat was raw, then collapsed in the straw, gasping for air. Her elbows and knees felt smeared with dirt, and the sharp tang of urine burned her nostrils. She curled up in a ball and sobbed, tears and sweat coursing down her cheeks.

For as long as she could remember, she had wanted to see the outside world. Now, she'd give anything to go back to Blackwood Manor. *Please, God,* she prayed. *If Momma comes and gets me, I'll do everything she says. I'll pray ten times a day and memorize the Bible verses. I'll get rid of my dolls and books and do whatever she wants. No more daydreaming, no more asking for a window that opens. I love Momma and I'm sorry for being bad. Please, God, please. I'll do anything. I miss my daddy and Abby.*

She pictured her cat curled up on her bed, waiting and wondering why she had left her all alone. The thought of Abby being sad and thinking she had deserted her was almost more than she could take. What would happen to Abby now? Who would feed her and love her and pet her? Not Momma. Momma didn't like cats. Then she imagined Daddy going upstairs to surprise her with a birthday present and finding her bedroom empty. He would want to know where she was. And after Momma told him what she had done, he would race over to the circus train to rescue her.

If Momma told the truth.

If Daddy wasn't dying.

With that thought, something turned over beneath Lilly's rib cage, and a horrible, heavy pain exploded inside her chest. All of a sudden, she knew she was going to be sick. She turned on her side and threw up, coughing and gagging on her own vomit. She spit over and over, then wiped her mouth and lay back. Her eyelids felt heavy. Her pulse thundered in her ears. She felt dizzy, like that time Daddy had to put mustard and warm dressings on her chest for three days. Then the world spun out of control and went black.

A shrieking whistle startled Lilly awake. She didn't know where she was or how long she had been sleeping.

"Daddy?" she cried in a weak voice. "I'm over here, Daddy!"

A dim light filtered in through the slats in the walls and fell over the metal bars of a cage. Straw stabbed her arms and legs, and the low thud of a powerful engine sounded in the distance. Then it all came back to her.

She was locked in a cage on a circus train. And Daddy wasn't here.

Lilly's eyes flooded and she sat up, her throat and chest burning, her neck stiff. When she could take a breath without coughing, she got to her knees and brushed herself off. Every muscle in her body hurt, her skin itched, and she had to go to the bathroom. Her belly felt like it was about to explode. She gathered the skirt of her dress around her waist, pushed her underwear to her knees, and squatted in a corner of the pen. Pee ran down the inside of her leg into one of her shoes. Now, not only was she dirty and cold, she smelled bad too. Using the already filthy straw, she did her best to wipe off her leg, then pulled her underwear up and sat in the opposite corner, counting the bars of the cage and trying not to cry.

The goats and llamas were lying down in their stalls, sleeping or munching hay. She peered between the slats in the boxcar and tried to look outside, but couldn't see anything. Somewhere a whistle screeched. Then the boxcar shuddered and lurched forward with a jolt, and the train rattled forward along the tracks. The llamas and goats got to their feet and nervously looked over their stall doors. Lilly gripped the cage bars with shaking hands.

"No!" she screamed. "We can't leave yet! My daddy is coming to get me!"

Little by little, the train picked up speed and traveled farther and farther away from Blackwood Manor. Lilly fell back on the dirty straw and sobbed, her head bumping against the cage wall. How would Daddy ever find her now? Terror and homesickness washed over her in violent, powerful waves. There was nothing she could do but wait and pray. Then again, Momma always said God would only answer prayers if they were sincere. Lilly had begged God to make Momma come back for her, but she never did. Lilly was still here, locked in this cage. If God didn't think her prayers were sincere then, when would he?

After what seemed like a thousand hours, the circus train slowed, groaning against the brakes. The iron wheels caught and screeched, caught and screeched, and the pistons hissed longer and louder. Finally, the train came to a shuddering stop, and the shriek of releasing steam pierced the air. The goats and llamas stood and swayed on unsteady legs. Lilly sat up, trembling and scared and cold.

Outside, iron latches lifted, doors slid open on their tracks, and men talked and shouted. Ramps and chutes clattered to the ground. When the side door to the boxcar slid open, Lilly moved to the back corner of the cage and curled up in a ball, trying to make herself smaller. Sunlight burst into the car, revealing floating dust and hay chafe, and the outside sounds got louder. She squinted against the light and put her hands over her ears, shaking all over. The shape of a man appeared in the doorframe and climbed into the car. He stretched and yawned, then went over to one of the pens and looked inside. Gray stubble covered his weathered face, and a faded black derby sat tilted back on his head. He scratched one of the llamas behind the ears, then moved down the center aisle to check the other stalls. When he came to the one across from Lilly, he leaned over the door, his back to her.

Lilly crawled forward and clutched the cage bars in her hands. "Hello?" she said in a quiet voice.

The man startled and spun around. When he saw her, his eyes went wide. "Jumpin' Jesus!" he said. "Who the hell are you?"

"I'm Lilly," she said. "Can you let me out? Please?" She watched his face, waiting to see if he was afraid of her.

"What in tarnation are you doing in there, kid?"

Her heart thumped so hard inside her chest she could barely speak. Was he pretending not to be afraid, like Daddy pretended? Or was he brave because she was in a cage? She swallowed and found her voice. "They put me in here."

The man took off his hat and scrubbed an age-spotted hand across his balding head. "Who put you in there?"

"A man with a moon face and a ponytail and someone called Viktor. He was . . . he was . . ." A burning lump filled her throat and she couldn't go on.

"A monster?"

She nodded, tears spilling down her cheeks.

The old man put his hat back on and straightened, his brow furrowed. He stood for a moment, scratching his neck and thinking, then hurried over to the open boxcar door and yelled out, "Hey, Dante, come over here a minute, will ya?"

A few seconds later, a big man with a red beard climbed into the boxcar. "What's going on, Leon?"

Leon pointed at Lilly and grinned, revealing crooked yellow teeth. "Look what we got here."

Dante knelt down and peered into the cage. "Well, well, what do you know," he said. "Looks like we got us a little stowaway." He smiled and put his fingers through the bars to touch her hair. She scrambled backward into a corner, frightened and surprised at the same time. Maybe Momma was right. Maybe circus people were used to monsters.

"She said Viktor put her in there," Leon said. He bent over to look at her. "And a man with a moon face and a ponytail."

Dante straightened. "Best leave her be, then. We don't need no trouble."

Leon turned away and moved down the aisle. "I'm just here to feed the critters and get them ready to unload."

"Please," Lilly cried. "You can't leave me here. My daddy is looking for me and I—"

Leon stopped and glanced back at her, his forehead lined with concern.

"Were you kidnapped?" Dante said.

Lilly shook her head. "Momma . . . she . . ." The words caught in her throat.

"What?" Leon said. He came back and knelt

beside the cage. "What'd your mother do, darlin'?"

Lilly forced the words out. "She took money from the man with the ponytail and left me with him." She broke down again, shoulders convulsing.

"I knew Merrick had something to do with this," Dante said to Leon. "She belongs to him now."

Lilly swallowed and gazed at him. "What is he going to do to me?"

"You mean you don't know?" Leon said.

Lilly shook her head, her chin quivering.

"Merrick runs the sideshow for The Barlow Brothers' Circus, The Most Amazing Show on Earth," Leon said. He stood and pulled a bale of hay from the stack, broke it open, and divided it among the goats and llamas. "Looks to me like you just joined the circus, kid."

"Leon's right," Dante said. "But don't cry, it's not so bad. You might like it here."

Lilly cried harder.

Two more men climbed into the boxcar and Dante moved away from the cage. It was Viktor and the moon-faced man with the ponytail.

"Don't scare her, now, boys," the moon-faced man said.

"Mornin', Merrick," Leon and Dante said in unison.

"Yes sirree, boys," Merrick said. "The gods are smiling on The Barlow Brothers' Circus today.

Damned if they ain't, sending us such a splendid young specimen. Isn't she stunning?"

The men nodded in agreement, and Merrick and Viktor made their way over to Lilly. She pressed herself against the back of the cage.

"Let's get a look at her in the daylight," Merrick said.

Viktor unlocked the padlock, knelt down, and reached into the cage. Lilly scrambled into a corner, away from his giant hands. He swore and stuck his head inside, stretching and reaching for her. She kicked him in the face. Her shoe collided with his already mangled nose and she heard a bony crack.

"Bloody hell!" Viktor yelled. He put his hand to his face and moved backward, out of the cage. Blood trickled over his lips. Then he reached in again, grabbed her by the arm, and yanked her out the door. Lilly twisted and screamed and tried to get away.

"Don't just stand there gawking!" Merrick shouted at Dante. "Help him!"

Dante grabbed Lilly's other arm and held on. Lilly thrashed and kicked and fought to break free. It was no use. She was no match for two grown men, and her lungs were closing again. She stopped struggling and gasped for air.

Merrick moved closer, his eyes gleaming. "You're a fighter," he said. "That's good. But I don't appreciate you kicking my star attrac-

78

tion in the face, even if it's already a mess."

"Let me go!" Lilly shouted. "I . . . want . . . to go home!"

"I'll say it one more time," Merrick said. "You are home. And you might as well learn to play nice, because you're not going anywhere."

"Yes . . . I am," Lilly cried. "My daddy is coming to get me and . . ."

"I'm afraid that's not going to happen, sugar."

Lilly coughed and gulped and tried sucking in more air. Then, for some reason, she suddenly remembered that cats hiss and llamas spit when they're afraid. She took the biggest breath she could muster, closed her mouth to gather her saliva, and spat at Merrick. A white blob landed on his cheek and slid down his face, leaving a wet trail.

He flinched as if slapped, then reached into his pocket for a handkerchief and, glaring at her, wiped his face. Then, without a word, he went over to the wall and yanked what looked like a short black whip from a nail, his expression getting darker and darker.

"Turn her around," he ordered Viktor and Dante.

"Come on, Merrick," Dante said. "You don't have to do this. She's just scared."

"Shut your damn pie hole and do as I say or I'll have you red-lighted!" Merrick yelled, spittle flying from his lips.

The men turned Lilly around and held her by

the arms. Viktor's fingers dug into her flesh, but Dante held on with gentle hands. Leon watched with sad, worried eyes.

"I'm sorry 'bout this," Dante whispered. "Just do what he says from now on."

Then the whip lashed across her back, ripping like fire over her shoulder blades. She arched her back and cried out. Merrick grunted and whipped her again. Once. Twice. Three times. The pain was hot and strong, like the flame on Momma's lantern. She writhed in agony and something warm ran down the inside of her leg. Her vision started to close in and her knees buckled, but Viktor and Dante held her up. Merrick grunted and she sensed him lifting the whip again.

Dante moved between them, blocking her body with his. "That's enough," he said in a calm voice. "You're going to kill her."

"He's right," Leon said. "She's just a little girl."

"Put her back in the cage!" Merrick snarled.

Viktor dragged her over to the cage and threw her inside. She landed on her back and hit her head. Pain shot up her spine. She rolled on her side in the straw, her shoulders burning and her breath hitching in her chest. Viktor closed the door and slammed the padlock shut.

Merrick hurled the whip down the aisle and paced the floor, his fists clenched. Then he bared his teeth and kicked the cage, denting it.

"I'll leave you in there for as long as it takes," he said. He pointed at Leon. "Old Leon here can bring you food for weeks. Got it?"

She nodded and gasped for air.

"Now you see who's in charge here?"

She nodded again.

"You've got a lot to learn, little girl," Merrick said. "And if you think we're something to be afraid of, try escaping and see who you run into. There are men out there just waiting to examine someone like you. More than one freak has been cut up and had their brains and body parts pickled and put on display." He paced the floor again, then stopped and addressed Leon, who had gone back to pulling apart another bale of hay. "Hey, Leon. What do you think the good people of this fine town would do if they saw this young lady wandering around their neighborhood?"

Leon busied himself putting hay into a stall and avoiding Merrick's eyes. "I can't say for sure."

"Of course you can," Merrick said. He smiled a mean, snake-like smile. "Come on, tell Miss Lilly the truth, for her own good."

Leon stopped working and eyed Lilly, a sad look on his face. "I suppose the folks in town might be frightened of her. Probably make fun of her too."

"That's right," Merrick said. "Or some damn fool might try to kill her just 'cause she looks different than they do. Ain't that right, Leon?"

Leon shrugged.

"Come on, old man. Tell Lilly what happened to your daughter."

Leon's shoulders dropped and he gripped the top of a stall door with one hand. He stared at his feet for a long time, then made his way over to Merrick. "He's right, Miss Lilly," he said. "It ain't safe out there for people like you." His saggy eyes brimmed with tears.

"Tell her why," Merrick insisted.

"'Cause people are afraid of what they don't understand. My daughter and me, we worked for Merrick and Mr. Barlow for three years. She was the most beautiful bearded woman you ever saw. Her eyes were blue as the sea, her blond hair soft as silk. But she made the mistake of falling in love with a townie and thinking she could live a normal life. I warned her against it and, well, it didn't work out so good. The other townies weren't never going to allow a freak to marry one of their own."

"Finish the story," Merrick said.

Leon pulled a red bandana from his pocket and wiped his forehead and eyes. "A week after the wedding, her husband . . ." He stopped and his face folded in on itself. Then he looked at Lilly, his chin trembling. "Her husband found her tied to the church steps with her face shaved and her throat slit."

Lilly swallowed and closed her eyes. The thought of someone slitting someone else's throat made her feel like throwing up. She remembered seeing Daddy going into the woods with a shotgun and coming out with a string of dead rabbits. He said hunters killed for food, but seeing the rabbits still made her stomach sick. This was worse. Is that why Momma kept in her in the attic? To keep someone from slitting her throat? But what if someone in the circus did it? If Daddy didn't find her soon, and she couldn't escape because someone might slit her throat, was she going to spend the rest of her life locked in this cage? Between her burning back and the idea that she was never going home again, it was too much. She put her hands over her face and felt herself going someplace else, someplace where it would all go away.

Merrick kicked the cage again. "Wake up."

She took her hands from her face and struggled to a sitting position. "What . . . What are you going to do to me?"

"You work for me now," Merrick said. "I run the sideshow, which is why most people come to the circus anyway. They might bring the kiddies to see the elephants and the lions, but what they really want to see are the freaks. And I have the best around. People will pay good money to see someone like you."

"But Momma said people would be afraid of me."

"Well, we'll find out, won't we? Now, if you're ready to cooperate, I'll let you out of that cage. We'll get you cleaned up and get you something to eat. Sound fair?"

She nodded.

"No more biting and trying to escape? No more kicking and screaming? If you try anything, I'll just lock you back up. Got it?"

She nodded again.

"Dante," Merrick said. "Go get Glory."

"Yes, sir," Dante said. He gave Lilly a worried glance and jumped out of the boxcar.

Merrick moved toward the center of the car, stood across from the open door and lit a fat cigar. "If you think about it, I'm doing you a favor. Your parents don't want you, and neither would anyone else. A lot of people look down on carnies. They don't trust us. But the circus is a place where a person can work for a living even if he's lost the possessions normal society likes him to have. People try to get a job somewhere else when they've lost their moorings, and more likely than not, they're turned away. Maybe the road is better than whatever they left behind, maybe they've got a troubled past, maybe they're just not cut out for the nine-to-five, or maybe they don't fit in among decent people." He took a drag on the cigar, then made his way toward Lilly again, smoke trailing from his lips. "Or maybe their family just don't want them around. But we take them in, all of them. Even people like you. So you see, it all depends on which side of the fence you're looking from."

Lilly didn't know anything about sides of fences. The only thing she knew for sure was that she wanted to go home more than anything in the world.

After a minute or two, Dante returned with a woman wearing a pink skirt, a sparkly, sleeveless blouse, and a pearl headband in her short, wavy hair. Her face looked soft and pink, but the rest of her skin looked as if someone had written all over it with different colored ink. Drawings of lions, angels, crosses, skulls, hearts, and flowers covered every exposed inch of her arms and legs, each image merging with the others to create one continuous design. Lilly couldn't take her eyes off her. When the woman saw her in the cage, she gasped.

"Where did she come from?" she said.

"We picked her up at the last stop," Viktor said.

"Picked her up?" the woman said. "What do you mean, picked her up?" She knelt next to the cage and Lilly watched her expression, waiting for her reaction. The only emotion on her face was concern. Maybe she was pretending like everyone else.

Merrick gave Viktor a withering look. "We didn't pick her up. We saved her. Just like I saved Viktor from that orphanage, remember?" He gestured toward Lilly. "Glory, meet our newest act."

Glory smiled at Lilly and in a gentle voice said, "What's your name, sweetheart?"

"I want my daddy," Lilly said, tears filling her eyes.

Glory glanced at Merrick and frowned. "Saved her, huh?"

"Mind your business, Glory," Merrick said. "It was a legitimate deal and I'm her legal guardian now. So are you going to help me with her, or do I have to get Josephine to do it?"

Glory stood. "No, keep Josephine away from her. I'll get her cleaned up and fed."

"That's what I thought," Merrick said. He jerked his chin at Viktor. "Let her out."

Viktor unlocked the padlock, opened the door, and stepped back.

Glory bent over in front of the cage, smiled, and crooked her finger at Lilly to come out. "It's all right," she said. "You don't need to be afraid."

"Watch out," Viktor said. "She's a wild animal."

Breathing hard, Lilly stared at Glory and tried to decide if she could trust such a strange-looking woman. Except for the odd drawings on her skin—What were they called? She couldn't remember—Glory looked normal, and her eyes seemed soft and kind. Lilly leaned forward and slowly crawled across the straw toward the door. Glory stepped backward to give her room and Lilly got out and stood. Her head hurt, her legs felt weak and shaky, and the whip marks on her back throbbed with pain. Glory closed the door and held out a hand. Lilly wrapped her arms around herself and moved away, her eyes lowered.

"Come on, honey," Glory said. "I'm not going to hurt you."

Lilly shook her head. Other than Viktor crushing her to his chest and the men holding her by her arms, the last time anyone had touched her was when she was a little girl, unable to wash and dress herself. Daddy never held her hand or hugged and kissed her, not even on her birthday. When he surprised her with Abby the kitten one year, she was so happy she reached out to hug him, but he drew away. And Momma only hit her. Thinking about her parents, Lilly went limp, as if she were about to collapse in a pile on the floor. Was she ever going to see them again?

"It's okay," Glory said. "You don't know me yet, but we'll be friends soon. Just you wait and see."

Lilly stared at her, trying not to cry.

Glory motioned for Lilly to follow her toward the boxcar door. Lilly did as she was told. But when they reached the door, she shrank back, blinking, and put her hands over her ears. The sounds were too loud and the light hurt her eyes.

A city of tents and people and animals filled a field of brown grass outside the boxcar. The big top lay flat on the ground while men worked all around it, putting the walls together and lacing up seams. An elephant carried long posts curled in its trunk across the lot, while another pushed posts upright with its forehead and the help of workers pulling ropes. Groups of men stood in circles and took turns swinging big hammers over their heads, bringing them back down on tent stakes, pounding them into the ground and filling the air with loud bangs. High poles stuck out from the big top's center and sides, like a giant bug with a hundred feelers. Men shouted and yelled to be heard above the noise. A group of dark-skinned workers struggled to hang over-sized banners in front of a tent across from a row of red-and-white-striped candy apple, popcorn, and hot-dog stands. Draft horses hauled wagons, equipment, and cages filled with monkeys, bears, lions, and tigers around the yard. Red and gold letters on wagons with sunburst wheels read: THE BARLOW BROTHERS' CIRCUS, THE MOST AMAZING SHOW ON EARTH. Two men on horseback galloped past the boxcar, kicking up clouds of dust.

Glory eased over the edge of the door down to the gravel, then smiled up at Lilly. "It's all right," she said. "Come on."

Lilly didn't want to, but she took her hands from her ears and climbed down. When she felt something warm on her arms and face, she looked up and squinted. It was the sun. Shielding her eyes with her hand, she looked from horizon to horizon. The sky was bigger than she had ever dreamed. And there were birds, flying like black arrows back and forth over the tents and people. She glanced up and down the railroad tracks. The train was so long she couldn't see the end. The parts she could see were made up of boxcars, flat cars, and passenger cars with windows. Men and women came out of the passenger cars and boxcars and made their way toward a tent with an orange flag. Next to the tent, a big tank belched steam.

"After you get her cleaned up and fed," Merrick said from the boxcar doorway, "bring her back to the train and we'll show her to Mr. Barlow."

Glory nodded and started walking. Lilly followed her away from the railroad tracks toward the lot, staring at the dust clouds kicked up by Glory's feet, the clumps of grass, the dandelions, and the stones. A bee landed on a dry clover blossom, and a tiny white butterfly flitted past her nose. She nearly tripped three times, unable to take her eyes off everything she was seeing. As they entered the lot, a man went by on horseback and the ground vibrated beneath her feet. The yelling and pounding of stakes grew louder, but she resisted the urge to put her hands over her ears. Every once in a while, one of the workers glanced up at her, and it made her stomach turn over. What if someone wanted to slit her throat? She hunched her shoulders and walked as close to Glory as she could without touching her, trying to make herself smaller. There was so much to see—tents and people and animals and flags and banners and posters—and she didn't want to miss anything. At the same time, she didn't want to look. It was too much and too close and too big and too loud.

"You okay?" Glory said.

Lilly bit her lip and nodded.

When they reached a line of tents at the far end of the lot behind the big top, Glory stopped, held open a tent flap, and waited for Lilly to enter. Inside, rows of buckets sat in front of suitcases, trunks, and racks of colorful costumes. Dressing tables and vanities and mirrors lined the back wall. Lilly's heart leapt in her chest. Was she about to see herself for the very first time? She dropped her eyes, unsure if she should she go over to the mirrors or run out of the tent.

Glory led her over to a bucket, picked up a cloth and a bar of soap from a table, and knelt down. She dunked the cloth and soap into the bucket and slowly made a move to wash Lilly's face. Lilly drew away, her chin to her chest.

"It's all right," Glory said. "I'm just going to clean you up a little."

Lilly stared at Glory. Why wasn't she afraid? Was it because she looked different too?

Glory sighed, then smiled and held out the cloth. Lilly slowly reached out and took it, then rubbed it over her face. It felt good.

"Are you doing okay?" Glory said. "I know this is a big change and it all must seem so scary."

Lilly clenched her jaw to keep her chin from trembling and shrugged.

"Did Merrick really save you from an orphanage?"

Lilly wasn't sure what an orphanage was, but she shook her head anyway.

"A hospital?"

Lilly shook her head again.

"Did he take you from your daddy?"

Lilly's eyes flooded. She shook her head a third time.

Glory frowned. "Where did he get you, then?" She took the rag, rinsed it, and handed it back to Lilly. "Can you tell me?"

"He . . ." she managed. "He gave Momma money and Momma left me with him."

Glory gasped. "He bought you?"

Lilly nodded.

"He bought you from your mother?" Glory's face grew as red as the ink heart on her neck. "But why would she—" She put trembling fingers over her lips.

Lilly shrugged one shoulder and started to cry.

"Oh, sweetheart, I'm so sorry." She reached for Lilly again, but Lilly took a step back.

Glory dropped her arms and gave her a weak but sad smile. "It's all right," she said. "I understand. You don't have to let me hug you. As a matter of fact, you don't have to let anyone hug you, or even touch you. If someone tries, you run away as fast as you can. Then tell me, okay?"

Lilly nodded and blinked back her tears, wondering if she should tell Glory about Merrick hitting her with a whip. Momma always warned her not to tell Daddy when she punished her, or the next time would be worse. If Merrick found out she told Glory he hit her, it might be the same. Lilly took the cloth again and washed the dirt off her arms and legs.

"We need to get you out of that filthy dress," Glory said. She straightened, went over to a trunk, and lifted the lid. "You can borrow one of Tina's dresses until the Monday man can get you some of your own. She won't mind." She pulled out a simple blue dress with puffy sleeves and a white belt. "This one should work. Do you need help putting it on?"

Lilly shook her head and took the dress. She unbuttoned the collar of the one she was wearing, then stopped and glanced at the tent door. What if someone came in and saw her naked?

"Don't worry," Glory said. "Everyone's headed to the cookhouse for breakfast."

Lilly gazed up at her and waited.

"Oh, sorry," Glory said, turning around. "Let me know when you're done."

Lilly took off her dress and let it fall to the ground. It was her favorite, the only thing she had left from home, and now it was ruined. She slipped the clean one over her head, pushed her arms through the sleeves, then realized she couldn't reach the top buttons in the back. If Glory helped with the buttons, she might see the marks from Merrick's whip. Maybe she wouldn't realize it was unbuttoned.

"I'm done," Lilly said in a small voice.

Glory spun around to face her. "Aw, look at you! And it's a perfect fit. Can I button up the back?"

Lilly glanced at the ground.

Glory knelt down and smiled at her. "It's all right. You can trust me."

Lilly clasped her hands into fists and turned around. Maybe Glory wouldn't see the marks. Hopefully, they weren't bleeding.

With gentle fingers, Glory started to fasten the first button. Then she stopped and gasped. "Who did this to you?"

Lilly closed her eyes. Lying was a sin, but right now she didn't care. "Momma," she said.

Glory went quiet and finished buttoning the back of the dress. When Lilly turned around, Glory's eyes were glassy.

"Listen," Glory said. "You have to do what Merrick says, okay?"

Lilly nodded. But how did Glory know it was Merrick who left the marks on her back?

"Promise me," Glory said. "You'll do what he says from now on."

"Okay."

Glory gave her a weak smile and stood. Lilly gazed up at her. She wanted to ask her a question but didn't know if she should.

"What?" Glory said. "You look like you want to say something."

"Can I ask you a question?"

"Of course, anything."

"How come you're not afraid of me?"

Glory frowned, her head moving back slightly. "What are you talking about? Why on earth would I be afraid of you?"

Lilly scuffed a shoe across the grass.

Glory knelt again. "What is it, sweetheart? You can tell me. We're friends, remember?"

Lilly lifted her chin and looked at Glory. "Momma said I'm an abomination. She said I'd make everyone sick and scared, that's why I had to hide." Her voice trembled. "Because I'm a monster and I'm cursed."

Glory pressed her lips together. Then she tried to smile, but tears filled her eyes instead. "Oh, honey. You're not a monster. Far from it. And you're not cursed. I hate to tell you this, but your mother wasn't telling the truth."

"But Momma says lying is a sin."

Glory got to her feet again. "Come here, I want to show you something." She started toward the mirrors.

Lilly couldn't move. Her hands grew clammy and she started to tremble. All those nights, all those hours, staring into the window glass trying to see her face, and now all she wanted to do was run and hide. What if Momma was right and she really was a monster? What if the sight of her own face made her scream? What if she looked like Viktor? She touched her tongue to her teeth— *one, two, three, four, five*—and tried to think. If she had a third eye, she would have felt it on her forehead. If her mouth was twisted or her nose was split in two pieces, she would have felt that too. Still, she wasn't sure she wanted to look in a mirror. Her mouth felt dry as dirt.

"It's all right," Glory said. "I promise."

Lilly kept her eyes lowered so she wouldn't see herself in the mirror before she was ready, and slowly followed Glory over to a dressing table filled with colored feathers, combs, brushes, earrings, necklaces, and glass bottles of all shapes and sizes. She counted the bottles to try to calm down. *One, two, three, four, five.* It didn't help. Her lungs grew tight. She couldn't breathe. She put a hand on her chest, the muscles in her neck loosening and tightening as she struggled for air.

Glory knelt in front of her. "It's all right," she said in a soothing voice. "Just relax and try to breathe slowly. Take a really deep breath and let it out, like this." She inhaled deeply and blew out a long, slow breath. "The same thing happens to one of my friends when she gets scared too. Just look at me and you'll be okay."

Lilly fixed her eyes on Glory and tried doing what she said. After six or seven breaths, her lungs loosened and her throat opened up. Her thundering heart slowed. Finally, she could get air without choking.

"Better?" Glory said.

Lilly nodded.

"Do you trust me now? Are we friends?"

Lilly nodded again.

"How about you turn around and let me fix your hair, then?"

Lilly thought about it for a moment. She couldn't remember the last time Momma had washed her hair, let alone combed or even touched it. And when Momma did her hair, she always pulled. But for some reason, Lilly didn't think Glory would be that rough. She turned, her hands in fists at her sides, and waited for Glory to touch her head.

With gentle fingers, Glory gathered Lilly's hair in one hand and, using a brush from the dressing table, worked out the snarls and bits of hay. It felt strange and strangely pleasant to have another person touch her hair, to feel the pull and tug of someone else's movements on her scalp. Goose bumps rippled across her skin and her heartbeat slowed. With the dirt and tangles out, Glory brushed her hair away from her face and fluffed the sides and top with her fingers. When she was finished, she moved in front of Lilly and smiled, one hand on her hip.

"Ready?" she said.

Lilly took a deep breath and nodded.

"Close your eyes and turn around."

Lilly squeezed her eyes shut and turned to face the mirror.

"Okay, open them," Glory said.

Lilly counted, curling and uncurling her fingers—*one, two, three, four, five, six, seven, eight, nine, ten*—then opened her eyes and, ever so slowly, raised her head to look in the mirror. When she saw her reflection, she drew in a sharp breath.

Looking back at her was a young girl with flawless skin, winter-white hair, and eyes the color of a summer sky. The only mark on her face was a small indent on her chin, from the time Momma pushed her and she fell into her bedframe. Her lips were such a light pink they were nearly invisible, and her lashes and brows looked dusted with snow. The navy blue dress looked black against her milk-colored skin. Lilly leaned forward and touched the mirror. Was it some kind of trick? But the girl in the mirror moved too, and their identical, pale fingers touched, tip to tip, on the glass. The color of their skin matched perfectly. But there was something else in her reflection too. Something that shook her to the core.

She looked like a doll.

A beautiful, perfect doll.

She wasn't a monster.

She wasn't an abomination.

She wouldn't have made anyone sick.

Momma had lied. And Daddy had too.

She stared at herself for a long time, tears flooding her eyes. Why had Momma kept her locked in the attic? And why had Daddy gone along with it? Did they hate her because God forgot to give her a color? Was it really that horrible? If they were only trying to protect her, why didn't they let her go downstairs? Why didn't they spend time with her? Why didn't they hug and kiss her? Like Momma said, no one in the circus cared what she looked like. So why did she? Why did Daddy? Why did the two people who were supposed to love her more than anything keep her hidden from the world? Were they afraid? Were they ashamed? Were they evil? Overcome, she put her face in her hands and collapsed on the ground, shoulders convulsing. Glory knelt beside her.

"See, honey," she said. "You're not a monster. Quite the opposite."

Sobs hitched in Lilly's chest. "But I don't

understand," she cried. "What's wrong with me?"

"There's nothing wrong with you. You're perfectly normal except for the color of your skin. That's all. And guess what? There are other people just like you. They're called albinos."

Lilly looked up, her chin trembling. "There are other people like me?"

Glory smiled and nodded. "I met someone like you a few years ago at Ringling Brothers. But she wasn't anywhere near as pretty as you. She said her skin was missing something that gave it color and she was born with the condition, just like you were. I can't remember what the *something* was called, but other than being really pale and having to avoid the sun, she was perfectly fine."

Lilly's face crumpled in on itself. "So why would Momma and Daddy . . ." She couldn't go on. Her grief was like a shroud she couldn't see through. It made it impossible to think straight. She wanted to lie down and go to sleep, to make this nightmare go away.

Glory took a handkerchief from the dresser and gave it to her. "I don't know, sweetheart, but I can see why Merrick wanted you. You're perfect, like a life-sized porcelain doll."

"What does he want me for?"

Glory stroked Lilly's hair. "Let me tell you a little story. When I was eleven, I ran away from home to join the circus. Of course I had to earn my keep, so for the first few years I worked for

Josephine, cleaning her sleeper car, sewing costumes, basically being her slave. Then, when I got older, Merrick gave me these tattoos and let me work for him in the sideshow. That's when I asked him to help my brother, who my parents had sent to a horrible place. He was locked up, just like you were. But Merrick got him out and saved his life, and I'll never be able to repay him for that. Now Viktor is one of our biggest attractions, and I'm . . ." She paused and furrowed her brow, as if rethinking what she was about to say. Then she sighed and went on. "What I'm trying to tell you is Merrick sees something in you, Lilly. That's why he bought you from your momma. He thinks he can make you a star. He thinks everyone is going to love you."

"I don't want to be a star," Lilly cried. "I just want to go home to my cat."

"I know," Glory said. "But this is your home now, remember?"

Lilly buried her face in her hands and cried harder.

CHAPTER 6
Julia

The trees surrounding Blackwood Manor were black and bare, making the estate look even grayer. The house seemed as overpowering as it did the day Julia left, grim and bulky, the color of the winter sky. It was a Victorian, neo-Gothic four-story, with mullioned windows, attic dormers, three chimneys, and a steep mansard roof. Dirty drifts of melting snow and dead leaves lined the stone foundation, edged the hedgerow between the yard and the back woods, and trailed the fences around the horse barn.

Julia climbed out of the taxi and took slow, calming breaths. The damp air smelled of mud and fungus, hay and horse manure. Just like she remembered. Had it really been three years since she left? It felt like yesterday. She wore pink pants and a tight sweater today, in defiance of her dead mother and the somber house. But now, she felt foolish. The cab driver opened the trunk, gave Julia her suitcase, then drove away and left her standing in the driveway.

The windows of the house were blank, reflecting the naked trees all around. The trees seemed taller and scragglier. Maybe they needed to be trimmed. Was she already thinking of things that needed doing? The house was hers now, all twelve bedrooms, the soaring ceilings, the grand staircases, the huge kitchen with flagstones worn smooth by passing feet. It was hers, but only if she stayed. That was what Mother wanted, and even in death, she demanded her way. And yet, Julia couldn't help wondering if this was a test. If she didn't stay, everything would be sold off and the money sent to charity. But while she wasn't sure she could live in the manor for the rest of her life, there was plenty of land and plenty of money to build a new house. It gave her a strange sense of satisfaction to know that, as much as Mother tried, she couldn't control everything.

She stared up at the estate, wondering what she would do with all that space. Would the rooms seem empty and quiet, or would they groan under the weight of bad memories? She pictured Mother's crystal in the dining room buffet, sparkling in the light of the chandelier. She pictured her father's whiskey bottles, lined up on a sideboard in his den. As a child, she had snuck into the den and peered into the mysterious decanters and flasks, trying to understand why her father found the liquid inside so appealing. She'd even pulled out the stoppers to take a sniff. But then Mother caught her, and she never went into the den again, or anyplace else in the house she wasn't allowed to go. A good whipping with a willow branch had a way of reminding you to do as you're told.

Now she could go wherever she wanted—into her father's den, into the third-floor bedrooms, into the attic and barn. With the cab gone, there was only silence. Silence from the trees and the house. Silence from the barn and fields. Where were the horses?

She shivered and wrapped her arms around herself. The house looked like it was waiting patiently, anticipating the moment when it could swallow her whole. Had she made a mistake? What was she going to do out here all alone, a good two miles from the nearest neighbor? And how in the world was she going to run a horse farm when her parents had never let her into the barn, let alone talked to her about the business? Then she remembered she had money, lots of it, and she could pay someone else to take care of the horses. Besides, she couldn't go back to Big Al's and her dingy little room above the liquor store. She couldn't go back to stealing, or being abused by Tom. She felt bad for leaving him without saying good-bye, but when she came home from work the day she got the letter, he was passed out on the couch after another bender. In the end it was for the best. She didn't have to explain and she didn't have to lie. And now she was free of him for good. She picked up her suitcase, wrapped her fingers around the front door key in her coat pocket, and strode toward Blackwood Manor, determined to make the best of whatever lay ahead.

Inside, the manor somehow seemed smaller than she remembered, but it was still enormous. The foyer alone was five times the size of her room above the liquor store. The house felt cold and damp, and she wondered if there were still rats in the attic. Mother and Father always denied the infestation, but growing up she had heard them at night, scurrying between rooms and in ceilings, scratching and gnawing on old plaster and rotted wood. The sounds of the old house had always kept her awake—beams creaking and shifting, pipes knocking and moaning—and her vivid young mind imagined someone, or something, living behind the walls.

She dropped her suitcase at the bottom of the stairs and drifted toward the kitchen, her footsteps echoing on the wood floors. She hadn't eaten since last night and now she was starving. After the attorney found out she had agreed to take over the estate, he called Claude, the barn manager, to have groceries delivered. Too bad Claude hadn't turned up the furnace too.

The smells of her childhood rushed back to her as she made her way through the house: lemoned oak, stone floors and wood fires, dusty furniture and silver polish. She passed the formal dining room and pictured Mother perched like a queen at the head of the table, casting a cold glare at anyone who dared slurp their soup or interrupt while she was talking. In the living room, moldy ashes lingered in the grates of the fireplace, and the familiar red tin of matches sat in the same spot on the mantel. A pair of reading glasses rested on an open book on the end table next to Mother's favorite wingback chair, as if she had just set them down and gone upstairs to take a nap. Suddenly, being alone in the house made Julia uneasy, as if she might turn and see Mother standing in a doorway, an acid smile on her wrinkled face, her hair tinted gold.

In the kitchen, she rinsed out the copper teakettle, filled it, and put it on the stove to boil. The water from the sink smelled the same—iron, wet stone, and a hint of algae, so unlike the chlorinated water in the city. How many times had she been in this kitchen, washing dishes and helping Mother cook? How many times had she begged to do more than cut vegetables or cheese, more than get the flour out of the pantry, or the milk and eggs from the refrigerator? She wanted to knead the bread and brown the meat for the soup. She wanted to frost the cake and roll out the piecrust. But Mother worried she'd ruin whatever they were making, so she never let her do any of those things. After all, it was a sin to let good food go to waste.

Julia grabbed an apple from the wooden bowl on the island and stood at the sink, looking out the window, her shoulders hunched against the chill. Outside, the winter garden was a tangle of leggy plants and overgrown weeds. Mother would turn over in her grave if she could see it.

Now more than ever, Julia felt truly alone. Her mother and father were gone, and nothing had been resolved. Now it never would be. Over the years she had pulled herself apart, piece by piece, trying to understand why she felt so unloved, and why it always seemed as though her parents were keeping things from her. Somewhere in the back of her mind, there were foggy memories of Mother swaddling her in blankets and kissing her cheek, and she could still picture Mother's blond hair and red lips as she sang lullabies and rocked her to sleep. But something changed as Julia got older, and she had no clue what it was.

Around the time Julia turned nine, Mother told her how she had prayed for a daughter and had spent most of her pregnancy in bed because she was so afraid of losing her. Then she went into a tirade about how disappointed she was to learn Julia's only goals in life were to disobey and argue with her. Sometimes it seemed like her parents had a separate life that had nothing to do with her, or she had been born into the wrong family. She used to fantasize that she was adopted, or that her parents were spies, or had changed their identities to hide from the mob. But that was only to distract herself from being sad. Maybe she would never know.

A sudden banging at the back door made her jump. The banging came again, more insistent now. She set the apple on the counter, headed toward the door in the mudroom off the kitchen, and looked through the glass. An elderly gentleman in a tweed fedora and brown jacket stood on the stone steps.

"Hello?" he called.

Julia opened the door a crack. "Can I help you?"

"Just stopping by to check on you, Miss Blackwood," the man said. He was short and thin, with a weathered face and watery blue eyes. "I don't suppose you remember me, do you?"

Julia shook her head. "I'm sorry, I don't."

The man looked uncomfortable, as if he were performing some unpleasant but necessary task. He glanced over his shoulder, as if plotting a quick getaway. "I'm Claude, the barn manager and groundskeeper. Worked for your parents for nearly twenty-seven years."

She smiled and opened the door wide. "Oh," she said. "I don't think we ever officially met. I wasn't allowed in the barn when I lived here."

Claude cleared his throat. "Well . . . I . . . ah . . . I remember you. I met you when you were just a little tyke. And I saw you playing around the yard. Your father, God rest his soul, used to talk about you all the time."

Julia was taken aback by the comment. Her father used to talk about her? All the time? Maybe Claude was just being nice. Maybe he was worried about losing his job. "How are the horses?" she said because she couldn't think of anything else to say.

"They're fine, Miss Blackwood, just fine. We've still got the best breeding mares around and five of the best stallions."

"That's nice," she said. "I look forward to seeing them."

Claude briefly dropped his eyes and scuffed his boot on the step. When he looked up again, something that looked like worry, or maybe it was fear, gathered behind his eyes. "You planning on redoing the place? Selling the horses or land, anything like that?"

Julia shrugged. "I don't know. I haven't had time to think that far ahead yet."

He forced a quick smile. "Okay. Just curious, is all."

"Maybe we can get together in the next day or two and you can start going over everything with me."

He nodded.

"Thank you for getting the groceries," she said. "And thanks for staying on and taking care of the horses. I'm sure you've done a wonderful job."

Claude seemed embarrassed by the compliment. He ducked his head and nodded once. "All right. As long as you're settled in, I'll be getting back home then. The keys to everything are in that drawer over there." He pointed at the cupboard next to the stove. "Including the key to the Buick in the garage."

"I'm afraid the car won't do me much good," she said. "I don't have a driver's license. Mother didn't allow that either."

"Oh," Claude said. He hesitated, his expression slack. "Well, if you need to go into town for something, let me know and I'll give you a ride."

"Thank you. I appreciate that."

"All right, then. Just give me a holler if you need anything else. Have a good night." He gave her a two-fingered salute, clomped down the steps, and started across the yard.

"I will," she said. "Night."

After Claude left, she berated herself for not asking him how to turn up the furnace. How could she be so dumb? She looked out the window toward the barn to see if he was close enough to come back, but he was getting in his truck. By the time she put on a coat and hat and ran after him, he'd be gone. Then she remembered the fireplace in the living room. Right now she was cold, hungry, exhausted, and overwhelmed. There would be plenty of time to figure everything out tomorrow, including how to turn up the furnace. She took eggs and milk out of the refrigerator and made scrambled eggs and toast, ate them standing at the island, then went into the living room to start a fire.

A stack of old wood sat next to the fireplace, bugs and cobwebs filling the cracks and crevices of the brittle bark. After she got the fire going, she took off her shoes and curled up on the couch. The cushions sank low where she sat, and the silence of the house rang in her ears. It was going to be a long night.

CHAPTER 7
Lilly

After seeing her reflection for the very first time in the mirror above the vanity in the dressing tent, Lilly sat on the ground, her head spinning and her stomach queasy. All this time, she thought she was a monster. All this time, her parents had been lying to her. All this time, she had been locked in the attic for no reason. She pushed herself up on wobbly legs and brushed the grass from her dress, the world a blur through her tears.

"You okay?" Glory asked her.

Lilly nodded.

"Come on," Glory said. "Let's go over to the

cookhouse and get some breakfast. That'll help you feel better. You must be half-starved."

Lilly didn't think she could eat anything, but she followed Glory out of the tent and across the midway. She thought about turning around and running away, but where would she go? Home? No one wanted her there. To the nearest town? Merrick and Leon said she wasn't wanted there either, unless someone was waiting to pickle her brains and put them on display. There was nowhere to go.

Walking beside Glory past rows of concession stands and circus wagons, she tried not to think about what might happen next. It was hard enough putting one foot in front of the other. On the other side of a row of wagons, three elephants stood with their heads down, their back legs chained to stakes in the ground. A man in bib overalls and a boy in a newsboy cap stood beside one of the elephants, studying something in the grass. Whatever they were looking at was gray and round, like a big rock. The man leaned against a long stick and the boy bent over at the waist, his hands on his knees, smiling. Then the boy sat on the ground and the rock moved. It got to its feet, shook its little ears, and flopped its small trunk up and down. It was a baby elephant.

Lilly slowed, unable to pull her eyes away. The boy laughed and the man rubbed the big elephant's leg, stroking its thick hide back and forth. The boy ran a hand down the baby elephant's forehead and along its trunk. The baby put its front feet on the boy's shoulder, then dropped to its knees and lay on its side like a big dog in the boy's lap, curling its head into his legs. Lilly couldn't believe what she was seeing. The boy laughed harder and scratched the baby's belly with both hands. Then he looked up at the man, who had caught sight of Glory and Lilly, and followed his gaze, grinning. To Lilly's surprise, he waved.

She dropped her eyes and walked faster. Had she been staring? Was she supposed to wave back? He looked a little older than her, but she had never seen another child, let alone a boy playing with a baby elephant. She didn't know what to do. What did he think when he saw her? Did he notice the color of her skin, or was he too far away? He had to belong with the circus; otherwise he wouldn't have been playing with the elephants. Maybe he was used to seeing people who looked different. But why did he wave?

"Never mind about him," Glory said. "Their kind don't get involved with the likes of us."

"Their kind?" Lilly said.

"Big-top performers. They don't get tangled up with sideshow acts."

Lilly frowned. "Tangled up?"

Glory smiled and waved a hand in the air. "Never mind. I'll tell you when you're older."

Farther along the midway, six animal wagons sat off to one side, each with a lion inside. Two of the lions sat up in their cages while the rest dozed in the heat, their sides heaving up and down. One slept with his massive head pressed against the cage wall, his brown matted mane spilling out between the bars. When Glory and Lilly walked past, he lifted his head, blinked, and watched them pass, his whiskers twitching. Lilly slowed and stared into his sad brown eyes. She saw how beautiful and perfect he was, locked in a cage and filled with sorrow. She saw his thick fur, his padded feet, his sharp teeth, his black nose. All of a sudden, the walled-in feeling of being locked in her room washed over her, and the heavy, horrible ache of missing home. The sensations were so strong they nearly brought her to her knees. It almost seemed as if she could feel the lion's longing to be free, as surely as she felt her own grief and fear. Maybe he dreamed of lying on cool grass and running through the open savannah in Africa, like she used to imagine escaping her room and going outside. Maybe he, too, missed his home.

With tears filling her eyes, she fought the urge to go over and unlock the cages. But the lions wouldn't be any better off than she was. If they tried running into the woods, someone would stop them. If they tried to fight back, someone would hurt them or shoot them. She moved toward the watching lion as if pulled in by an unseen force. She wanted to reach in and touch him, to let him know that if it were up to her, he would be free.

"What are you doing?" Glory yelled. "Get away from there!"

Lilly stopped, startled out of her trance. "I just wanted to—"

"Lions are man-eaters," Glory said. "He could take off your hand with one bite!"

Lilly moved away from the lion and continued on beside Glory, watching him until they were out of sight. Hearing Glory talk about the lions the same way Momma used to talk about her made her sad, as if the lions were something to be hated and feared. They were wild animals who wanted their freedom, and to be left alone. That was all.

After leaving the lions, they headed to the back lot, toward a tent nearly as big as the big top, but not as tall. As they got closer, Lilly dragged her feet and fell behind Glory. The tent sidewalls were rolled up, and voices and laughter floated out over the lot. People at tables filled the tent, people who might stare and make fun of her, people who might be afraid and try to hurt her. Lilly's chest constricted and she stopped walking, struggling to pull in air. Glory stopped to look back at her.

"It's okay," she said. "There's no reason to be afraid. This is the cookhouse, where everyone eats. One thing you'll learn is that the circus travels on its stomach. It's what keeps us moving." She pointed to a flag on top of the tent. "See that flag? When it's orange, the cookhouse is open. When it's blue, it's closed."

Lilly didn't care about the cookhouse or the flags. She didn't want to go in there. Glory returned to where she stood.

"Listen," Glory said, kneeling beside Lilly in the grass. "If there's one thing you need to know about circus folk, it's that we're strangers in every town we go, so we only have each other. Sure, we got our own set of rules so we can get along, and not everyone follows the rules. But when the chips are down, we protect our own. And you're one of us now. You're part of our family. No one is going to hurt you. I know it's hard, but try to calm down and breathe slowly."

Lilly thought about reminding Glory that Merrick had hurt her, but she couldn't talk. Her lungs were too tight and her throat felt like it was closing. She drew in a shaky breath and blew it out, long and slow, over and over and over, counting each inhale and exhale. After what seemed like forever, her thundering heart slowed and her chest loosened.

"Okay now?" Glory said.

Lilly nodded.

Glory gave her a weak smile, then straightened and started walking again. Lilly followed.

Inside the cookhouse, a canvas curtain divided the tent down the center. On one side of the curtain, checkered tablecloths and silverware, salt and pepper shakers, and ketchup and mustard bottles covered the tables. On the other side, the tables were bare, their wooden surfaces stained and scratched and dented. Groups of men and women sat eating and talking at the tables with tablecloths and silverware, while only men sat at the bare tables, all with sweaty faces and dirty hands, grimy shirts and torn overalls. To Lilly's surprise, children sat here and there among the adults at the tables with tablecloths. And other than the men in white jackets and aprons behind the food counter, everyone was dressed in ordinary clothes. For some reason, she thought they would be wearing costumes.

The smell of cooking grease and fried food filled the air, and people with trays lined up in front of a counter filled with eggs and bacon and toast. Following Glory over to the food line, she noticed a giant man at the end of one table, his head and shoulders towering several feet above his fellow diners. Beside him, a second man looked thin as a skeleton, his skin stretched tight over his face. At a table filled with platters of pancakes and bacon, a fat woman with a purple bow in her curly blond hair took up an entire bench. Across from the fat lady, a tiny girl with glossy black hair stood on a stool feeding a man with no arms.

Lilly dropped her eyes and followed Glory's feet. Her stomach went wobbly and her chest felt tight again. How did a person live with no arms? And why was that girl so small? Her head seemed too big for her neck, and her legs and arms looked extra short and chubby. Was she an elf, or a doll come to life? Lilly wanted to run out of the tent and never come back. There were too many sights and sounds and smells, too many strange faces and bodies, all crammed together in one place. She wanted to go home. She wanted to be in her safe little room with Abby. Thinking of her cat again, her eyes and throat burned. Was anyone taking care of her? Or did Momma leave her in the attic to starve?

Trying not to cry in front of everyone, Lilly followed Glory into the food line, the world a blur through her tears. Glory handed her a dented tin plate and she took it with shaking hands.

"Have whatever you want," Glory said. "There's sausage and eggs, bread and jam, pancakes, hash browns, and ham."

Lilly didn't think she could eat. Her stomach cramped with grief and fear and nerves, but she took a pancake and piece of toast to be polite. At the end of the line, an oily-haired man with a smoldering cigar in the corner of his mouth sat on a stool taking tickets. When Glory and Lilly reached him, he looked Lilly up and down.

"Who's this?" he said with a scowl.

"She's with me," Glory said.

"Where's her ticket?"

"She doesn't have one, Bob, and if you don't like it, you can take it up with Merrick."

Bob studied Lilly with narrowed eyes. He paused for a long second, then took Glory's ticket and jerked his head to one side, telling them to move along.

Lilly gripped her plate with trembling hands and followed Glory toward the far side of the cookhouse. Heads lifted to watch her pass, and thousands of eyes followed her across the tent. Women whispered behind raised hands, and children giggled and stared.

When they finally reached an empty table with a checkered tablecloth, Lilly almost dropped her plate while getting into her seat. She set it on the table and put her hands in her lap, thankful to be sitting down. Glory sat next to her, her plate full of toast and sausage.

"It's a good thing we're far enough from town so there aren't any rubes around," Glory said. "Otherwise, we'd be boiling hot in a closed-up tent. Because God forbid the townies see a freak for free."

Lilly said nothing and stared at her food. Her chest was getting tight again and she was starting to feel dizzy. She couldn't get enough air.

"Are you all right?" Glory said.

Lilly bit her lip and nodded. The last thing she

wanted to do was draw attention. She took a deep, trembling breath, held it for a second, then let it out, trying to calm down.

"Listen," Glory said. She picked up her knife and began cutting the sausage on her plate. "I know you're scared. I would be too. But most everyone here is friendly, and I'll let you know who isn't." She gestured toward the back of the cookhouse with her knife. "Like Josephine over there. It's best to stay away from her."

The woman Glory called Josephine sipped coffee alone at a table and surveyed the room, her lips and fingernails painted red, gemstones sparkling from every finger, a rainbow of bracelets lining both wrists. She was dressed in a flowered robe, with glittery barrettes in her thin gray ringlets. Her large, hooked nose and close-set eyes reminded Lilly of a story she'd read about a giant rat. A thin man with black hair approached her table, set a plate of food in front of her, then stood off to one side like a servant, his hands behind his back.

Glory noticed Lilly staring at Josephine. "Just stick with me, okay?"

Lilly nodded, her chin trembling. She thought about asking why she needed to stay away from Josephine but couldn't find the right words. There were so many things to get used to, so many things to learn and fear. She was having a hard enough time sitting up straight and breathing.

Just then, two girls in yellow dresses approached and sat across the table from her and Glory. They looked exactly the same, with high cheekbones, matching black dots above their lips, and red hair parted down the middle and combed over one side, half obscuring one blue eye.

"Who's this?" the girls asked Glory at the same time. They picked up their forks and started eating identical piles of hash browns, bacon, and scrambled eggs.

"This is Lilly," Glory said. She addressed Lilly. "Ruby and Rosy are my friends. You can trust them."

The twins set down their forks and reached across the table to shake Lilly's hand. "Pleased to meetcha," they said in unison.

Lilly tried to smile, but kept her hands in her lap.

The twins withdrew and gave each other a confused glance. Then one of them said, "We're with the sideshow too. Sometimes with the freaks, sometimes with the cooch show."

Glory's brows shot up. "Ruby!" she said.

Ruby shrugged. "The lot lice know about the cooch show." She leaned forward and grinned at Lilly. "That's the girlie show, in case you were wonderin'."

"Jesus, Ruby," Glory said. "The circus kids know what the cooch show is, but Lilly didn't grow up in the circus. I don't think she's ever even been to one, have you?" She looked at Lilly.

Lilly shook her head.

"That's what I thought," Glory said. She frowned at Ruby and Rosy. "Merrick picked her up at the last stop. And it wasn't her decision."

The twins' faces fell in unison. "Oh," they said.

"Right," Glory said. "So take it easy, will you?"

"Sorry," Ruby said. She started eating again.

"So, kid, what do you think of this spread?" Rosy said. "Pretty amazing, huh? We don't get paid a lot, but we're guaranteed three squares a day."

"Well, from what I hear," Ruby said, "this spot is wide open, so things might get a little wild later. Guess the patch men greased the rails of the local officials good last night, so this isn't going to be no Sunday school show. But Josephine isn't happy 'cause Mr. Barlow promised two of her girls to the sheriff without asking."

"Josephine isn't happy unless she's running the show," Glory said. "It's her way or the highway."

Rosy addressed Lilly. "You stay away from that one, you hear? First she'll reel you in like she's your best friend, then before you know it, she'll have something over you and turn you into one of her—"

Glory shot Rosy a hard look. "Too soon," she said.

"Oh," Rosy said. "Sorry."

"Do you know what your act will be?" Ruby asked Lilly.

Across the way, the man and boy Lilly had seen with the elephants waited in the food line, trays in hand. They gave their tickets to Bob, then made their way to the other side of the tent, toward the tables with saltshakers and tablecloths. Lilly couldn't help staring. The boy had touched and played with a baby elephant. He had to be someone special. So why in the world did he wave at her? Did he think she was a normal girl?

"Lilly?" Rosy and Ruby said at the same time.

Lilly blinked and looked at the twins. "What?"

"I was wondering if you know what you'll be doing," Ruby said. "What's your act?" She shoved a piece of bacon in her mouth and chewed, the black dot above her red lips moving 'round and 'round in tiny circles.

Lilly shrugged and gazed at Glory, a question on her face.

"We don't know yet," Glory said. "Merrick hasn't decided. After breakfast he wants to show her to Mr. Barlow."

Lilly thought Glory sounded worried, or maybe it was sad.

Then the thin black-haired man who gave Josephine a plate of food appeared at their table and jerked his chin at Glory. "Josephine wants to know about the girl." The skin on his face was stretched tight over his cheeks and his eyes looked bigger than normal, like they were about to pop out of his head.

"She's with Merrick," Glory said.

"Where'd she come from?" the man said.

"If Josephine wants to know," Glory said, "she can ask Merrick."

The man grinned but said nothing. Then he winked at Lilly and walked away.

Lilly stared at her food again, growing more nd more nauseous. She thought about saying she couldn't eat, then picked up her toast and nibbled on the crust, trying not to be sick.

After breakfast, Glory took Lilly back to the train so Merrick could show her to Mr. Barlow. On the way there, they passed a tent surrounded by hay bales and water buckets, and a group of men with an elephant in the mouth of an open-sided barn. Three of the men held ropes that went up to a pulley attached to a pole above the elephant's head, then came down and tied around the elephant's front feet and the top of its trunk near its mouth. A fourth man with a stick commanded the elephant to sit up and the three men pulled on the ropes, yanking the elephant's front feet and head in the air. Two other men shoved a round stand under the elephant's rear end, forcing it to sit down.

Lilly came to a halt and put a hand over her stomach. The walled-in feeling of being locked up and the heavy, horrible ache of missing home twisted in her chest again. But this time there was something else too, something that felt like terror and pain.

Glory stopped and looked back at her. "What's wrong?"

"What are they doing to that elephant?" she said.

"Trying to teach it new tricks," Glory said. "They've been having trouble with that one."

"It looks like . . . like they're torturing it."

"It doesn't hurt her."

Lilly searched Glory's face with watery eyes. "How do you know?"

Glory gazed at her for a long moment, then started walking again. "I don't," she said in a quiet voice.

Lilly stared at the ground and followed. She couldn't look at the elephant again. Just like when she saw the lion, she could feel every twinge of the elephant's fear, every stab of pain and confusion. The weight of it pressed in all around her, as if she were being swallowed by mud or quicksand.

When they neared the train, Glory slowed. "Listen," she said. "We're on in a few hours and Mr. Barlow is like a bear with his leg caught in a trap before we open the doors. So don't speak unless you're spoken to."

Merrick was waiting for them outside one of

the passenger cars, pacing and wringing his hands. Unlike the rest of the passenger cars, which were green or brown or gray, this one was painted a glossy red and trimmed with decorative black scrolls. Tasseled curtains hung in the windows below gold lettering that read: THE BARLOW BROTHERS' CIRCUS. Beside Merrick, two men stood on either side of the car steps. One was bald, with mean-looking eyes and hairy arms. The other seemed as big as a horse, his short-sleeved shirt stretched over his chest like it was about to rip open. His black hair was in a knot on top of his head.

"You see those men?" Glory said under her breath. "Don't ever mess with them. They're Mr. Barlow's strongmen. They protect him and work as patches when things get rough with the townies."

Lilly could only nod.

"What took you so long?" Merrick said. Before Glory could answer, he grabbed Lilly by the arm and took her up the metal steps to a platform between Mr. Barlow's car and the next. Glory started up the steps behind them, but Merrick told her to wait outside. Then he lifted his chin, cleared his throat, and rapped on the door. Lilly waited beside him, her heart kicking like a jackrabbit in her chest.

"Enter," a baritone voice called from inside.

Merrick opened the door and told Lilly to enter

first. Fancy light fixtures decorated the shiny wood walls of the car, along with two upholstered chairs, a velvet sofa, a round table, and flowered rugs scattered here and there like playing cards. A small sink, countertop, and cupboards sat against one wall, and two wooden fans whirred on the ceiling. Behind a beaded curtain, an open doorway led into another room. The smell of smoke, old wood, and warm dust filled the air, reminding Lilly of her bedroom back home. Homesickness washed over her and she was overcome by a sudden falling sensation, as if the weight of her head had grown too heavy for her neck and was pulling her over. Somehow she stayed upright and gritted her teeth until the feeling passed.

A man in a suit, cufflinks, and shiny shoes sat in a red chair, a plate of eggs and a cup of coffee on the round table in front of him. His waxed blond mustache twitched over gray teeth that looked too big for his mouth.

"What is it?" he said.

"I picked up a new act at the last stop," Merrick said. "Something we've never had before."

"Step forward," Mr. Barlow said to Lilly.

Lilly did as she was told. Her mouth felt full of sawdust.

"What's her billing?" Mr. Barlow said.

"I'm not sure," Merrick said. "Got any ideas?"

Mr. Barlow spun a finger in the air and ordered

Lilly to turn. Moving slowly so she wouldn't get dizzier, she did as she was told.

Mr. Barlow took a sip of coffee and stared at her, drumming his fingers on the table. Then he rose from his chair. "Alana!" he shouted, making Lilly jump. "Come out here!"

In another room, someone groaned and bed-springs squeaked. "Whaat?" a female voice whined.

Mr. Barlow scowled. "Come here," he said. "And don't make me say it again."

"Ahhh, Christ on a cracker," Alana mumbled. Then she called out in a cheerful voice, "I'll be right there!" More sounds came out of the room—feet hitting the floor, a heavy sigh, jewelry clinking, a drawer being opened and closed. After a long minute, Alana pushed the beaded curtain to one side and entered the room in a white robe, open at the waist, and undergarments made out of lace. Lipstick smudged her mouth like red fingerprints, and her long hair was a tangled mess of blond curls. The pink of her nipples showed through the thin fabric of her brassiere. Behind her, a small brown dog trotted into the room.

Alana smiled at Mr. Barlow. "What is it, dear?"

Lilly lowered her eyes. Didn't anyone care that Alana was nearly naked?

When the dog saw Merrick, it barked and charged at him, baring its teeth and growling, its

127

hair raised. Then it suddenly came to a halt and eyed Lilly. It dropped its head, went over to her, sat up on its hunches, and pawed the air, begging to be picked up and petted.

"Well, I'll be damned," Alana said. "She's never done that before. Chi-Chi hates everybody but me." She went over, kneeled next to the dog, and gazed up at Lilly. "You want to pet her?"

Lilly nodded, got down on one knee, and touched the dog's little head. Chi-Chi rolled over to expose her tiny tan belly, her tail wagging wildly. Lilly rubbed the dog's belly and, for the first time in what seemed like forever, smiled.

"I've never seen her act like that with anyone," Alana said. "She even tries biting Syd if he gets too close." She glanced over her shoulder. "Isn't that right, darling?"

"If that idiot dog bites me, I'll stomp it into the ground," Mr. Barlow said.

Alana ignored him and directed her attention back to Lilly. "Have you always had a way with animals?" She scratched Chi-Chi's chest with long pink fingernails.

Lilly shrugged.

"I don't believe I've had the pleasure," Alana said. "What's your name, honey?"

Before Lilly could answer, Mr. Barlow said, "We're trying to come up with her show name. That's why I called you out here, not to play with that stupid dog."

Alana rolled her eyes and kept scratching Chi-Chi. "Well, what's her act? Where is she going to be working?"

"Where the hell do you think?" Mr. Barlow said. "In the freak show!"

Alana pressed her lips together and stopped petting the dog. She straightened and pulled her robe closed, tying it tight at the waist. "Call her whatever you want," she said. "You will anyway."

"Goddammit!" Mr. Barlow said. "Sometimes I wonder why I keep you around."

Alana shot him a cold smile and strolled back toward the bedroom. "You know perfectly well why you keep me around."

Mr. Barlow caught her by the arm. "Stay here. I need ideas."

Alana pulled away and plopped down on the velvet sofa, pouting. Chi-Chi flipped over onto her feet, scurried over to the sofa, and jumped up to sit beside her owner. Alana took a cigarette from a silver case on the table, put it between her smudged red lips, lit it, and blew out a stream of smoke with more force than necessary. Then she cocked her head slightly and fixed her eyes on Lilly, thinking.

"Well, she's perfect," she said. "When I saw her, the first thing I thought of was a porcelain doll." She took another drag from her cigarette, crossed her legs, and leaned forward. "How about 'The World's Only Living Porcelain

Doll' or 'A Real Porcelain Doll, Alive and Breathing'?" Smoke curled from her mouth when she talked.

"Not exotic enough," Mr. Barlow said. "We want to shock and amaze people, not bore them to death."

Alana rolled her eyes again, then took another drag from her cigarette. "How about 'The Swan Girl'? Or we could put her in a wedding dress and call her 'The Ghost Bride.' "

"I think we should bill her as some kind of princess," Merrick said.

"That might work," Alana said. "She's different because her skin is so white, so you'd need something that makes sense, like 'The Frozen Princess' or 'The Ice Princess.' "

"I've got it!" Mr. Barlow said. " 'The Ice Princess from Another Planet!' "

Alana shook her head and leaned back in the sofa, one arm across her middle, the other bent at the elbow, her cigarette in the air.

Mr. Barlow ignored her. "It's perfect, right?" he asked Merrick.

Merrick shrugged and mumbled something under his breath.

"What's that?" Mr. Barlow said.

"Nothing," Merrick said.

"He said it's stupid," Alana said.

"Shut up, Alana," Mr. Barlow said.

Anger pinched Alana's face. She crushed her

cigarette out in an ashtray, got up, and went back to the bedroom. Chi-Chi jumped off the couch and followed her.

"You think it's stupid?" Mr. Barlow asked Merrick.

"No, but I'm not sure what being an ice princess has to do with being from another planet. Is she supposed to be an alien? Because that's not what I had in mind."

"Well, the name of this circus might be the Barlow Brothers'," Mr. Barlow said. "But I'm the only brother left. Not to mention, I'm the one paying the bills around here. Do yourself a favor and remember that."

Merrick clenched his jaw, his temples moving in and out. "You know damn well your brother had every intention of leaving me his half," he snarled.

"Maybe, maybe not. The only thing I know for sure is he didn't have time to change his will between making a move on Alana and drowning in that river. You're my cousin, Merrick, and only a second cousin at that. You're lucky I let you run the sideshows."

"I own the sideshows."

"No, dear boy, you don't. You might own a few of the acts, and Viktor will always be loyal to you, but I own the tents and the banners and the stages. I own the ticket booths and employ the people who run them."

"Maybe so, but Lilly's my act. I should decide her billing."

Mr. Barlow jutted out his chin and took a step closer to Merrick. "Listen, pisshead. Without me you wouldn't have a circus for her act. I own the big top and the animals and the wagons. I pay the people who set it all up. I even own the train that hauls your sorry ass from one show to the next. Now get the hell out of my car before I throw you out!"

Merrick stomped over to the door and yanked it open, his face the color of beets. He ordered Lilly out and slammed the door behind them. Glory was waiting outside, sharing a cigarette with the bald strongman.

"Let's go," Merrick said. He stormed toward the other end of the train.

Glory gave the cigarette back to the strongman and hurried to catch up. Lilly followed. "What happened?" Glory said.

Merrick ignored her and kept going, his hands in fists. Then he stopped and let loose a string of curses. "That arrogant bastard might know what he's talking about when it comes to the big top. But he doesn't know a damn thing about the freak show."

"What did he say?" Glory said.

Merrick started walking again. "I don't want to talk about it."

"Well, I've got to get ready for my performance," Glory said. "I'll take Lilly over to the twins' car. She can stay there for now. They've got room."

Merrick shook his head. "No, she's staying with us."

"But—" Glory started.

Merrick stopped again and glared at her. "No buts. I'm not giving her the chance to try to escape."

"Escape and go where? She's just a little girl."

"I don't care," Merrick said. "She's staying in our car where we can keep an eye on her, and that's final. It's either that, or back in the stock car with the goats and llamas."

Glory gave Lilly a worried glance. "Okay," she said. "But I'll take her to the dressing tent with me while I get ready."

"No, you won't make it back to the train before the show opens without the rubes seeing you." He started walking again. "Now come on."

Glory and Lilly trailed Merrick past the next three cars, then climbed the steps of the fourth and waited while he unlocked the door. The inside of the car looked the same as Mr. Barlow's except with faded, torn furniture, dull paneling, and no ceiling fans. Dirty glasses filled the small sink, and a set of yellow curtains hung in the open doorway between the two rooms, their edges stained gray. The air felt hot and thick, like the air in Lilly's attic bedroom in the middle of summer.

Lilly did not like the place.

Merrick tromped over to a sideboard, opened a bottle, and poured brown liquid into a glass. Glory picked a newspaper and a rumpled blanket off the couch and straightened the pillows.

"You can sleep here," she said to Lilly. She lifted an overflowing ashtray off a table piled high with magazines and brushed fallen ashes to the floor. "Sorry it's such a mess."

Standing frozen by the door, Lilly didn't know what to do or say. This was her new home, whether she liked it or not. She pictured her old room, her lumpy bed, her stained pillow, Abby sleeping on her woolen blanket. The sudden realization that this was final, that she was never going to see any of it again, that she was never going to see Abby again, hit her like a sledgehammer. It was the worst feeling in the world. Her eyes flooded and her lungs started to close. She tried counting the floorboards to calm down, but it didn't help. Glory saw what was happening, came over, and knelt beside her.

"It's okay," she said. "Just breathe. I know it's a lot to get used to, but I'll take care of you, I promise."

After several long minutes of struggling to get air, Lilly's chest finally loosened and she stumbled over to the sofa and collapsed into it, her face smeared with tears and sweat. Her vision grew blurry and she closed her eyes. She was exhausted and wanted to disappear into sleep, but her mind wouldn't stop spinning. She needed to come up with a plan, she needed to get out of there and go home.

Maybe this afternoon, when the circus opened and Merrick and Glory left the car to go to work, she could sneak out and follow the railroad tracks in the other direction, toward Blackwood Manor. She had no idea how long it would take to walk home, but she didn't care. Maybe she could steal some food and a blanket, and sleep in the woods at night. At least it wasn't winter. She pictured herself crossing her parents' fields and walking across the lawn, marching up the steps and knocking on the front door. Daddy would answer, surprised and happy to see her. Momma might be mad at first, but if Lilly promised to be good, promised to stop asking for things she couldn't have, and promised to memorize the Bible and say her prayers every night, maybe Momma would let her stay. Then she thought of something else and started to tremble.

What if Daddy wasn't happy to see her? What if he knew all along Momma was going to sell her to the circus? After all, he let Momma lock her in the attic. If he really loved her, he wouldn't have done that. And what if he really "wasn't long for this world"? What if he really was dying?

The thought made her feel like she was falling off a cliff, her arms and legs limp and useless, her hair fluttering around her face and head. She buried her face in a pillow and sobbed.

Glory knelt beside her. "It's all right, go ahead and cry. You have every right to be sad and mad and scared and all of those things. It's not fair what your momma did to you. When my parents dropped Viktor off at the asylum, I was six and he was five, but, God help me, I remember thinking how glad I was that they were leaving him there instead of me. Because he was crying so hard and I—"

Merrick slammed his glass on the sideboard. "For Christ's sake, Glory," he snarled. "Quit your blubbering. The show starts in an hour and you need to get ready."

Glory got to her feet, wiping her palms on her skirt. "Don't you think it'd be okay if I sit this one out? Others have missed shows before. I should stay here with Lilly and—"

With that, Merrick flew across the room and slapped her hard across the face. She staggered backward and nearly fell but managed to stay on her feet. Lilly sat up, breathing hard. Glory put her hand to her cheek and gaped at Lilly, her eyes wide with shame and fear. Then, without a word, she hung her head and went into the other room.

"You better be getting your things together!" Merrick yelled. He went over to the sideboard and poured himself another drink. Lilly watched from the sofa, her fingers digging into the cushions.

A moment later, Glory came out of the other room with what looked like a miniature suitcase in one hand. A red mark in the shape of a hand-print colored her cheek and she gazed at Lilly with glassy eyes. "I'll be back as soon as the show is over. I'm sorry. I can't stay."

Lilly wanted Glory to stay more than anything, but there was nothing she could do. She watched her leave, then curled up in a corner of the sofa, wondering what would happen next. Merrick locked the door behind Glory and disappeared into the other room. Somewhere a door opened and closed. Lilly held her breath and listened. Was there another way out of the car in the other room? The only things she heard were the violent thud of her heart and what sounded like water running. She got up, tiptoed across the room, and tried the door that led outside, even though she knew it was locked. She tried the windows. It was no use. Everything was bolted shut. She sat down again and tried to think.

Then the door in the other room opened and closed again, and Merrick whistled as he moved about in there. A few minutes later, he came out in a suit and tie, his hair slicked back from his cratered face. The smell of shoe polish and cologne filled the room, reminding Lilly of Daddy. Merrick poured another drink, came over

137

to the sofa, stood over her, and grinned. She swallowed and pushed her back into the cushions.

"You and I are going to make a lot of money together," he said. "But right now, I've got to get over to the sideshow." He swallowed the contents of his glass and headed for the door.

As she watched him go, the tightness left Lilly's shoulders. After he left, maybe she could pound on a window to get someone's attention, or break it and crawl out. Then Merrick realized his glass was still in his hand and went over to set it on the sideboard. She tensed again and, before she knew what was happening, he rushed toward her, clawed hands outstretched. She screeched and tried to scramble off the sofa, but he clamped his fingers into her upper arms and dragged her into the other room. She thrashed and kicked and clawed, but couldn't get away.

He hauled her past a chair piled with clothes and a bed covered with tangled blankets, then opened a wooden door and shoved her into a small room. She stumbled and fell between a wall and a toilet, and he slammed the door, casting the room into blackness. A horrible stench filled her nostrils and she gagged. She got to her feet and pounded on the door, screaming for him to let her out.

"Sorry, kid," he said through the wood. "But the show must go on."

CHAPTER 8
Julia

The morning after her return to Blackwood Manor, Julia woke with a start, her head bent at an odd angle against the arm of the overstuffed couch. At first, she didn't know where she was. Then she recognized the marble fireplace and the ornate tin ceiling of her late parents' living room. Now the living room, the entire house in fact, belonged to her. It felt surreal and a bit unsettling. She sat up, stretched, and rubbed her stiff neck. The room was cold and gray, and she could almost see her breath. Sometime during the night the fire had gone out. She stood, walked over to the windows, and pushed back the velvet curtains. Warm shafts of sunlight burst through the glass, illuminating the dusty air and creating blocks of light on the red Persian rug. A strong wind pushed against the window frame and creaked against the panes. Mother's dead rosebushes scratched along the sill.

Outside, the brown front lawn stretched out for what seemed like forever toward a line of towering oak trees, a white plank fence, and the one-lane road that led into town in one direction and the Adirondack foothills in the other. A band of black starlings filled the swaying tree branches and a gray pickup truck lumbered along the way, its exhaust like swirling ice in the air. Even in the sunshine, everything looked lonely and cold.

After she got the fireplace going again, she went into the kitchen and turned on the teakettle. The first thing on her to-do list was to figure out how to turn the furnace up. Then she could start exploring. She opened the drawer beside the stove and stared at one of the great mysteries of her childhood—Mother's keys. She could still picture the key ring hanging from Mother's apron, brass and iron clinking as she strode up and down the stairs, through the rooms and halls like a cat with a bell on its collar. While growing up, Julia had often wondered why were there so many keys on the ring, and where Mother kept them at night. Could it be they were in this drawer all along? No, it was impossible. Mother never let them out of her sight. How many times had she seen Mother reading or knitting, one hand checking to make sure the keys were still tied to her apron? A hundred? A thousand?

Julia took a deep breath and touched the keys, half expecting to hear Mother's chiding voice warning her to leave them alone. But there was no voice, no electric shock, no scolding slap of an invisible, cold ghost hand. She picked up the ring and was surprised to find it weighed more than expected. There were seventeen keys, each one unique—short and long, brass and iron, thick and thin, ornate and plain. And now, like everything else in Blackwood Manor, they belonged to her. She took the keys, grabbed her suitcase from the foyer, and went up to her old room.

The second floor featured a long center hallway, with two hallways leading off each side. Julia's bedroom was at the top of the stairs, the first door on the left. As she suspected, it was locked. She tried five different keys before finding the right one, then finally turned the lock and opened the door, thinking briefly how odd it was that she didn't know which key belonged to her old room. The bedroom was freezing and looked exactly the same as it did the night she left, except for the cobwebs hanging from the stuffed calico elephant on the shelf above her headboard, and the dust graying every surface, including the pictures of dogs and cats taped to her dresser mirror.

She entered and stood in the middle of the room, shivering and still holding her suitcase, a thousand memories flooding her mind. This was where she had spent countless lonely hours—banished for the smallest violation of Mother's rules. Or doing homework, wishing she had a brother or sister, sobbing into her pillow after being picked on in school. After a long minute, she turned around and walked out. She didn't have to stay in her old bedroom. She could stay in a different one. After all, there were six on this floor alone.

She closed the door, put the key in the lock, and started to turn it, then changed her mind. There was no longer any reason to keep her old bedroom locked. Not that there ever was, except for Mother's insistence it be that way. She carried her suitcase toward the end of the hall, Mother's keys jangling against her hip. The sound reminded her of lying in bed every night, the clinking of keys outside her bedroom as Mother checked the doors up and down the hall. For what, Julia had no idea.

She stopped in front of the room opposite her parents' bedroom, what Mother called "the playroom," the only other bedroom she was allowed in while growing up. As usual, the playroom was unlocked. Inside, gray light filtered in around the curtains, and a mint green rug embroidered with roses and leaves covered the plank floor like a thick layer of lime sherbet. A brass daybed with ruffled pillows and a white comforter sat against one wall, opposite a blue painted armoire between two tall windows. Unlike Julia's bedroom, this one had been kept free of dust and cobwebs.

As a child, she had spent hours in the playroom, combing her dolls' hair, feeding them bottles, rocking them to sleep, kissing their foreheads. Thinking about it now gave her heart a strange twist. Mother was the one who taught her how to cuddle babies and lay them gently into their beds. She was the one who told her to pat the dolls' backs and sing them to sleep. Now, Julia couldn't imagine it. She pushed the image of Mother from her mind and concentrated on the here and now. Trying to figure out the woman who had brought her into this world at an age when most mothers were watching their children get married or sending them off to college wouldn't change anything. Mother was who she was, and now she was gone.

She set her suitcase next to the armoire, pushed open the drapes, and looked out a window. The playroom overlooked part of the side yard, where six gnarled apple trees ringed a small lawn. Whenever she was being too loud or trying Mother's patience during summer vacation, she was sent there to play while the grown-ups drank iced tea and whiskey at a wicker table on the terrace. Over the tops of the apple trees, the butter-colored horse barn and white paddocks sat surrounded by brown fields. Three horses grazed in a round pen while two men looked on. One stood with his hands on his hips, the other had his foot on the bottom fence plank, his arms crossed and resting over the top. The man with his hands on his hips looked like Claude, but she had no idea who the other one was. Then she noticed the gray pickup truck she had seen on the road earlier sitting in the barn driveway. Maybe the other man was the veterinarian.

She opened her suitcase, found a thicker sweater, and put it on, wondering if Claude knew how to turn up the furnace. She had no idea if the house was heated with wood or coal, or where the thermostat was located. After all, she was only a teenager when she left, and she had never been interested in those things anyway. Not that anyone would have explained them to her if she'd asked. Somewhere in the back of her mind, she remembered her father going into the basement to "adjust the valves," but she wasn't sure what that meant. If Claude didn't know what to do, she'd have to figure it out herself, or hire someone. She brushed her hair in the mirror, pulled it into a ponytail, and went back downstairs. In the kitchen, the teakettle was screaming. Hot water boiled from its spout and sizzled on the flame beneath it. She turned off the burner and, without thinking, grabbed the teakettle handle.

"Shit!"

She dropped the teakettle on the stove and went over to the sink to run her red, tender palm under the faucet. How was she ever going to take care of this place if she couldn't even make tea without messing it up? She stared at the running water, wondering if she should quit while she was ahead. Someone knocked on the mudroom door and she jumped.

"Shit," she said again. She shut off the water, wiped her hands on her pants, and went into the mudroom. Maybe it was Claude and she could ask him about the furnace. She opened the door. It wasn't Claude.

A man in rubber boots, a black toque, and a green barn jacket stood on the steps with his back to her, watching the horses in the round pen.

"May I help you?" Julia said.

The man spun around and took the toque from his head. "Sorry," he said. "You caught me daydreaming. I'm Fletcher." He grinned and thrust out a hand. "Fletcher Reid. I'm here to see Miss Blackwood."

He was tall and lean and looked to be in his late twenties, with a square jawline and chocolate-colored eyes. His short, sandy hair stuck out in all directions above his tanned, rugged face.

She shook his hand. His handshake was sturdy, his skin rough. "I'm Miss Blackwood," she said.

His brows shot up. "You're the new owner?"

"Yes."

"But you're so . . . so . . ."

Heat rose in her cheeks. "I know. I'm too young to own this place."

His face filled with instant regret. "Oh. No, I'm sorry. It's none of my business. Please forgive me." He glanced over his shoulder as if plotting a quick getaway, then gave her a broad smile. "Um . . . can we start over?"

She shrugged one shoulder. "Sure."

He shook her hand again. "I'm the vet."

She hesitated, surprised. For some reason, she expected the veterinarian to be old, like Claude, with a bristled face and age-spotted hands. She couldn't have been more wrong. He looked like one of the surfers she used to watch on Long Island. "Pleased to meet you," she said. "I'm Julia."

"Pleased to meet you too, Julia. Claude and I were wondering if you'd come over to the barn and take a look at the horses."

"Me?"

He nodded.

"Is something wrong? Because I don't—"

"No, it's nothing like that. A buyer is interested in a couple of our, I mean your, stallions. We were wondering if you wanted to sell or not."

She frowned. Why were they asking her to make decisions already? She had just arrived and didn't know the first thing about horses. "I don't know . . . I . . ." She groaned inside. Suddenly, she couldn't string two words together. *He's going to think I'm an idiot.* "Whatever you think will be best for the farm. I trust you and Claude to make the right decision."

"All right," he said. "I know what Claude is thinking, but he said we had to ask you first. Are you sure you don't want to come and take a look? They're some of our best stallions yet. Perfect specimens from Blackwood Farm's most famous lineage. When you see them, you'll know what I mean."

She thought about it for a moment, then shrugged. There was no harm in looking, and she had to go over to the barn sooner or later, not to mention she needed to ask Claude how to turn up the furnace. "Okay."

"Better grab your coat," he said. "It's a cold one out there today."

She opened the door wide and stepped back. "Please, come in and stay warm while I get it."

He entered the mudroom, closed the door behind him, and waited with his hat in his hand at the edge of the kitchen while she went to get her coat. "Nice house," he called after her. "It's got a great kitchen."

She grabbed her coat from the foyer closet and hurried back to where he stood. "You've never seen it?"

He shook his head. "Mrs. Blackwood was an odd duck. She never allowed us inside. If we needed something we had to call on the barn phone."

She pushed her arms into her coat and buttoned it up. "That sounds about right. My mother loved rules."

He grimaced. "Sorry. I didn't realize the former owner was your mother. I thought she was a long-lost aunt or something."

She smiled. "Don't worry. If anyone knows how odd my mother was, it's me." She started to take her crocheted beanie out of her coat pocket but changed her mind. It was dirty and the edge was starting to unravel. Then she realized her coat wasn't in much better shape. If Fletcher and Claude knew how she'd been living the last three years, they'd never take her seriously. She stuffed the beanie back in her pocket, at the same time realizing she couldn't go over to the barn wearing Keds. She quickly scanned the mudroom for something to wear and, for the first time since her return, noticed Mother's barn boots in their usual spot beneath the bench. She slipped off her sneakers and pushed her feet into the rubber boots as if she'd done it a hundred times, despite the fact that they were two sizes too big. Somehow, it felt wrong to put them on. She stood and did her best to ignore the hollows and lumps in the soles, misshapen from years of wear and tear beneath Mother's bunioned feet.

"Claude didn't tell you I was Coralline's daughter?" she said, trying to act calm and composed.

"If there's one thing about Claude," Fletcher said, "it's that he does his job and keeps his mouth shut. He never breaks the rules or gets into anyone's business."

"Well, that's good to know. So why didn't you call me on the barn phone?"

"It was disconnected after your mother, mean, Mrs. Blackwood, passed. Claude didn't see any reason to have it working again until you arrived."

She started toward the door. "Makes sense to me. I'll call and have it connected again."

He grinned, put on his toque, opened the door, and held it for her. They left the house and she walked beside him toward the barn, her hands in her pockets. Her hair whipped in her eyes, and a cold wind made her nose run, making her wish she'd worn her hat despite its appearance. Maybe later she'd find a more suitable coat and hat in the house, until she could buy new ones anyway.

Unfazed by the harsh wind, Fletcher turned his face to the sun and strode across the lawn, scanning the distant horizon. Then he turned his head and smiled at her, as if going out to the barn together was something they did every day. Unlike Julia, who hated awkward silences and always tried to fill them with conversation, he seemed completely at ease with the silence between them. Somehow, walking side by side was enough.

Then again, she didn't like small talk either, so she was glad he wasn't commenting on the weather or landscape. Life was too big and too short and too important to talk about the lack of rain or the latest gossip. She wanted to know how people felt about themselves and one another, whether they were happy or sad. She wanted to know what made them feel loved and what hurt them to the core. She wanted to know about their past, how they got where they were, and their relationships with their mothers and fathers and siblings. She wanted to know if she was the only mixed-up person in the world who felt completely and utterly alone. But she couldn't ask Fletcher about any of those things, and she had to say something.

"How long have you worked at Blackwood Manor?" she asked.

"I don't just work here. I work at farms all over the county."

"Of course," she said. *Maybe sometimes it's better to keep your mouth shut.* "Well, how long have you been the vet here?"

He twisted his mouth to one side, thinking. "Around three years, I think."

"So you started right after my father died."

"A couple months before, if I recall. Your father was great with the horses. He really knew his stuff."

She shrugged and smiled, not sure what to say. Other than seeing him heading over to the barn or working outside on fences and equipment, she never knew that side of her father.

"If you don't mind me asking," he said. "Where have you been the last few years? Away at school? Claude never told me Mr. and Mrs. Blackwood had a daughter."

Julia swallowed. She didn't want to lie, but she didn't want to tell him the truth either. "I'd rather not talk about it."

150

"Sorry. Sure." He shoved his hands in his pockets. "So when was the last time you were around the horses?"

"It's been a while. I wasn't allowed in the barn when I was growing up."

He jerked his head back, his eyebrows raised. "What? Why not?"

She hunched her shoulders against the cold, or maybe it was against her emotions. "Like I said, my mother loved rules. She said it was too dangerous for a young girl to be in the barn, and it was a business not a playground. I'm pretty sure she didn't want me in there because she thought I'd cause trouble or ruin something."

Fletcher looked down at his feet as he walked, his brows knitted. "That's too bad. Most young girls love horses. It would have been good for you."

She studied him out of the corners of her eyes. What made him think she needed something good for her? Did she look that beaten down?

When they reached the round pen, Claude tipped his cap in her direction. "Morning, Miss Blackwood."

"Please," she said. "Call me Julia."

Fletcher rested one arm on the fence. "So, what do you think?"

Inside the pen, three horses ran back and forth, their tails held high, like black flags in the wind. Their coats shined like oil and their hooves pounded hard on the dirt, making the earth beneath Julia's feet tremble.

Seeing the horses up close, a memory came to her. She was nine years old and home sick from school. Normally, Mother was always home, but that day she had an important appointment in town. Father was supposed to check on Julia when he came in from the barn around noon, but as usual, he went into his den and locked the doors. When Julia crept down to the kitchen to get something to drink, she looked out the window above the sink and saw a black horse in the garden, trampling the tomatoes and eating the lettuce and carrot tops. She ran to the den to get her father and started to knock on the door, then stopped, her knuckles on the wood. On the other side of the double doors, her father was weeping, his favorite record—"Little White Lies"—turned up loud.

She stood for a moment, sick and scared and not knowing what to do, then hurried back to the kitchen, put on her shoes, and went outside. At the edge of the woods, she picked a bunch of clover, then went over to the garden and slowly approached the horse, her hand outstretched. The horse yanked up its head and snorted, startled by her presence. Talking soothingly, Julia took one step at a time toward it, not making any sudden moves. Finally, the horse took a step forward and nibbled at the pink blossoms in her hand, its soft lips like velvet on her palm. When the horse moved closer, munching the clover and looking down on her with big brown eyes, Julia stepped backward and the horse followed. She kept going until they reached an empty paddock outside the barn, then opened the gate and led the horse through. After putting the rest of the clover on the ground, she shut the gate, went back to the horse, and ran her fingers through its black mane. The horse nickered and rubbed its heavy head against her side, loving the attention.

Overcome by the horse's show of affection, she wrapped her arms around its muscular neck and pressed her nose into its warm hide. It was the first time she had ever touched a horse and, somehow, it seemed as though she could feel its strength, radiating like the warmth of the sun into her skin. It was like nothing she had ever felt before. On her way back to the house, confusion stirred in her mind. Why would her parents keep her away from such wonderful creatures? It didn't make sense.

After that encounter, she looked out her bedroom window every day, aching to be with the horses. Once in a while, when Father wasn't watching and on the rare occasion Mother was out, she snuck over to the fences near the back of the barn. But she only dared stay a few minutes. Sometimes the horses came over to eat clover out of her hand or let her pet them, but other times they were too busy grazing, running, and sleeping. Either way, she was happy just to be near them. When she ran away from home three years ago, the horses were the only things she missed about Blackwood Manor.

Now, seeing these stallions—her stallions—up close, she was surprised to feel the old longing return with such undeniable force. "They're beautiful," she said, a lump forming in her throat.

"We have a buyer interested in the black one, and the one with the white blaze," Fletcher said. "But it's up to you if you want to sell or not."

"Not sure if you're aware," Claude said, "but your father bred a lot of blue-ribbon winners in his time. Course, it was Mrs. Blackwood who bought the stud that started it all. But these are some of our best stallions yet. All you have to do is say the word and we can keep them and rebuild our reputation."

Julia had no idea what to do. Her head was spinning with memories and doubts and insecurities. Of course she wanted to keep the horses, but could she really run this farm? Could she really take care of these beautiful animals and make the right decisions for their future? "Umm . . ." she started. Then she noticed Fletcher studying her, as if trying to read her mind, and her face flushed with embarrassment.

Fletcher grinned and turned toward Claude. "Maybe we should give Miss Blackwood a minute to catch her breath," he said. "After all, she just got here. I know you told the buyer we'd have a decision right away, but the buyer can wait."

Claude scowled and pushed his thumbs into his belt.

Julia breathed a sigh of relief and smiled at Fletcher to show her gratitude. "Can I have a day or two to think about it? I haven't decided anything yet, if I'm selling the horses or keeping them. I haven't even unpacked yet."

Claude's frown deepened. "You're the boss," he said. "But I'm telling you right now, selling these studs is a big mistake."

Fletcher gave Julia a bemused uh-oh look, then directed his attention at Claude. "I'm sure Julia will take your advice into consideration. And I'll let the buyer know she'll be making a decision soon." Then he winked at her and said, "How about a tour of the barn since you're out here?"

She nodded. "Thanks, I'd like that." She waited to see if Claude was going to say anything else, but he busied himself stomping dirt around the base of a fence pole, brooding silently. "I'm sorry for not making up my mind right now," she said to him, "but I will. And I know you've got work to do, but after I have a look around, could you please show me how to turn up the furnace? The house is freezing."

Claude moved away from the fence pole and started toward the manor, his face dark. "Yes, ma'am," he said. "I'll take care of it right away."

"You don't have to do it right now," she said.

Claude ignored her and kept going, his head down.

When he was out of earshot, she glanced at Fletcher. "Did I say something wrong?"

Fletcher shrugged. "I have no idea. But I have to admit, I don't think I've ever seen him that cranky."

CHAPTER 9

Lilly

Trying to catch her breath, Lilly kicked the door and pounded on the walls inside the tiny, dark bathroom inside Merrick's sleeper car. The rough wood tore at her knuckles, and the heavy stench of old urine made her gag.

"Let me out of here!" she screamed.

Muffled voices filtered in through the outer walls of the car as performers and workers left the train on their way to work. She shouted again, then forced herself to stand still on trembling legs, trying to hear above her own labored breathing. Nothing. She closed her eyes and struggled to pull air into her lungs without gagging. *They'll come back,* she thought. *When the show is over, they'll come back.* She pushed her thumbnail into each fingertip—*one, two, three, four, five*—over and over again, trying to calm down. After what seemed like forever, her lungs loosened and her breathing returned to normal. But then her muscles started to cramp, like a hundred knives in her legs, and the lack of oxygen made her dizzy. She reached blindly for the toilet and sat on the closed lid, her jaw clenched and her shoulders hunched.

A little while later, the distant sounds of the big top found their way into the car from outside—music pulsing, people whistling, clapping, shouting, several collective intakes of breath and a smattering of nervous shrieks. An elephant trumpeted and children laughed. To distract herself, Lilly tried to picture the circus in her mind, the clowns and zebras and elephants and balloons. But what once seemed like a dream had turned into a nightmare, and all she could think about was Abby and going home. She put her head in her hands. There was nothing she could do now but wait.

After a while, the outside sounds changed from laughter and happy shouts to quiet talking and the distant clang of metal doors. Finally, the show was over and, hopefully, Glory was on her way back to the car. Lilly stood and pounded on the door again, even though she knew no one would hear. Her jaw ached from gritting her teeth and a sharp, stabbing pain throbbed at her temples. She could hardly breathe, she couldn't move, and she didn't know what she would do if she wasn't let out soon. At last, she heard muffled voices outside the car, footsteps coming up the steps, and the door to the passenger car opening. She put her ear against the door and strained to listen.

"Lilly?" a voice called out. "Where are you?" It was Glory.

"I'm in here!" Lilly shouted, her voice raspy and hoarse. She banged on the door with both fists.

Footsteps raced across the bedroom floor. The handle on the bathroom door rattled.

"Hold on," Glory said. "I'll get you out." Footsteps hurried across the floor again, and Glory's muffled voice said, "Where's the key, Merrick?"

Merrick's muffled voice answered, but Lilly couldn't make out his words.

Finally, a key rattled in the lock and the handle turned. The door opened and light sliced into the dark bathroom. Lilly blinked and covered her eyes with one shaking hand, briefly blinded by the glare. Then she bolted across the bedroom and living room, and headed for the exit. Merrick blocked her way, grabbing her by the shoulders.

"Where do you think you're going?" he said.

She yanked herself from his grasp and hid behind Glory, breathing hard.

"Leave her alone," Glory said.

"She's trying to escape again," Merrick said.

"Because you locked her in the toilet!" Glory shouted.

Merrick took a step closer and pushed his face into Glory's, his chin jutting out. "She needs to learn who's boss around here, just like you did."

Glory moved away from him, almost stepping on Lilly's toes. "Well, you don't need to lock her up like an animal to prove it."

Merrick scowled at her as if fighting the urge to hit her again, then turned away and took off his jacket, mumbling under his breath. He loosened his bow tie and fell into his chair. "I need a drink."

Glory shot a Lilly a wide-eyed look and jerked her chin toward the sofa, then went over to the sideboard and poured Merrick a glass of whiskey. Lilly went to the sofa and sat on her hands, unable to stop shaking. Glory flashed her another worried look, her lips pressed together in a hard, thin line. Lilly wasn't sure if Glory was warning her to keep quiet, or if she was concerned about something else, but she planned on staying still and silent anyway. Merrick was just like Momma, and if he was trying to teach her a lesson, it worked. Glory took the drink to him, pushed a footstool over to his chair, took off his shoes, and lifted his feet onto it. Then she knelt beside his chair.

"Is there anything else I can do for you?" she said. "Are you hungry?"

Merrick took a long swig of his drink, then looked at Glory with amusement. At first Lilly thought he was going to thank her, or give her a kiss. Instead he abruptly sat up and threw his drink in Glory's face. Lilly jumped and shrank back into the sofa, her heart racing again. Glory gasped and blinked, her mouth open in shock.

"Yeah," Merrick said to Glory in a mocking voice. "There's something else you can do for me. You can stop telling me what to do." He put the empty glass on the arm of the chair, then stood and stormed into the bedroom.

Still on her knees, Glory gazed at Lilly with sad, tear-filled eyes, whiskey dripping from her hair and face, mascara running down her cheeks. Lilly hung her head and started to cry.

After locking her in the bathroom, Merrick kept Lilly prisoner in his sleeper car for three days. Glory brought her wash water from the changing tent, meals from the cookhouse, and fresh clothes from the Monday man, who stole clothes from clotheslines in nearly every town. And when Merrick finally let Lilly out, it was time for her to go to work.

After breakfast in the cookhouse, Merrick took her over to the sideshow to see the new canvas banner being hung outside the freak-show tent to

160

announce her act. When they arrived, Mr. Barlow—in a top hat and jacket—and Alana—in a powder blue dressing gown—were there, watching the painter put the finishing touches on the giant image. Merrick swore under his breath when he saw it.

Lilly stared up at it, not sure what to think. In the image, she was ten feet tall, with her chin held high and her pale hand around a sparkling staff, like a white version of the bad queen in *Sleeping Beauty*. A winter scene surrounded her as she stood in front of an icy spaceship and an igloo. She couldn't imagine why Mr. Barlow wanted people to think she was from another planet. What was she supposed to do and how was she supposed to act? And what happened if everyone found out they were lying? She thought about asking Merrick, but changed her mind. She'd ask Glory later.

"It's perfect, don't you think?" Mr. Barlow said to no one in particular.

Alana stood beside him, her fingers and neckline dripping with jewels. She hooked an arm through his and twisted her red lips, staring up at the canvas. "I don't know, darling," she said. "It seems kinda . . . what's the word . . . off."

"No, no," Mr. Barlow said. "It's just what I wanted."

"For my show," Merrick said.

Mr. Barlow kept his eyes straight ahead. "Yes,

it's just what I wanted on my banner, on my tent, on my circus lot." He swore under his breath, then turned on his heels and walked away, swinging a silver-tipped cane and taking Alana with him. "Come along, darling. Let's celebrate with a little champagne."

Merrick watched him go, his face growing crimson. Then he grabbed Lilly by the arm and dragged her toward the sideshow performers' dressing tent. "You better pull this off, or you'll pay for it."

Now, the freak show was starting in a few minutes and she stood trembling in her undergarments in front of a mirror inside the dressing tent while Glory fastened a fake diamond crown on her head with white bobby pins, then tied beads throughout her hair. Her hair was freshly washed and curled, and it spilled over her shoulders like a wedding veil.

"Your dress will be here any second," Glory said.

"What am I supposed to do in the show?" Lilly said, her teeth chattering.

"Just stand there and let the rubes look at you," Glory said. "That's all. I'll be in the booth right next door and the only thing between us will be a canvas curtain. If you need anything, I can be there in two seconds flat."

Lilly wanted to ask what she might need, but she couldn't find the right words. She stared at her reflection, trying to remember how to breathe. Everything about her was white or silver—her hair, the beads, her skin, the crown on her head. The only color was in her eyes, which looked like blue stones in snow. Behind her in the mirror, the canvas flapped open and a dwarf came into the dressing tent, a pair of high-heeled shoes in her hands, a shiny dress draped over her shoulder. Her hair was as white as Lilly's, her face thick with beige makeup and pink rouge.

"Merrick sent these over," she said, showing Glory the shoes. "He wants her to look taller."

"Lilly," Glory said. "This is Penelope Dupree, our very talented seamstress and sideshow performer extraordinaire."

Lilly tried to smile at Penelope. It felt more like a twitch.

"Ah, yes," Penelope said. "I've heard about you, Lilly Blackwood. Mrs. Benini, who owns the snow cone and cotton candy stand with her husband, Tony, wants to have you over for a home-cooked meal some evening. Elizabeth Webb, who runs the grease joint, says you can play with her kids anytime. And Madame Zelda, otherwise known as Mrs. Daisy Hubert from Queens, our gypsy fortune-teller, says you're a Leo, and you've got wonderful things in store."

Lilly tried to smile again, but she didn't know what to say. The woman, like everyone she'd met besides Merrick, was being so nice. And all she wanted to do was go home, back to her room and Abby.

Glory and Penelope helped her into the dress. It was silver and white, with long, beaded sleeves and a billowing hoop skirt. Glory buttoned up the back, and Lilly pushed her feet into the shoes, holding on to the vanity to keep her balance. She had never worn high heels before, and when she straightened, she nearly fell.

Glory caught her by the arm and grinned. "You'll get used to them," she said.

"Never did like the things, myself," Penelope said, lifting her skirt to show Lilly her feet. Her long red toenails hung like claws over the front edge of brown sandals. Lilly gaped at her, speechless. She didn't think Penelope could wear regular shoes, let alone heels. Penelope laughed and dropped her skirt, then got on her knees to check the hem of Lilly's dress. When she got up, she said, "You look beautiful, just like a princess."

Lilly gazed at herself in the mirror. Despite the fact that her hands were sweaty and her stomach felt full of rocks, she decided Penelope was right. She looked like a princess from a fairy tale. But what would the people from town think— What did Glory call them? Rubes? Townies?— when they saw her white skin and spider-web hair? Would they be afraid? Would she make them sick? Would they hate her like Momma and Daddy did? She touched her thumbs to the tips of each finger over and over and over—*one, two, three, four, one, two, three, four.*

"Now remember," Glory said. "We're on until the show opens in the big top. The circus performance lasts about two hours. Then we do another show after it closes for the people who didn't catch us the first time around."

Lilly nodded and followed Glory out of the dressing tent and across the back lot, trying to breathe normally and walk without twisting her ankles in the high heels. Behind the big top, the circus performers and animals were getting ready for the show. Women in tutus and pink tights, men in red jackets or white leotards with gold-lapeled shirts. White-faced clowns in bald caps and oversized shoes, firemen's pants and suspenders, hobo hats and patched trousers, their orange and red hair sticking out in all directions. Women and girls in sequined costumes practicing atop white horses with plumes of pink and white feathers between their ears. Draft horses harnessed to parade wagons, dancing nervously in their hitches. Llamas and zebras and animal handlers, lions and bears and monkeys in cages, leggy giraffes and elephants with tasseled headgear. The boy who waved at Lilly was there too, dressed in a tuxedo and standing next to the baby elephant.

Despite her nerves, Lilly slowed, unable to pull her eyes from the spectacle. The sun reflected off the sparkling sea of glittering jewels that seemed to cover everyone and everything. It was like a picture book come to life, but a thousand times brighter. Then she noticed the boy in the tuxedo staring at her and she looked away. What did he think when he saw her dressed like a princess and heading over to the sideshow? Did he think she looked pretty, or more like a freak? Why couldn't she be like him and the rest of the big-top performers, beautiful and normal, admired for what they could do, not judged for what they looked like?

"Come on, Lilly," Glory said. "We can't be late."

Lilly gripped the sides of her skirt in her fists and concentrated on walking without tripping. It was all she could do to put one foot in front of the other, and not just because of the high shoes. Momma said she was a monster and people would be afraid of her, and now Merrick was putting her onstage for the entire world to see. What if Glory and everyone else were lying to her? What if Momma was right and she really was an abomination?

On quivering legs, she followed Glory into the back entrance of the freak-show tent and along a narrow, dimly lit walkway behind a row of canvas curtains. Glory called it the "backstage." The inside of the tent felt hot and musty, and smelled like mold, wet grass, and a strange, smoky perfume. Squinting in the shadowy passageway, Lilly fought the urge to turn and run. She didn't want to do this. Not now, not ever. The heels of her shoes sunk in the soft earth and she had to lift the hem of her dress so she wouldn't step on it. Then Glory stopped and pulled aside one of the first canvas curtains, revealing a raised stage covered with a flowered rug. In the center of the stage, a woman with a black beard sat on a chair in a zebra-patterned skirt and a jeweled brassiere, her hem pulled up to reveal her hairy thighs. Her eyebrows were dark and bushy, and a thick layer of hair covered her arms and back.

"This is my friend, Hester," Glory said. "Otherwise known as The Monkey Girl."

Hester waved a hairy hand.

Lilly nodded and tried to smile.

Behind the next curtain, a curly-haired woman with no legs sat on a round, one-legged pedestal. She was wearing a string of pearls and a pink blouse, and the bottom of her torso filled the entire tabletop, like an oversized vase or lamp. Using her arms, she turned herself around to say hello, the pedestal shaking back and forth beneath her. Lilly worried it would topple over.

"This is Dina the Living Half Girl," Glory said.

"Nice to meet you," Dina said.

Lilly swallowed. "You too."

Behind the next curtain, Aldo the Alligator-Skinned Man stood wearing nothing but a pair of silver shorts that looked two sizes too small.

Brown scales covered his hairless head and thin body. He smiled and gave Lilly a two-fingered salute.

Next, a woman in a long skirt and green brassiere stood with a white veil over her head. When she turned and lifted the veil to say hello, Lilly gasped and stepped back. A naked baby hung from her middle, it arms and legs limp, its head buried deep in her stomach.

"Don't worry, it's not real," Glory whispered. "The baby is made out of rubber and glued to her skin. This is Belinda the Woman with Two Bodies and One Head."

Lilly nodded once and tried to look friendly, but she couldn't help staring. Why would Belinda make herself into a monster on purpose? Did she want people to be afraid of her? What if someone tried to lock her up or slit her throat? What if they wanted to put her body parts on display? After they left Belinda, she asked Glory what would happen if the townies found out the baby was fake.

"Shhh . . ." Glory said, and lowered her voice again. "All sideshows have fake acts. We just don't say it out loud. Ever. We call it a gaff, or pulling a Margarite Clark."

"A Margarite Clark?"

"Never mind," Glory said. "You'll learn soon enough. Just don't talk about it. Not until the lingo comes natural to you anyway."

"But what if the fake baby scares someone?" Lilly whispered. "What if they don't want to see it?"

Glory chuckled. "If they didn't want to see things like that, they wouldn't pay money to come inside the freak show."

Lilly shook her head, a question on her face.

"In the freak show it's okay for the townies to stare at something they think they shouldn't," Glory said. "They don't have to, and actually aren't supposed to, look away. But thank God that's the case, or we'd be out of a job."

Lilly had to think about that. She still didn't understand, but it didn't matter. Right now she had more important things to worry about, like trying to keep her breakfast down.

One by one, Glory introduced her to other attractions in the freak show—Zurie the Turtle Boy, Dolly the World's Most Beautiful Fat Woman, Mabel the Four-Legged Woman, Magnus the World's Ugliest Man, Spear the Living Skeleton, Stubs the Smallest Man in the World, Brutus the Texas Giant, and Miles the Armless Wonder. Behind the third to the last flap, Ruby and Rosy stood back-to-back wearing blond wigs and matching lavender dresses joined at the hip, as if the skirts had been sewn together to make one garment.

"You already met Ruby and Rosy," Glory said. "Today they're The Siamese Twins."

The twins waved. "Hey, Lilly," they said at the same time. "Go get 'em, sweetie!"

Lilly wasn't sure what she was supposed to get, but she forced a smile and waved anyway. Glory let the curtain drop and kept going.

"What are Siamese twins?" Lilly said.

"They're twins connected from birth on one part of their body, like the hip or shoulder or head."

"But Ruby and Rosy aren't connected," Lilly whispered.

"Siamese twins are hard to find."

"So it's another Margarite Clark?"

Glory smiled. "That's right. You're a quick learner." She stopped in front of the second to the last curtain. "Well, this is your spot. Don't forget, I'm right next door."

"Where's Viktor?" Lilly said. "I thought he was in the freak show."

"Viktor is the star attraction over at the ten-in-one. And in The Barlow Brothers' Circus that means the acts not for the weak of heart." She lowered her voice to a whisper again. "You should see the gaffs Merrick's got going over there. He's got pickled punks, a fake mermaid, and a mummified devil baby in a tiny coffin with horns and tail. The female rubes nearly faint when they see it."

Lilly thought about asking what pickled punks were, but changed her mind. She couldn't imagine acts more shocking than the ones she'd just met. And right now, she didn't care. In a few minutes, crowds of people would be entering the tent to see the freak show and stare at her. She was about to find out the truth. Was she a monster? Or had her parents had been lying to her after all? The only thing she knew for sure was that she had no idea what was going to happen next. Glory pulled aside the canvas and held her hand while she climbed the steps to the stage. At the top, Lilly turned to look back at Glory, her stomach doing flip-flops.

"What am I supposed to do now?" she said.

"Make a game of it. You're from another planet, remember? Stare at the rubes like you've never seen anything like them in your life."

Lilly thought about saying she really *hadn't* seen anything like them in her life, but it didn't matter now. It was all she could do to stand upright. "Do I move around or stand still?"

"You can move, but act like a princess, like the rubes are beneath you and you don't have time for them. And you don't speak English, so don't talk to them. If anyone tries anything, just yell and I'll come right over."

"Wh-what do you mean? What would they try?"

Glory shrugged. "You never know. Rubes can be strange. But don't worry, you'll be fine." She let the curtain drop and left Lilly all alone.

Lilly moved to the center of the stage and

looked around, her arms and legs trembling. White sheets, silver ribbon, and glitter-covered stars hung on the side and back walls, and mounds of cotton and white felt covered every floorboard. A white chair and pearl-covered table sat below a hanging light made of sparkling crystals, reminding her of the one she'd seen in her parents' living room. Thinking about her parents' house, something cold and hard twisted in her chest. Leaving her attic bedroom and walking through Blackwood Manor seemed like a lifetime ago. And in all her fantasies of escape and imagined journeys, she never pictured herself ending up like this—a freak in a circus sideshow.

The viewing area behind the rope in front of the stage stood empty, waiting to be filled with townies wanting to examine her with their eyes. She stared at the murky, open space, her heart in her throat. It seemed gigantic and dark, like an open mouth made of grass and canvas, waiting to swallow her whole. She pulled her eyes away from it and counted the stars on the wall. *One, two, three, four, five, six, seven, eight, nine—*

The canvas behind her flipped open and she jumped.

It was Glory.

Glory smiled and pointed at a rod wrapped in white ribbons and silver beads, leaning against the sidewall. "I almost forgot. Your scepter, my queen."

Lilly picked up the pole with shaking hands and nodded her thanks. At least she had something to hold on to if she felt dizzy.

A whistle screeched outside and someone shouted, "Doors!"

"Here we go!" Glory said, and disappeared.

Outside the tent, thousands of footsteps walked and ran and stampeded into the midway. Children laughed and squealed and shouted. Grown-ups scolded and told them to slow down. A man on a stage outside the freak-show tent started his pitch to the incoming crowd. Glory said he was called the professor, and his job was to lure the townies into the sideshow by giving them a taste of what they would find inside.

"Ladiiiies and gentlemennnn," the professor shouted. "Step right up and get a look at the wonders we've got waiting for you inside! The big show starts in sixty minutes, in sixty minutes, so you've got plenty of time to see our show and get your place in line for the big top. There's plenty of time to see the oddities and spectacles behind these walls! Come one, come all, this is the show you've been waiting for, the one you'll be talking about next week. We've got the sights of a lifetime here, folks! We've got the half girl who giggles and talks and walks. Your mind will fail to believe what your eyes will see! She's not all there, but she's in here, and she's alive! See Zurie the Turtle Boy, with the head of a human and the body of a turtle. Have you seen Stubs the World's Smallest Man? What about Belinda the Woman with Two Bodies and One Head? They're all here, and they're all alive and inside. They all perform, they all entertain— one act after the other until you've seen them all. Have you seen Dolly the World's Most Beautiful Fat Woman? You won't believe the size of her thighs! This is the biggest show on earth for so little money. Come in now. There are no charges on the inside. Remember, you stay as long as you like and leave when you so desire. Oh wait, there's more! I almost forgot! We have a new act, folks, a new act. This is the only show in the world with this act. You won't see it anywhere else. We've got Lilly the Ice Princess from Another Planet. Our very own Syd Barlow captured her from the farthest corners of the earth, and she's here, inside and alive. Don't miss it! You'll be talking about her for the rest of your lives, folks!"

Lilly could hear the townies getting closer and closer, the excited voices, the laughing and talking and shouting. The shadows on the tent walls grew bigger and wider and darker, the shapes of bonnets and hats and heads and shoulders and balloons and children crowding one another for space. Sweat slicked Lilly's hands and her knees felt wobbly. She wanted to get off the stage, flee out of the back of the tent, and keep running until she couldn't go any farther. She gripped the scepter in one hand and counted the seams in the canvas behind the viewing area. *One, two, three, four.* If she could escape out of the tent, where would she go? And what would she do when she got there? Maybe she'd end up dead like Leon's daughter. Or maybe Merrick would send Viktor after her. *Five, six, seven . . .*

Outside, the professor kept shouting. "That's it, folks, step right up. My good friend here will take your money and give change if you need it. That's right, line up right here. There's no hurry now. These freaks aren't going anywhere. They'll stay inside this tent until you've seen them all."

Then the canvas entrance flapped open and a slice of sunlight burst into the viewing area. Lilly couldn't see the door, but it seemed as if she could feel the townies coming into the tent. The air grew thinner and hotter, and she could feel the presence of other humans, other beings, other bodies. A thousand smells filled the air all at once—cologne, popcorn, sweat, cigarette smoke, roasted peanuts, hot dogs, soap, leather, perfume, lace. It felt almost as if the townies were pushing in on her, trying to smother her, even though they were nowhere near her stage. Her breath grew shallow and tight in her chest. *One, two, three, four.*

At first, the townies made their way into the tent talking and laughing. Then, little by little, they grew quiet as they looked at the first freaks. Women whispered and gasped in surprise, men talked in hushed voices and laughed nervously.

Lilly gritted her teeth and stared at the grass on the other side of the rope, waiting for the first person to appear. What would their reaction be when they saw her? Would they recoil in fear? Would they cry? Would they laugh? Would they be sick? Would they jump onstage and try to hurt her? Would she be able to stand here and let them gawk without screaming? What if she couldn't do what Merrick wanted her to do?

Just when she felt like she was about to pass out from terror, a little girl came into view, wearing a faded jumper and pulling her father by the hand. When she saw Lilly, she let go of her father's hand, stopped, and put her pale fingers to her mouth. She drew closer to the rope and stared up at Lilly with wide brown eyes. Lilly steeled herself, waiting for her to cry or scream. She touched her tongue to her clenched teeth. *One, two, three, four . . .*

Behind the father and the little girl, more townies squeezed into the viewing area. What seemed like a hundred faces looked up at Lilly. A sea of mouths twisted and moved and chewed and smiled and scowled and laughed. A thousand eyes stared and squinted and widened and blinked and gaped. Sweat broke out on Lilly's forehead. Her mouth went dry.

The little girl took another step closer. "Daddy, is she really a princess?"

The father took her hand again. "No, honey," he said.

"But she has a crown," the little girl said.

"That doesn't mean anything." The father pulled her away and moved on.

"But, Daddy, I wanted to . . ." The little girl's voice trailed off.

Little by little, the first group of townies left while more streamed into the viewing area. Some walked slowly and others hurried past, as if they had changed their minds about coming into the freak show. Most people stopped to study Lilly for a few minutes before moving on. A frowning mother covered the eyes of the young child on her hip and refused to look at Lilly while the man she was with pointed and whispered in an older child's ear.

"They don't need to be seein' things like this," the mother hissed.

"Stop your frettin'," the man said. "It's all in good fun."

"Yeah, well, it ain't gonna be fun when they wake up with nightmares later."

The man rolled his eyes and moved on.

A freckle-faced boy stood in front of her stage for what seemed like forever, staring at her with droopy eyes and chewing his gum with his mouth open. Lilly had no idea what to do, or what he was waiting for. She tried not to look at him, but he was hard to ignore. Three groups of townies came and went before he finally left. When he did, she breathed a sigh of relief. Then, during a quick break in the flow of gawkers, a little old lady in a flowery hat stopped to let her tiny black dog relieve itself near the back wall of the viewing area, and a horrible smell filled the tent.

After a while, Lilly's feet started to go numb in her shoes, and her calves began to ache. Her head felt like it was about to explode from clenching her jaw. When the crowd finally started to thin, her chest began to loosen and her heart-beat slowed. The grass in the viewing area was flat and muddied, trampled by thousands of feet. She took a deep breath and let it out slowly, her shoulders dropping. At last, her first show was almost over. And no one had screamed or cried or gotten sick or tried to slit her throat. Then, suddenly, there was a shriek and a crash in the direction of the entrance, and the sound of a body hitting a stage.

"Get the hell out of here!" someone yelled. And then, "Are you all right, Dina?"

A boy laughed and others joined in.

A girl giggled and said, "Come on, you guys. Leave her alone."

Lilly's heartbeat picked up speed again. What was going on? What had happened to Dina the

Living Half Girl? Did someone try to hurt her? A few seconds later, a group of teenagers hurried into the viewing area. The boys laughed and playfully punched one another in the arms and the girls tittered. The girls wore puffy-sleeved dresses, and one had on a red beret over her long blond curls. The boys were in cuffed trousers and crisp shirts. Their eyes were glassy and bloodshot, the same way Daddy's eyes used to look when he drank too much whiskey. Somewhere a woman was crying. Was it Dina? What had the teenagers done to her? Then the girl in the red beret saw Lilly and stopped.

"Jeepers," she said. "Look at her. Is she really made of ice?"

"Naw," a boy said. "She's covered in white paint."

"Even her hair?" the girl in the beret said.

"It's a wig," the boy said.

"She's supposed to be from another planet," a second boy said. "That's stupid."

"She's kind of pretty, though," one of the girls said.

The girl in the beret made a face. "I think she's hideous."

Another girl wrinkled up her nose. "She stinks too."

"She looks like a corpse," the girl in the beret said. "Maybe that's why she stinks."

The girls laughed, and the first boy moved

closer and grabbed the rope in front of Lilly's stage. "Are you alive, freak?"

Lilly blinked at him. She had no idea what to do. Beads of sweat rolled down her neck and back. Then, before she knew what was happening, the boy ducked under the rope and climbed onto her stage. She stepped backward and her heels caught in her dress. "Glory!" she cried.

The boy smirked and reached for her hair. "Is this real, freak?"

The canvas wall between the platforms yanked to one side and Glory stormed onto Lilly's stage, her face contorted with anger. "Get the hell out of here!" she yelled.

The boy jumped down, crawled beneath the rope, and rejoined his friends, who were laughing hysterically. But instead of leaving, they moved toward the back wall of the viewing area, mocking Glory and Lilly and pointing.

"Go back to your cave, ya freaks!" the boy who climbed onstage shouted.

"Yeah, ya ugly freaks!" the girl in the beret shouted. She began to chant and the others joined in. "Freaks, freaks, freaks! Ugly, stupid freaks!"

The other sidewall between the stages pulled aside and Rosy and Ruby poked in their heads. "Are you all right, Lilly?" Rosy said.

"Leave her alone!" Ruby shouted at the teenagers.

They ignored her, still laughing and chanting.

Then the boy who climbed into Lilly's stage bent over as if tying his shoe. When he straightened, a strange look came over his face, a cruel, yet nervous, smirk. He raised his arm and threw something at the stage. A handful of wet dirt hit Lilly in the chest and splattered over her white dress, and chunks of grass landed in her hair. Another boy joined in, laughing as he reached down to get more mud. But instead of mud, he picked up the dog poop and threw it at Lilly. A thick gob of it hit her above one eye and ran down her nose. She dropped the scepter and stood there stunned, her hands up, her eyes and mouth squeezed shut, unsure if she should run or scream. The stench of dog poop made her gag.

The teenagers' laughter came to a halt, and in the sudden silence that followed, one of the girls said, "Oh my God, is that dog shit?"

Lilly stood frozen, a bulge of terror rising in her mind. Momma had been right after all. She made them sick. They hated her. They thought she was an abomination.

One of the girls began to laugh again, a lone, almost frightened, sound. Lilly opened her eyes and shrank back, cowering in disgust and shame. Then the others joined in, the girls giggling, the boys snickering, all of them laughing at her. She let the noise wash over her, dimly aware of Glory saying something and reaching for her. A gut-wrenching flood of homesickness washed through her, and a horrible cry tore from her throat. She put her hands over her face, realizing too late that she was smearing the feces over her cheeks and eyes. She gagged and staggered backward, her only thought to run, to get out of the tent so they would stop laughing at her. But it was like trying to run through molasses. It seemed as if everything had slowed to a crawl. Even the laughter seemed to deepen and slow. She shoved past Glory and her feet tangled in her skirt and she fell off the front of the stage, losing her heels and landing in a tangle of white dress, mud, and dog shit. The boys sprang on her like a pack of hungry wolves, pulling at her hair and clothes. She curled into a ball and covered her head with her arms.

Glory jumped down from the stage with the scepter in her fist. "Get out of here!" she screamed. "Leave her alone!" The teenagers raced toward the other end of the tent and Glory chased after them, swinging the scepter in the air. "If I see any of you in here again, I'll kill you!"

Hester the Monkey Girl and Aldo the Alligator Skinned Man came running to help.

"Are you okay?" Hester said, reaching down to help Lilly up.

Lilly knew only one thing: She had to get out of there. She scrambled to her feet and bolted barefoot toward the end of the tent where she and Glory had come in. When she couldn't find a way backstage, she ran out the front entrance through the middle of the crowd, sending the shocked townies left and right, spreading them like Moses spread the Red Sea. Women gasped and stepped back as if she had the plague while men put their arms out to protect them. Children cried out in fear. And Lilly saw them all, how beautiful and perfect they were, wrapped in sunlight and the normal world. She saw the pretty dresses, the rosy faces, the dark lashes, the blond and auburn hair. She hated them and wanted to be them, all at the same time.

Someone stuck out their foot and she tripped and fell on her hands and knees. She started to crawl along the sawdust-covered lot in her white princess dress, her dog shit–covered hair hanging in her face. Tears of shame and sorrow blurred her vision and she collapsed on the hot earth, breathing raggedly, not caring what happened next. On the ground in front of her, a pair of shiny black boots appeared. With what little strength she had left, she looked up.

"What the hell did you do?" Merrick said, glaring down at her.

Before she could say anything, he yanked her up by the arm and dragged her toward the back lot, around the stakes and lines of the big top. Behind the giant tent, the performers, animals, and clowns waited in line for the opening parade. Everyone turned to watch Lilly and Merrick—

women in tutus and pink tights, men in white leotards and red jackets. White-faced clowns and women and girls in sequined costumes. All looked on with curious eyes. At the end of the waiting procession, the boy in a tuxedo stood next to a man in work clothes, holding a line tied to the baby elephant.

Then Lilly tripped and fell again, her head and right shoulder hitting the ground with a bone-jarring thud. For a brief second, as she lay on her side, a cloud of dust nearly obscuring her vision, she saw the boy in the tuxedo drop the rope and start toward her, his face filled with surprise and concern. But the man in work clothes put a hand on his shoulder to stop him and led him back to the baby elephant. The boy glanced over his shoulder at Lilly and retook his place in line, frowning.

Merrick grabbed Lilly by the hair, yanked her to her feet, and dragged her away. She reached up with both hands to claw at his wrist, but he wouldn't let go. Over at the big top, the circus band started, the back entrance opened, and the grand parade made its way into the giant tent, greeted by the cheers and applause of an adoring crowd.

CHAPTER 10
Julia

The evening after Julia's first full day as the new owner of Blackwood Manor, the wind picked up and the house grew dark and cold, despite the fact that Claude had turned up the furnace. But it was far from silent. Creaks and groans seemed to come from every beam and floorboard, pipes knocked, radiators whispered, and the shutters rattled against the windows. Every once in a while, as she sat by the living room fireplace trying to make sense of the papers from the lawyer, Julia thought she heard rats in the walls. Doing her best to ignore the unsettling noises and pushing away images of a rodent infestation, she studied investment statements and deeds, a copy of her parents' last will and testament, page after page of legal mumbo jumbo, and bank statements that made her gasp. She knew her parents had money, but until now, she had no idea how much. If nothing else, it put her mind at ease to know she could keep paying Claude and Fletcher to help with the horses. And she could send Danny and his family a nice check so he wouldn't have to dig for food in the Dumpster behind Big Al's anymore. Maybe she'd even send one to her old boyfriend Tom, without a return address of course.

She had already made the decision that she would keep the farm running and, if possible, she would gut the house and turn Blackwood Manor into something fresh and new. She certainly had the money to do it. But first she had to sort through everything, to make some order of all the possessions, the thousands of items that seemed to fill every corner. There were too many memories, too many rooms, too much furniture, too many drawers and cupboards and hiding places. It was going to take weeks, if not months, to go through it all.

Her mind whirled in a hundred different directions at once, and yet, she couldn't help thinking about the horses and the tour of the barn Fletcher had given her earlier. Growing up, the scent of hay had been a familiar one, but inside the barn it was stronger and sweeter than she imagined. Mixed with the bakery-like fragrance of molasses and grain, and the musky aroma of the horses, it gave the barn a strangely cozy feel that, to her surprise, she found quite pleasant.

While showing her around, Fletcher had explained that Blackwood Manor raised Thoroughbred and Quarter horses for showing and racing, horses that displayed great foundations and descended from famous bloodlines. At its peak, he said, Blackwood Manor held eighty head of the best stock produced in the state, including their most famous stud, Blue Venture. Julia didn't understand everything he was talking about, but she appreciated his willingness to educate her. The only thing she knew for sure was that every horse was more beautiful than the last. And she couldn't believe they belonged to her.

When they reached the end of the center aisle, Fletcher entered the last stall. The horse inside nickered and turned toward him, nostrils quivering. It was black as night, with a glossy mane and a tail that touched the floor. Julia watched over the door as the horse sniffed Fletcher's shirt and hair, then nuzzled his neck like an overgrown puppy. Fletcher laughed and scratched the horse's cheeks and neck with both hands. Clearly, they were fond of each other.

"This is Bonnie Blue," Fletcher said. "Blue for short. She's your top producer and most valuable mare." The horse nickered again. "Why don't you come in and say hi?"

"Who?" Julia said. "Me?"

Fletcher grinned and glanced over her shoulder as if looking for someone. "I don't see anyone else out there. Don't worry, she's gentle as a lamb."

Julia took a deep breath, unhitched the door latch, and entered the stall. She wanted to pet Bonnie Blue more than anything, but it had been a long time since she'd been near a horse and she knew they could sense fear.

"Put your hand out, palm up, like this," Fletcher said, demonstrating.

Julia held out her hand and Bonnie Blue sniffed her palm, then rubbed her head on Fletcher's arm. "I don't think she likes me," Julia said.

"Sure she does, don't you, girl? Watch this." He took a step back and stood in front of the horse. "Shake, Blue."

Bonnie Blue lifted her front leg, extending it toward Fletcher. He grabbed her hoof with one hand and shook it like a dog's paw.

Julia gasped. "Wow. How did you teach her that?"

He let go of Blue's hoof and scratched her between the eyes. "It was easy. She's smart. They all are. But Claude wouldn't be happy if he knew I was teaching her tricks, so let's keep it our little secret."

"Okay. But why would he be upset about that?"

"Because it can be dangerous if you don't know what you're doing. Why don't you give her a scratch and get to know each other. After all, she's yours now."

Julia touched the side of Blue's neck and smiled, inhaling the mare's wonderful musky smell. Her coat was as slick and soft as it looked. Blue stopped nuzzling Fletcher and gazed at Julia with curious eyes. Then she put her muzzle near Julia's ear and sniffed, her charcoal-colored nose and lips like warm velvet against Julia's skin. She blew out a strong breath over Julia's neck, moving Julia's hair and giving her the shivers. Then she bumped her massive head against Julia's shoulder, nearly knocking her over.

Fletcher laughed. "There. You just got the Bonnie Blue stamp of approval."

Julia smiled and ran her fingers through Blue's mane. "I don't think I've ever seen a more beautiful horse."

"She's pretty special, that's for sure. And her foals are always perfect." He moved to Blue's side. "Come here, I want you to feel something." He took Julia's hand, laid it against Blue's belly, and pushed. Something pushed back. Then Blue's belly moved in and bounced once, like a rubber ball.

Julia gasped and pulled her hand away. "What was that?"

"Blue's next foal." Fletcher winked at her. "And your first one."

A wide smile spread across Julia's face. On one hand, it was almost too much to take in all at once—the house, the barn, the horses, the business, a new foal. On the other, it was the most wonderful thing she had ever heard. This foal would be the first born under her owner-ship. It would belong to her and no one else, not even her parents.

Now, as she sat in front of the roaring fireplace

surrounded by legal forms and listening to the house creak and groan, she tried to imagine taking care of the farm and making the right decisions for the horses. It was amazing and terrifying at the same time. The grounds and house were one thing, but Blue and her baby and the rest of the horses were living creatures. How would she ever manage it all? What if one of them got sick or injured and she didn't see the signs? What if Claude wasn't around and she didn't call Fletcher in time? The idea that this was a test crossed her mind again. Maybe Mother wanted to prove once and for all that bad things happened if you didn't follow the rules. But what Mother didn't know was that Julia planned on following the rules. Except this time, they were going to be her own.

She tried pushing the worries from her mind and concentrating on the paperwork, but her eyes grew blurry from reading and her head hurt from trying to make sense of everything. She put down the papers and decided to explore instead. She had no idea what time it was, but the sky outside the windows was black. Mother's key ring beckoned from the end table next to the couch, as if every scrolled bow held the potential to reveal secrets. She stood, picked up the key ring, and started toward the far side of the house, knowing all along Father's den was the first place she'd go.

Wrapping her sweater around herself, she padded down the hall, switching on lights as she went. The floor creaked beneath her feet and lamplight flickered off the smooth oak paneling and dusty picture lamps above paintings of horses and dogs. How many times had she tiptoed down this hallway as a child after one of Mother's tirades, hoping her father would let her into the den? How many times had she heard him, throwing things and crying behind the double doors? How many times had she wanted to ask what tormented him? A hundred? A thousand?

She stopped in front of the den and ran her fingers along the engraved oak doors, the hair rising on the back of her neck. What would she find on the other side? Suddenly, she felt like a little girl again, her knees trembling. Mother would surely disapprove of what she was about to do, and for reasons she couldn't explain, it still felt wrong to invade her father's space. But, she reminded herself, Mother and Father were dead and gone. Blackwood Manor was hers now, along with everything in it.

She fingered the keys, trying to decide which one to try first. They were all so different. Surely, Mother had them made that way to ensure she'd be the only person who knew which key unlocked which door. A lot of good that did her now. Julia slipped the key with a circular medallion engraved with the letter *B* into the lock and turned it. The tumblers clicked and the wooden doors creaked inward a few inches. She gave them a gentle push and they swung all the way open, squeaking on their hinges.

Lamplight from the hallway fell across the plank floor of the den, revealing the dusty fringe of a Persian carpet and illuminating a wide middle section of the room. Julia stood for a long moment. Maybe she should wait until tomorrow, when she wasn't so tired and overwhelmed. But she had too many things to do and too many rooms to go through to put anything off. She took a deep breath, entered, and switched on the lamp on top of her father's piano-sized desk.

Mahogany bookshelves covered the back wall, every space crammed with books and maps and files and papers and folders. A sideboard lined with dusty liquor bottles and etched tumblers sat against another wall, and a green upholstered couch sat against the opposite wall next to a silent grandfather clock. Her father's wingback chair slumped behind the desk, its faded brown leather wrinkled and worn. The air in the room felt close and musty, scented with the stale, sour tinge of cigar smoke and old whiskey. Except for the dust that seemed to cover everything, the den looked like her father had walked out yesterday.

For a few seconds, Julia was too stunned to do anything. How would she ever go through it all?

And why hadn't Mother cleaned and straightened the den after Father died? One of Mother's pet peeves had been his unwillingness to part with anything, and she had warned him a hundred times not to drop a cigar on his papers and books. Because if there was one thing Mother was deathly afraid of, it was fire. She used to have a fit when Father burned leaves and brush in the burning spot in the side yard, and she always reminded him and Julia that sinners would burn in the fires of Hell. So why hadn't she cleaned up the den for safety's sake, if nothing else?

Now Julia had no choice. She had to start somewhere. Maybe that was Mother's plan. Maybe it was further punishment for her part in his death. She took a deep breath and walked slowly around the perimeter of the room, scanning the bookcases and reading book titles. The shelves groaned under the weight of hardcovers on horse breeds, horse diseases, first aid, training techniques, and veterinarian terms, along with stacked file boxes bearing names like Blue Venture, Preston's First Run, Dakota Point, Shy Dundee, Whiskey's Pride, and Fame's Fortune. Another section held trophies, ribbons, and framed pictures of horses with blue and red ribbons on their halters.

Julia gave the last few shelves a quick glance, then blew the dust off the gramophone player and opened the lid. A record sat on the turnstile, the needle halfway across the track as if someone had turned it off in the middle of the song. She squinted at the name of the record: "Little White Lies." *Of course,* she thought, and closed the lid. She moved to the desk and stood staring at it. A film of dust covered the top of the desk, the blotter, the pens in the penholder, the green desk lamp, and the ashtray overflowing with ashes and cigar butts.

She went to the sideboard to examine the dusty liquor bottles, looking for reinforcement. A glass tumbler held the remains of dark liquid, thickened into what looked likc a solid sludge. All the bottles were partially empty, except for two bottles of unopened brandy. She picked one up, wiped the dust off with the edge of her sweater, opened it, and took a good swig. It burned her throat and warmed her stomach, and was just what she needed. She took the bottle to her father's desk and sat down in the leather chair, ignoring the dust wafting out of the seat.

And then she saw the picture.

It was her sophomore photo in a silver frame edged with gold filigree, taken for the yearbook ten months before her father died. High school seemed like a thousand years ago. She picked up the picture, blew away the dust, and bit her lip, trying to hold back a sudden flood of tears. Unlike other people's homes, where pictures of every milestone adorned the walls—kindergarten

and birthdays, weddings and graduations—
Blackwood Manor displayed none of those
things. Mother said photographs were meaning-
less and vain. She never bought Julia's school
pictures to hang in the house, and they didn't
even own a camera. But somehow her father had
gotten a copy of her school portrait and kept it on
his desk. And she never knew. She brushed the
rest of the dust off with shaking fingers and used
her sweater sleeve to clean the smeared glass.

In the picture, her skin was flawless, her white-
blond hair was pulled back into a ponytail, and
her expression was somber. Anyone else might
have thought it was a snapshot of a typical teenager having a bad day. After all, there were no
telltale signs of the difficult times she had at
home, or the taunts she endured because Mother
didn't allow her to wear the latest styles. But
Julia could see the sadness in her eyes.

She set the picture down, blinked back her
tears, and opened the middle drawer of the desk.
Inside were the usual things: pens and pencils,
paper clips, rubber bands, stamps. She tried a
side drawer and found a stack of unused
envelopes, stationery with the Blackwood Farm
letterhead, and a box of dried-out cigars. The
drawer below that was locked. She tried Mother's
keys, but none of them fit. The rest of the drawers
were filled with papers heaped willy-nilly—
invitations to various events, statements, bills,

and legal documents. She searched the other drawers for the key to the locked one, but found nothing. Frustrated, she stood and looked around the room. Where was that key?

Just then, something bumped and skittered across the ceiling above her head. She looked up. Another, louder thump made her jump. Then there was a grinding noise, like an animal chewing wires inside the second-floor walls. *I've got to get rid of those rats,* she thought. She glanced around the room one more time, then decided to call it a night. She was exhausted, and the weight of all she had to do, and everything she had to figure out, settled on her like chains.

CHAPTER 11
Lilly

After Lilly bolted from the freak-show tent, Merrick dragged her back to the train and locked her in the bathroom to punish her for letting the townies see her for free. Shaking all over, her hands and face and hair smeared with dog shit, she threw up in the toilet, then sat on the lid and sobbed. The stench was overwhelming and she couldn't stop gagging. After what seemed like forever, footsteps hurried into the car and someone unlocked the door. It was Glory.

"Oh my God," she said. "Are you all right?"

Lilly shrugged and got up from the toilet, her eyes burning and swollen.

"Did Merrick hurt you?"

Lilly shook her head.

"Come on," Glory said. "Let's get you cleaned up. I've got buckets of water outside." She grabbed a bathrobe, a washcloth, towels, and a bar of soap, then led Lilly outside and around to the other side of the car, where no one could see them. She helped her out of the filthy princess dress and gave her the washcloth and soap, then watched with sad eyes while Lilly scrubbed her face and hands.

"I'm so sorry that happened to you," Glory said. "I swear I've never seen rubes act like that. It was so . . . so vicious."

A burning lump formed in Lilly's throat, but she had run out of tears. "It's me," she said. "Momma was right. I'm a monster."

"No," Glory said in a firm voice. "It wasn't you. They tipped Dina over and threw half-eaten hot dogs at Belinda. They're just a bunch of horrible, stupid kids who don't know any better. I promise, being in the sideshow is not always like that. If it was, I wouldn't have anything to do with it."

Lilly didn't know what to say. It didn't matter if the sideshow was like that or not. She never wanted to do it again. And the fact that she had no choice made her body feel heavy and slow, as if her arms and limbs and heart had turned to stone. She washed her hair and dried it with a towel, too exhausted to think beyond the next few minutes.

Glory helped her into the robe, then knelt down to help her roll up the sleeves. She gazed at Lilly with tears in her eyes. "I'm sorry I didn't protect you. I said I would, and I failed. I hope you know I really care about you, and I'll try to do better from now on."

Lilly bit her lip and said nothing. Between the shock of what happened in the freak-show tent and the way Glory was looking at her, she felt like she might disappear into thin air, or collapse in a heap in the grass. All at once, she was overcome. "I want to go home," she cried, a sob bursting from her throat.

Glory's face crumpled in on itself and she held out her arms. At first, Lilly hesitated, then she collapsed into Glory's embrace, her shoulders convulsing. Glory held her tight, rocking her gently back and forth. "It's going to be okay, sweetheart," she said. "Everything's going to be all right. I promise."

A thousand different feelings overwhelmed Lilly, including surprise and relief at the calming effect of Glory's arms wrapped around her. It reminded her of snuggling her beloved cat, Abby, except the warmth and comfort she felt seemed twice as powerful. Little by little, she stopped shaking. And even though she was too exhausted to cry, tears sprang from her eyes. So this is what it felt like to be hugged by another person. And maybe, just maybe, this was what it felt like to be loved.

The following night, Merrick insisted Lilly stand next to him on the platform outside his car as the circus train traveled to the next spot. When he forced her out the door between his car and the next, she gripped the railing, trembling and hanging on for dear life, certain he was going to throw her off, even though Glory had reassured her that Merrick would never red-light someone he'd paid good money for. Then, as they approached the outskirts of the next city, Merrick pointed out houses with boarded-up windows and breadlines outside churches. He made sure she saw the CLOSED signs on warehouses and the hobos along the railroad tracks—men and women, young and old—gathered around fires built in trash cans.

"People are starving out there," he said. "So you might want to remember how good you've got it. The promise of three square meals a day is the biggest reason some people join the circus these days."

The morning after a show in Massachusetts, during which Lilly got through her act without running out of the tent or having anything thrown at her, Merrick called a taxicab for her, Glory, and himself. When Lilly asked where they were going, Merrick said he wanted to show her a place called Danvers State Hospital. In the backseat of the cab, Lilly paid no attention to the fact that it was her first time riding in an automobile. The only thing she wanted to know was why Merrick was taking her to a hospital. Was he going to let doctors poke and prod her to see if she was normal? Was he going to sell her to someone who wanted to pickle her body parts and put them on display? She looked up at Glory with worried eyes, her fingernails pressed into her palms. Glory patted her arm and said everything would be fine.

Twenty minutes later, they arrived at a castle-sized stone building with what seemed like a thousand windows and steep roofs. They entered through a set of giant doors into a foyer and followed a nurse into a long hallway. The hallway was empty and quiet, except for the *clack-clack* of the nurse's white shoes. The farther into the massive building they went, the more Lilly worried Merrick was going to leave her there. To calm herself, she made her feet go in step with the nurse's. *One, two, three, four, five.*

As they neared the end of the first long hallway, she heard a low murmur, like a hundred voices talking in the distance. Then it grew louder and louder. When they reached a set of thick double doors surrounded by rubber strips, the nurse stopped and smiled sympathetically at her.

"Now, it gets a bit unruly in here, but don't worry, you won't be staying in this area. Is it all right if I call you Lilly?"

Lilly's heart skipped a beat, then thumped hard and frantic in her chest. She gaped up at Glory, suddenly trembling.

"That's not what we're here for," Merrick said to the nurse. "We're looking for a relative."

"Oh." The nurse looked at Lilly again, confusion written on her face. "I'm sorry, I thought—"

"You thought wrong," Glory said.

Lilly went limp with relief. Merrick wasn't leaving her there after all. The nurse nodded and unlocked the door. Before they even went through to the other side, Lilly clamped her hands over her ears. What she thought was talking was wailing and crying and shrieking. The room was full of women in gray gowns with scraggly hair and scratches on their faces and arms. Some were strapped to their beds, and one of them screamed for help over and over. The room smelled like old urine and spoiled food. Bugs scurried up the windowless walls. A woman with a bloody nose smiled and came toward them. Lilly edged closer to Glory and kept her head down, her eyes on the nurse's feet.

After leaving the frightening, noise-filled room, they passed through a short hallway into another area, this one quieter, with women lying in beds and staring at the ceiling, reading, or talking in small groups. The nurse stopped in the aisle and addressed Merrick.

"Anyone look familiar?" she said.

Merrick scanned the room, then shook his head. "Not this time."

Afterward, in the cab on the way back to the train, he said to Lilly, "Do you know why I took you there?"

Lilly, who was leaning against Glory in the backseat and trying to forget what she'd seen, shook her head.

"Because I want you to know if you try to run away, chances are you'll end up starving and homeless, and the cops won't waste any time sending you to a place like that or worse. That's the first thing you need to remember. The second thing you need to remember is that I visit orphanages and asylums all the time looking for my next act. Kristi the pinhead came from the Waverly Hills Sanatorium in Kentucky, and I discovered Aldo the Alligator Man in Willard State. So if you give me a hard time about doing what you're told, having you committed would be a piece of cake."

Lilly said nothing and stared out the window. It was pouring outside, the green and brown smudges of trees and electric poles blurring past the rain-streaked glass. The clouds hung low and heavy, like ashes in the sky. She tried counting the trees along the side of the road but couldn't see past her tears. The world was nothing like she imagined, and she would have given anything to be back in her attic room, even if it meant dealing with Momma. A surge of homesickness plowed through her, so strong it nearly made her cry out.

Later that night, as Merrick snored in the bedroom, Glory and Lilly sat on the couch, talking about the visit to the hospital.

"He's right," Glory said. "You're better off with us, even though it's not the easiest life sometimes. With the circus, at least you'll have a place to lay your head at night, three square meals a day, the chance to see the country, and friends who look out for you." She gave her a smile that looked sad and forced. "And for the most part, you'll be treated like a person."

Lilly was glad that Glory was trying to make her feel better, but she couldn't push the images of the women in gray nightgowns out of her head. Visiting the hospital was going to give her nightmares for sure. "What kind of place was that? What was wrong with those women?"

"Danvers is an asylum for crazy people. You know, people who don't know the difference between what's real and what's not? But some people are sent there because their families want to get rid of them, like my brother, Viktor. My parents put him a place worse than that."

"Why? Is he crazy?"

Glory shook her head and began picking at the tiny balls of fuzz on her skirt. "No, he's not. My parents left him there when he was five because some people think when a person looks different on the outside, they're different on the inside too." She looked at Lilly. "But we know that's not true, right?"

Lilly nodded.

After showing Lilly the breadlines, the hobos, and Danvers State, and making sure she understood what would happen to her if she misbehaved, Merrick allowed her to walk the lot alone in the evening, when the shows and concession stands were shut down and the big top was empty. But only if the train wasn't loading up to move on to the next destination, and they were far enough away from the nearest village so the townies wouldn't see her for free. Glory thought it would be a good time for Lilly to start making new friends, because once the business of the day was over, everyone was ready to unwind and have fun. Maybe she could visit Mrs. Benini, or ask Penelope to introduce her to Elizabeth Webb's children. But Lilly had other plans. She wanted to find the animal tents, or what Merrick and Glory called the menagerie.

On her first night of freedom, after Merrick and Glory took a cab into town to go to a club, she stepped out of the sleeper car wearing a pleated dress and black Mary Janes—one of several outfits from the Monday man. The sun was setting in the August sky, coloring the clouds purple and pink and orange, and the first stars appeared in the distance. Crickets chirped in the long, dry grass surrounding the dusty lot, and the dark shapes of birds flitted through the dimming light. It felt strange and a little scary to be outside without Glory or Merrick, so she stayed near the car for a few minutes to build up her courage.

Outside the neighboring passenger car, four men in polo shirts and pressed trousers set up a table and chairs while a pretty blonde came down the steps carrying a deck of cards and two bottles of brown liquid that looked like whiskey. Another woman called out from an open window to ask how many glasses they needed. The men and women were thin and beautiful and graceful, like the ballerinas Lilly used to read about in her books. Glory said they were the trapeze artists.

When Lilly felt brave enough, she moved away from the car and made her way along the length of the train. After passing the trapeze artists and another passenger car, she stopped to pet three goats nibbling on weeds near a telephone pole. Were they the goats from the boxcar where Merrick had locked her in a cage? Had they heard her screaming and crying? One of the goats lifted its head and rubbed its face against her hip, then went back to eating. Another came over and nibbled gently on the edge of her dress, wagging its short tail. The third one sniffed her shoes and socks and legs, then licked her hand with its scratchy tongue. It was almost as if they were saying, yes, we know who you are.

Glory said the goats were allowed to wander the lot during off hours because, according to Mr. Barlow, they brought good luck. She also said circus people believed the color green and whistling in the dressing tent were bad luck, a bird flying into the big top meant death for a performer, and the trapeze artists and tightrope walkers sewed crosses into their costumes to keep from falling. Lilly wondered what Momma would think of the circus performers using crosses that way. Momma said people were put on earth to serve God, not the other way around. So why did the performers think He would keep them safe?

Thinking of Momma made her stomach hurt, so she pushed her from her mind, gave the goats another scratch, and kept going. What seemed like a thousand different noises floated out the open train windows, each sound changing and blending into the next as she passed, until it faded and dissolved all together—a tinny voice on a radio, someone singing, people arguing, a harmonica, a man yelling, a dog barking, coins clinking, laughter, clapping, triumphant shouting.

Farther along the tracks, a scratchy, up-tempo tune came from the open doorway of a boxcar, the loudest music Lilly had heard so far. She slowed. Was someone having a party? Dolly the World's Most Beautiful Fat Woman and Penelope the Singing Midget sat on wooden crates inside the boxcar, laughing and fanning themselves with paper fans. Wearing a feathered headband and a sequined blouse, Dina the Living Half Girl smoked a cigarette on top of an overturned wine barrel while talking to Spear the Living Skeleton. Ruby and Rosy laughed and danced with Aldo the Alligator Man, and two midgets, all four drinking from brown bottles. The twins wore long, beaded necklaces, grass skirts, and nothing else, their bare breasts bouncing up and down in time with the music. Lilly dropped her eyes and walked faster, hoping no one noticed her.

A gathering of men in dirty clothes huddled some distance from the train, smoking and passing around bottles. Inside another open boxcar, a dwarf sang and played a miniature guitar while Hester the Monkey Girl laughed and watched Magnus the World's Ugliest Man trying to teach his dog to play dead. Stubs the Smallest Man in the World sat on the lap of Belinda the Woman with Two Bodies and One Head, a hardcover book in his tiny hands. Hester caught sight of Lilly and called out, asking her to join them. Lilly smiled, shook her head, and kept going.

For some reason, she wanted to be with the animals more than the people. She couldn't describe how she felt about the animals or why she had such a strong need to see them, because she didn't understand it herself. But it was one of the reasons she was brave enough to venture out for the first time on her own. Maybe she was drawn to them because they understood what it was like to be locked up, with no control over what happened next. Maybe it was because her cat was the only one who had never let her down. Or maybe her love of animals was part of who she was, like the way her left foot turned in slightly, the way her fingers were long and thin, and the way her skin was white as snow. Whatever the cause, seeing the baby elephant and the other animals was the only thing she cared about right now.

When she finally reached the animal tent, she slowed, suddenly unsure. What if someone yelled at her for being there? What if they told her to go away and not come back? Then she remembered nearly everyone was done for the day, resting up for tomorrow and relaxing in boxcars and open tents, looking for relief from the heat. Hopefully, no one would be inside the menagerie at this hour.

She took a deep breath and slipped in through a side flap, staying close to the shadows. On the other side of the tent, the elephants loomed large and gray, like dark mountains against the canvas. Across from the elephants, zebras, horses, and giraffes stood behind low ropes, sleeping or chewing hay. Camels and llamas lay in a circular bed of straw in the center of the tent, and wagon dens with lions, chimps, and bears lined one wall. The sweet-sour tang of hay and animal dung filled the air, and the only sounds were munching, snorting, thumping, and shuffling.

With every sense on high alert, Lilly slowly moved through the aisle and approached the elephants, stepping as lightly and quietly as she could until she reached the first one. She tilted her head back to stare up at the massive creature. It gazed down at her with amber eyes, a low, rumbling noise vibrating deep in its throat, like the loud purr of a colossal cat. The elephant was mottled and gray, wrinkled and cracked and furrowed from the top of its head to its enormous legs and platter-sized feet. Its toenails were as big as potatoes. Dark swathes of green ran across its ears and knees, like the mold on the bars outside Lilly's old bedroom window. Black hairs and deep ridges lined its trunk, and the tops of its ears looked thick and rubbery, then grew thinner and thinner until the bottoms resembled a tattered old leaf.

The only thing between Lilly and the elephant was a rope, hanging across the front of the two-sided stall. A heavy chain wrapped around the elephant's back ankle, then attached to a thick stake in the ground. Looking up at the powerful beast, the walled-in feeling of being locked in her room returned, and the heavy, horrible ache of missing home. The sensations were so strong they nearly brought her to her knees. It was almost as if she could feel the elephant's misery, like she had with the lion, except this time, there was something else too, something that felt like tenderness. Was it possible that this powerful animal cared about people, even after everything they had done to it, even after they had caged it, tied it in ropes and chains, and forced it to perform? Lilly's eyes grew moist. More than anything, she wanted to go into the stall and comfort the elephant, to stroke its head and explain she understood what if felt like to be held prisoner, and to still love someone who hurt you. But she didn't dare.

She moved along the front of the stalls to the second elephant, which seemed even bigger than the first. This one looked half-asleep, its long lashes drooping, its eyes almost closed. She kept going and stopped in front of the third elephant, lying on its side in the straw. Next to it, the baby elephant stood picking at a pile of hay with the end of its little trunk. Lilly gasped quietly and put a hand over her mouth. The baby was even more beautiful up close. When it saw her, it lifted its trunk and reached toward her, a fingerlike lip at the end of its trunk wiggling and moving. Lilly smiled and held out her hand, hoping the baby would come closer. But there was a chain around its hind leg and it couldn't move forward. Suddenly, the mother elephant startled, sat up, and leapt to her feet faster than Lilly thought possible. Lilly scrambled backward, her heart racing.

"Hey!" a voice yelled, and a boy tumbled between the mother's tree-sized legs and fell in the straw between her feet.

It was the boy she had seen with the baby elephant on her first day, the one who waved at her and wanted to help when Merrick dragged her away from the freak show. He scrambled to his feet. When he saw Lilly, his eyes went wide.

"What the hell are you doing in here?" he said.

Heat climbed up Lilly's cheeks. She thought about running, but she was spellbound by the elephants and didn't want to leave. Before she could decide what to do, the baby elephant reached for her again. The mother held the baby back with her trunk, keeping her eyes on Lilly and trying to push the baby behind her. She looked like the same elephant Lilly had seen tied to ropes in the half-open barn, the one the men were trying to teach new tricks. The boy came out from beneath the mother elephant and put a hand on her giant, wrinkled leg.

"It's okay, Pepper," he said to the mother elephant. "Back. Get back, girl."

Pepper stepped backward and grumbled, a deep, vibrating sound in her throat. Then she lowered her head and checked to make sure her baby was okay, examining its ears and legs and belly with her trunk.

"That's it," the boy said. "Steady, girl. Steady." He patted Pepper's leg, then moved toward Lilly, frowning and brushing straw from his clothes. "What are you doing in here?" he said again, this time with less irritation.

She swallowed, searching for the right words. Would he get her in trouble, or would he be nice? Maybe he was wishing he'd never waved at her, now that he'd seen her up close. "I-I just wanted to see the elephants," she said.

He put his hands on his hips. "You know these are wild animals, right? They can be dangerous. You can't just come in here whenever you want."

"I'm sorry," she said, and turned to leave.

"Wait," he said.

She faced him again. To her surprise, he was grinning.

"I thought you came in here to see the elephants?"

She gave him a weak smile, relief washing through her.

"You want to meet them up close?" he said.

She nodded.

"Well, come on, then," he said. "Crawl under the rope."

Quivering with excitement and nerves, Lilly did as she was told. When she was on the other side, she stayed close to the rope.

The boy patted the mother elephant's leg. "This is Pepper. She's five tons of pure talent." He gestured for Lilly to move closer and she edged forward. "Pepper, someone is here to meet you." Pepper gazed down at Lilly, the baby huddled between her legs, her giant ears fanning back and forth. "Steady, girl," the boy said. Then, to Lilly, "Put out your hand."

Lilly extended her hand and Pepper reached out with her trunk, the rubbery, fingerlike lip tracing the inside of Lilly's palm. Lilly could hardly believe what was happening. Her heart raced with excitement. Pepper sniffed Lilly's fingers as if checking to see if she could be trusted, then lifted her trunk, whooshed it past Lilly's face, and snuffled her cheek. Lilly grinned and shivered, trying not to move. Then Pepper grasped Lilly's thumb with her trunk and shook it, and Lilly laughed.

"She likes you," the boy said.

Speechless, Lilly couldn't stop smiling.

"Guess how old she is," the boy said.

Lilly shrugged. "Ten?"

"Nope, she's thirty-four."

Pepper let go of Lilly's thumb and opened her

mouth in what looked like a smile. The baby came out from between her legs and Pepper started to sway, keeping time with the movement of her trunk. The boy urged the baby forward and told Lilly to come closer. Lilly hesitated and looked up at Pepper, unsure.

"Don't worry," the boy said. "They trust me. My father is the boss elephant man, the supervisor of the pachyderms. He can shoe horses, drive a ten-horse team, lay out a canvas, and clown if he has to, but mostly he takes care of the bulls. He feeds them, waters them, and checks for injuries and sickness. He helps the trainer and the veterinarian too."

Lilly raised her brows. "Pachyderms?"

"A pachyderm is an elephant."

"Your father takes care of bulls too? I didn't know there were cows in the circus."

He laughed. "No, we call the elephants bulls. Doesn't matter if they're girls or boys."

"Oh," Lilly said. She had to think about that. She edged toward the baby and placed a gentle hand on its wide gray head. Short black hairs bristled from the top of its forehead like a stiff brush. Lilly's heart filled with wonder and delight and something that felt like joy. Her cheeks hurt from smiling so much. She never thought she'd have the chance to touch a real, live elephant, let alone a baby elephant.

"This is JoJo," the boy said.

The baby curled his trunk around Lilly's arm and pulled her closer. She laughed again.

"Wow," the boy said. "He really likes you!"

Lilly ran her free hand over the outer edge of JoJo's ear, amazed at the warmth and softness of his thick skin. The boy rubbed JoJo's temples and forehead.

"They like to be petted here," he said. "And on their trunk."

Lilly rubbed JoJo's trunk, which was still wrapped around her arm, then ran her hand up and down between his eyes.

"All right, JoJo," the boy said. "That's enough. Let her go."

The baby unfurled its trunk and moved beneath his mother, rubbing its little ears on her legs. Lilly couldn't take her eyes off of him.

"Come on," the boy said. "I'll introduce you to the others." He slipped beneath the rope and made his way over to the next elephant. Lilly followed.

"This is Petunia, she's twenty-four," the boy said. "And the one on the end is Flossie, JoJo's aunt. She's the oldest of the group at sixty-three, and the biggest. Mr. Barlow claims she's three inches bigger than Jumbo." He grinned at Lilly. "And I'm Cole."

She glanced down at her shoes. "I'm Lilly."

"Nice to meet you, Lilly." He kicked stray piles of hay closer to Flossie, then rubbed her trunk.

What is he thinking? she wondered. *Is he going to ask why I'm so white and how I ended up in the circus?* "So what were you . . ." she started. "Why were you laying in the hay with Pepper and JoJo?"

He shrugged. "I like to be with them. It helps me think. Sometimes my father lets me sleep in their stock car."

Lilly's eyes grew wide. "They don't step on you?"

He shook his head. "Naw, they're used to me."

"You're lucky." She slipped under the rope and moved closer to Flossie. "I just wish they didn't . . ."

"Didn't what?"

"I wish they didn't have to be chained."

Cole frowned. "I know, but my dad says it's for their own good." He ducked beneath Flossie to scratch her belly. "If they got loose and got in trouble, who knows what would happen. Someone might hurt them. People get mad at animals for acting like animals all the time."

Something cold and sad twisted in Lilly's chest. Momma said the bars on her bedroom window were there for her own good too, and Merrick said if she ran away someone would hurt her because of the color of her skin, something that wasn't her fault. It seemed like she had more in common with the circus animals than the people. No wonder she could feel their pain.

"If you want, you can come see the elephants whenever I'm here," Cole said. "Just don't let Mr. Barlow or the trainers catch you."

Lilly couldn't believe what she was hearing. "Really?"

"Sure. Just stay away from the other animals. I haven't spent as much time with them, so I'm not sure which ones to trust."

She fought the urge to jump up and down, glad he was still scratching Flossie so he wouldn't see her excited grin. "Okay. Thanks."

Just then, the tent entrance flapped open and someone came into the menagerie. Lilly stood rooted to the ground, trying to decide if she should run or hide under the elephant with Cole.

"Hey!" a man yelled. He marched toward her, his face angry. "What are you doing in here?"

Cole scrambled out from beneath Flossie, crawled under the rope, and stood in the aisle. "It's okay, Dad," he said. "She's my friend."

Lilly felt a strange flutter in her belly. Cole had called her his friend. And he said she could spend more time with the elephants. It seemed almost too good to be true.

CHAPTER 12
Julia

The day after going into the den and finding the locked drawer and her high school photo on her father's desk, Julia made her way up to the third floor, hoping to find a way into the attic. She needed to figure out how the rats were getting in before the infestation got any worse. With Mother's keys on her belt loop, she hurried up the second flight of stairs, something she hadn't done since she was a little girl, when she used to stomp up and down the steps to see how many times she could get away with it before Mother scolded her for forgetting the third floor was off limits.

Except for the thick coating of dust and cobwebs hanging from the crown moldings and ceiling lights, the layout was the same as the second floor, with a wood paneled grid of hallways lined with red Turkish runners, brass sconces, and closed doors. Starting at the far end of the main hall, Julia stuck her head inside each soundless room, unable to shake the feeling that she was in an abandoned hotel. Every tight, narrow chamber was exactly the same, with double windows, a mahogany bed, a mirrored dresser, a dust-covered duvet, and a red and green Tiffany lamp on a bedside table.

She had no memories of visitors heading up to there to sleep, and could barely recall her parents having company. She also had no knowledge about the history of Blackwood, if it had been in the family before her parents owned it, or the age of the building. As a child, she hadn't cared. But now it was easy to imagine a time when elaborate feasts and grand parties were held in the dining room and the sweeping front lawn, couples dancing and drinking before treading upstairs arm in arm to make love in the beds, or to argue, laugh, and cry within the privacy of the third-floor rooms. She pictured lovers meeting secretly, couples fighting, men taking advantage of women, drunks being put to bed, women weeping in chairs next to windows, men playing cards and smoking. It was quite possible that someone, maybe more than one someone, had died up here. Could it be that rats weren't the ones making noises at night? Could it be that Blackwood Manor was full of ghosts? The idea made her shiver.

She pushed the morbid thoughts away and walked to the end of each hall, looking for a way up to the attic. If rats were getting in somewhere, the attic would be the logical place for them to hide. She searched for another door or staircase, but found none. She checked the ceilings for a trapdoor. Still no luck. It didn't make sense. How did her parents get up to the top floor? Thinking she had missed something the first time, she looked in every room again.

Then, in the bedroom at the end of the last hall, she noticed there were two closet doors instead of one. She hurried toward it, then slowed. What if she found a nest full of rats in the attic? Or a loft full of bats? With a strange mixture of excitement and fear, she opened the first door. It was a closet, empty except for a dusty pair of men's dress shoes with crumbling laces. When she slowly opened the second door and peered inside, the light from the bedroom revealed a narrow space the size of a large bathroom or small dressing room, decorated with wainscoting and fleur-de-lis wallpaper. Haphazard piles of hatboxes and shoeboxes lined one wall. She opened the door all the way and let out a screech.

A nude, headless woman stood in the back corner, partially obscured by shadows.

Then Julia realized her mistake and laughed, her fingers over her mouth. It was a dressmaker's dummy. She stepped through the door, pulled a string on a bare bulb, and the room flooded with gray light. Unlike the eight-foot ceilings in the rest of the house, the ceiling in the small room was less than six feet tall. And if she stretched out her arms, she could touch two walls at the same time. At the far end of the space, next to the dummy, a hand-carved table with lion legs atop ball and claw feet sat beneath a cloth tapestry embroidered with a stone cottage surrounded by iris and lilies. Why anyone would hang a tapestry in such a small room was beyond her. She put her hands on her hips and glanced around. What had this room been used for? It felt chillier than the rest of the house and she couldn't imagine why. Maybe it had been someone's private sitting area or changing room. It almost seemed like a hidden chamber. A hidden chamber for what, who knew?

She picked up one of the hatboxes and blew a layer of dust off the lid. Just as she was about to open it, someone called her name downstairs. It was either Claude or Fletcher, she couldn't tell which. She switched off the light, left the room, closed the bedroom door, and hurried toward the staircase.

Claude waited at the bottom, his face dark.

Julia stopped on the top step, surprised to see him in the house, let alone on the second floor. "What is it?" she said.

"Sorry for barging in unannounced," he said, sounding winded. "I knocked, but no one answered."

"I was in one of the bedrooms. What's going on?"

"We need to call Fletcher. One of the mares is foaling."

She started down the steps. "The phone is in the kitchen."

Claude hurried down the stairs and Julia followed. He ran into the kitchen and went straight to the phone on the counter next to the pantry door. She couldn't help noticing he knew where to find it. He dialed the number and waited, his hat twisted in his fist, his wind-reddened brow furrowed. Without saying hello or announcing who he was, he said, "Bonnie Blue's in trouble."

Julia drew in a sharp breath, then rushed into the mudroom and put on boots and a jacket.

"All right," Claude said, and hung up the phone. He put on his hat and marched toward the door.

"Is he coming?" Julia said.

"He's half an hour away," Claude said. "And he might be too late." He yanked open the door and went out.

She followed. "Is there anything I can do to help?"

Claude said nothing and sprinted across the lawn. Julia did her best to keep up.

It started to snow.

In the barn, Bonnie Blue lay on her side in the straw, panting, her neck and sides wet with sweat. The other horses nickered and whinnied and thumped against their stalls, sensing something was wrong. Julia stood in the doorway of Bonnie Blue's stall and watched Claude, unable to stop the trembling that worked its way up and down her limbs.

"Is there anything I can do?" she said.

"Nope," Claude said. He moved straw out from around Blue's backside with his foot and lifted her tail. A small white hoof stuck out beneath her tail, like a child's fist wrapped in white plastic.

"What's wrong with her?"

"Her labor's taking too long," Claude said. "That foal should be out by now and Blue's getting weak. I checked to see if the foal was turned wrong, but I can't tell. It's too big."

Julia could hardly breathe. If that beautiful horse and her foal died, she wasn't sure she could take it. Not just because Blue and her foal were her responsibility now and she already felt a special connection to them, but because horses had always seemed so strong and majestic to her, like they were supposed to live forever. Seeing a horse die, a pregnant one at that, would be a tragedy from which she wasn't sure she'd recover. And if this was going to be her initiation into the ownership of Blackwood Manor Horse Farm, maybe she should give up now.

"Is it okay if I come in?" she said.

"It's your barn," Claude said.

She entered the stall and, stepping carefully around Blue, knelt beside her head. "Shhh . . ." she said. "Everything's going to be all right." With gentle fingers, she pushed Blue's forelock away from her eyes and rubbed her forehead slowly, hoping to distract her from pain. Blue moved her head ever so slightly in Julia's direction and nickered softly. Julia's eyes filled and a burning lump formed in her throat. It seemed like Blue recognized her.

Waiting for Fletcher, Claude paced the stall, his hands in fists, and, every few minutes, checked under Blue's tail. Julia blinked back tears and kept stroking Blue's forehead and ears, talking to her in a soothing voice. Every now and then, Blue closed her eyes, her breathing slowed, and Julia's heart nearly stopped.

After what seemed like an eternity, the barn door opened and slammed shut, and Fletcher ran up the aisle. "What's going on?" he said, out of breath.

"I think the foal's too big," Claude said. "Either that or something else is wrong."

Fletcher came into the stall, rolled up his sleeves, and felt Blue's stomach. Then he went around to her rear end, knelt, and pushed her tail aside. "One of the foal's front legs is back too far." He pulled on the little hoof and let it go back in, sliding his fingers in beside it. "It's okay, Blue," he said in a calming voice. "You'll be all right. Just hold on a little longer." Slowly, he put his hand inside the mare, waited a second, then gently pushed his arm in almost up to his elbow. Blue stiffened and groaned. "Hold her hind legs," he said to Claude. Claude got into position and Fletcher looked at Julia with serious eyes. "Do you think you can hold her head down?"

Julia nodded.

"Get between her crest and withers and firmly put your hands on the side of her neck beneath her mane," Fletcher said. "This is going to be painful, so she might try to stand and we need to keep her down. Don't worry, you won't hurt her."

Julia went around the top of Blue's head and knelt beside her neck.

"Ready?" Fletcher said.

"Yup," Claude said.

Julia nodded again, sweat breaking out on her forehead.

Fletcher pushed his arm in farther and Blue's body contracted in pain. She grunted and panted and moaned.

"It's okay," Julia whispered to Blue, holding her neck down with both hands. "You're going to be all right. We're trying to help."

Fletcher grimaced and reached in farther. He felt around for what seemed like forever, then finally said, "Got it!" and started slowly pulling. Blue stiffened and snorted loudly, nostrils flaring. Little by little, Fletcher's arm came out all the way, the foal's second hoof in his fist. Suddenly, Blue went limp, exhausted. "Let her go," Fletcher ordered Julia and Claude. Julia lifted her hands, and Claude released Blue's back legs. Still gripping the second hoof, Fletcher grabbed the first hoof with his other and

and pulled. "Come on, Blue, push!" he yelled.

Blue's belly contracted and she lifted her head and pushed while Fletcher pulled. The foal's hooves and front legs came out up to its knees, and Claude broke the white bag around them and yanked it away so Fletcher could get a better grip. Then the foal's head came out and Blue went limp again. Fletcher kept pulling while Claude drew away more of the white sack from around the foal's eyes and mouth.

"Come on, Blue," Julia whispered. "You can do it."

Blue moved her head, her stomach contracted again, and finally, Fletcher pulled the foal out all the way. He let go and stood while Claude drew away the rest of the sack. The wet foal lay in the straw, its sides fluttering up and down, its head down, its neck limp. It was oil black like Blue, with perfect white socks halfway up to its tiny knees. But its ribs stuck out, it looked half-starved, and it wasn't moving. Julia swallowed and knelt in the straw, certain the foal was dying.

Bonnie Blue and her foal lay tail-to-tail in the stall, both motionless except for quick, shallow gulps of air. Julia's heartbeat thudded in her brain, like her veins were about to burst. She felt like she couldn't breathe or speak or move. How could this be happening? How could these beautiful horses, a mother and her newborn baby, be dying? To her horror and shock, Fletcher and Claude seemed unfazed. If this was what it was like to own Blackwood Farm, she didn't want any part of it.

Fletcher checked between the foal's hind legs. "It's a filly."

Julia looked at him and waited for the bad news, amazed he could be so detached. He was a veterinarian, trained to save sick and injured animals. Why was he just standing there? Then, to her surprise, the filly rolled onto its belly and lifted its head, its long limbs stretched out like saplings. But even if it survived, she thought, how would it ever stand on such bone-thin legs? It seemed impossible. The filly's head doddered like an old man's, as if taking one first and final look at the world. Julia couldn't take it. She looked at Blue, who still lay on her side, her eyes closed. *Oh God, not you too*. Hot tears fell down Julia's cheeks.

Then Blue lifted her head, rolled onto her belly, and curled her legs beneath her. The filly lifted its tiny wet head higher, then glanced at its mother and inched forward in the straw, struggling to get closer to her. Blue gazed back at her filly and nickered. The filly inched toward her, every effort a little bit stronger. And then Julia recognized the look in their eyes, the look she had studied so many times between mothers and daughters, the look that lit up their faces with affection and recognition of their unconditional love. Her breath caught in her chest.

"Well, Miss Blackwood," Fletcher said, smiling at her. "What's your new filly's name?"

Even Claude was smiling.

Julia put a hand over her mouth to stifle a sob. Miraculously, Blue and her filly were going to be okay.

CHAPTER 13

Lilly

1937

Lilly lay on her bunk inside the stifling hot car, staring into the darkness and listening to the other sideshow women mumble and snore in their sleep. She was on top of her covers, her cotton nightgown pulled up to her thighs, her long hair piled above her head on the pillow. The train had stopped a few hours ago, and she had been with the circus long enough to know that the smell of bacon, eggs, fried potatoes, and strong coffee meant the flying squadron—the first section of the train to arrive in town—had already set up the cook tent. The roustabouts were laying out the lot, Cole's father—his name was Hank—and the rest of the menagerie workers were feeding hay and grain to the animals, and the cooks were getting ready to serve the first meal of the day—made from meat, vegetables, flour, milk, sugar, and butter delivered earlier that morning—to the hundreds of workers and performers employed by The Barlow Brothers' Most Amazing Show on Earth.

Despite the fact that the inside of the sleeper car felt like an oven and her horsehair mattress was full of lumps, she was grateful for both. She'd been sharing this car with the other women for the past four years, and she had Glory to thank for it. Because when Lilly turned twelve, Glory gave Merrick a choice. Either he allowed Lilly to move out, or she would leave him. Lilly knew Glory was doing it to protect her, but she never thought it would work. At first, Glory tried convincing Merrick it was an issue of privacy. But by that point, Lilly had already spent two years on the couch listening to them in the bedroom, talking and arguing and laughing. The first time she heard them having sex, she put a pillow over her head and cried, certain Merrick was hurting Glory but too terrified to do anything about it. When Glory came out of the bedroom the next morning and saw the worried look on Lilly's face, she assured her that she and Merrick had only been playing a game and she was fine. Then Lilly walked in on them naked one afternoon and Glory gave her "the talk" about the birds and the bees. After that, Lilly put her head under the pillow every night, just in case. So when Glory told Merrick she was worried Lilly might catch them doing something "inappropriate," he laughed. It was already too late for that.

But then Glory packed her bags and stood in the doorway with tears in her eyes, and Merrick surprised everyone by letting Lilly move out. He still kept a close eye on her—threatening to send her away if she messed up, talking to her like she was a possession instead of a person—but she was no longer a regular victim of his physical abuse. When she was living with him, the slightest slipup or wrong word set him off, and he kept control with insults, the backside of his hand, and sometimes, his fists. Lilly tried talking Glory into leaving with her, but for some reason, Glory refused. Half the sideshow performers said Glory stayed with Merrick because she thought she could change him, the other half said it was because he saved her brother, Viktor, from a lifetime in an asylum.

After Lilly moved out, she asked Glory nearly every day if she was okay. Sometimes Glory looked happy and acted fine, and other times she seemed sad and distant. On the days when she was quiet, she wore more makeup than usual, or combed her hair in a different way to hide the bruises. Lilly eventually realized Glory loved Merrick, despite the way he treated her. And sadly, she knew what it was like to care about someone who misused you. Even after everything Momma and Daddy had done to her, the fact that they never returned her love still broke her heart.

Now, everyone would be getting up soon, and the other sideshow performers in the car—Dolly the World's Most Beautiful Fat Woman, CeeCee the Snake Enchantress, Hester the Monkey Girl, and Penelope the Singing Midget—would be climbing down from their beds, asking one another what town they were in today. After all, it was easy to forget, considering The Barlow Brothers' Circus covered fifteen thousand miles and a hundred and fifty shows every season.

Lilly knew two things for sure. They were somewhere in Pennsylvania, and when Merrick returned from scouting out new venues for the past week, he was going to have it out for her again. Even now, despite the fact that she'd been with the sideshow six years and was one of his star attractions, the money she brought in was his to keep. He was her boss and legal guardian, and three meals a day and a place to sleep was all he owed her. She'd asked a hundred times to be paid like the other performers, but he always reminded her that he could get rid of her as easily as he had acquired her.

This time, though, she was going to be in trouble

for turning away a line of townies—or as she now called them, rubes. And that was one thing you didn't do. You didn't get between Merrick and his take, especially when you were one of his main acts—The Albino Medium. Not to mention she had broken the golden rule—"The Show Must Go On."

Merrick came up with the idea for The Albino Medium after he convinced Mr. Barlow that the rubes were more interested in Dina the Living Half Girl and Mabel the Four-Legged Woman than The Ice Princess from Another Planet. And Alana loved the concept so much she wanted to help with the act and persuaded Mr. Barlow to give Lilly her own tent.

At first, Lilly thought being The Albino Medium would be better than being in the freak show, where the rubes stared and heckled and spit at her, toddlers cried out in fright, and little old ladies tried poking her with canes. Kids and adults alike threw popcorn and peanuts and half-eaten candy apples at her, laughing when she ducked, hooting when something hit her. And when Merrick put her "out front" to lure rubes into the tent, women touched her face, drunk men grabbed her chest, and teenagers pulled her waist-long hair. More than one tried to yank it out.

But after the first few weeks of her new act, she grew to hate the fact that people thought she was real, and she felt horrible seeing rubes part with their hard-earned money in the hopes of hearing from a deceased family member on the "other side." Some people were so desperate they paid with jewelry or what looked like their last dollar. Sure, there were a lot of fake acts in the sideshow—The Devil Baby, The Fee Gee Mermaid, The Woman with Two Heads—but that didn't make her feel any better. Day after day of countless pained faces, all them looking at her with hope and enthusiasm, praying to hear from deceased mothers, fathers, lovers, children, was almost more than she could bear.

How long had it been since the first clueless rube had come into The Albino Medium's tent and asked to speak to a departed loved one? Two years? Three? It felt like a hundred. Thinking about it now, as she lay in her bunk alone with her thoughts, anguish welled up inside her chest. But she fought it and pushed it back down, packing it away. It was better to be numb.

And yet. And yet. She wasn't numb. She felt like one of the lions or elephants, a caged animal being forced to perform. She used to work the gig on the same schedule as the rest of the sideshow, but then the lines grew longer and longer, and some of the rubes willingly missed part of the big top to see her. Now, her tent was open all day, from the opening of the doors to the final curtain, with two short breaks to rest and have a meal. At the end of those long days, her emotions were spent, and the only thing that made her feel better was spending time in the menagerie.

If it were up to her, she would have gotten a job with Hank taking care of the bulls, mucking out stalls, filling water and feed buckets, giving them treats and patting their trunks—the smallest and perhaps only bit of comfort they would find in the circus. The circus trainers and performers claimed to love the animals, but as soon as the show was over they put them back in their stalls and cages and forgot about them until the next performance. Sure, the animals were fed and housed, and examined by a vet if they were hurt or ill, but Lilly and Cole were the only ones who talked to them, played with them, and gave them extra scratches and rubs. And they did it every night.

Last night in the menagerie, when she told Cole she had turned away the line of rubes, he begged her to hide in his car until Merrick cooled off. But she refused. It wouldn't be fair to get him involved. He was her best friend and everyone knew it and accepted it, maybe because they had been children when it first began. But that meant if Merrick didn't find Lilly in her car, Cole's car would be the first place he'd look. Now, she wondered if she'd made a mistake. Maybe she should have taken Cole up on his offer. At least he'd be there to protect her.

Part of her hoped no one would tell Merrick, but she knew better. Anyone who held back that information would be in trouble too. And then there was Viktor, whose loyalty rested with Merrick no matter how badly he treated his sister, Glory. Everyone had warned Lilly over the years never to bad-mouth Merrick in front of Viktor, or to do anything that might affect Merrick's bottom line. Now she wondered if Viktor would be the first one to tell Merrick what she had done. The other women said they couldn't blame her for shutting down her act, but she knew it wouldn't matter to Merrick.

Thinking about it now, she could hardly believe what happened. To trick the rubes waiting to see The Albino Medium, Alana went down the line with a ledger and wrote down the name of the departed loved one each rube hoped to reach, in the guise of a money-back guarantee. She only did a few at a time because the waiting area tent next to The Albino Medium's tent only held ten people. But unbeknownst to the rubes, Alana wrote the names down twice, once in her ledger and again on another slip of paper, which she moved to her pocket unseen. And if the rube was a mark—a townie with a fat wallet, singled out by the ticket seller with a friendly slap on the back that left a chalk mark—it was noted on the paper too, so Lilly could offer a more "in-depth" reading for an extra charge. After ushering ten rubes into the waiting area tent, Alana transferred the list to Merrick, who gave the names to Lilly one at a time. Sometimes, when Merrick was gone, Leon, the old man who found her locked in the animal cage all those years ago, took his place.

The inside of The Albino Medium's tent was decorated with red and black curtains, shiny beads, mirrors, and dark rugs. The only light came from three candles in pewter holders on a round, antique table in the middle of the tent, with two chairs on either side—one an elaborately carved throne for Lilly, the other a cane-backed chair for the rube. Pierre—a midget who used to work as a clown until he broke his pelvis during the "baby in a burning building" act—hid inside a wardrobe with sliding panels, where he could clap, whistle, or play the harmonica or tambourine without being seen. Sometimes he snuck out of his hiding place to touch the rubes with wool-stuffed evening gloves, or to produce a glowing light or other moving object in the dark, like a woman's hankie on the end of a stick. Other times, a "spirit baby"—a stuffed shape concealed beneath the tabletop and attached to a stick worked by Lilly's foot—peered over the edge of the table when called from the netherworld. And when Lilly asked a spirit to ring the bell beneath a glass globe in the center of the table, Pierre rang a bell inside the wardrobe.

It was a clever setup, and word quickly spread that The Albino Medium was authentic. But every time the bell rang or the tambourine jingled, every time Lilly relayed a special message from the great beyond and the grieving person's facial expressions changed from sadness to surprise, from doubt to gratitude, guilt clawed at her throat. It was a lie, all of it. And seeing the rubes' tear-stained faces broke her heart.

It was late yesterday afternoon when a strange-acting man came into the tent, his hands stuffed in his jacket pockets, a wool scarf over his mouth, his hat pulled down over his forehead. At first, Lilly thought wearing a scarf in the middle of summer seemed odd. Then she reminded herself that she had done readings for a woman in bathing trunks, an old lady dressed like a gypsy, and someone in a chicken costume. She had seen men in women's skirts, toddlers wearing cat ears, and boys with earrings. Nothing surprised her anymore.

She gestured for the man to sit down across from her and thought briefly how the scarf did little to hide the smell of alcohol on his breath. Then, like a trained animal, she began her spiel in a low, even voice. "Hello and welcome. Before we begin, let me tell you a little bit about what I do. I've been communicating with the dead since the age of four and eventually came to realize I needed to share my gift. Messages from the beyond can come in the form of music, voices, and other sounds. What I'd like you to do is close your eyes and think about the person you're hoping to hear from. While you're doing that, I'll try to connect with the spirit world. Then I'll ask you some questions, to which you must answer either yes or no. Are you ready to begin?"

The man stared at her but said nothing. Candlelight flickered in his bloodshot eyes.

"Is there someone special you'd like to hear from today?" she said.

The man shifted in his chair. "Yes," he mumbled.

"All right," she said. "Please think about your loved one while I concentrate on—"

"I'm looking for my daughter."

Alarms went off in Lilly's head. Leon had told her the next name on the list was Barbara, the rube's dead wife. Her mind raced and she tried to come up with a new plan. If she got this wrong or Leon mixed up the names, it could mean big trouble. "I see," she said. "Please know that I'm very sorry for your loss. Perhaps we should start by—"

"She's not dead."

Lilly frowned, confused. "Okay," she said. "Um . . . You do understand I'm here to help people connect with their departed loved ones, right? Are you sure you're in the right tent?"

He nodded. "I'm in the right tent. My daughter's name is Lilly."

Lilly's breath caught in her chest. What in the world was going on? She studied the man's eyes, trying to remain calm. He held her gaze. She opened her mouth to ask who he was and what he wanted, then reminded herself there were thousands of girls named Lilly. "I see," she said again. "Is Lilly lost? Did she run away?"

The man shook his head. "I came here to tell her I'm sorry. I had no idea what her mother was going to do."

Lilly stiffened. *No. It couldn't be.* "Please," she said, suddenly light-headed. "Just close your eyes and I'll try to—"

"I want her to know I'm glad she got out and I hope she's happy."

Lilly leaned back in her chair, her heart about to explode. She didn't know what to say. It had to be coincidence. It just had to be. Then the man pulled down his scarf and she jumped to her feet. "What are you doing here?" she cried.

Her father stood and moved toward her, his face thin and white in the dim light. "I came to see you."

For a dizzying second, she wondered if he was a ghost. Maybe he really did die after Momma took her out of the attic. Maybe Momma had been telling the truth all those years ago when she said he wasn't "long for this world." She moved away from him on watery legs, until her back bumped into the tent wall. Beads rattled against the canvas. "What do you want?"

"I want you to know I'm sorry. And I still love you."

She put a fist over her churning stomach. "I-I waited for you. I thought you'd come looking for me."

He glanced at the floor, his face grave. "I know. And I don't blame you if you hate me. But I did the best I could."

Tears flooded her eyes. "Did you try to find me?"

He shook his head. "Your mother never would have let me bring you back home."

Lilly gripped the sides of her skirt in her fists and struggled to keep her voice steady. "Why would you listen to her after what she did to me?"

He pressed his lips together and stared at her, but said nothing.

"You were my father," she said. "You were supposed to protect me."

"I'm know, and I'm sorry. Your mother made me—"

Lilly couldn't believe what she was hearing. What kind of father allows his wife to lock up his daughter and sell her to the circus? "Made you what?" she said, her voice rattled by fury. "Choose her over me?"

With that, Pierre climbed out of the back of the wardrobe. "What's going on?" he said. "Are you all right, Lilly?"

She scrubbed the tears from her face, confused and furious and mad at herself for crying. Her father didn't deserve to know he affected her that way. "Yes, I'm fine."

Pierre looked up at him. "I think you should leave, sir," he said in a firm voice.

"I just want to talk to her," her father said. "I want to explain—"

"No," Lilly said. "You don't get to explain anything. You had your chance. It's been six years and *now* you come looking for me? For what? To clear your conscience? It's too late for that." She pointed at the exit. "He's right, you need to leave. I don't need you anymore."

"Lilly, please," her father said. "I—"

"Get out!!" Lilly screamed.

He studied her face with sad eyes for what seemed like forever, then dropped his shoulders and trudged out of the tent. When he was gone, Lilly crumpled to the ground and buried her face in her hands, shoulders convulsing. Pierre put a hand on her shoulder.

"Are you okay?" he said.

She shook her head. "Shut it down."

"What?"

"Shut down the act. I can't see anyone else today."

"Are you sure? Merrick will have a fit. Who knows what he'll do."

She looked at Pierre, her temples pounding and her face wet with tears and sweat. "I don't care what he does. Whatever it is, it won't hurt as much as this."

Now, Lilly lay awake in her bunk, waiting to see what Merrick would do when he found out the midway had been packed with a long line of rubes waiting to see her, and she had turned every last one away. Pierre was right; there was no telling what Merrick would do. She tried to stay calm by counting the boards in the ceiling above her. *One, two, three. four.* It didn't help.

She turned on her side, trying to decide if she should tell Merrick before someone else did. Maybe he'd understand if she explained what happened. Maybe he'd even be glad she kicked her father out. After all, buying a child from its mother couldn't be legal. She could lie and tell him her father wanted to know where he was, and that he threatened to call the cops. Then the boxcar door screeched open on its iron tracks and slammed into the opposite wall. The other women startled and sat up in their beds.

"Everybody out!" Merrick bellowed.

The women swung their legs over the sides of their bunks, wrapped their robes over thin nightgowns, and slipped their feet into worn slippers. With her hair in curlers, Dolly the

World's Most Beautiful Fat Woman rocked back and forth on her cot, trying to get enough momentum to push herself up. Hester went over and put a hand under her arm to help. Lilly got down from her bunk, put on her bathrobe, helped Hester with Dolly, then followed the women toward the exit.

"Not you," Merrick said, pointing a riding crop at Lilly.

Lilly stopped, her stomach turning over.

"I'm sorry," she said. "My father showed up and I . . . I couldn't pull myself together afterward."

The other women got out of the car and stood in the open doorway, their faces lined with fear and worry.

Merrick glared at her. "Your father is dead."

Lilly shook her head. "No, he's not. My mother was lying. He came here looking for me. He wanted to know where you were and said he was going to call the cops."

"I don't believe you. If he came looking for you, where is he? Why are you still here?"

Lilly's chin trembled. "I told him I wanted to stay, and he left."

"Of course he did. He doesn't want you either." He yanked the door closed behind him and moved toward her, his face snarling and red. "But I don't give a shit if the Pope came into your tent! You don't turn paying customers away!"

"I'm sorry. It won't happen again, I promise."

He stopped, and for a second she thought he just wanted to scare her, but then he lunged forward and whipped the riding crop across her bare forearm. It felt like a hot poker, burning through her flesh and muscle. A red welt erupted on her white skin, like a streak of fresh blood. She put a hand over it and gritted her teeth, determined not to cry out. He lifted the crop again and she ran to the end of the boxcar. He chased after her.

Trapped, she turned to face him. "Go on," she cried. "Beat me all you want. You won't kill me. You won't ruin your biggest moneymaker!"

He stopped as if considering what she'd said, then raised the crop, his teeth bared, and hit her again and again, harder with every blow. She curled into a ball to try and protect herself, but it was no use. The crop whipped across her hands and arms and shoulders like a burning flame on her skin. Somewhere, in the back of her mind, she was thankful for her bathrobe, otherwise her arms would have been bare in her sleeveless nightgown. Then the boxcar door slid open again and suddenly, Merrick flew backward, as if yanked by an unseen force. His eyes went wide and his mouth dropped open. Lilly looked up to see what happened. Viktor held Merrick by the scruff of his jacket, the top of his head nearly touching the boxcar ceiling.

"What the hell are you doing?" Merrick bellowed, struggling to get out of his grip.

Behind Viktor, Glory stood with Mr. Barlow and his strongmen, her face contorted with anger and fear.

"If you mark her up, what good is she?" Mr. Barlow yelled. "We wouldn't even be able to use her in the cooch show!" He gestured for Viktor to let go. Viktor did as he was told.

Merrick straightened his shirt and shot Viktor a withering look. "What, you're siding with him now?"

"Sorry, boss," Viktor said. "Glory said you were in trouble."

Merrick pushed his hair from his sweaty brow. "I can handle myself. And Lilly works for me, remember?"

"In my tent, in my circus," Mr. Barlow said. "She eats my food, sleeps in my train. I'd say at this point she's more my property than yours."

Merrick glowered at him, breathing hard, his jaw clenched. For the first time ever, he looked speechless. He eyed Lilly, as if trying to decide whether or not to keep beating her. "You ever turn away another rube, your next job will be in the back lot *behind* the cooch show!" he shouted. Then, finally, he turned and stomped out of the boxcar, swearing under his breath. Viktor, Mr. Barlow, and his strongmen followed.

Lilly slumped in the corner, her shoulders and

back screaming in pain. Her skin felt split open where the riding crop had whipped across her arms.

Glory helped her up. "That son of a bitch," she said. "As soon as I knew he was headed over here, I got Viktor. I've never seen Merrick that pissed off. When Mr. Barlow saw us running, he came too."

Lilly raked her hair way from her face and started toward her bunk. "Who told him what happened?"

Glory shrugged. "I don't know."

Just then, Cole climbed into the boxcar and rushed over to Lilly. "Are you all right?" he said. He wrapped an arm around her and helped her sit on the nearest bunk.

"Yeah," she said.

"I'll take her over to the menagerie," Cole said to Glory. "We've got wound salve over there."

Glory nodded and helped Lilly stand again. Together, she and Cole led her over to the door. Cole jumped out, then reached up to help Lilly down. But instead of setting her on the ground, he scooped her into his arms and carried her toward the midway. Lilly wrapped her arms around his neck and rested her head on his chest, his heartbeat hard and strong against her ear.

As they made their way across the lot toward the menagerie, past Petunia and Flossie pushing tent poles into place with their trunks and heads, past workers and roustabouts putting up canvas and concession stands, several of the men stopped to watch Cole and Lilly pass, probably wondering if she were drunk or dead. After getting a good look, they went back to work without saying a word. They'd seen plenty of strange things in the circus, and they knew better than to stick their nose in a performer's business.

In the menagerie, Cole laid Lilly on a clean blanket inside Pepper's stall, then went to get the salve. Pepper lowered her trunk and snuffled the length of Lilly's body, as if trying to figure out what was wrong. She made a low, quiet moaning noise that sounded almost like crying. JoJo was in the stall next door, having grown too big to share a spot with his mother. He stuck his trunk around the front of his stall and sniffed the air.

Lilly sat up and petted Pepper's trunk. "I'll be okay," she said. "Don't worry."

Cole returned with the healing salve and knelt beside her. She lowered her bathrobe from her shoulders and slid her arms from the sleeves. Working slowly and gently, he smoothed the cream over the red marks on her arms and hands. She gritted her teeth and tried not to cry out.

"Thankfully the skin isn't broken," he said, checking her face and neck for injuries.

Then she remembered she was naked beneath her nightgown and heat crawled up her cheeks. She thought about him carrying her across the midway and wondered if her breasts had jiggled against his chest. Cole moved behind her to put salve on her shoulders and back, his hand sliding beneath her thin straps. He slid his fingers into the low back of her nightgown and lifted it away from her skin.

She pulled away. "Hey."

"What?" he said.

"I'm . . . I'm not wearing any . . ."

"I'm looking for whip marks," he said. "Not trying to see your ass. We're practically brother and sister, for Christ's sake."

She sighed and let him look, her face burning as she thought about him looking farther down than necessary. Not only was the thought of him seeing her rear end embarrassing, but the fact that she said something about it made her feel like a fool. He held the material away from her skin and reached in to apply the salve. Despite the pain and her embarrassment, his warm hands felt good on her back.

"I think that's it," he said. "Unless you can feel any I didn't reach."

She shook her head, pulled up her bathrobe, and pushed her arms into the sleeves. The salve stuck to the material, but she didn't care. She didn't want to sit there half naked any longer than necessary. "Thank you," she said. "It feels better already."

Cole put the lid on the ointment and wiped his hands on the blanket. "You're welcome. But I wish you had stayed in my car last night. Then he never would have had the chance to hurt you."

"I know," she said. "You're right."

He gave her a weak smile. "Of course I'm right. I'm always right. In case you have figured it out yet, I'm the smartest person you know."

She grinned. As usual, he knew how to make her smile.

Then his face grew serious again. "What do you think will happen now?"

She shrugged. "Things will probably go back to normal. Merrick's not going to shut down his biggest draw."

"Yeah, well, we need to figure out a way to get you away from that bastard."

"Good idea," she said. "And since you're the smartest person I know, why don't you come up with a plan?" She was trying to make a joke, but Cole stared at her, somber and thinking.

CHAPTER 14

Julia

The morning after Bonnie Blue delivered her new foal, Julia woke with a start. She opened her eyes but lay motionless, trying to figure out what had woken her from a deep sleep. For a dizzying second, she thought she was back in her room above the liquor store. Then she recognized the red brocade curtains and the mullioned windows of Blackwood Manor and remembered she was home. Her dreams had been filled with rats and secret rooms and headless women. But something else had startled her awake.

The world outside the window looked gray, and the air in the room felt cold on her face. She studied the early-morning light and tried to read what was different about it. The tree branches outside looked hazy and the house seemed quieter than normal. Too quiet. Then she realized the furnace wasn't humming. The tips of her fingers and toes felt chilled, and the end of her nose too. She could see her breath. She sat up and immediately drew the covers up around her neck. The room was freezing.

She jumped out of bed, wrapped the goose-down comforter around her shoulders, and went over to the window. The floor was like frost against her feet and a thick layer of ice covered the window glass. Outside, the world was a blur—the trees and buildings like dark smudges on a white blanket.

Shivering, she threw the comforter back on the bed, got dressed as quickly as possible, and hurried into the dark hallway. The house felt like an icebox. She flicked a switch. Nothing happened.

"Shit," she said.

The power was out. Which meant the furnace had quit working. Squinting in the semidarkness, she made her way down to the living room and built a fire in the fireplace. In the kitchen, she lit the burners on the gas stove, then opened the back door to look out toward the barn.

A thick layer of ice encrusted everything— the snow-covered lawn, the trees, the fences, the telephone poles and wires, the barn and out-buildings. Broken limbs and splintered branches littered the ice-covered yard, and electric wires swayed toward the earth as if pulled by a magnetic current. In the woods across the fields, tree branches snapped and crashed to the ground, as if a thousand hunters were randomly shooting off guns. Julia had never seen or heard anything like it. She leaned out farther to look around, and the grapevine arbor above the doorway suddenly snapped and cracked, then fell at her feet with an ice-shattering crash.

She gasped and shut the door, then went to the kitchen and tried the phone. The line was dead. What was she supposed to do now? And what about the horses? Were they okay? Would Claude show up to take care of them? Most of the horses would be fine without food and water for a few hours, but what about Blue and her baby? Could they take this cold?

She went into the living room, sat on the couch in front of the fireplace with an afghan around her shoulders, and tried to think. If Claude or Fletcher didn't show up in the next few hours, she'd have to go over to the barn herself. That was all there was to it. She couldn't let the horses, especially Blue and her filly, whom she had named Samantha Blue, fend for themselves. They were her responsibility now, and if anything happened to them, she'd never forgive herself.

Unable to stop shivering, whether from cold or nerves she wasn't sure, she went upstairs and put on an extra sweater, then went down to the kitchen, made tea and eggs on the gas stove, and ate them at the table with the afghan around her shoulders. Afterward, she curled up on the couch and waited, getting up every ten minutes or so to look out the mudroom door and check the barn driveway for Claude's truck. It was never there.

By noon, the crash of branches outside had lessened, but neither Claude nor Fletcher had shown up to check on the horses. She found a flashlight in a kitchen drawer and went upstairs to her parents' bedroom to search for warmer clothes. Hopefully, she'd find a pair of her father's flannel-lined trousers and his heavy barn coat, unless Mother had gotten rid of them.

Her parents' bedroom was on the list of rooms she wasn't allowed to enter as a child, so she'd only seen the inside twice: once when she knocked on their door crying after getting sick in bed, and again during a thunderstorm that shook the entire house. Both times, Mother ushered her back to her own bedroom, refusing to let her inside. Now, she couldn't help wondering if she was about to find out why.

After two tries, she found the right key, unlocked the door, and stepped inside. Like the rest of the furniture in Blackwood Manor, the bed, dressers, and armoire were mahogany carved with scrolls, leaves, floral swags, and lions' heads. The posts of the four-poster bed were as big around as trees, with marble finials and fluted columns. Matching brocade lamps with tasseled fringe sat on the bedside tables, and religious paintings and crucifixes adorned every flocked wall. Julia remembered the night of the thunderstorm; Mother opening the door and lightning flashing on a portrait behind her shoulder—Jesus on the cross, his eyes rolled back in his head, blood running from an open gash in his ribcage. Afterward, Julia had nightmares for weeks. And she never went to her parents' bedroom again, no matter how sick or scared she was.

Oddly, the rest of the rooms in the house—the ones Julia used to be allowed to enter anyway—were free of religious images and crosses. Even stranger, Mother agreed with Father that the common areas, where they occasionally entertained clients, were no place for them. Father said he didn't want the house filled with spiritual things because he didn't want to push religion on others. But Julia always sensed his impatience—bordering on resentment—with Mother's beliefs, especially when she insisted on turning every serious conversation into a Bible lesson and praying on the rare occasion they went out to dinner. He'd go along with it for a while; then he'd roll his eyes and change the subject. For reasons Julia never understood, it was the only time he stood up to Mother, and the only time Mother conceded.

Now, Julia couldn't decide if the bedroom looked like it belonged to a religious fanatic, or someone who made her living in a brothel. Everything was red except the furniture—the flocked wallpaper, the curtains, the rugs, the shams, the bed skirt and duvet. Maybe it was decorated that way to match the blood of Jesus. Maybe red was Mother's favorite color. If she had a favorite anything.

Julia shook her head to clear it and made her way over to an armoire. Who cared why the bedroom was decorated in red? As soon as she could, she was getting rid of all of it. Besides, there was no time for reflection now. The horses needed her. Thankfully, the armoire was unlocked. She shined the flashlight inside. Dresses and minks and trousers and jackets hung in a neat row, as if their owners had put them there yesterday. Surprised to find more of her father's things, she pushed the clothes along the hanging pole until she found his heavy barn jacket. She took it out, threw it on the bed, and opened the drawers of the gentlemen's dresser to search for trousers and a heavy sweater. Traces of her father's aftershave drifted out from neatly folded undershirts and monogrammed handker-chiefs.

She could still picture her father coming in from the barn, hanging his cap and coat in the mudroom, taking off his boots, and stretching his tired feet. She used to watch him in silence, waiting for him to acknowledge her presence. How she had longed for him to ask about her day, or tell her something about his. But every night it was the same. First he washed his hands in the water closet next to the mudroom; then he patted her head and trudged into the dining room to pour himself a whiskey or brandy. No "Hi, how was school?" or "What did you do today?" Right up until the day he died, he never took the time to find out who she was and what she cared about. And it broke her heart.

She could see him sitting at the table, waiting for Mother to appear with dinner and her steely glare. She remembered the time Mother told him to go back outside and park the old tractor behind the barn so passersby would only see the new one. The time she found out he had sold a colt five hundred dollars below the asking price to one of his friends. The time she wanted to press charges against one of those "wretched wandering bums" for stealing water from a horse trough. "They spread disease," she said. Without a word, Father got up and refilled his glass, listening to Mother go on and on while Julia ate dinner in silence. Sometimes she wondered if she were invisible.

In the second to the last bottom drawer of the gentlemen's dresser, she found a stack of wool sweaters. She chose the thickest one, tossed it on the bed with the jacket, then opened the deep bottom drawer. Inside were the flannel-lined trousers Father wore out to the barn in winter. She pulled them out and held them up one by one, trying to figure out which pair would fit over her pants without falling off. When she took out the last pair, a yellowed newspaper page came out with them. It fluttered to the floor and slipped beneath the dresser as if blown by an unseen breeze. She got down on her knees and reached for it, dust and cobwebs sticking to her hand, then gently pulled it out and sat up to read it.

Then she saw the book at the bottom of the trouser drawer.

It had a plain leather cover and a brass clasp to keep it closed, like a logbook or diary. Julia dropped the newspaper, lifted the book from the drawer, and touched the dry leather. A shiver ran like a current down her spine. What was it? And why had her father hidden it in his dresser?

She took a deep breath and opened the book to the first page. In her father's handwriting, the first words read:

We have buried our firstborn. May she rest in peace. God speed her soul to heaven. And may God help us for what we have done.

Julia gasped. *Our firstborn? God help us for what we have done?* Who was her father talking about? Her parents never mentioned a sister. And what on earth had they done?

She quickly turned the page and read the next entry.

I can't bring myself to write the words. It's too difficult. The only thing I can do right now is ask God for forgiveness.

"Forgiveness?" Julia said into the silent room. "Forgiveness for what? What did you do?" She flipped to the next page, desperate to read more.

Someday, I'll record the truth. But not now. Not today. It's too raw, too soon, too painful.

She looked through the rest of the book. The pages were blank. She reread the first entries, then groaned and put the book back in the drawer. With confusion spinning in her head, she got up and looked around, suddenly overcome by the feeling that she was in a bad B movie. She had a sister. A sister who died. And her father blamed himself and Mother for something to do with her death. It seemed impossible. Unbelievable. And yet. And yet. Maybe that was why her parents were so unhappy. Maybe that was why Mother prayed and Father drank. Maybe that was why they acted like she didn't exist unless she was getting into trouble. Maybe they didn't want to look at her because she reminded them of her dead sister.

She scrubbed her hands across her face. My God, what other secrets did Blackwood Manor hold? What other lies had she been told? She picked up her father's clothes and left the bedroom. Whatever sins had been committed in the past would have to wait. Right now, the horses—*her* horses—needed her.

CHAPTER 15
Lilly

A week after Lilly's father showed up in The Albino Medium's tent and Merrick beat her with a riding crop, The Barlow Brothers' Circus set up near a farming town outside of Des Moines. Word among the performers was that it was the hottest week on record in Iowa's capital city, and the air was breathless. When Lilly passed the menagerie on her way to the dressing tent before her first opening of the day, she noticed the sidewalls were rolled up and Cole and his father were carrying water buckets around to the animal cages. Rivers of sweat slicked their red faces and plastered their shirts to their chests.

Watering the animals was the roustabouts' job, along with circling the lot with the water wagon to fill the performers' wash buckets, spray the ground to keep the dust down, refill the drinking barrels, and hose off the elephants. She went inside to see what was going on. The big cats were panting harder and faster than usual, and flies swarmed around the horses, chimpanzees, and bears.

"What's happening?" she asked Cole.

"Mr. Barlow refuses to bring in extra water," he said. "So we're hauling in as much as we can from a nearby pond."

Lilly wanted to hug him. One of the things she loved about him was that he cared about the animals as much as she did. "I'll help you after the show's over."

"Thanks," he said. He mopped his brow on his shirtsleeve and refilled the water trough in the bear's den. "But between me, my father, Dante, and Leon, I think we've got it."

"Are you sure?"

He nodded. "You're going to be exhausted after spending all day in that hot tent. I'll make sure you've got an extra water bucket in the dressing tent when you shut down for your break."

"Thanks," she said. "And I'm coming over here later anyway, so I'll help if you still need it."

A half hour later, she sat at a vanity inside the women's dressing tent, fanning herself and holding up her hair while Dolly the World's Most Beautiful Fat Woman fastened the clasps of her six-stranded pearl choker. The choker and pearl earrings were costume jewelry, designed to match the pearl barrettes in her hair, but Merrick reminded her every chance he got not to break or lose them. Dolly finished fastening the necklace, then collapsed in a chair and wiped a chubby forearm over her dripping face.

"God Almighty, I'm sweatin' like a whore in church," she said.

Merrick pulled aside the tent flap and stuck in his head. "Move it, Lilly, the rubes are gettin' restless. We've got to open the doors!"

Lilly sighed. "I'll be right there." She looked in the mirror to check her hair and jewelry. As usual, Glory had outdone herself. Lilly's hair was coiffed high and smooth on top and pulled back on the sides, with fine white wisps curling at her temples and ears, the rest hanging in perfect ringlets down her back. Her white chiffon and satin dress enhanced the illusion of an ethereal creature not of this earth. She dabbed the sweat from her brow with a handkerchief, stood, and started toward the exit.

"Thanks for the help, Dolly," she said.

Dolly waved her away. "Anytime. Go get 'em, hon."

From the dressing tent, Lilly followed Merrick across the back lot to The Albino Medium's tent. When they passed the end of the midway near the freak-show marquee, she caught sight of a figure dressed in black, sitting on the platform out front with a sack over its head.

"Is that a new draw?" she asked Merrick.

"Yeah, Mr. Barlow thinks it'll pique curiosity

if the professor says we're gonna unveil a freak in the ten-in-one that's not advertised on the front of the show. For an extra charge of course."

"What is it?"

"A half-and-half, the biggest drawing gaff ever to work a midway."

She gaped at him. "You mean a half man, half woman?"

"Yup, but like you, it's as phony as a three-dollar bill."

Lilly wondered briefly if pretending to be a half-and-half would be easier than lying to people about their late loved ones. But being a half-and-half meant showing your private parts to the rubes, and she wouldn't want to do that either. She entered her tent and took her place in the chair. Merrick made sure Pierre had everything he needed inside the wardrobe, checked to make sure the "spirit baby" attached to the underside of the table was working, then went out to wait for the first list of names from Alana.

A short time later, the entrance opened, the curtain pulled to the side, and the first rube came into the tent. Over the next few hours, Lilly pretended to speak to the dead while Pierre rang the bell or played the harmonica and tambourine inside the wardrobe. By noon, the inside of the tent felt like an oven and rivers of sweat dripped down her back. On her lunch break, she undressed in the dressing tent and rinsed off with a fresh bucket of water, making a mental note to thank Cole for it later. After her break, a bearded man in a newsboy cap, white shirt, and bow tie entered her tent and sat down, his hands in his lap. He was smirking, as if trying not to laugh. Lilly tensed, sensing trouble. The majority of the rubes who came in looked scared, nervous, or heartbroken. She'd never seen one this happy.

"Sure is hot today," the man said in a low, guttural voice. "And from what I hear it's not letting up anytime soon!"

"Yes, it is warm," she said. Then she cleared her throat and began her pitch. "Hello and welcome. Before we begin, let me tell you a little bit about what I do. I've been communicating with the dead since the age of four and eventually came to realize I needed to share my gift. Messages from the beyond can come in the form of music, voices, and other sounds. What I'd like you to do now is close your eyes and think about the person you're hoping to hear from. As you're doing that, I will try to connect with the spirit world. I'll ask you some questions, to which you must answer either yes or no. Are you ready?"

The man grinned and said nothing.

Then he leaned forward slightly and the candle flames flickered in his cobalt blue eyes. Lilly lowered her gaze to the table, trying to hide her smile. She'd recognize the eyes of her best friend anywhere. It was Cole, in a fake beard and someone else's clothes.

"What are you doing here?" she whispered. Then, so Pierre would hear, "Is there someone special you're trying to reach today?"

Cole screwed up his mouth, trying to come up with an answer. Lilly worried he wouldn't remember the name he'd given Alana while waiting in line. Then, finally, he said a little too loudly, "Yes, I'm hoping to hear from my first cousin twice removed. It's very important and I miss him something terrible." Then he whispered, "There's a farm pond beyond the trees in the field on the other side of the train. I'm taking the bulls over there tonight to cool off. You in?"

Lilly drew in a quiet breath and tried to keep up the charade so Pierre wouldn't get suspicious. "Please close your eyes and let's begin." She paused for a long moment and, trying not to laugh, said in a serious voice, "There is a visitor here . . . this visitor has a message for you. I don't know, I can't be sure, but he seems to be a relative of yours, not a close one. The two of you were good friends. Do you understand this?"

"Yes," Cole said.

"I can feel his presence," Lilly said. "It's very strong." Then, louder, "We invite whoever is here to join us. We're not here to harm you. We're here with the utmost respect for you and any spirits who might be with you. Please try to give us some sort of sign that you're near. Can you make a noise to let us know you hear us?"

Pierre knocked three times on the wardrobe door.

"What was that?" Cole said.

Lilly pressed her lips together to keep from laughing. "It's a sign from someone on the other side," she said. "Oh . . . hold on just a moment. I'm getting a name. Is it Frank? Fred? No, it's . . . it's Ferdinand. Do you recognize this name?"

"Yes," Cole said. "That's my cousin!" He winked at her.

Lilly smiled. "Ferdinand wants you to know he acknowledges your summons. But you need to be careful. Does that make sense to you?"

"Yes," Cole said. "Yes, it does. What else does he want to tell me?"

"Shh . . ." Lilly said. She closed her eyes. "Give me a moment."

"All right."

"He's saying something about your usual place," she said. "Something about meeting at midnight." She opened her eyes. "Do you understand that?"

"Yes!" Cole said.

"He wants to know if this pleases you," she said.

"Indeed," Cole said, his smile lighting up his face. "It pleases me very much."

• • •

After the doors were closed for the night and the last of the rubes had left the lot, after the clowns had wiped the final traces of face paint from their foreheads, and the animals were put back in their pens, everyone gathered outside the train to celebrate Dina the Living Half Girl's birthday. The night air was thick with humidity, and a waxing moon cast long shadows from trees lining one side of the lot, turning tents and wagons into dark, otherworldly looking shapes.

Mrs. Benini, co-owner of the snow cone and cotton candy stands, made a white birthday cake with strawberry frosting, and Madame Zelda, the gypsy fortune-teller, brought homemade apple moonshine. Rosy and Ruby decorated an open-air tent with rugs and tables and pillows for sitting, and Magnus the Ugliest Man Alive helped Brutus the Texas Giant hang lanterns in the trees. Normally, the big-top performers steered clear of the sideshow parties, but Lilly persuaded Cole to come anyway.

"Everyone!" she called across the crowd. "This is my friend Cole. Please make him welcome."

Aldo the Alligator Man lurched forward, his hand outstretched. "We know who he iz," he said, his eyes shining. "He's alwayz welcome here." He shook Cole's hand, pumping it vigorously up and down while swaying on drunken legs. "Right, everybody?"

The party guests whistled and laughed. Cole grinned and put a hand on Aldo's shoulder to steady him. Glory winked at Lilly, and heat rose in Lilly's cheeks. Aldo threw his arm around Belinda the Woman with Two Bodies and One Head and they staggered off. Rosy and Ruby pulled Cole into the crowd and Lilly followed, amazed by how happy she felt.

After the cake was cut and eaten, someone brought out a record player and the roustabouts fashioned a dance floor out of boxcar ramps. Wine bottles were passed and mason jars were refilled with moonshine, and it didn't take long for Lilly's head to start swimming. She retreated beneath one of the trees to catch her breath. Cole came over to find her.

"You okay?"

"Yeah," she said. "But I think I've had enough moonshine."

He laughed. "Me too. It's potent stuff."

She circled the tree to the other side and sat down, leaning against the bark. Cole sat beside her and they both grew quiet. She started to ask if he was still taking the elephants over to the farm pond when off to her left, a woman moaned. Lilly and Cole got to their feet at the same time and looked at each other with alarm. The woman moaned again and a man grunted. Cole and Lilly moved toward the sound, then stopped in their tracks. In the long grass, a man lay between a woman's bare legs, his pants down, his scaly buttocks moving up and down. It was Aldo and Belinda.

Lilly put a hand over her mouth to stifle a laugh and she and Cole went back to the party. Magnus the World's Ugliest Man was carrying a half-conscious Dina out of the tent toward the train, and Rosy and Ruby lay on either side of Brutus the Texas Giant in the pillows, alternating between kissing him and running their fingers up and down his chest. "The Way You Look Tonight" by Fred Astaire was playing on the record player, but the makeshift dance floor was empty except for Penelope the Singing Midget and Stubs the Smallest Man in the World slow dancing with their heads on each other's shoulders.

"Looks like the party's dying down," Cole said.

Just then, running hooves pounded off to their right and a man yelled, "Look out!"

Two zebras headed straight for Cole and Lilly, followed by three men with whips and lead lines. Cole stepped into the zebras' path and waved his arms to slow them down. The first zebra veered off to one side and slid to a stop between the train and the party tent. The second zebra followed and they reared up on their hind legs, squealing and kicking each other, hooves and tails flying. The first zebra bit the second zebra in the neck, and the second zebra spun around and kicked him in the head with his back hooves. The first zebra retreated, frantic and galloping toward Lilly and Cole. The men caught up to the second zebra and threw a rope around its neck. It tried to get away, but they held on and wrestled a halter onto its head.

Lilly hurried toward the zebra racing toward her and Cole.

"What are you doing?" Cole shouted.

Lilly ignored him. She cut the zebra off before it turned toward the lot, and held out her arms. "Slow down now," she said. "Easy, easy."

The zebra slowed to a trot, then a walk, then stopped in front of Lilly, head held high, ears twitching. The men holding the other zebra stood stock-still, watching with wide eyes. Lilly sensed Cole behind her, moving closer. She held her hand out toward the zebra, palm up.

"Come on, I won't hurt you," she said in a soft voice. The zebra lowered its head and sniffed her hand, its muzzle like velvet on her skin. Ever so slowly, she took a step toward it and reached up to rub its forehead.

"Come on, Lilly," Cole whispered behind her. "Step away from him before—"

"Shhhh," Lilly said to Cole as much as to the zebra. "Stay right there. Everything is going to be all right."

She rubbed the zebra's face until it lowered its head and its striped shoulders relaxed. When it blinked as if falling asleep, Lilly moved closer to scratch the length of its neck, up and down, back and forth, her nails raking through its black and white hair. After another minute, during which the zebra looked like it was in a trance, she stopped and started walking toward the menagerie. The zebra lifted its head and followed, his nose near her shoulder. The men with the other zebra waited until she passed, then trailed them at a safe distance. Cole followed too. When they reached the menagerie, she led the zebra inside and back into its stall. After giving it another good long scratch, she moved out of the stall and latched the door. Cole stood watching, his mouth hanging open.

"You know that's a stallion, right?" he said.

She shrugged. "No, the only thing I know is he was hurt and afraid."

"Jesus, Lilly. You could have been injured."

"I'm fine."

The men secured the other zebra a few stalls away and came over to Lilly and Cole.

"How the hell did you do that?" one of them said. He was slightly taller than Cole, with wavy hair and broad shoulders. Lilly recognized him and the others as acrobats, a troupe called The Flying Zoppe Brothers. Normally they wouldn't have given Lilly, or any of the other freaks, the time of day.

"I've never seen anything like it," one of the other brothers said.

Cole glowered at them. "How the hell did the zebras get out?"

"Mr. Barlow wants us to incorporate horses or zebras into our act," the wavy-haired brother said. "We thought we'd see what we could come up with."

"Without the equestrian director's help or permission," Cole said. It wasn't a question.

"We thought we could handle it," the third brother said.

"Well, working without an animal handler was your first mistake. Your second and biggest mistake was trying to do anything with two stallions. Someone could have been killed."

"We didn't know they were stallions," the third brother said.

"Obviously," Cole said. "Next time, get permission from the equestrian director and he'll have a trainer help you. I don't want you or the zebras getting hurt." Lilly could tell he was angry, but in pure Cole fashion, he still tried to be nice.

The wavy-haired brother jerked his chin at Lilly. "Maybe we should get her to help."

Lilly's eyes went wide. "Me? Why?"

"Because in my twenty-plus years in the circus," he said, "I've never seen an animal react to anyone like that zebra reacted to you."

Cole looked at her. "He's right," he said. "And a stallion no less. Most people have no idea how dangerous they can be. My father made sure I respected stallions by telling me about a woman who had her throat ripped out by one. She died on the spot. And you walked up to that one like you were walking up to a puppy."

Lilly shrugged. "Guess it was a good thing I didn't know any better then."

"Who knows what might have happened if you hadn't distracted him," the wavy-haired acrobat said. "And Mr. Barlow would've murdered us if he got away." He held his hand out to Lilly. "Thanks for your help."

Lilly smiled and shook it. "You're welcome," she said.

Later that night, after everyone was asleep, Lilly pulled her hair into a messy bun on top of her head and put on a shirtwaist dress with short sleeves. She grabbed a pair of sandals, snuck out of the sleeper car, and looked up and down the train, stretched out a half mile on each side of her car, to make sure no one was watching. Some of the car windows were open, and on the lot, tent sidewalls were rolled up. Roustabouts and workers slept on the ground outside, trying to stay cool. Somewhere a waltz played, tinny and haunting. A warm breeze caressed her bare arms, and a fine sheen of sweat broke out on her forehead as she hurried over to the menagerie. She wasn't sure if it was from heat or excitement.

When she entered the animal tent, the elephant stalls were empty and Cole was nowhere to be found. She slipped beneath the back wall and looked around. Beyond a line of trees in the distance, a gabled barn sat high on a hill, moonlight glinting off its metal roof, giving the illusion that it was covered with snow. Cole said he was taking the bulls to a farm pond, so she walked toward the barn. When she got closer to the line of trees, a small light flickered amid a gathering of bulky shadows moving slowly near the edge of the field.

The elephants.

"Cole?" she called as loud as she dared.

"Over here," he said.

She hurried toward his voice, walking as fast as she could in the moonlit dark. When she tripped over a clump of grass, a memory flashed in her mind—her very first time outside, following her mother across the field toward the circus, with no idea where she was going or that her life was about to change forever. This time, though, she knew exactly where she was going. She found her footing and shook her head to clear it. She didn't want to think about unhappy things right now. And besides, thinking about her past wouldn't change her future. There was nowhere she'd rather be than with Cole and the elephants.

Using their trunks, Pepper and Petunia and

Flossie pulled bark and branches and leaves from the trees and shoved them in their mouths, making low, contented noises in their throats and munching loudly. JoJo, despite the fact that he was bigger than his mother, ran clumsy circles around them, delighted by his first taste of freedom. Cole waited inside the trees.

"I thought we were meeting at the tent?" she said.

"I wasn't sure if you were coming. Besides, I knew you'd find us."

"I told you I was coming."

"You did? I didn't know if that was you, or my cousin Ferdinand."

She punched him playfully on the shoulder. "Haha. Very funny. Okay, enough teasing. Where's the pond?"

He laughed and led her along the tree line toward a wide gate leading into another field. The elephants followed. He picked the padlock, unwrapped the chain, and opened the gate. "After we're all through, close it behind us," he said to her. "And there were cows in this field earlier, so be careful where you step."

He went through the gate and the elephants trailed behind him. Flossie first, followed by Pepper, JoJo, and Petunia. As their massive, dark bodies lumbered past Lilly, just feet away from where she stood—their tree-trunk-sized legs moving slowly but surely, their long, tufted tails swaying back and forth, their big floppy ears fanning—tears filled her eyes and her heart cramped in her chest. Even after six years of spending time with them nearly every day, she was still amazed by their size and beauty. And tonight there were no chains around their legs, no ropes or walls keeping them in. It seemed as though she were witnessing a parade of gods, reluctant to share their worldly secrets with her because she didn't deserve to know.

When all the elephants were clear of the gate, she pushed it closed, then sprinted to catch up with Cole. In the distance, moonlight reflected off the farm pond's smooth surface, making it look like glass. The elephants snorted and grunted and rumbled as they walked, their giant legs swishing through the long grass, their platter-sized feet thumping the earth.

"What do you suppose they're saying to each other?" she said.

"I think they're enjoying this," he said. "They seem curious and happy, but maybe a little on edge too."

"But they trust you."

"They trust you too."

"You think so?"

"Yes, you have a way with them. I've always thought so. But I'm beginning to think you have a way with all animals, especially after what you did with that zebra."

She smiled. The idea made her happy.

When they were far enough away that no one could see them from the train, Cole turned up the flame in the lantern and led the elephants and Lilly over a slight berm, down to the edge of the farm pond surrounded by grass, cattails, and areas of flat rock. Beyond the pond, the land rose enough to hide them from anyone who might be looking out the farmhouse windows.

"Are you sure it's safe?" she asked.

Cole nodded. "I went for a swim after getting water from it this morning. It's deep and clean, and I think it's spring-fed." He set the lantern on a rock.

The older elephants didn't hesitate. Flossie, Petunia, and Pepper flattened a stand of cattails and waded in, their trunks swishing back and forth in the pond. Dirt and dust floated off their backs, coating the water with a thin, brown film. JoJo put in his front feet, but hesitated. The adult elephants went in deeper and deeper, until the water was nearly up to their eyes, their humped backs like small, mountainous islands. Flossie and Petunia ducked beneath the surface, the ends of their trunks sticking out of the pond. Pepper lifted her trunk, blew a brown shower over her head and back, then snorted at JoJo, as if telling him to come on in. JoJo moved toward her and when the water touched his belly, he bent his knees, dove in, and surfaced a few feet away, his trunk spraying in the air.

Lilly and Cole laughed, delighted by the spectacle. Then they grew quiet and watched the magnificent beasts in the pond, splashing and swimming and rolling. The elephants' joy was as palpable as the humidity in the night air, and Lilly felt like one of the luckiest people on earth. She was with her best friend, witnessing these glorious creatures act like the wild animals they were born to be. After everything she'd been through, she never dreamt it was possible to feel this happy. Even though it wasn't her choice to join the circus and she despised her job, she wouldn't give up this moment for anything in the world.

Cole took off his shoes and started unbuttoning his shirt.

"What are you doing?" Lilly said.

"Going swimming."

"You're crazy," she said.

He smiled and pulled off his shirt. "Well, I'm hot too." When he started unbuckling his belt, she looked away, went over to a flat-topped boulder, and sat down. She plucked a tall stalk of timothy from the grass and concentrated on pulling off the blades. Despite the fact that she had seen numerous men—freaks, clowns, and performers alike—in various stages of undress, the thought of seeing Cole in his undershorts unsettled her.

The other sideshow women always joked that with Lilly's perfect features and Cole's fair complexion and muscular physique, the two of them would make beautiful, angel-haired babies. Lilly shushed them and said she didn't think of Cole that way. He was her best friend and that was it. Except it wasn't entirely true. She wasn't sure when her feelings for him had started to change or when she stopped ignoring them, she only knew they had. And she wasn't sure what to do. They had been best friends for nearly six years, but he wasn't in love with her. She was a fifteen-year-old albino who worked in the sideshow, and at eighteen, Cole was the lead performer in the elephant show. He could be with anyone he wanted. The trapeze artist, Natasha, was his age, and so was Chloe the tightrope walker. They were beautiful girls with perfect figures, smooth, rosy skin, and shiny hair, who wore fancy costumes covered with feathers and glittering jewels. She had seen them watching Cole out of the corner of their eyes, sizing him up and down and whispering behind their hands, wondering why he spent so much time with a freak and paid so little attention to them. She wondered too.

"You coming in?" he said.

She glanced at him and laughed. "No."

The lantern light reflected off his bare chest and muscular shoulders, and heat rose in her cheeks. She wanted to watch the elephants, but went back to picking apart the timothy instead.

"Come on," he said. "Don't be a chicken. It's hotter than Hades tonight."

She looked up at him again. "I'm not chicken, I just . . . I don't have my swimsuit with me."

He raised one eyebrow. "Since when do you own a swimsuit?"

She grinned. He knew perfectly well she didn't own a swimsuit. Then, before she knew what was happening, he rushed over, scooped her into his arms, and headed for thc water. She screeched, then put a hand over her mouth. What if someone heard?

"Put me down!" she said as loud as she dared. She pushed against his bare shoulders, trying to get him to release her. But he was too strong.

"I'll put you down," he said, laughing. "Right in the water!"

"Okay, stop!" she said. "I'll go in. Just let me take off my sandals."

He set her on the bank and straightened. "That dress will weigh you down and wrap around your legs. Better take that off too."

She took off her sandals and tossed them up on the bank, toward the rock where she'd been sitting. On one hand, she wanted to cool off and play in the pond with Cole and the elephants. She wasn't afraid of the water. On the other hand, she had never been swimming in her life and wasn't crazy about the idea of being in her underwear in front of Cole. She had changed her clothes in front of men and women alike getting ready for the sideshow. But this was different.

An image of them naked together flashed in her mind, and a strange sensation fluttered in her abdomen. She turned away and undid the thin belt around her waist, then pulled her dress over her head, thankful she had worn her long-legged panties. She stood for a minute, her dress bunched in her hands over her brassiere, then took a deep breath and turned to face Cole, her heartbeat thudding in her ears.

To her surprise, he was gone. He was already running into the pond, his long legs cutting through the water. She let out her breath and watched him dive in, disappear, and surface a few yards away. JoJo moved toward him, his mouth open in what looked like a smile. Cole swam over and climbed on JoJo's back. His tanned skin looked even darker now that it was wet. Lilly looked down at her arms. They were white sticks, like the limbs of a skeleton. She fumbled with her dress and hurried to put it back on.

"What are you doing?" Cole said. "I thought you were coming in. Come on, it feels great!" He slipped off JoJo's back and swam toward shore.

"I don't know how to swim," she said.

"That's all right," he said. "I'll teach you." He rose out of the water and took her hand. She hesitated, then dropped her dress in the grass and followed him into the pond. The water was cold. She drew in a sharp breath and scrunched her shoulders. Pebbles and mud squished between her toes. He led her in farther, laughing. "Don't worry, you'll get used to it."

When she was in up to her waist, he told her to lie across his arms and paddle with her hands while kicking her legs. She leaned forward, but when her stomach and chest touched the water, her breath caught and she straightened. It felt like ice on her hot skin. Cole smiled and waited patiently. After a minute, she gathered the courage to lean across his arms again, and this time the pond didn't feel as cold. He held her up and she kicked and paddled, doing her best to follow his instructions.

"You're doing great," he said.

Then her face accidentally went under and she swallowed a mouthful of water. She put her feet on the bottom and stood, coughing and wiping her face.

"You okay?" he said.

She nodded and, when she could breathe again without coughing, said, "It's harder than I thought."

"It takes practice. Hold on, I want to try something." He moved toward the elephants, who were soaking near the center of the pond like submerged boulders.

"Pepper, come," he said. Pepper lifted her head and seemed to float toward him. He gestured toward Lilly and Pepper swam in her direction and emerged next to her at the edge of the pond, water dripping from her wide head and body, like a barge rising from the deep.

Lilly reached out to touch Pepper's trunk. "Hi, beautiful."

Pepper wrapped her trunk around Lilly's waist and picked her up, pulling her off the bottom of the pond. Lilly gasped with delight and put a hand on Pepper's forehead for balance. Pepper lifted her over her head and placed her on the back of her neck. Cole's eyes went wide with surprise.

"Did you give the lift command?" he said.

"No," she said. "I thought about it, but she did it before I could say anything."

"That's amazing! I've never seen her do anything without being told."

Lilly smiled. "Maybe she likes me."

"Of course she does."

Cole swam over to Petunia, who was up to her shoulders in the water, and climbed on. He steered her toward the middle of the pond and Pepper followed. Lilly hung on to Pepper's ears, lolling from side to side as the water washed up and over her legs and waist. She felt perfectly safe because, somehow, she knew Pepper was aware of her limitations. JoJo and Flossie came too. Moonlight reflected off the rippling waves as the massive gray beasts moved gracefully across the pond, lined up one after the other in their own private parade. The only sounds were the elephant's grunts and snorts, and water lapping against their bodies.

Cole looked over his shoulder and smiled at Lilly, but neither said a word. She felt like she had died and gone to heaven. Her heart felt about to burst with happiness and awe. Never in a million years did she think she'd be riding an elephant across a pond. It felt like a dream.

Cole turned Petunia back to the other shore, and when the water was shallow enough, he slid down from her back. Lilly did the same, and Cole was there to catch her.

"Come here," he said. "I want to try something else." He took her hand, pulled her toward the shoreline, and looked back at the elephants. "Pepper, come." Pepper did as she was told and followed them out of the pond. Cole stopped on the grassy bank and Pepper came to a halt beside him. "Steady," he said to her.

"What are you doing?" Lilly said. She squeezed the water out of her hair and looked around for her dress. When she saw it, she picked it up and held it out, trying to figure out which end was up.

"Never mind about that right now," Cole said. "I need you to come over here."

Lilly dropped the dress and went to his side. "What?"

"Stand in front of Pepper and give the command 'back.' " He positioned Lilly in front of the waiting animal.

"Why?" Lilly said. "What are you—"

"Just humor me, okay?"

Lilly shrugged, looked at Pepper, and said, "Back."

Pepper moved back.

"Now say, 'Go on,' " Cole said.

"Go on," Lilly said. Pepper moved forward.

Cole grinned. "Tell her to stand up."

"Why?" Lilly said. "I don't understand the point of me telling her what to do. She's a trained circus elephant. She knows all the commands."

"Standing on their hind legs is uncomfortable for elephants. Pepper's trainer and I have a hard time getting her to do it. Most of the time she refuses."

Lilly regarded Pepper. She didn't want to tell her to do anything. Pepper wasn't supposed to be here, in this remote field in the middle of Iowa. She was supposed to be free, wandering through rainforests and jungles, not shackled to a post, traveling all over the country inside a boxcar, or doing tricks for a tent full of oblivious rubes. Every time she was with the elephants, Lilly imagined she could feel their sadness as if it were her own. Not just Pepper's, but Flossie's and Petunia's and JoJo's too, even though he had no idea what he was missing.

In the moonlight, she could see the scars from the bull hook on Pepper's head and shoulders. She could see the welts on her ankles from the chains. She could see the pain and sorrow in her intelligent amber eyes. With something that felt like lead in her heart, she knew there was nothing she could do to help them beyond showing them kindness whenever possible.

"I don't want her to do something that makes her uncomfortable," she said.

"It doesn't hurt her," Cole said. "It's just difficult, like us standing on our heads."

Lilly sighed. As long as it didn't injure Pepper, she supposed there was no harm in going along with Cole's game. Then Pepper could get back to swimming. She opened her mouth to tell her to stand, but before she could utter the word, Pepper lifted her front feet and stood on her hind legs.

Cole's mouth fell open. "Holy shit!" he said. "How'd you do that?"

"How did I do what?"

"I didn't hear you give the command."

"How do I tell her to get down?"

Before Cole could answer, Pepper dropped her front feet and went back to standing on all fours.

Cole laughed. "That's incredible! She'll do

anything for you. It's like she can read your mind or something." He called Flossie out of the pond. She came out and stood on the grass. "Tell her to lie down."

Lilly shook her head. "I don't want to," she said. "I don't like making them perform. Let them go back in the pond. They were having fun."

"Just one more time," Cole said. "Then we'll stop."

Lilly told Flossie to lie down. Flossie dropped to her elbows and knees, then rolled over on her side.

"I knew it!" Cole shouted.

"Knew what?"

"Flossie hates lying down. I have no idea what it is or how it works, but after what you did with that zebra and these elephants today, I have no doubt you have a gift, Lilly. It's real. And after we show Mr. Barlow, you won't have to be The Albino Medium anymore."

Lilly made a face. She didn't have a gift. The elephants liked and trusted her. That was all. Her cat, Abby, used to be the same way. She did what Lilly wanted because they loved and trusted each other. Maybe people didn't give animals enough credit. They were smarter and had more feelings than anyone realized. "You're out of your mind. Besides, Mr. Barlow already has an elephant trainer."

"Yeah, but you saw how he trains the bulls with

chains and ropes. And the only way the trainer knows how to make them mind is by using a bull hook."

Lilly dug a toe into the grass, trying to sort through her feelings. Even if she didn't believe what Cole was saying, maybe she could make the elephants' lives easier by getting them to do tricks without being beaten or tortured. "Okay. Let's say you're right. How are we going to convince Mr. Barlow? And what about Merrick?"

"Don't worry," he said. "Just leave everything up to me."

Then, before she knew what was happening, Cole was in front of her, his warm hands on her shoulders. He pulled her close and kissed her long and hard on the lips. At first, she resisted, unsure if he was kissing her out of excitement or something else. Then he wrapped his arms around her and pressed his bare chest against her. Their naked stomachs touched and the strange flutter in her pelvis returned, stronger than ever. He kissed her harder, and she kissed him back, melting into his arms.

This.

This was want she wanted more than anything in the world. Somewhere in the back of her mind, she heard water splashing as Pepper and Flossie reentered the pond. The balmy night caressed her skin as Cole's warm hands lowered the straps of her brassiere. Then they were naked in each other's arms on the grassy bank and Cole moved above her, his wet body skimming hers. She shivered and he looked into her eyes, as if asking permission to kiss her again. She'd always wondered what Glory meant when she said desire was a powerful thing. Now she knew.

She pulled Cole to her and kissed him with an open mouth. He groaned and kissed her lips and neck and breasts and stomach. She trembled and arched her back. He moved up to kiss her neck again and she wrapped her arms around his head. Then they began to make love beneath the stars, while the elephants frolicked and swam in the pond, enjoying their one night of freedom.

CHAPTER 16

Julia

After finding her father's journal the day after the ice storm knocked the power out, Julia put her father's barn jacket on over her sweaters and pulled his lined trousers on over her pants. She put on an extra pair of socks and Mother's boots, then carefully stepped out the mudroom door. Using a fireplace poker to break though the ice-encrusted snow, she slowly made her way across the yard to the barn, hunched over like an old woman with a cane, trying not to slip and fall. If anyone had seen her there, wearing baggy clothes, mens' gloves, and rubber boots, her hair hanging out from beneath an oversized newsboy cap, they would have thought she was a crazy person escaped from the loony bin.

The crack and crash of breaking trees echoed from the woods across the empty fields like random gunshots, though not as often as they had earlier that morning. Halfway to the barn, she looked toward the tree line beyond the nearest pasture. Nothing broke the surface of the ice and snow. At the back of the property, a low jungle of underbrush and evergreens hung weighed down under inches of ice, like praying monks with giant white hoods.

Suddenly, the stillness was interrupted by a loud whooshing sound, like the roar of rushing water. A huge crash filled the air behind her, like a thousand exploding windows. She jumped and spun around to look at the house, her pulse pounding in her ears. At first, she saw nothing. Then she realized what made the noise. A massive sheet of ice had slid from the roof above the mudroom door and crashed to the ground, shattering on the planters and steps.

If she had been on the steps, the ice would have hit her for sure. She looked up at the steep roof of the house and barn. If she was going to check on the horses without getting struck by a sudden avalanche of loose ice, when she was close to the buildings, she had to hurry.

When she reached the barn, she hammered the office door handle with the fireplace poker to break the ice around it, working as fast as she could before another roof-full of ice gave way. After several good blows, the ice broke free. She tried the handle, but the door wouldn't budge. She shoved her shoulder into the wood several times, until, finally, the ice along the frame split and the door wedged open. She broke the rest of the ice and pushed her way into the office. Even inside the barn, her breath billowed out in the freezing air. She pictured Samantha Blue shivering in the cold, ice hanging from her tiny nostrils, and rushed into the main part of the barn. The horses pushed their heads over their stall doors to see who was there. When they saw her, they whinnied and nickered. She hurried over to the first stall and looked inside. The hay cradle was empty and a thick sheet of ice covered the water trough. With her heart in her throat, she ran down the center aisle toward the empty door of Bonnie Blue's stall. Why wasn't she looking out?

When Julia reached the stall, the blood drained from her face. Bonnie Blue was down in the straw, Samantha Blue on her side next to her belly. Julia held her breath and stared at them to see if they were breathing. They weren't moving.

She was too late. She clamped a gloved hand over her mouth to stifle a sob. Then Blue raised her head and blinked. Samantha Blue woke up, lifted her head, then let it fall against her mother's belly as if she were too tired to get up. Julia let out a sigh of relief and her thundering heart slowed. Samantha saw her and struggled to stand, her long legs stiff and clumsy, like the limbs of a wooden puppet. Bonnie Blue pulled her hooves beneath her, got to her feet, and shook the straw from her mane. She nickered and came over to the stall door.

Julia unlocked the stall and went inside. She smiled and gave Bonnie Blue and Samantha a good scratch and a kiss, then used the fireplace poker to break the ice in the water trough. Blue started drinking immediately while Samantha nibbled at the pocket on Julia's jacket. Julia scratched her between the ears, gave her and Blue another kiss, then went out to get some hay. The other horses whinnied and kicked at their stall doors.

"Don't worry," Julia said to them. "I'm coming."

She pulled a bale of hay from the stack near the hayloft ladder and tried breaking the strings with her hands, but they were too strong and tight. She dragged the bale out to the aisle, pushed her foot against it to keep it from moving, and tugged a string from one corner with two hands. She had seen Claude undo a bale that way, but it was harder than it looked. Finally, the string came off and the bale loosened. She yanked the other string off and the bale broke into sections, like a deck of thick cards. She picked up the hay slices and divided them between the stalls, then broke the ice in all the troughs. The horses began to eat and drink right away, then thanked her by nudging her with soft noses, nuzzling her neck, and sniffing behind her ears. Remembering what Fletcher said about horses generating heat by eating hay, she broke up ten more bales and divided them between the horses. When she finished, she stood in the center aisle and looked around, finally warm inside her coat. For the first time in her life, she felt loved and needed.

"You're mine," she said to the horses. "And I promise to do my best to take care of you from now on."

Outside, an engine sounded in the distance. It was getting closer. Julia went into the office, scraped a patch of ice off the window, and peered out. A vehicle pulled into the barn driveway, came to a stop, and the driver got out. It was Claude.

Ever so slowly he made his way toward the office, his arms out as he tried not to fall on the ice. She opened the door to let him in.

"What are you doing out here?" he said. His scowling face was red from the cold. She couldn't tell if he was concerned or angry.

"I came out to check on the horses." Despite Claude's sour mood, a smile played around her lips. She had taken care of the horses all by herself.

Claude harrumphed and went into the barn. She followed.

"They're fine," she said, hoping she sounded confident. "I broke the ice in the troughs and fed them hay. But thanks for coming out."

"Just doing my job." He tromped down to Bonnie Blue's stall and looked over the door. Julia peered in too. Blue chewed on a mouthful of hay while Samantha nursed, her fuzzy, short tail wagging like a dog's.

"Any idea when the power will come back on?" Julia said.

Claude shook his head. "Nope, it's out all over."

"Do I need to worry about the pipes in the house freezing?"

"If you think it'll help."

She furrowed her brow. Why did he have to be so ornery? She was starting to wonder if he had always been a man of few words, or if he had something against her. "Is there anything we can do to prevent it from happening?"

Claude opened the stall door, closed it behind him, and checked Samantha's navel. "Hope for warmer weather."

Julia crossed her arms over her chest. If he wasn't going to be friendly, maybe she could at least get some information out of him. "Can I ask you something?"

Claude ran a hand over Blue's back and checked her bag. "What?"

"Were you working for my parents when my sister was born?"

Claude straightened and kept his eyes on the horses, but Julia saw him flinch. It was the tiniest of movements, like a quick startle or a wince from a pulled muscle. Someone else might not have noticed. But she did.

He ran a hand under Blue's neck. "I worked for your parents for twenty-seven years."

"So you know about my sister."

Claude came out of the stall, locked it, and started down the aisle. "I heard Mrs. Blackwood lost a child a few years back."

Julia drew in a quick breath and followed him. "Do you know what happened?"

"Nope." Claude went into the office, got a bottle of iodine out of the medicine chest, then went back to Blue's stall.

She went with him. "But you must know something. Fletcher said you and my father were friends."

Claude entered Blue's stall, got on his knees, and put iodine on Samantha's navel. "Did he?" He put the lid back on the iodine, got to his feet, and met Julia's eyes for the first time since his arrival. "Listen, I worked for Mr. and

Mrs. Blackwood for a long time. But I have a policy never to get involved in my employer's personal business." He dropped his eyes and opened the stall door, practically pushing her out of the way. "And that includes yours." He went down to the tack room.

She followed. "I just thought—"

He stopped and turned to face her. "If you want to help with the horses, that's fine. They belong to you now. I can't tell you what to do. But I've got to get Blue and her filly out of that stall and put in fresh straw. I don't have time for gossip."

Blood rose in Julia's cheeks. Suddenly she felt foolish, standing there in her father's barn coat and oversized boots, the fingers of her gloves flopped over like a child playing dress up. She searched Claude's face, trying to think of something to say. His eyes looked guarded. She wasn't going to get anywhere with him. Not today anyway. She'd have to prove herself first. "All right," she said. "I want to help."

He retrieved a miniature halter from the tack room, went back to Blue's stall, and tried to put the halter on Samantha. At first, she resisted, pulling away her little head and moving backward, her tiny hooves dancing in the straw. Then Claude wrapped an arm around her shoulders and rubbed the halter up and down her neck.

"It's all right," he said in a calming voice. "No

one's going to hurt you. See, it's just a halter." He moved the halter over her ears and cheeks as if petting her with it.

To Julia's surprise, he sounded gentle and kind. "What are you doing?" she said in a quiet voice.

"Showing her she doesn't need to be afraid of the halter by getting her used to the feel of it." He continued rubbing the halter gently over Samantha's face while Blue stood watching and eating hay, unconcerned.

After a few minutes, Samantha let him slip the halter over her head and buckle it. Once it was on, Claude let go. Samantha shook her head and pranced around the stall a few times, then pushed her nose beneath her mother's belly to nurse. Claude clipped a lead line onto Bonnie Blue's halter, asked Julia to open the door, and led the mare out of the stall. Samantha followed, her tiny hooves clip-clopping on the cement aisle. After Claude deposited Blue and her filly into another stall, he got a wheelbarrow from the far end of the barn and handed Julia a pitchfork.

"Might as well learn how things work from the ground up," he said.

Julia took the pitchfork and went to work mucking out Blue's stall. If this was the only way she'd prove herself and get information out of Claude, it was going to be the cleanest stall he'd ever seen.

CHAPTER 17
Lilly

Two days after Cole and Lilly took the bulls swimming in the farm pond, Lilly stood in front of Pepper in the center ring of the big top while Cole watched from a few yards away in the hippodrome, or outer track. Mr. Barlow waited beside him, chewing the end of a fat cigar, his face twisted in irritation. Next to Mr. Barlow, Cole's father Hank held a bull hook in his hands, just in case.

"This better not be a waste of my time," Mr. Barlow said.

"It won't be," Cole said. "We only need a few minutes, that's all." He nodded once at Lilly. "Go ahead."

Lilly took a deep breath and gazed into Pepper's eyes, trying to concentrate and silently begging her to do what she asked. If this went as planned, she could quit being The Albino Medium. She'd be working with Cole and the elephants, and hopefully, there'd be less need for training ropes and bull hooks. Pepper looked bored and a little confused. Lilly opened her mouth to give a command, then went over and gave Pepper's trunk a good rub instead.

"Please don't let me down, beautiful," she whispered. "This is for both of us."

Pepper made a deep, rumbling noise in her throat, snuffled Lilly's neck and hair, and gave her a big mushy kiss with the end of her trunk. Then she started to sway.

"Okay, I've seen enough," Mr. Barlow said. "The elephant likes her, so what?" He started to walk away.

"No, wait," Cole said. "Just watch."

Lilly moved back into position and said, "Up."

Pepper stopped swaying, lifted her feet, and stood on her hind legs.

"On your head," Lilly said.

In one fluid motion Pepper rolled forward and balanced on her head and front feet, her giant back legs in the air. Lilly glanced at Mr. Barlow to see his reaction, but his face gave nothing away. Cole and Hank, on the other hand, were grinning like fools.

"Down," Lilly said.

Pepper put her back legs down, got on her knees, and rolled over on her side. Lilly took a step toward her, told her to get up, and said, "Lift." Pepper got up on all four feet, curled her trunk under Lilly like a swing, and lifted her gracefully over her head onto her neck. Lilly smiled and put an arm in the air, imitating the other big-top performers. Cole and Hank started clapping.

Just then, the elephant trainer stormed into the

arena. "What in the hell is going on here? What are you doing with my bull?"

"I believe this is *my* bull," Mr. Barlow said. "But I've been asking myself the same question." He addressed Cole. "What exactly is going on here?"

Cole gaped at Mr. Barlow as if he were the dumbest man on earth. "Didn't you see what just happened?" he said, throwing his arm out toward the center ring. "Lilly is a natural. Nine times out of ten, Pepper refuses to stand on her head, but she does it for Lilly every time. The elephants respond to her like no one I've ever seen before. If you put Lilly under the big top with Pepper, they'd be your star attraction for sure!"

Mr. Barlow took the cigar from his mouth and scowled. "Lilly is already a star attraction. And so are the elephants. So why would I combine them and lose one? That's not good business sense, my boy. But I suppose that's why I'm the owner of this circus and you're not." He waved a dismissive hand in the air. "Now get her down off that bull, take it back to the menagerie, and forget about this nonsense. We've got a show in two hours."

Lilly slid down Pepper's side to the ground and stood beside her, surprised by the depth of her disappointment. Somewhere in the back of her mind, she knew Mr. Barlow would never allow her to perform with the bulls, but Cole had been so *sure* about the plan, she'd begun to believe in it too. Now she had to settle back into the fact that she'd be The Albino Medium forever.

Anger and frustration lined Cole's forehead. "If Lilly is one of your star attractions," he said, "maybe Merrick should start paying her."

With that, Mr. Barlow's face went dark. "As long as Merrick pays me my share of her take, I don't give a damn what he does with his." He gave Hank a disgusted look. "I'm surprised you were part of this."

"He wasn't," Cole said. "He brought Pepper over here, that's it. I didn't tell him why."

"Enough out of you," Mr. Barlow snarled at Cole. "This circus has been running for over twenty years now, without any help from young, smartass whippersnappers like you. Now get back to work before I fire the lot of you!" He stuffed the cigar back in his mouth and marched out of the big top.

Lilly looked at Cole and shrugged, blinking back tears.

CHAPTER 18

Julia

The evening following the ice storm, after Julia and Claude were finished with the horses and Claude had left for home, Julia took an oil lantern into her father's den to search for more information about her late sister. The electricity was still out, and ice-encased branches trembled outside the windows, rattling against one another like bones. But despite the fact that she could see her breath in the freezing room and she was exhausted after cleaning stalls half the day, she couldn't ignore the burning need to find the truth.

She set the lantern on the desk, opened the middle drawer, and searched inside for the key to the locked drawer. It had to be in there somewhere. She reached into the back corners, felt along the lining for the shape of a key, and came up empty-handed. She tried picking the lock with a bobby pin but had no idea what she was doing. She shoved a letter opener between the desk frame and the top of the locked drawer to pry it open. The letter opener broke in two and she jammed her fist against the wood.

"Shit!" she hissed. She dropped the letter opener and examined her knuckles. Divots of ripped skin flopped open on each one, exposing raw flesh underneath. Now, along with blisters on her palms from shoveling horse manure, she had scrapes on her knuckles too. Swearing again, she covered her knuckles with her other hand until they stopped throbbing, then carefully searched through the papers in the rest of the drawers. She took them out one by one and held them close to the lantern, squinting to read the fine print. They were business letters, indecipherable doctors' prescriptions, pay stubs, old bills, and receipts. Nothing of any significance.

Frustrated, she stood and looked around the room as if the answer was hidden there. Lantern light flickered off the walls and bookshelves, reflecting in the trophies and picture frames like tiny flames. She made her way along the shelves and scanned the titles. Then, starting at the bottom of the first bookcase, she riffed through the pages of each book before returning it to the shelf and moving on to the next. The dusty pages made her sneeze. She worked fast, trying to keep warm, and anxious to find the key to the locked drawer, or hopefully, more clues about her sister and what her parents might have done. Along with numerous volumes on horse breeds and veterinary medicine, there were novels, poem collections, reference books, and outdated encyclopedias.

She climbed on a footstool to examine a set

of six antique books with worn leather spines sitting between elephant-shaped bookends on the top shelf of the center bookcase. The dust was thicker on these books than the rest, and the pages were thin and yellowed. When she picked up the fourth book, she was surprised to discover it weighed almost nothing, despite the fact that it was the same size as the others. She got down from the footstool, opened the book, and gasped.

The center of the book had been cut out to form a box inside the pages, and a small pile of yellowed newspaper clippings and other papers filled the space, stacked like pressed flowers in a haphazard pile. She took the book over to the desk and sat down, trembling with anticipation. Blowing into her hands to warm them first, she took out one of the clippings and opened it with gentle fingers, careful not to rip the paper.

The headline of the article read: CIRCUS COMES TO LANGHORNE, PENNSYLVANIA. Below the headline, grainy black and white pictures showed two men in tuxedos and two women in evening gowns holding the halters of four white horses. In the middle of the horses, a man in a top hat and long fur coat smiled at the camera. Julia scanned the article. Why had her father felt the need to hide an article about a circus? She picked up the next item. It was a ticket stub from The Barlow Brothers' Circus. She looked at the article again. It was the same circus.

The next clipping featured a photo of what looked like a pretty white-haired woman in a white dress and pearl choker. Her hair was swept back with pearl barrettes and she looked off in the distance, her mouth in a thin line as if she were trying not to cry. The caption below read: THE ALBINO MEDIUM. Another article announced the circus was coming to Saratoga, New York, and pictured what looked like the same woman sitting on the curled trunk of an elephant. This time she was smiling, one bejeweled arm in the air, her ballet-slippered feet pointed downward. There were more articles and ticket stubs from different towns in New York, Pennsylvania, Vermont, and Connecticut, all to The Barlow Brothers' Circus.

Julia's mind raced. Her father never took her to the circus. So where did all the ticket stubs come from? Why was he so interested in this particular circus? And why did he feel the need to hide these articles and ticket stubs? Why did it seem like most of the articles featured the pretty albino woman? Was it a coincidence? Did they have an affair? Is that why he went to the circus so much? Was that why he drank, because they couldn't be together? Was his transgression, coupled with the loss of their first child, the reason behind Mother's misery?

Julia put the clippings and ticket stubs back in the book, shivering and more confused than ever.

She wanted to stay in the den to keep searching for clues and the key to the locked drawer, but it was too cold. She needed to get back to the fireplace. Not only that, but she hadn't eaten since morning and her stomach cramped with hunger. She left the book on the desk, grabbed the lantern, and headed into the hall.

In the living room, she knelt in front of the fireplace, trying to get warm and staring into the flames, thinking, thinking. A quiet desperation gathered beneath her ribs. She had to know more. About her dead sister. About her father's secrets. About her parents and what they had done. A piece of burning bark stuck to the grate in the fireplace, turning gray and curling toward the chimney, hypnotizing her.

Three insistent knocks on the mudroom door made her jump. She got to her feet. Who could possibly be at the door at this hour, and in this weather? Claude had left hours ago. Maybe someone's car had broken down and they wanted to use her telephone. Three more knocks, louder and more demanding with every blow. She hurried across the living room toward the kitchen, then stopped, suddenly nervous. If someone needed help, they'd be at the front door, not the side door. And she was alone in the house, two miles from the nearest neighbor. She blew out the lantern and waited to see if the person would give up and go away.

"Julia?" a man's voice called.

It was Fletcher.

She let out a sigh of relief. "Coming!" she called out, feeling a little foolish. She relit the lantern, went to the mudroom, and unlocked the door to let him in. He blew into the house and stomped his boots on the rug, his face ruddy below a fur-lined aviator hat. He smelled like winter and hay and woodsy cologne. Julia's heart lifted at the sight of a friendly face.

"What are you doing way out here at this hour?" she said. "Did you stop by the barn? Is everything all right?"

"The horses are doing great," he said. "But I wanted to make sure you're okay too."

She smiled. "I'm fine, thanks. A little cold, but fine."

"Do you have the fireplace going?"

"Yes."

He hunched his shoulders and shoved his gloved hands in his coat pockets. "Brrr. It's freezing out there. Is there anything I can do for you? Bring in more firewood? Check the faucets?"

She frowned. "Check the faucets? For what?"

"You should let them drip so the pipes won't freeze."

"Claude didn't tell me that."

He grinned. "I told you, Claude doesn't talk much."

"I know, but I specifically asked him about

306

the pipes freezing." She briefly considered asking if he knew anything about her dead sister, then remembered he'd only been working at Blackwood Manor a few months before her father died. Fletcher hadn't spent enough time with him to learn anything about her family. "I was glad Claude made it over here to check on the horses, though."

"Yeah, you can always depend on Claude for that." He took off his gloves, went into the kitchen, and turned on the faucet just enough to make it drip. Then he looked at her and waited.

"What?" she said.

"Do you want to show me where the rest of the faucets are?"

She thought about showing him the eight bathroom faucets, but changed her mind. If all she had to do was make them drip, she could handle it. "That's all right, I can take care of them."

He shrugged. "Okay. What about wood, do you have enough?"

"I think so."

"Try not to open the fridge too much," he said. "Your food will stay cold longer that way."

She glanced at the refrigerator. "Okay."

"Of course you can always set it out on the steps, it's certainly cold enough out there."

"The refrigerator? I don't think I can lift it." She smiled and he laughed.

"Ah, that was a good one," he said. "You got

307

me." He put his gloves back on and went to the door. "Well, I guess I better get going. It's going to be a treacherous drive home."

She thought about asking him to stay for a while, but didn't want him to think she was flirting. After all, he could be married for all she knew. But then he started to open the door, and she realized she didn't want to be alone. The words came out before she could stop them. "Why don't you come in and get warmed up before you head back out? There's food if you're hungry, and brandy."

He grinned, closed the door, and took off his gloves again. "Brandy sounds good."

"Okay." She went to the cupboard and grabbed two juice glasses. "I'm not sure where the snifters are."

"No worries. I'm a vet, remember? I've been known to drink out of cow troughs if I'm thirsty enough."

She made a face. "Yuck."

"Hey, don't knock it until you've tried it. It's especially good when it's been sitting in the sun for a few days. Gives it that little extra zing."

Shaking her head and laughing, she led him into the living room. The fire was dying down. She set the juice glasses on the coffee table in front of the couch. "Would you mind throwing on a few more logs while I get the brandy?"

"Not at all."

She hurried toward the den to fetch the brandy, surprised at how happy she was to have a visitor. After the ice storm, worrying about the horses, finding out she had a sister, and the mysterious discoveries in her father's den, maybe having company would get her mind off things for a little while. When she came back into the living room, Fletcher was leaning back on the couch like he belonged there, relaxed and enjoying the fire, one ankle crossed over his knee.

She held up the brandy bottle and smiled. "It's old, but it should be fine."

"Well, I guess we'll find out, won't we?" he said.

She filled the glasses halfway, handed him one, and sat on the couch beside him. He took a swig and grimaced a little.

"Is it horrible?"

"No, it's fine."

"You didn't look like it was fine. You made a face."

He grinned. "I have a confession to make. I'm not a brandy drinker. Beer is normally my spirit of choice."

"Then why did you—"

"Because a night like this calls for brandy." He drained his glass, set it on the coffee table, and swallowed, trying to keep a straight face. "And you looked like you needed some company."

Her cheeks grew warm and she fixed her eyes on the fire. Why did he always assume he knew what she needed? "Would you like another?"

"No, thanks." He sat forward, his elbows on his knees, and gazed into the fire.

She sipped her drink and watched him out of the corner of her eye, wondering why he agreed to stay. If she didn't know better, she might have thought he took her up on the brandy just to spend time with her. But that was impossible. He was a veterinarian with a college degree and she had never graduated high school. Someone as handsome and accomplished as he surely had a girlfriend, or a fiancée, or a wife. Maybe even a couple of kids and a dog. She shook her head and tried to think rationally. He had come here to check on the horses and only took her up on her invitation because he was kind. That was it. And truth be told, she was grateful to meet someone kind at Blackwood Manor. Maybe he was right, maybe she did need company.

Despite her earlier decision not to ask if he knew anything about her parents and sister, she changed her mind. Kind people liked to help others. And she certainly needed help. Maybe he'd heard something while working here—if not from Claude, from someone else. After all, he knew the other horse farmers in the area, and people loved to talk. "Can I ask you something?"

He grinned. "Am I single? Yes."

Her face grew hot again. "That's not what I was going to say."

"How come I'm not married?" He raised his palms as if confessing a crime. "I guess I just haven't found the right person yet. After all, it takes a special woman to appreciate someone like me. I'm handsome, charming, well educated. And who could resist a guy who wears shit-covered boots and sticks their hands up cows' asses all day?" He leaned back, put his arm across the back of the couch, and cast her a wry smile. "What about you? Are you single, or will I have to fight someone for your affections?"

She couldn't seem to answer him. She had forgotten how to breathe, as if taking in air no longer followed letting it out. Suddenly she felt like they were too close. But he didn't move and neither did she. He gave her a bemused look. Then gradually, his expression changed and grew more serious. She felt like she might dissolve under his scrutiny. She stood, picked up their glasses, and headed toward the kitchen. "You should probably go," she said. "It's late and I need some sleep. Thanks for your help."

He got up and followed her. "No problem," he said, sounding puzzled. She went to the sink and he went to the door. "I'll come back tomorrow and check the pipes."

"All right, I'll see you then. Thanks again."

"Night." He smiled awkwardly and let himself out into the freezing night.

After he was gone, she leaned against the counter and tried to clear her head. She had no idea if he was trying to be funny or sincere. And to her surprise, she felt like a schoolgirl with a new crush, with sweaty palms and quivering knees. But that was impossible. She had just met him. She didn't even know if she trusted him. Hell, after everything she'd been through, she didn't trust anyone.

CHAPTER 19
Lilly

Three weeks after Cole tried to convince Mr. Barlow to put Lilly in the elephant act, The Barlow Brothers' Circus landed its biggest venue yet, in a town outside New York City on the Fourth of July weekend. It was their first time performing at that spot, and Mr. Barlow and Merrick barked orders nonstop.

Inside the dressing tent, Glory finished fixing Lilly's hair and helped her with her pearl necklace. "Are you nervous?" she said. "Mr. Barlow says everything has to go off without a hitch so we can come back next year."

"No," Lilly said. "But the bigger the venue, the more people I have to lie to."

"I know," Glory said. "But even if what you're doing isn't real, at least it makes the rubes happy to think they're talking to their lost loved ones."

"That's what I keep trying to tell myself," Lilly said. "But what happens when everyone finds out I'm nothing but a gaff?"

"You need to quit worrying ahead," Glory said. "It won't change anything."

Merrick stuck his head inside the tent. "Let's go, Lilly."

She stood, gave Glory a hug, and left with Merrick.

Over the next few hours, the rubes coming inside The Albino Medium's tent ran the entire gamut, from men looking to connect with their long-departed mothers, to little old ladies desperate to hear from their dead cats. When Pierre meowed from inside the wardrobe and the gray-haired lady with the sweet smile sitting across from Lilly started to cry, it was all she could do not to get up and walk out. Until the chance to do something else had presented itself in the form of working with the elephants, she hadn't fully realized how weary she was of this gig. And she knew in her heart of hearts the day would come when she would make a mistake and someone would peg her as fake. Then there would be hell to pay.

After the gray-haired lady left, Merrick gave Lilly two names instead of the usual one, because the next rube insisted on trying to reach two dead family members. As soon as Merrick left, a big, surly man in a worn jacket and dungarees limped into the tent. He looked to be about forty, his grimy face covered with two or three days' worth of beard, his hair sticking out in all directions, the smell of stale beer and cigarettes wafting from his clothes. Scowling, he fell into the seat across from Lilly, then sat forward, his elbows on the table as if ready to arm-wrestle a sworn enemy.

Lilly swallowed, her mouth suddenly parched. "Hello and welcome," she said. "Before we begin, let me tell you a little bit about what I do. I've been communicating with the dead since the age of four and eventually came to realize I needed to share my gift. Messages from the beyond can come in the form of music, voices, and other sounds. What I'd like you to do is close your eyes and think about your departed loved one. While you're doing that, I'll try to connect with the spirit world. Then I'll ask you some questions, to which you must answer either yes or no. Are you ready to begin?"

"Name's John," the man said.

She blinked at him, confused. "Is that your name, or the name of the person you hope to reach?"

"Mine."

"All right, John. Please relax, close your eyes,

and think about the person you'd like to hear from today."

"I'll do no such thing," John said.

Lilly tensed. *Here we go,* she thought. *My first difficult rube of the day.* "I'm sorry," she said. "But perhaps you misunderstood. Would you like to tell me something about yourself? Maybe that will—"

"I lost my wife and son in a car wreck a year ago. But you already knew that, didn't you?"

She shook her head. "No, I didn't know, but I'm very sorry for your loss. It must be extremely hard for you. If you'll give me a chance, I can try to reach them for you."

John fixed his watery gaze on her. "It was my fault 'cause I was drinking, and I been trying to tell them sorry ever since." He cleared his throat. "I been to all sorts of people sayin' they could talk to my wife and boy, that they could bring them into the room so I could ask their forgiveness. That's all I want. I just want to say I'm sorry." His face contorted in misery.

"I understand," she said. "Why don't we see if I can help?" She closed her eyes and waited a few seconds before continuing, guilt churning in her stomach. The agony on John's face burned itself into her memory next to the thousands of other rubes she had tricked into believing she could speak to their loved ones on the other side. "I'm seeing the figure of a young woman.

She's very pretty. I believe her name is Lisa . . . no, that's not right. It's Lynette."

"Stop it," John said in a hard voice.

Lilly opened her eyes. "Excuse me?"

"I said stop it."

"I'm sorry, I don't understand. Is something wrong? Sometimes it takes a little while to get—"

"Yeah, something's wrong," John interrupted. He glared at her. "You're a fake, just like the rest of them. Mediums, spirit guides, séance holders. Every last one of y'all is a goddamn fake!" He spit the words out like poison.

"I'm sorry," she said again. "But I—"

"I just wanna know one thing. What kinda person takes a hardworking man's money and lies right to their face about their dead kin?"

She shook her head. "I . . . I don't know. But if you'll just . . ."

John shot to his feet and slammed his fists on the table, rattling the candleholders and bell globe. "Don't lie to me!" he shouted, his chest heaving in and out. "I know this is a setup!"

Lilly got out of her chair and backed away, starting to shake. "Now listen, John. If you'll just calm down, we can give you your money—"

John stormed over to the wardrobe and yanked on the door handles. When they didn't open, he smashed his fists through the wood, reached in, and dragged Pierre out by the scruff of his shirt. "Who's this?" he snarled.

"Let go of me!" Pierre shouted. He tried punching John in the stomach, but his short arms wouldn't reach. John lifted him in the air and shook him.

"Don't!" Lilly shouted. "Please! It's not his fault!"

Just then, the back entrance flew open and Merrick rushed in, threw an arm around John's broad neck, and tried to wrestle him to the ground. Pierre yanked himself from John's grasp and scurried out of the way, his face white as a sheet. John pulled away from Merrick, then turned and threw a punch at him. Merrick ducked and John fell forward, landing on his knees. Then he found his footing, stood, and upended the table with one swipe of his arm. The candles toppled over and the glass bell globe shattered on the hard earth. The legless "spirit" baby flopped upside down from its wooden attachment beneath the table, its stuffed arms hanging limp next to its yarn-covered head. Pierre stomped on the candles to put them out, and Merrick threw his arms around John's shoulders. Nearly twice his size, John tore Merrick off his back, pushed him to the ground, and punched him in the face. Then he got up and tore down the curtains and stars and mirrors. Merrick groaned and rolled over on his side.

"Stop!" Lilly said. "Please, John! Stop!"

John bellowed like a madman and ripped

317

down one of the sidewalls, nearly bringing the entire roof down with it. Then he wrenched down the wall facing the midway, revealing the interior of the tent to the line of waiting rubes. Women gasped and stepped back, and men moved forward to protect them.

John gaped at the crowd, his eyes wild, pieces of canvas and ripped curtains in his hands. "They're stealing your money!" he yelled. "It's all fake!"

Mouths dropped open in confusion and shock. Faces contorted in anger. Several men shook their fists and demanded a refund, while others grumbled amongst themselves.

Merrick struggled to his feet and held up his hands. "Now, now," he said, blood gushing from his nostrils. "Can't you see this man is intoxicated? And at a family gathering, no less! He doesn't know what he's saying!"

"Then why are you asking for names before we go in?" a young woman called out.

"Yeah," a man yelled. "What's that for?"

"That's for a money-back guarantee, just like we told you," Merrick said. He pointed at Alana, who stood between the tent and the rubes, her notebook clasped to her chest, her slack face the color of ash. "She's the only one who sees the names until the end of the day. We're also keeping track of every spirit The Albino Medium contacts because we're trying to break the world record. And when you fine people read about that in the papers, you'll know you and your loved ones had a hand in making it happen. Your family will be famous!"

"Hogwash!" a man shouted.

"You're lying!" someone else yelled.

"Damn right, he's lyin'!" John shouted. He trudged over to the wardrobe and yanked out the stuffed glove. "See this? This is what that midget touches you with, all the while the albino's tellin' you your feelin' a ghost!" He yanked out the harmonica and bell and tambourine and threw them on the ground. "See? It's all rigged!"

With that, Merrick lunged at John like a battering ram and shoved him backward into the broken wardrobe. John collapsed in a heap of arms and legs and splintered wood. The rubes closed in to get a better view of the action, gawking and standing on their tiptoes to see over one another's shoulders and heads. Several men stepped forward, their chins raised, their hands in fists. Lilly moved away from them, her breath coming shallow and fast. She wanted to run, but there was nowhere to go. She, Merrick, Alana, and Pierre were surrounded. John shook his head, then clambered out of the smashed wardrobe and staggered to his feet.

"You sons a bitches!" one of the rubes shouted. "I want my money back!"

"Me too!" a woman yelled.

This brought more angry shouts from the crowd. Finally, Mr. Barlow's patches pushed their way through the gathering and stormed toward the tent. Patches normally calmed unhappy customers by offering free tickets to the big show, or—if the problem rube was male—giving them a free pass to the special "event" in the back lot behind the baggage wagons, which was accessible only by word of mouth. But once in a while, they had to use force. This was one of those times.

At first, John thought the patches were angry rubes, coming forward to back him up. Then they charged him and his eyes went wide, looking around frantically for an escape route. Before he had a chance to run, one of the patches grabbed his wrist, twisted it behind his back, wrapped a muscular arm around his neck, and dragged him away from the now-leaning tent. John sputtered and clawed at the patch's arm, but couldn't get away. The other patch stood between Lilly and the crowd with his arms crossed, daring the rubes to try something. Merrick raised his hands again and spoke to the irritated mob.

"Okay, folks, okay. Everything's fine. The heckler has been removed from the area. If you've already paid to see The Albino Medium, we'll give you a full refund. She won't be doing any more readings this afternoon. Everyone else, it's time to move along. There's nothing more to see here."

The rubes who already paid grumbled and moved toward Alana, shoving and pushing to get in line for their refunds. The rest were reluctant to leave, afraid they might miss something.

Merrick waved them away. "Go on now," he said. "Move along."

Mr. Barlow pushed his way through the stragglers. "What the hell is going on over here?" he asked Merrick.

Merrick turned his back to the rubes and kept his voice low. "Someone outed her. The rubes heard everything."

"Jesus Christ," Mr. Barlow said. "What did she do now?"

"I didn't do anything," Lilly said. "That rube had his mind made up before he came into my tent."

"His mind made up about what?" Mr. Barlow said.

"Me being a fraud," Lilly said.

Several women in the refund line heard what Lilly said and gasped, then turned to spread the word, whispering behind their hands.

"Shut up, you dumb bitch," Merrick hissed at Lilly.

"I don't care," she said. "I don't want to lie to people anymore. I can't."

"I don't give a damn what you want," Merrick said. "You do what I tell you to do. Without me, you'd still be locked in your parents' attic, half out of your mind. I saved your sorry ass and I own you." He glared at her, daring her to speak.

She said nothing. There was no point.

He dismissed her with a wave of his hand. "Go back to the train and stay there. After we fix the tent, you're on again."

Mr. Barlow scanned the collection of angry rubes, his brow creased. "It's too late for that," he said. "Word is out she's a gaff and it'll spread like wildfire. Once the cops hear about it, we'll get heat for sure." He cursed under his breath and balled his hands into fists. "And at our biggest venue." He pointed a finger at Merrick, anger flickering in his eyes. "Come up with a new act for her. In the meantime, she can recoup your losses by working for Josephine in the cooch show."

CHAPTER 20

Julia

Two days after the ice storm and Fletcher's surprise visit, the weather warmed and everything began to thaw. Water dripped into the already soaked ground, and snow and ice fell off roofs and buildings in giant, wet chunks. Tube-shaped pieces dropped from branches and wires, and dark patches of green grass and wet stone became visible beneath fields of translucent ice. The power came back on and the furnace sprang to life in the basement of Blackwood Manor. The house ticked as it began to warm.

Julia wrapped a sweater around herself and watched the wet scene from the kitchen window, sipping a cup of hot tea and honey. Over at the barn, a truck and horse trailer backed into the driveway. At first, she thought it was Fletcher's truck, but a man she'd never seen before got out and went into the office.

Fletcher had stopped in the previous day to check the pipes like he said he would, but he only stayed a few minutes. A client was waiting at another farm and he couldn't be late. He was polite but business-like, and Julia didn't know what to say other than thank you. She thought about apologizing, but for what, she wasn't sure. For their awkward exchange? For asking him to leave so quickly? For sending him out on the ice-covered roads after he'd been kind enough to check in on her? He was the one who made the decision to venture out to Blackwood Manor on such a treacherous night. She hadn't asked him to come. And it wasn't her job to keep him safe. Besides, even if she had wanted him to stay, for safety reasons or otherwise, the last thing she needed was for Claude to think something was going on between them. Still, she hated the thought of him being mad at her.

Over at the barn, the man got back in his truck, backed the trailer up to the main door, got out, and went into the office again. Julia furrowed her brow. What was going on? Claude hadn't said anything about a new horse being delivered or any of them being sold. And he wouldn't make those decisions without asking her anyway. Would he? She stared out the window, paralyzed by indecision. She didn't know whether to go over there and ask, or wait and see what happened. Then, before she could make up her mind, the man got in his truck and drove away, and Claude let some of the horses out in the main paddock. The horses ran and kicked and rolled in the snow, enjoying their freedom after being stuck in the barn during the storm. Bonnie Blue raced out of the barn and galloped around the perimeter of the fence, her head held high, her nostrils flaring. She looked desperate, whinnying and calling out, waiting for someone to answer.

Julia's heart dropped.

Where was Samantha?

She set her cup down on the counter so hard it nearly cracked, then hurried into the mudroom, threw on boots and a jacket, and flew out the door. If something had happened to Samantha, she wasn't sure she could handle it. She rushed across the yard, sidestepping icy patches and puddles until she reached the barn, then yanked

324

open the office door. She ran through the office and burst into the center aisle, searching frantically for Claude. He was putting straw in one of the stalls.

"Where's Samantha?" she said, her voice rattled by fear. "I saw Blue outside alone and she's beside herself!"

Claude stopped spreading the straw and looked at her, confusion written on his face. "She's with a nurse mare."

"Why?" Julia said. "Blue is frantic!" Her racing heart slowed, but only a little.

Claude gave her a stern look, as if she should know the answer. "Blue is one of our top producers. We need to breed her again as soon as possible."

"What does that have to do with taking Samantha away from her?"

"We need Samantha to stop nursing so Blue will go into heat again."

"But Samantha is only three days old. She's too young to be taken from her mother!"

Claude shrugged. "That's the way it's done. Blue will get over it. She always does."

A surge of sorrow and anger welled up in Julia's chest. She knew hard decisions sometimes had to be made when working with animals, but taking a three-day-old foal away from its mother was ridiculous and cruel. For the first time in her life, she was so mad she didn't care what

Claude or anyone else thought. The horses belonged to her now, and she had pledged to take care of them. "Where is she?" she asked again.

He lifted his chin, indicating the other end of the barn. "In with the nurse mare who delivered last night."

"What's a nurse mare? Explain it to me like I'm in first grade."

Irritation furrowed Claude's brow. "A nurse mare is a horse who just foaled and is able to produce milk. We use nurse mares to nurse other foals, foals that might be worth money. Like Blue's filly, Samantha."

"So the nurse mare is taking care of two babies?"

"No, just Blue's."

Julia frowned. "What about the nurse mare's foal? Where is it?"

Claude went back to spreading straw.

"Where is it? Tell me."

He looked at her, his face flat. "We send nurse mare foals to auction."

"Is that what that truck was doing here? Picking up the nurse mare's foal?"

Claude nodded.

"So you took Blue's three-day-old filly away from her and gave it to the nurse mare, then took the nurse mare's newborn away from her and sent it to auction?"

He took off his gloves and fixed hard eyes on her. "The sooner you learn that nurse mare foals are by-products of the racing industry and the pharmaceutical industry, the better off you'll be. Some farms let nurse mare foals starve, club them to death, or sell them for skin and meat. We don't do that here."

"Well, how do you know the foal won't be sold for skin and meat at the auction?"

"I don't."

Julia bunched her hands into fists at her sides. "Go get it."

He gaped at her. "Beg your pardon?"

"I want you to put Samantha back in Blue's stall with her. Then I want you to go get the nurse mare's foal and bring it back here."

Claude sighed loudly and shook his head. "Sorry, but that's not how it's done, Miss Blackwood. This is a business, not a place for bleeding hearts."

"Well, I own this business now and we're doing things my way. No more taking foals away from their mothers and no more sending newborns to auction."

Claude straightened his shoulders and jutted out his chin. "We're trying to make money here. We raise racehorses and show horses, not barnyard pets."

"I don't care. I've seen the books and we've got plenty of money. And while I'm in charge, we're not taking babies from their mothers. We'll have to figure out another way to make things work."

Just then, Fletcher came into the barn. "What's going on?"

Claude came out of the stall and yanked off his gloves. "Ask her," he said, and stormed away. He exited through the open barn door, got in his truck, slammed the driver's side door, and sped out of the driveway, gravel shooting from his back tires.

Fletcher looked at Julia, eyebrows raised. "Where's he going in such a hurry?"

Despite her conviction that she was doing the right thing, she was on the verge of tears. Her knees shook as adrenaline left her body. Putting her foot down and saying what she thought was exhausting. "To get the nurse mare's foal and bring it back here."

"What? Why?"

"I don't want foals taken from mares or sent to auction," she said. "Ever."

Fletcher crossed his arms and leaned against the wall, his face somber. "Okay. But that means more time between births and fewer horses to sell."

"I don't care. Blackwood Farm is doing perfectly fine, and if we have to get by on less in the future, we'll figure that out when the time comes. But I refuse to make money that way. Now, will you please help me give Samantha back to Bonnie Blue?"

He put on a pair of gloves and studied her, the

hint of a grin on his face. "Yes, Miss Blackwood."

She turned and started down the aisle in the other direction.

"Hey, where are you going?" he said. "I thought you wanted help taking Samantha to Blue?"

"You can do it," she called over her shoulder. "Their stall needs to be cleaned." She entered Blue's stall and got to work.

In truth, she needed to be alone. The thought of foals being taken away from their mothers, ripped without warning from everything familiar and loved, then starved, clubbed, or sold for meat, tore her heart to shreds. Tears filled her eyes as she imagined Blue and the nurse mare, scared and confused and frantic, wondering why someone had taken their babies. She could almost feel the horrible, heavy pain in their chests, the terror and helplessness in their minds. It didn't matter that they were animals. Mares still possessed the maternal instinct. She had seen it with her own eyes when Bonnie Blue looked back at her newborn filly. It was love at first sight. Her mother had never looked at her that way, but Julia had studied enough interactions between mothers and daughters to recognize unconditional love when she saw it. Then another thought hit her and she had to stop working.

How many foals had been taken away from their mothers at Blackwood Manor Horse

Farm? How many horses' hearts had been broken because of her parents' greed? How could anyone be that callous year after year after year? What kind of people were her parents anyway?

CHAPTER 21
Lilly

Wearing a white silk gown, kitten heels, satin evening gloves, and a white feather boa, Lilly shivered in front of a cracked mirror in the cooch show dressing tent, despite the fact that it was well over ninety degrees outside and the inside of the tent felt hotter still. She hadn't eaten a thing all day, and her empty stomach twisted with nerves and bile. Behind her, half-naked women wiped red lipstick off their lips, scrubbed beauty marks from their cheeks, and peeled tassels off their nipples. They were done for the night, and now it was time for the final cooch show act—Lilly Blackwood. It was all she could do not to throw up.

Earlier, Josephine had insisted Rosy and Ruby add color to Lilly's face, so Ruby drew a beauty mark above Lilly's mouth while Rosy lined her eyes with black liner and applied fake lashes.

"What did Cole say about Mr. Barlow putting

you in the cooch show?" Ruby said. She patted a makeup brush into a pot of rouge and brushed it over Lilly's cheeks.

"He punched a hole in the wall of a boxcar and nearly broke his hand," Lilly said.

"Oh God," Ruby said. "Did you tell him it was only until Merrick comes up with a new act for you?"

Lilly nodded, a burning lump growing in her throat. She had tried to tell Cole that no matter who saw her naked, she was still the same girl who came to him in the menagerie at night. She was still the same girl who snuck into his sleeper car when no one was looking, and followed him into the fields to make love beneath the stars. It was hard enough knowing she was being forced to appear naked onstage, but the thought of losing Cole was more than her heart could bear. He wasn't a prude by any means, but what would he think of her after she revealed herself to the world?

"And?" Rosy said. "What did he say?"

Lilly's eyes filled. "He said he needed some time alone and walked away."

"Jeepers," Ruby said. She dabbed a tissue in the corner of Lilly's eyes to stop her makeup from running. "Well, he can't be mad at you for it."

Lilly shrugged.

"You know," Rosy said, applying lipstick to Lilly's lips. "Some men find it exciting to think about other men ogling their woman's body." She winked playfully and grinned.

"Yeah," Ruby said. "For some reason, the thought of dating a cooch show girl gets their engines running. In case you hadn't noticed, practically all the single men in this dog and pony show are after us."

"That's right," Rosy said. "And some of the not-so-single ones too." The twins giggled.

Lilly loved them for trying to make her feel better, but it didn't work. "I only want one."

Ruby grabbed another tissue. "Aww, don't cry, sweetie. He'll come around."

When the twins were done putting on the makeup, Lilly thought she looked like a clown. But she didn't have the heart to tell them that. Besides, she didn't care. Maybe the audience would think she looked like a clown too, and her career in the girlie show would be over before it began.

Now, her mind raced as she sat in front of the mirror, trying to figure out how she could sabotage her act without getting caught. Nothing came to her. She was supposed be over in the cooch show tent already, waiting in the wings. She got up and pulled back the dressing tent door to peer out. Maybe she could make a run for it. But one of Mr. Barlow's strongmen kept guard outside, protecting the girls and watching for rubes trying to sneak a free peek beneath the canvas walls.

Across the narrow passageway, the cooch show tent glowed red, and Ruby's and Rosy's silhouettes danced and wiggled across the stage. Snare drums and a trumpet played sexy music, and men hooped and hollered for the twins to take it all off. The longer the music went on, the rowdier the men got.

"You ready?" the strongman said to Lilly.

She steeled herself and stepped out of the changing tent, her limbs trembling. The strongman led her over to the back of the cooch show tent and pushed aside the entry flap. She swallowed the acid in her throat, went inside, and followed a short, dim corridor to the wings of the stage, where three overturned crates, two with cushions and one topped with ashtrays, glasses, and bottles of liquor, sat against the back wall. Watching from behind the curtains, her face grew hot as the twins shimmied across the pockmarked platform in G-strings and lace brassieres, a string of red lights illuminating their rouged faces. Like everything else they did, they moved and danced in perfect unison. Then they stopped and leaned forward, shaking their shoulders and covering their breasts with their hands. The men hollered and groaned.

"Show us what you got!" a man yelled.

The twins straightened, pouted coyly, and shook their index fingers back and forth.

Then the snare drum rolled and the twins faced

each other and slid each other's bra straps down from their shoulders. They winked at the audience, rotated on their tiptoes, bent over again, and let their breasts swell forward in the loose cups of their brassieres.

"Come on," another man shouted. "I paid good money for this!"

The twins shrugged, turned away from the audience, and reached behind their backs to undo their bra clasps. In perfectly timed identical movements they glanced over their shoulders, winked again, and let their brassieres fall to the floor.

"That's it!" someone shouted.

"There you go, girls!"

"Turn around, honey!"

The twins spun around with their hands over their nipples, opened their red-lipped mouths in mock surprise, and took their hands away, letting their breasts drop. The men whooped in delight.

"Lord have mercy!"

"Sweet Jesus!"

The twins did another quick little dance, then curtsied and ran off the stage, smiling and blowing kisses to the audience. The men cheered and whistled and clapped. Lilly's neck and chest ignited with a strange mixture of shame and panic. She was next, and she didn't think she could go through with it. On the opposite side of the stage, Josephine sauntered out from behind the curtain and asked for a big hand for Rosy and Ruby. The men hollered and applauded. The twins hurried down the stage steps, entered the wing, and stopped beside Lilly, laughing and out of breath.

"You look gorgeous," Ruby said.

"Like a movie star," Rosy said.

"I think I'm going to be sick," Lilly said. She was starting to feel dizzy.

Onstage, Josephine raised a hand to quiet the men.

"It's your lucky night, fellas," she said. "Because we've saved the best for last. Tonight you're going to see something you'll never forget, something so shocking you'll be talking about it for weeks. This one is so special, boys, we're asking you to pay another quarter to stay. I can't say any more than it's our last girl of the evening, and you won't want to miss her. Just hand your quarter to that fella right there, and he'll let you stay for this final act. That's it. Just one more quarter and you'll see something you'll be talking about for the rest of your lives."

"Listen," Rosy said to Lilly. "The first time's the hardest. But once you see those men turn into little boys at your feet, you might like it."

"I doubt it," Lilly said.

"Just remember what we taught you," Rosy said. "Start with a slow, sexy strut, and make sure you smile."

"And play with your hair a little," Ruby said.

Lilly nodded, suddenly incapable of speech.

"And now," Josephine announced to the audience, "our very own, the beautiful, the alluring, the angelic, the *virginal* Miss Lilly Blackwood!"

Lilly stood frozen, unable to put one foot in front of the other. Her heartbeat thundered in her ears, blocking out all sound. Josephine grinned like a wolf, one arm outstretched, and waited for her to come up the steps. Lilly's vision started to close in and the ground swayed beneath her feet.

"Go on, Lilly," Ruby said. "You can do it."

"Quick," Rosy said. "Give her a swig before she runs."

Ruby grabbed a bottle of whiskey from the overturned crate and, before Lilly could protest, held it to her lips and told her to drink. Lilly took a big sip. The alcohol burned her throat and ignited her chest. But she didn't care. If it helped her get through this, she'd drink the entire bottle. She took several more good swallows, then pushed it away and coughed. She'd had her share of booze over the years, but never on an empty stomach, and she could already feel it slithering through her veins, warming her arms and legs.

"There you go," Ruby said. "That'll take the edge off. Now go on."

"I . . . I can't," Lilly stammered. "I can't do it."

"You have to," Rosy said. "You know what Merrick will do if you don't."

"Come on," Ruby said. "Show him you're stronger than that."

For a second, Lilly thought about taking the beating. Anything would be better than undressing in front of a crowd of drunken men. Then she remembered what Merrick said about entertaining rubes in a tent behind the baggage wagons and something shifted in her head, like reason and logic and sanity coming unfastened deep within her. She felt it in her chest too, like a loosening of her lungs and heart. Her breath felt bottomless. She wasn't sure if it was the whiskey or a sudden case of indifference, but something pushed her toward the stage. She almost laughed, wondering what the men's reactions would be when they saw the color of her skin. Maybe they'd go running out of the tent and spread the word that the Barlow Brothers' had a disgusting freak in their girlie show. Maybe it would be the last time she'd have to do this.

Holding up the hem of her silk evening gown, she marched up the steps on unsteady legs. Josephine winked at her and left the stage. When the music started, Lilly took a deep breath and stepped into the spotlight.

A collective intake of breath filled the tent, and there was a moment of awed silence. Standing men sat down hard in their chairs and sitting men stood, wide-eyed and gawking. Lilly was right. The rubes didn't want to pay good money to see a freak take off her clothes. They wanted busty blondes, sultry redheads, and voluptuous brunettes, not a ghost with a headful of spider-web hair. Relief washed through her. There was no need to get naked after all.

Then the men started whistling and clapping, and Lilly's heart sank. She glanced nervously at Ruby and Rosy, who were watching from the wings. Ruby smiled and made a circular motion with her finger. Lilly turned around, her back to the audience, and tried pulling herself together, a bulge of terror rising in her mind. Merrick and Mr. Barlow had forced her up there, up there in front of a group of men who might be fearful of her, up there in front of men who might want to hurt her as badly as they wanted to see her naked. And now she was supposed to undress and put herself on display for them.

It'd been years since Momma's words rang in her ears, but she could hear them now, like a returning nightmare from her youth, calling her an abomination and telling her it was a grievous sin to expose her naked body to anyone, even herself. And suddenly it broke, the horrible realization that she had been cheated out of a normal life came over her, and a soundless cry tore from her chest. Her only thought was to run, to get off the stage and get out of the tent. All at once, the whiskey rebelled inside her empty stomach and she knew she was going to be sick. She turned and her feet tangled in her dress and she almost fell. Then she recovered and headed toward the steps, a hand over her mouth.

Someone in the audience began to laugh, and another man joined in. Others shouted angry words.

"Is this some kinda joke?"

"Get that freak off the stage!"

"We want our money back!"

An empty popcorn box hit Lilly in the head. She hunched her shoulders and put her arm up to protect herself until she reached the stage steps and scrambled down them. At the bottom, she fell on her hands and knees and vomited in the flattened grass, her hair hanging in her eyes.

"Oh my God," Ruby said.

Rosy knelt beside her. "Are you okay?"

The twins helped her up and Josephine rushed back onstage to calm the angry crowd. Dizzy and disoriented, Lilly broke free from the twins and stumbled along the wing. She went out the back flap and hurried into the dressing tent. Somewhere in the back of her mind, she heard Josephine calling the twins back up onstage.

Trembling and trying to catch her breath, she collapsed inside the dressing tent. After a long minute, she got up, trudged over to a mirror, and wiped the red lipstick from her mouth with shaking hands. Using more force than necessary, she scrubbed the melted mascara from around her eyes and cheeks. She'd done a lot of things to survive over the past six years, but she refused to take her clothes off in front of a roomful of men. She just couldn't. And if Merrick and Mr. Barlow thought they could force her to entertain rubes in the tent behind the baggage wagons, she'd run away. There was no other choice. She'd take her chances in the real world, or join a different circus. Maybe, if she begged him, Cole would leave with her.

Behind her in the mirror, the canvas flap whipped open and Merrick stormed into the tent. She got off the stool and backed away. No matter what happened next, her conscience was clear.

"Who the hell do you think you are?" Merrick shouted, his face snarling and red. "You think you can just do whatever you want around here?"

"I was sick," she said. "The twins gave me whiskey and I—"

"I don't give a shit if you were dying! You made a laughingstock out of Josephine and the entire Barlow Brothers' Circus!" He launched forward and grabbed her arm. "I warned you what would happen if you didn't do what you were told. Now you're going behind the baggage wagons with the rest of the whores."

"No," she said. "You can't make me. I won't do it!"

He bared his teeth and dragged her toward the rear of the tent. "You will, and I'm going to be the one to break you in."

He shoved her behind a stack of steamer trunks, then seized her again, lifted her off her feet, and crushed her to his chest. Her kitten heels fell off and for a moment she hung suspended, her bare toes scraping the tops of his boots. He shook her hard and set her down. When her feet touched the grass, she tried to get away, but he grasped her face, turned it toward his, and pushed his wet mouth over hers. She clamped her lips shut and tried to wrench free, but he wrapped his arms around her and held on tighter. The sour tang of whiskey and tooth decay filled her nostrils and mouth. She twisted and turned and kneed him in the crotch.

He groaned in pain and loosened his grip, then slapped her across the face and shoved her backward with an angry grunt. She landed hard on her back and scrambled to her knees, trying to crawl away. But before she could get her feet beneath her and run, he grabbed her ankles, dragged her backward, flipped her over, and held her down.

"Let me go!" she screamed, pushing against his chest. She swung at his head, her small fists colliding with his rock-hard jaw, his muscular neck, his granite temples. He grabbed her flailing arms with one rough hand and pinned them above her head, his face red with exertion. She bucked and twisted and tried to bring her knee into his crotch again but couldn't lift her legs beneath him. He ripped open the front of the silk gown as if it were paper and tore off her underwear. Then he undid his pants and forced himself between her legs.

"You don't tell me what to do," he said. "I tell you. You belong to me, remember?"

She thrashed beneath him, using every ounce of strength she had left to try and push him off. But it was no use. His full weight, nearly twice hers, pinned her to the ground like a moth beneath a rock. She could barely breathe. She turned her head and closed her eyes, then felt herself going somewhere else, like a dropped coin spiraling to the bottom of a lake. Away from this, away from him, away from what he was doing to her. She saw a black hole and felt herself falling in. Deep in the center of her soul, a diminutive, secret place split wide open. It was the only part of her she'd managed to keep hidden and protected, even while people stared and made fun of her in the freak show. Now, without any warning, it was exposed and vulnerable, lingering for just a moment, like a trailing wisp of black smoke, and then it was gone. She let out a high, keen shriek, like the long, final wail of a dying animal, until she tasted blood at the back of her throat.

Suddenly, Merrick stopped and stared down at her as if he had no idea who she was, his shocked face that of a man suddenly exorcised of a demon. Then, with a hard, low grunt of surprise and pain, his head jerked to the left and he fell to one side, his body limp. Behind him, Cole stood with a bull hook in his hands, his face contorted with rage.

He dropped the bull hook and knelt beside her. "Are you all right?" he said.

Lilly gathered her torn gown over her trembling legs, rolled on her side, and curled into a fetal position, fighting the urge to jump up, grab the bull hook, and bash in Merrick's head. The newly dead space at the center of her soul began to shift and change. Then it shriveled, closed, hardened, and turned to stone.

Cole scooped her off the ground and carried her out of the tent. "You're going to be okay," he said. "I've got you."

She leaned against his shoulder and closed her eyes, her teeth chattering.

He kissed the top of her head. "I'm so sorry, Lilly. I never should have let you go through with it. I should have protected you." His voice sounded strangled, as if he had to force the words out. "I hope I killed the bastard."

She looked up at him. "No, don't say that. Mr. Barlow will have you red-lighted."

"I don't care."

Neither of them spoke again as he carried her through the back lot. Above the ghostly roofline of the big top, above the yellow and orange flags and colored lights, a smattering of stars twinkled in the evening sky. The circus was starting to close down and the jovial finale music floated out into the night. Laughter and shouts sounded in the distance as the rubes started toward the exit, happily making last-minute stops at the side-shows and concession stands before returning to the normal world.

When Cole and Lilly reached the train, he passed her car and kept going.

"Where are you taking me?" she said.

"You're staying with me from now on. You're done with Merrick and that damn sideshow."

CHAPTER 22

Julia

After Julia told Claude and Fletcher no more foals would be taken from their mothers at Blackwood Manor Horse Farm, she took a glass of brandy into her father's den to resume her search for the missing key and clues about her dead sister. She wiped the dust off the record player, turned it on, and put the needle at the beginning of "Little White Lies." When the tinny, old-timey music filled the room, she stood there, frozen. Suddenly she was a little girl again, hearing her father's curses and cries between the lyrics, Mother's voice telling her to get away from the den doors. She knew if she turned around, shc would see her father at his desk, his hand wrapped around a whiskey-filled tumbler, his dark-ringed eyes wet with tears. She switched off the record player, took a swig of brandy, and turned around. The desk chair was empty.

After another long sip of brandy, she sat at the desk and ran her fingers beneath the middle drawer to see if the key was taped to the wood. It wasn't. She got on her hands and knees and looked beneath the desk. Cobwebs hung from the wooden legs and dust bunnies tumbled away from her breath. There was no key. She reached into dusty vases and searched beneath anniversary clocks and trophies. She took horse pictures and certificates down from the walls and looked behind the frames. She rolled up the edges of the rugs, lifted lamps, felt below windowsills, and tested floorboards to see if any were loose. Nothing. Feeling defeated, she sat back down at the desk and tried to think, her hands tented beneath her chin. *If I wanted to hide a key,* she wondered, *where would I put it?* Nothing came to her.

She sighed and reached for her high school

photograph. She still couldn't believe her father had it, let alone kept it on his desk. Upon closer examination, she noticed the photo had shifted downward the tiniest bit, exposing the top edge of what looked like another picture behind it. She turned the frame over and, using her fingernail, bent open the metal points used to hold the mat in place, then took out the mat and a thin piece of cardboard between it and the picture. As suspected, there was another photo behind the first. It took her a few seconds to realize who it was, but when she did, her eyes went wide.

Mother smiled in the professional-looking portrait, wearing a crisp white blouse and a necklace with a silver cross. Her light hair was pushed back in a headband, the rest falling in soft waves over her shoulders. She couldn't have been any older than eighteen or twenty. Apparently, Mother hadn't always been opposed to pictures. Imagining her as a young woman had always been difficult for Julia, but here was proof that Coralline Blackwood had once been fresh, vibrant, and beautiful. Still, Julia had trouble connecting the wide, genuine smile of the woman in the picture with Mother. She had never seen her smile like that. What had changed? Was it the loss of her first daughter that turned her into the woman Julia remembered? Or was it the affair, or obsession, or whatever it was her husband had with the albino and the circus? And why had Father covered Mother's picture with hers?

She laid both photos on the desk, mother and daughter side-by-side. The shape of their faces and their features were nearly identical, the arch of the brows, even the way one eye was the tiniest bit lower than the other. She had never noticed the similarities before, but now it seemed eerie how much they resembled each other. They could have been the same person living in separate eras. No matter how much Julia might have fantasized in the past about coming from a different family, there was no denying she was Coralline Blackwood's daughter.

With a thousand questions running through her mind, she returned the pictures to the frame and started putting it back together. Then she stopped. A small key had been taped to the front of the cardboard behind Mother's photo. Her heart-beat picked up speed as she peeled off the key, removed the tape, and tried it in the locked drawer. It fit and turned. She held her breath and pulled open the drawer. A polished, wooden box sat alone and perfectly centered in the bottom, in stark contrast to the chaos in the rest of the desk. With shaking hands, she carefully lifted the box and put it on the blotter, relieved to see it didn't have a lock.

She opened the lid and found a velvet drawstring purse and a red leather camera case.

She took out the drawstring purse and opened it. Inside was a pearl necklace, matching earrings, and a silver hairbrush wrapped in yellowed newspaper. She stared at the white strands in the brush. *It couldn't be, could it?*

She took out the camera case and set it on the desk. The clasp was broken and the brittle leather felt like grit on her fingertips. Working gently she took the camera out of the case. Written in blue ink inside the case lid was a name: *Lilly.*

Was that Father's mistress? If so, why did he have her things?

A thin piece of folded cardboard sat on the bottom of the box. Julia took it out and unfolded it. Red and blue paint flecked off the creases of a poster from The Barlow Brothers' Circus. On the front, two clowns smiled and waved next to a pale-looking elephant standing on its hind legs. A woman dressed in a white evening gown sat in the elephant's curled trunk, smiling with one arm in the air. It looked like the same woman from the newspaper clipping.

Julia picked up the camera and turned it over in her hands. It was a silver and black enamel Kodak with three round knobs on the top. Despite its age, it looked brand new. She released the lens, looked through the viewfinder, and pushed the exposure level. To her surprise, the camera clicked and the shutter closed. She wound the advance knob.

The camera had film inside.

• • •

The morning after finding the camera inside the locked drawer of her father's desk, Julia woke up with a splitting headache. That second glass of brandy was a bad idea. Then again, it wasn't every day you found out you had a dead sister and your father might have had an albino mistress. Not to mention wondering why your parents needed forgiveness for something to do with your sister's death, and putting your foot down about something you believed in. All those jumbled up emotions felt like having the stomach flu—complete with trembling knees and the desire to throw up. If being the owner of Blackwood Manor Horse Farm was going to be this draining, maybe she wasn't cut out for the job.

The leaden sky outside her window mirrored her frame of mind. Rain clouds hung like gray waves above the treetops, as if ready to break open and flood the earth at any second. If it were up to her, she would have stayed in bed all day. But there were too many things to do. Too many things to figure out and untangle. She crawled out from under her warm covers, got washed and dressed, and went downstairs. After a quick cup of tea, she put the camera and case from her father's desk in her purse, threw on a coat and hat, and went out the mudroom door toward the barn. Hopefully, Claude would still give her a ride somewhere, no matter how mad he was about retrieving the nurse mare foal. The thought of riding alone with him for any length of time sounded as appealing as chewing sawdust, but how else would she get into town? Besides, she wanted to ask him a hundred questions, including if he knew anything about the camera. If they were in the truck together he wouldn't be able to walk away.

When she was halfway across the lawn, Fletcher came out of the barn and ambled toward her, smiling. *How could he be so cheerful on this crappy day?* she wondered. When he reached her, she forced a smile and kept walking.

He stopped and turned. "Hey."

"Morning," she said.

He followed her. "I was coming over to the house to see you."

"Why? What do you need?"

"I want to show you something."

Without looking at him, she knew he was grinning. She could hear the smile in his voice. *What is it with him anyway? Why is he always so happy? It's annoying.* "What?" she asked.

"Come over to my truck and see."

"Can it wait? I have errands to run in town and I need to ask Claude for a ride."

"It'll only take a second," he said. "Besides, you're the boss around here and I need your okay. Just give it a quick look and I'll run you into town after."

She stopped and looked at him, sighing. Riding into town with him would be a lot better than riding with Claude, and she wasn't really in the mood to ask Claude questions anyway. If he was mean and rude, she might say something she'd regret. Maybe by the time they got back she'd feel braver and have a better outlook. "Okay. What do you want to show me?"

Fletcher's smile widened. "Great," he said. "Follow me." He led her across the lawn, toward a horse trailer hitched to his truck. On the way, they passed Claude fixing a gate near the barn driveway. He glanced up at them, then put his head back down, his eyes on his work. Julia clenched her jaw, a knot of dread twisting in her stomach. In her head, she was tough, but in reality she hated the thought of anyone being angry at her, even someone as ornery as Claude. And if he was still upset about the foals, he might not be willing to talk about anything.

She trailed Fletcher along the side of the horse trailer and followed him around to the back, wishing they could get this over with so she could go into town and find a place to get the film in the camera developed. Maybe the pictures would help answer some of her questions. Fletcher unlocked the ramp and let it down, then gestured for her to follow him up it. He was still smiling, but there was a strange tightness in his eyes, a rare glint of unease she had never seen before. Normally he seemed to swagger around the barn like the jocks who used to make fun of her in school, sure of the world around him and his place in it. Seeing him like this made her nervous. She didn't think she could handle any more surprises. Steeling herself, she went up the ramp, peered inside the trailer, and gasped.

Lying in a bed of yellow straw, a newborn foal the color of coal lifted its head and blinked up at her. When it saw her and Fletcher, it struggled to its feet on wobbly legs and pushed its tiny muzzle over the door.

Julia smiled and rubbed its fuzzy forehead, forgetting about Claude, her late sister, and the film in the camera. "Is this the nurse mare's foal?" she said. "I thought Claude brought it back last night."

"He did," Fletcher said. "This one was born over at the Thompson Farm early this morning. The mare rejected it."

She frowned. "How come?"

He shrugged. "Sometimes it just happens. No one knows why. It was the mare's first."

She looked at the orphaned foal's sweet face and felt an instant kinship with it, immediately berating herself for being so caught up in her own problems she almost refused to listen to Fletcher. "But how will it survive without its mother?"

He leaned over the door and scratched the

foal's neck. "I was hoping you'd take care of it."

Her eyes went wide. "Me? I don't know any-thing about—"

"I'll help you."

"I don't know," she said. "I might do something wrong. Then it will get sick, and I've got so much to do in the house and—"

"After what you did yesterday, telling Claude not to take any more foals from their mares, I figured you wouldn't mind me bringing this little one here. It was either that or the auction. And its chances of survival after that wouldn't be good."

She took a deep breath and gazed at the newborn. She had no idea what was involved in taking care of a foal, but she couldn't turn away this beautiful baby and send it to auction. She looked at Fletcher. "What about you? Why can't you take care of it?"

"I'm on the road every day. A newborn needs to be fed about every two hours for the first week, then every four to six hours after that."

She gaped at him. "For how long?"

"After a few weeks she'll show interest in solid food, but you'll still have to bottle-feed her for a while."

"She?"

"Yes, it's a filly."

She studied the filly's innocent, trusting eyes. There was no other choice. She had to take the poor thing in. "Okay," she said.

"Okay what?"

"I'll take care of her."

Fletcher grinned and unhitched the trailer door. "Great, let's get her in the barn. I picked up some fresh cow's milk on the way here, but it has to be watered down a bit."

She feigned surprise. "You already picked up milk? What if I had said no?"

He winked at her. "I knew you wouldn't."

The filly backed away from the opening doorway, frightened by the strange sights and sounds. Julia stepped off the ramp to get out of the way while Fletcher went into the trailer and rubbed the filly's neck and ears and sides. At first, the filly wasn't sure what was going on. But the more Fletcher rubbed, the more she leaned into him like a dog enjoying a scratch. Eventually, Fletcher straightened, clicked his tongue, and exited the trailer. The filly followed him down the ramp on spindly, wobbling legs, then bounded behind him toward the barn, her short, fuzzy tail held high.

Julia followed and Claude turned to watch them go by, a scowl on his face. She forced a smile and waved at him. He nodded once, then went back to work. Halfway to the barn, the filly stopped, looked back at Julia, and waited for her to catch up. When she did, the filly jumped and kicked a hind leg in the air, as if happy she was there. She stayed beside Julia as they followed Fletcher into the barn, and Julia's eyes grew moist. Maybe she was imagining things, but it seemed like the little horse already loved her.

Julia left her purse in the barn office and went to help Fletcher put the filly in an empty stall. He filled a bottle with watered-down milk and showed Julia how to hold it, then watched her feed the newborn, his hands on his hips, a satisfied look on his face. Julia grinned like a fool as the filly slurped and licked and tugged on the nipple.

"You're a natural," Fletcher said.

"You think so?"

"Sure, she took right to you."

Claude came over to the stall and peered over the door. "What's this all about?"

"I brought this filly over from the Thompson Farm," Fletcher said. "The mare rejected it."

"So now we're taking in culls?" Claude said, his voice hard.

"She took a liking to Julia," Fletcher said.

Claude shook his head and walked away, mumbling under his breath. Julia looked up at Fletcher, her eyebrows raised.

"Don't worry," he said. "He'll get over it."

"I don't know. First I said I don't want foals taken from mares, and now this. I'm afraid we might never get along."

"He just doesn't like change," he said. "Your mother . . . sorry, I mean Mrs. Blackwood . . .

even said it took a while for him to listen to her after your father died. And now you're in charge after he's been running the show on his own for a while. He's a little hard around the edges and set in his ways, but he'll come around."

She studied Fletcher's face, trying to imagine him having a heart-to-heart with Mother. Maybe he knew more about Blackwood Manor and her parents than she thought. "Did my mother confide in you often?"

He laughed. "Ah, no. It was more like her yelling and swearing at Claude for not listening."

"That sounds more like the Mrs. Blackwood I remember." She grinned. "Do you think it will help if I swear at Claude?"

He laughed again. "No, you're doing a good job at keeping a balance between respecting his expertise and letting him know you're the new boss."

"Thanks," she said. "You have no idea how much I needed to hear that."

"Anytime."

Fletcher's words bolstered her confidence, but she knew it was fleeting. Maybe she should ask Claude about the camera now, before she lost her nerve.

"Take the bottle for a minute, will you?" she said. "I'll be right back."

Fletcher took the bottle and she left the stall, went into the office, and got the camera and case out of her purse. She found Claude working near the hayloft ladder, spearing hay bales with a handheld hook and stacking them in a pile. She stood in the aisle and cleared her throat to get his attention. He glanced over his shoulder to see who was there, but said nothing.

"Can I ask you something?" she said.

He lifted a bale of hay and kneed it into place among the others. "You're the boss."

She took the camera out of the case and held it up. "Have you seen this before?"

He stopped working, took off his cap, wiped a sleeve across his sweaty brow, and squinted at the camera. Then he put his cap back on and said, "Nope."

"Are you sure?"

"I'm sure." He impaled another bale and put it on top of the stack.

"So you have no idea who it belongs to?"

Claude shook his head.

"Well, I found it inside a locked drawer in my father's desk. I've never seen it before and I don't remember my parents ever owning a camera."

"There was no need. They had professional photographers for the horses."

She made a face. "Don't you think that's odd? They never had a family portrait done or took pictures of their daughter, but they paid someone to take pictures of their horses?"

Claude shrugged and turned away. "To each their own."

She watched him for a moment, unsure if she should press him further. Then she decided to go for it. What did she have to lose? He already disliked her. "What about Lilly?" she said. "Did my father ever mention anyone by that name?"

For a fraction of a second, Claude froze. A casual observer might not have noticed, but Julia did. Then he bent over, impaled another bale of hay, and shoved it into place. "Nope."

"Was that my sister's name?"

"Don't know."

"What about The Barlow Brothers' Circus? Ever heard of it?"

He shook his head. "Doesn't ring a bell."

She opened her mouth to ask him another question, then changed her mind. She wasn't going to get anywhere with him. Not like this, anyway. Maybe after she had the film developed and figured out if the pictures would help solve the mystery, she'd bring the newspaper clippings and other things she found over to the barn. Maybe then he'd understand she was serious about learning the truth. "Will you let me know if you remember anything? Please?"

"Yup."

She sighed and went back to the new filly's stall. Fletcher was coming out, an empty milk bottle in his hand, and the filly was asleep in the hay.

"She'll need to eat again in two hours," he said.

"When we come back from town I'll show you how much water to put in the milk."

Julia nodded, briefly entertaining the idea of telling him everything. She felt so alone with all of it and could have used someone to talk to. Maybe Mother had let something slip while he was working here. Then, in the next instant, she changed her mind. She had no concrete evidence to support her harebrained theories, just her own gut feelings, cryptic messages in a journal, hidden ticket stubs and articles about a circus and an albino woman, a brush full of white hair, and a locked drawer with a camera inside. It all sounded so absurd. And the last thing she needed was for Fletcher, the one person willing to help her right now, to think she was foolish or crazy.

In Fletcher's truck on the way to town, "Love Me Tender" played on the radio while Julia stared out the window trying to figure out how everything tied together. *If* everything tied together. What had her parents done that needed God's forgiveness? How did her sister die? Was she stillborn? Sick? Or was it something else? Who was the albino, and what did she have to do with her father? Who was Lilly? Her sister? Her father's mistress? How had her father's secrets—whatever they were—affected his relationship with her and Mother? And how had her sister's death affected her parents' relationship with her? Were they afraid to get too close, afraid to love her in case they lost her too? No, that wasn't it.

For the thousandth time, she pulled herself apart piece by piece, trying to figure out why she felt so unloved. Then she pictured the long-legged filly asleep in the straw back at the barn, rejected for unknown reasons by its mother. She and the filly were kindred spirits. Maybe that was why she had to take the newborn in, and why it made her eyes water knowing they already loved each other unconditionally.

Fletcher turned down the radio. "A penny for your thoughts," he said, pulling her out of her trance.

She blinked and tried to smile. "Just day-dreaming, that's all."

"Well, we're getting close to town. Where do you want to stop?"

"I need to get a roll of film developed."

"Okay, we can drop it off at the drugstore. Anything else?"

"I'd like to grab a few things at the super-market if we have time."

"All right." He drummed his fingers on the steering wheel, keeping time with the song on the radio.

"Do you know how long it takes to get film developed at the drugstore?" she asked.

He shook his head. "I'm not sure. What have you been taking pictures of?"

She was caught off guard by the question. "Nothing."

He laughed. "Well, that doesn't sound very interesting. Remind me to have something else to do if you ever want to bore me with your photographs."

"That's not what I mean." She picked at her thumbnail, unsure if she should tell him the truth, at the same time knowing she would. "I found an old camera in the house."

He grinned and widened his eyes. "Ooh, a mystery!"

"It *is* a mystery," she said. Her tone was harsher than she intended.

His smile disappeared, and he directed his attention back to the road. "Okay. Got it."

"Sorry. It's just . . . my parents were a little . . . strange . . . and difficult. Now I'm trying to find answers to questions I've been asking my entire life."

"No, I'm sorry," he said. "I didn't mean to make light of it. I can tell you've been struggling with something, but I don't want to pry. Just let me know if there's anything I can do to help."

She bit her lip and turned toward the window again. He was being so nice, but she didn't feel like explaining. Not yet anyway. And she wouldn't even know where to begin. Besides, he was still a stranger. A very kind, very handsome stranger, but still a stranger. Thankfully, he didn't press any further.

After they dropped the film off at the drugstore, Fletcher ran into the hardware store while she picked up a few supplies at the supermarket. When they returned to the barn two hours later, the new filly was awake and hungry, and Claude was in a stall with Bonnie Blue and Samantha. Julia and Fletcher stopped at Blue's stall to see what was going on.

"Everything okay?" Fletcher asked Claude.

"Right as rain," Claude said. "Just checking her bag. Samantha's nursing a lot. Probably going to be seventeen hands."

"Better give Blue extra grain then," Fletcher said.

"Already doing it."

Fletcher glanced at Julia and shrugged, and they made their way down to the new filly's stall.

"Has he always been that grumpy?" she said. "Or just since I got here?"

Fletcher threw his hands in the air. "I don't know what's gotten into him lately. I mean, he's always been focused on work, but he's never been that temperamental toward me."

"It's my fault."

"No, it's not. I told you he doesn't like change."

"That's not what I mean."

"What then?"

"He knows something. Something he doesn't want to tell me."

"About what?"

"My parents."

"What about them?"

"I'm not sure. But I'm going to find out."

Julia spent the following week in the barn feeding the orphaned filly—she had named her Molly—every two hours. She picked up Molly's bony, wiggling body and hugged her to her chest like Fletcher had taught her—one arm around her front, the other around her tail—so Molly would think Julia could lift her no matter how big she grew. Then she lifted Molly's legs one by one to get her used to having her feet picked up to trim her hooves. In between feedings, Julia spent time getting to know the other horses and cleaning out stalls.

Whatever section of the barn she was working in, Claude stayed on the opposite end. He was civil and polite, but it was obvious he was avoiding conversation. Julia left the barn long enough to shower, change, and get something to eat, but her first priority was taking care of Molly. Everything else, the house, the questions about her dead sister, and any other secrets her parents had been hiding, would have to wait. Near the end of the second week, Molly started nibbling hay and playing with Samantha and the other foals in the turnout pen, and Julia nearly burst with pride.

The following Monday, Julia was cleaning out Molly's stall when Fletcher leaned in and held out a yellow envelope. "I stopped by the drugstore today," he said.

Without missing a beat, she yanked off her gloves, snatched the envelope out of his hand, pushed open the stall door, and handed him the pitchfork.

He jumped out of the way. "You're welcome."

She hurried along the aisle toward the door, the envelope gripped in her hand. "Sorry," she called over her shoulder. "Thanks."

Ten minutes later, she was at the kitchen table, the yellow envelope on the tablecloth in front of her. Nerves fluttered in her stomach. What if the pictures showed her father in the arms of another woman? What if they were photos of her dead sister? What if they were a record of the sin committed by her parents referenced in her father's journal? What if they were more pictures of horses and she had gotten herself worked up over nothing? No, that wouldn't make sense. If they were horse photos, the camera wouldn't have been locked in a drawer. She took a deep breath, picked up the envelope, and tore it open.

The first black and white image showed a circus tent surrounded by circus wagons and draft horses hitched to drays loaded with poles and rope. The second photo was of a circus midway, crowds of people shoulder to shoulder between a row of freak-show banners and a line of striped tents with signs that read: COTTON CANDY, SALT WATER TAFFY, AND CANDY APPLES. The women and girls were in light summer dresses, and the men and boys wore white shirts, straw hats, and newsboy caps. A water tower rose in the background and the air looked filled with dust. The grainy scene reminded Julia of old photos in her high school history books. She squinted to read the words on the big top in the distance, and could only make out: BIG SHOW and MAIN ENTRANCE.

The next picture showed the interior of an enormous three-ring big top, with tall poles and rigging and ladders leaning left and right from the ground up through the canvas roof, like the colossal masts of a giant ship. Thousands of people filled the bleachers, and a man in a white suit stood frozen mid-step in one aisle, a tray around his neck like a cigarette girl. Four elephants lay on their sides inside the center ring, and zebras, llamas, and camels circled the other two. Men in dark suits gripped long sticks beside the animals, ready to keep them in line. What looked like the ringmaster in a jacket and top hat stood near the center ring, his back to the camera, one arm in the air.

There was another shot taken inside the big

top, this one with empty bleachers and an informal gathering of performers posing here and there in separate groups. Six men in band uniforms holding clarinets, a tuba, French horns, a trombone. A group of clowns made up of midgets, children, and adults, in white faces, hobo clothes, bald caps, ruffled collars, dunce caps, police uniforms, and firemen's hats. Four pale women in grass skirts, flower leis, and bikini tops. A line of girls in long dresses holding their sequined skirts out like fairy wings.

The next photograph showed a group of freak-show performers. A man wearing nothing but shorts and socks, his wrinkled skin covered in dark scales. A fat woman in a silk dress bunched at the top and bottom like a drawstring bag. A giant man in a cowboy hat. Several midgets in tuxedos and evening gowns. A woman with no arms or legs on a pedestal. A man as thin as a skeleton. A woman covered in tattoos.

The fifth snapshot was of a pale woman in a leotard and ballet slippers standing between two elephants. One of the elephants looked like it had been painted white, and the woman resembled the albino in the article Julia had found earlier. Her curled white hair ended at her waist, and her porcelain skin looked flawless. With one hand on the elephant's trunk, she looked at the camera, her smile soft and content. If Julia was right and this woman was her father's mistress, she could understand why he was drawn to her. Seeing her in an actual photograph instead of a grainy newspaper clipping or hand-drawn circus poster proved she was a stunning, almost ethereal beauty, with huge, soulful eyes and a heart-shaped face.

The next picture was the same albino woman in a lace dress and a man in a suit and tie. Performers from the other pictures surrounded them, holding up bottles and glasses and smiling at the camera. It looked like the woman and man were kissing—she was standing on her tiptoes and they were holding hands—but the giant man behind them playfully held a straw hat in front of their faces. Julia squinted at the photo and examined the man's hands to see if they looked familiar. She couldn't tell.

Hoping the next picture showed their faces, she held her breath, expecting to see her father looking back at her. But it was another group shot featuring tight rope walkers and pretty girls on horses, children in clown and cowboy costumes, girls playing drums in skimpy sailor uniforms. The last picture showed the albino woman with a plump, white-haired baby on her lap. This time she was in normal, everyday clothes, and the baby, who looked to be about three months old, was laughing and holding a patchwork elephant in her chubby little fists.

Julia gasped.

It looked like the same calico elephant on the shelf in her old bedroom upstairs.

She sprinted up to her old room, grabbed the dusty patchwork elephant off the shelf, ran back downstairs, and set the photo and elephant side by side. The elephants were identical, right down to the button eye and braided tail made out of yarn. She tried to remember where she got hers, but nothing came to her. It had been one of her favorite toys for as far back as she could remember, and Mother always made sure it was in her bed every night. It could have been purchased at the circus, but it looked handmade.

With a hundred questions spinning in her head, she took the photos of the woman back to the den, opened the circus poster, and looked at the woman on the elephant. They had to be one and the same. She knelt on the floor and went through the newspaper clippings again, laying them out on the rug. When she found what she was looking for—the clipping featuring The Albino Medium—she read the first sentence of the article and put a hand over her mouth. The Albino Medium's name was Lilly, the same name written inside the camera case. Trying to figure out what it all meant, Julia could hardly think straight. Had her father taken her to the circus when she was a baby, introduced her to his mistress, and purchased the elephant there? Is that why she couldn't remember ever going? Or was the baby on Lilly's lap her dead sister? If the camera belonged to Lilly, how did it get in her father's desk? And why hadn't Father gotten the film developed?

CHAPTER 23
Lilly

After Cole knocked Merrick over the head with the bull hook for attacking Lilly in the cooch show dressing tent, he took Lilly into his sleeper car and laid her gently on the sofa. Shivering, she held the torn evening gown together as best she could and lay back on a pillow, the muscles in her legs and arms aching, the inside of her thighs scraped and sore. Her cheek felt hot and swollen. Cole helped her into one of his long-sleeved shirts, wrapped a blanket around her shoulders, then sat beside her on the edge of the sofa to wipe the blood from her split lip with a clean, wet handkerchief.

"I shouldn't be here," she said, her voice shaking. "When they find Merrick, Mr. Barlow and his strongmen will be searching for me and this is the first place they'll look. I should hide over at the menagerie."

Cole shook his head. "If you hide, you'll look guilty, and you didn't do anything wrong. And what happens if they find you over there all alone? You think they'll take it easy on you?"

"No, but if Merrick is dead, I don't want you tied up in this mess."

"If he's dead, I'm not going to let you take the rap for killing the son of a bitch. I'm the one who hit him over the head, and I'd do it again if I caught him trying to . . ." Fury flickered in his eyes and he looked away.

"Shhh," she said. "It's okay." She put a hand on his cheek and turned his face toward her again. "You saved me. I'm fine."

He took her hand in his and gazed at her with sorrowful eyes. "When they get here, they'll see . . . they'll see what he did to you."

Tears filled her eyes. "How did you . . . how did you know I was in trouble?"

"When I heard you ran off stage, I knew Merrick would be furious. I tried to get to you before he did, but I . . . I'm sorry, Lilly." He brushed a lock of hair from her forehead with gentle fingers. "For everything."

Just then, Hank plodded out of the bedroom, his eyes swollen with sleep, his hair sticking out in all directions. "Cole?" he said. "What's going on?"

Before Cole could answer, Mr. Barlow's strongmen barged into the sleeper car.

370

• • •

A short time later, Lilly and Cole stood inside Mr. Barlow's car, the strongmen guarding the exit. Smoking a cigar, Mr. Barlow scowled from his seat at the table while Alana sipped coffee on the couch, her bare legs crossed, one foot bouncing up and down. Chi-Chi had curled up in the crook of Lilly's arm and was nuzzling her neck. Lilly scratched the dog's ears to avoid eye contact with Mr. Barlow and Merrick, who sat at the table with an ice pack held to his head. Along with the bruises on her face and her sore muscles, she could feel every taut muscle in her neck, every burning vein beneath her skin. Until now, she hadn't realized how much she wished Merrick dead. On one hand, she was distressed to find him alive. On the other, she was relieved. At least Cole couldn't be charged with murder.

"I don't give a good goddamn!" Mr. Barlow shouted at Cole. "If you want her in the show with you and the bulls, you're paying Merrick for her!"

"Otherwise it's kidnapping," Merrick said.

Cole glared at Merrick with hateful eyes. "What are you going to do about it, you piece of shit?"

"Shut up, both of you!" Mr. Barlow said. "I'm the judge and jury in this circus and you know it."

"That's right," Merrick said, lifting his chin. He winced in pain, then repositioned the ice pack on his head. "So what's the punishment for assault?"

"What's the punishment for attempted rape?" Cole hissed.

Merrick grinned, his lips crooked and bloody. "It wasn't rape, it was training. Someone had to get her ready for her next job."

Cole lunged at him, his hands in claws, his face contorted with fury. The strongmen caught him and held him back.

Mr. Barlow slammed a fist on the table. "I told you to shut your pie hole and let me handle this, Merrick!"

Merrick grumbled under his breath.

"What's that?" Mr. Barlow said. "You got something to say? Say it out loud."

"I said she belongs to me," Merrick said. He looked at Cole. "So unless you want to be red-lighted for assault and kidnapping, and your girlfriend here wants to pay off her debt by entertaining rubes behind the baggage wagons, pay up."

"No," Cole said. "I'm not paying for my wife."

Lilly stopped petting Chi-Chi and looked up.

Mr. Barlow's face went sour. "What the devil are you talking about, boy?"

"As soon as Lilly is feeling up to it, we're getting married," Cole said. "You said yourself the bulls are your biggest draw. If you try to stop me from marrying Lilly, we'll leave, and you'll have a hard time getting JoJo to listen to anyone else. And if I go, my father goes. Ringling Brothers put an offer on the table months ago because they know he's the best bull man around, but he turned it down because he didn't want to desert your bulls and he knew I wouldn't leave without Lilly."

"The other performers won't like you marrying a sideshow gal," Alana said.

"They don't have a problem with Lilly," Cole said. "Even if they did, I wouldn't care."

Mr. Barlow dropped his shoulders and looked at Merrick. "I can't stop them from getting married. This is a business, not a dictatorship. I'd have a rebellion on my hands."

Merrick shot to his feet and threw the ice pack on the floor. The bag split open and pieces of ice scattered everywhere. Chi-Chi buried her head beneath Lilly's arm.

"She's my property!" Merrick shouted. "I paid good money for her!"

"And you've made it back tenfold," Cole said. "You haven't paid her a red cent in six years."

"Because she's been nothing but trouble from day one!" Merrick said.

"That's a lie," Cole said. "She—"

"Everybody shut up!" Mr. Barlow said. He put his hands to the sides of his head, as if his skull were about to explode. "I don't want to hear another word out of any of you." He glowered at Cole. "Go ahead, marry her and put her in the elephant show. But I'm warning you, she's messed up every act she's ever been in, so if anything goes wrong or ticket sales drop, it'll be both your heads on a platter." Then he addressed Merrick. "He's right, you got your money out of Lilly and then some. It's time to move on. She's an employee of my circus now, and I don't own any of my employees."

Lilly couldn't believe what she was hearing. Standing there in a ripped evening gown with a swollen face, melted mascara under her eyes, every muscle aching and sore, it was all she could do not to cry tears of joy.

A week later, Lilly and Cole were married some-where in the middle of Louisiana, beneath a giant willow near a slow-moving creek. Glory, Ruby, and Rosy hung candle-filled mason jars from the moss-covered branches, the roustabouts lugged benches over from the big top, and sideshow and big-top performers alike gathered around to bear witness. The circus band played the "Wedding March," and the Tallest Man on Earth—a self-ordained minister—performed the ceremony. Hester the Monkey Girl let Lilly borrow a wedding dress she'd been saving since she was fourteen—a simple white gown with a beaded bodice, cap sleeves, and a lace-tiered skirt—and Cole wore the equestrian director's best tuxedo. The guests arrived wearing everything from tuxedoes and band uniforms to evening gowns, flapper dresses, tutus, and hula skirts. After the ceremony, Lilly and Cole made their way between the cars as the train traveled to the next destination, accepting congratulations and offers of food and drink. Then everyone herded them into a private sleeper car—gleefully vacated by Mr. and Mrs. Benini, owners of the snow cone and cotton candy stands—and left them alone. At midnight, Lilly lay in Cole's strong arms, amazed that her life had turned out so well.

If Momma hadn't sold her to the circus, she never would have met Cole. And right now, in this moment, she was so content and grateful, forgiveness almost seemed possible, like a shimmering jewel waiting for her to reach out and take it. But then she remembered the pain of all she had been through and everything she had endured, and the idea of mercy left her mind. Some wounds cut too deep. What her parents had done, locking her in the attic for ten years and selling her to the circus, was unforgivable. It wasn't like Momma was here asking for forgiveness anyway. She didn't think she had done anything wrong. Lilly wondered what Momma would think if she could see her now, loved by friends, happily married, and about to work with elephants under the big top. Would she be proud of her, or did her hatred run so deep it overshadowed anything good?

For the next two weeks, Cole and Lilly worked on the elephant act inside a practice ring set up at the back end of each stop. Every now and then, Mr. Barlow checked in to see how it was going and seemed delighted with their progress. Pepper especially seemed to read Lilly's mind. Wherever Lilly walked or ran, she followed, trunk in the air, mouth open in a smile. If Lilly lifted her foot, Pepper lifted a foot. Without a spoken word of instruction, Pepper stood on her hind legs or scooped Lilly up with her trunk and gently placed her on her neck behind her ears. Cole and his father had never seen anything like it. And Lilly was happier than she ever thought possible. But sometimes she noticed Merrick watching from the corner of a nearby tent, his face tight, anger radiating from his pores like heat from a desert. It unsettled her.

Finally, the big day came for Lilly to make her first appearance under the big top. Dressed in a white leotard with a flowing chiffon skirt decorated with silver crystals and beads, her hair braided into a soft bun, she walked barefoot over to the big top, her white ballet slippers in her hands. Cole had left their car earlier to help his father bring over the elephants, and the other performers and animals were already lining up outside the connecting entrance to the arena, waiting to be summoned by the shrill note of Mr. Barlow's whistle to start the grand parade.

Her stomach twisting with nerves, Lilly searched the lineup for Cole. The other bulls were there, but Cole and Pepper were nowhere to be seen. She hurried over to ask Hank what was going on.

He started to answer, then looked over her shoulder behind her. "Here they come now."

Lilly turned, anxious and excited all at the same time. But when she saw Cole and Pepper, her heart sank. Something was wrong. Pepper was white as a sheet and Cole looked miserable. She rushed toward them.

"What happened?" she cried. "What's wrong with her?"

"Nothing's wrong with her," Cole said. "Mr. Barlow had new posters made featuring you with an albino elephant."

Lilly's mouth fell open. "But how . . ."

"Whitewash."

Pepper's eyes were red and watery, irritated from the paint.

"You poor thing," Lilly said. She gently touched Pepper's trunk. "How could he?"

Just then, Mr. Barlow strode toward them, smiling in his top hat, white jodhpurs, and red jacket. "It's a full house," he said. "Thanks to you and this beautiful elephant here. Now hurry up and get in line. Just remember, keep her away from the rubes. We don't want any trampled children, no matter how annoying they are."

Lilly wanted to say something to him about whitewashing Pepper, but starting an argument before her first show would only make her more nervous. She put on her ballet slippers and Pepper lifted her onto her back, then they started toward JoJo, Flossie, and Petunia. A team of black Percherons hitched to the lion wagons danced sideways when they passed, and the clowns stared up at them, their eyes wide in their painted faces. The other performers watched with shocked expressions. Cole climbed up on JoJo and instructed Lilly to bring Pepper up beside them. Lilly did as she was told.

"This is it," Cole said. "You ready?"

"I'm scared," Lilly said. "What if—"

"You'll do fine," he said. "You've rehearsed it a hundred times. Just stay calm and remember, Pepper will know if you're on edge."

Mr. Barlow's whistle shrieked inside the tent, the band began to play, and the grand parade began moving forward. Lilly took a deep breath and gripped Pepper's bejeweled headpiece with one sweaty hand. With Hank beside them in case anything went wrong, Lilly and Pepper and Cole and JoJo entered the big top in front of Flossie and Petunia. Having never been inside the big top during a performance, Lilly couldn't believe how many people lined the bleachers. Sunlight filtered in through the bale rings and canvas ceiling, illuminating thousands of faces and heads and hats and hands. When the audience saw Pepper and Lilly, there was a collective gasp. Everyone clapped wildly and stared with open mouths.

As the parade made its way around the hippodrome, Lilly smiled and waved at the audience, every sense on high alert, her skin tingling with a strange mix of euphoria, disbelief, and fear. The trapeze artists and tightrope walkers, the Bally girls and lion tamers, the acrobats and stilt walkers, all strutted their stuff while the jugglers juggled and the clowns skipped and danced and played tricks on one another. It seemed as if the parade itself was mirroring her thoughts and feelings, a hundred colorful pieces all jumbled up and jumping around, making it impossible to know where to look and what to think.

Every once in a while, she glanced at Cole for reassurance, and he winked at her. He had told her once that as a third-generation circus performer, for him the traditions were keener, the lights a bit brighter, the pull of the ring stronger than nearly anything else. He was never interested in anything but performing. And now she understood why. The excitement of the audience felt like electricity running through her body, and instead of the fear of ridicule, she felt nothing but adoration from the rubes. Who wouldn't want to be the girl in the sparkling costume riding the beautiful elephant?

After the parade and the rest of the show, it was time for Lilly and Pepper's act. Two clowns carried a red pedestal covered with white stars into the center ring, and Mr. Barlow hushed the crowd to make a special announcement.

"Ladies-s-s-s-s-s and gentlemen-n-n-n-n-n!" he shouted in a deep voice. "Now it's time for the act you've all been waiting for! This is the act you've seen on the posters, folks, the one I risked my life to get in a jungle in Thailand, the one you'll be telling your grandchildren about! And now I introduce to you, for their first ever performance in the Barlow Brothers' Circus, Lilly the Albino Princess from Siam and her Albino Elephant, Pepper!" He raised his arm and looked at the back end.

Lilly swallowed and glanced down at Cole standing beside Pepper. Cole winked up at her and gave her a nod. She brushed her feet against Pepper's side and urged her forward, past the trapeze artists making their way out of the hippodrome after their act. When she and Pepper entered the big top, she raised one arm and, despite her nerves, smiled at the audience. The band played "Jungle Queen" as Pepper carried her into the center ring, her trunk curled

380

in salute. Then Pepper lifted Lilly from her head and placed her on the pedestal. The crowd clapped and whistled.

Lilly raised her arms in a V and turned to address each section, a smile glued on her face. Then she jumped down from the pedestal and faced Pepper, who waited patiently. Lilly nodded once and Pepper rose on her hind legs, her front feet in the air, and trumpeted loudly. The rubes laughed and applauded.

Lilly made a downward gesture with her hand and Pepper dropped down on all fours. Then she nodded again and pointed at the ground, and Pepper leaned forward, tucked her head toward her chest, pushed her back feet into the air, and did a headstand. With a dramatic flair, Lilly smiled and extended her hand, inviting the audience to adore Pepper. They cheered and roared with applause. Then Lilly lay on the ground in front of Pepper's trunk, directly beneath her raised haunches, and little by little, the crowd grew quiet in breathless anticipation.

Ever so slowly, Pepper dropped her hind-quarters and sunk lower and lower, until her massive bulk covered everything but Lilly's head. Women gasped and covered children's eyes. Pepper waited a moment, then pushed herself into a sitting position and rested a front foot on Lilly's skull. A smattering of small shrieks burst from the audience. Pepper raised her trunk in triumph, then, ever so slowly, lifted her foot. Lilly got up, waved to the audience, and, smiling in delight, rubbed Pepper's broad belly. The whitewash felt hard and dry and for a terrifying second, Lilly thought she had rubbed it off. Still smiling, she glanced at Pepper's belly and breathed a silent sigh of relief. The whitewash was still there.

She skipped toward the other side of the ring and glanced over her shoulder as if expecting Pepper to follow. But Pepper got down on her knees and rolled over on her side as if taking a nap. The bandmaster signaled the band to play a lullaby and laughter rippled through the crowd. Lilly put her hands on her hips and went over to Pepper, frowning and pretending to be frustrated. Pepper lay still as a stone. Lilly shrugged, climbed up on Pepper and lay on her side, her hands folded beneath her head, her eyes closed. The lullaby played on and the audience grew quiet again. Then Lilly sat up and stretched, pretending to yawn. The rubes laughed. Lilly stood, shook her head, made her way along Pepper's side, jumped down from her neck, and started walking away.

Pepper sat up and caught Lilly around the waist with her trunk. Lilly opened her mouth in mock surprise. People chuckled nervously, unsure if it was part of the act. Pepper got to her feet, still holding on to Lilly, and pulled her toward her. Lilly put her hands over her mouth and pretended to be afraid. The band started a fast number, then moved into a waltz. Pepper let go and Lilly strolled away, smiling and dancing around the perimeter of the ring, moving her arms in time with the music. Pepper followed, her head and trunk swaying back and forth. The audience laughed and clapped.

Lilly danced around the ring one more time, then led Pepper over to the pedestal and climbed on while Pepper lowered her massive bulk to the ground. Lilly stepped onto the back of Pepper's neck and remained standing, her knees slightly bent, her arms out for balance. Pepper pushed herself up and promenaded around the ring, her trunk held high while Lilly smiled and blew kisses to the audience. Out of the corner of her eye, she caught sight of Cole watching from the back end, a wide grin plastered on his face. After several times around the ring, Pepper took Lilly back to the pedestal and waited for her to slide off.

Everyone clapped and started to stand, but Lilly put up a finger to let them know there was more. A drum roll started, and she raised her arms and nodded once. Pepper stood on her hind legs again and Lilly lowered her arms. Pepper bent forward, wrapped her mouth around Lilly's head, and lifted her from the pedestal. The crowd gasped and a woman screamed. Lilly extended her arms, palms up to let everyone know it was part of the act, and the rubes went wild.

With Lilly still hanging from her mouth, Pepper climbed onto the pedestal and stood with her back arched, all four feet crowded together. She curved her trunk around Lilly like a swing and released her from her mouth. Lilly hooked an arm around Pepper's trunk, smiled, and pointed her toes. Pepper raised her trunk, holding Lilly aloft, and stood on her hind legs. The audience exploded with delighted cries.

Then Pepper deposited Lilly on her head, climbed down from the pedestal, and departed the big top to the cheers of a standing ovation.

CHAPTER 24

Julia

After seeing the newly developed pictures from the camera in her father's desk drawer, Julia couldn't sleep. The wind had come up and the house shutters clattered against the sills. The tree branches rattled against the windows, and she swore she heard rats in the house again, scurrying through walls and thumping along ceilings. The unsettling noises seemed to echo the thoughts in her mind, banging and leaping and ricocheting inside her skull.

Why did her father have Lilly's things in his

desk? Who was the baby in the picture? Her, or her dead sister? It was hard to tell if the baby looked as much like Mother as she did, but maybe her sister was a result of the affair, and therefore her half sister? Was it possible her father's business trips to buy and sell horses were a cover-up for meeting Lilly and his other daughter? Is that why her parents were so unhappy? And what had they done that needed forgiveness? More importantly, how was she ever going to put all the pieces together and learn the truth? When she finally fell asleep after three a.m., her dreams were filled with clowns and elephants and sideshow freaks.

The next day, a heavy rain lashed the trees and buildings, turning the estate grounds into a muddy mess. Julia pulled a wool toque over her head and made her way over to the barn to ask Claude if he knew how to get into the attic. Something had to be done about the rats before they multiplied, and the attic seemed like the logical place to start. By the time she made it to the barn office, her pants and hair were soaked and she wished she'd waited until the rain let up. She found Claude bent over in a stall, cleaning out a horse's hoof.

"Do you know how to get into the attic?" she said. "I keep hearing rats and I need to figure out how they're getting in and where they're nesting."

"Nope," he said. "Never been up there."

"Well, I can't find a staircase or a trapdoor anywhere," she said. "Don't you think that's odd?"

Claude shrugged and kept working.

"Could you come over to the house and help me look? Maybe set some traps?"

"Busy right now."

"I know. Just come over when you're finished."

He straightened and bent over again to pick up the horse's other front foot. "Can't today. I've got to clean up the broken branches in the yard before it storms again."

"It's pouring out."

"Need to catch up on paperwork then."

Julia's shoulders dropped and she sighed. She had tried to be pleasant, but her patience was wearing thin. "Are you upset with me for some reason? Other than making you bring the nurse mare's foal back and taking in the orphan? I know that's not how you've been doing things around here, but I—"

"Nope."

"Then why won't you talk to me? Why won't you look me in the eye? Why is helping me find a way into the attic too much to ask?"

He dropped the horse's leg, straightened, and regarded her, his face void of emotion. "I'm just trying to do my job, Miss Blackwood."

"Well, it's seems like you're annoyed with me, or avoiding me, or . . . I don't know." She threw her hands in the air. "Are you upset because I'm here? I know you don't like change and you think I'm too young to be your boss, and I'll admit I've got a lot to learn but—"

He shook his head, his mouth in a hard, thin line.

"What is it then?" she said. "You seemed fine when I first arrived. But after that your attitude changed. Did I say something wrong?"

"Nope." He stared at her, unyielding, resolute.

She couldn't shake the feeling he was hiding something. Maybe he knew about her father's affair, or whatever it was that her parents had done to her sister. Maybe he kept her at a distance because he didn't want her to ask questions. Why else would he avoid talking to her? Then another thought hit her and she drew in a sharp breath. *Oh dear God, maybe he and Mother were having an affair.*

"Did you think my mother was going to leave the farm to you?" The words came out before she could stop them.

He clenched his jaw, his temples throbbing in and out. "I'll pretend I didn't hear that."

"I'm sorry. I shouldn't have said it. But I don't know what else to do. I don't know how to prove to you that I'm a good person. Maybe I should give up." She turned and started to walk away. "Never mind, I'll ask Fletcher for help."

"Miss Blackwood?" Claude called out.

Julia turned around, hoping he had changed his mind. "Yes?"

"The rat poison is on the top shelf in the tack room."

She deflated. "Okay," she said. "Thanks." She thought about saying she needed to find out where the rats were before she figured out how to get rid of them, but changed her mind. There was no point in irritating him further. She left the barn and went back to the house, gusts of rain hitting her face like a thousand tiny bullets. Maybe Claude's disregard for her was simpler than what she imagined. Maybe after working for her parents for twenty-seven years, he had become just like them. Whatever the case, they needed to learn how to get along before things got any worse.

She hung her wet coat up in the mudroom, changed into dry clothes, found a flashlight in a kitchen drawer, and went up to the third floor again, determined to find a way into the attic. Perhaps she missed the attic door the first time around. After all, there were so many rooms and doors and closets. This time she searched every bathroom and bedroom, felt along walls and thumped the insides of closets, examined every ceiling for pull-down trapdoors. Again, she found nothing.

In the last bedroom at the end of the main hall, she entered the odd little extra room and pulled the string on the bare bulb. She set the flashlight on the claw-foot table and pushed aside the hatboxes to get closer to the walls. Then she stopped, suddenly uneasy. The headless dressmaker's dummy seemed to be watching, judging her for searching the house. It almost felt like Mother was scrutinizing her from the great beyond. Before proceeding any further, she dragged the dressmaker's dummy out of the little room and draped a sheet over it. Then she went back in and ran her fingers along the wainscoting to see if she had missed the outline of a short door, even though it seemed like an odd place for an attic access in a home as large as Blackwood Manor. Because judging by the house's footprint, the attic had to be enormous.

Again she was reminded that she had no idea about the manor's history, who had built it or how old it was. Her parents never talked about the past, so it should have come as no surprise that she knew nothing about their house. And now, knowing her parents had secrets to hide, it made sense. Then she had another thought. Maybe she couldn't find the way into the attic because someone knew she'd discover more than rats. After all, attics were like personal history museums, where people stored remnants of bygone days. And sometimes the answers to family secrets.

More determined than ever, she stood on her

tiptoes and felt along the tops of the walls. The corners and ceiling edges felt solid and thick. She pressed her hand along the back wall, moving toward the center where the tapestry hung over the claw-foot table.

And then she saw it.

The tiniest of movements.

The tapestry stirred.

She put a hand on the edge of the tapestry. It felt cold, as if cooled by an icy breath.

She grabbed the claw-foot table and dragged it away from the wall. It was heavier than she thought, but a sudden rush of adrenaline made it seem effortless. Her flashlight clattered to the floor, but she ignored it and reached up to take the tapestry rod down, fighting the urge to rip it off the wall. To her surprise, the rod was nailed to the wood instead of resting on brackets. Then she noticed a cord in the space between the rod and the top of the tapestry, dangling next to one of the hanging tabs. It was the same dark red as the wallpaper, and if she hadn't been trying to take down the rod, she never would have seen it. She lifted the bottom of the tapestry, found the tasseled end of the cord, and pulled. The tapestry rolled up like a window blind.

Julia gasped and stepped back.

There was a door in the wall.

CHAPTER 25
Lilly

Four months after her first appearance with Pepper under the big top, Lilly stood next to Cole inside Mr. Barlow's car, a protective hand over her lower abdomen. Merrick sat on a stool near the kitchen counter, staring at her and spitting tobacco juice in the sink.

"What do you mean she can't work?" Mr. Barlow bellowed. "We're bringing in the biggest takes we've had in years. She can't quit now!" He slammed his hand on the table, rattling the tumblers and nearly knocking over a bottle of bourbon.

"She's not quitting," Cole said. "She's just—"

"We're going into the slow season," Lilly interrupted. "I'll be ready to work again next summer."

"I don't give a good goddamn what season we're in," Mr. Barlow said. "We'll lose revenue without her and that elephant!"

"I refuse to put my wife and unborn child in danger," Cole said. "If something happens to her, you'll lose the act for good."

"Any possibility the baby might be albino?" Merrick said.

Cole and Lilly ignored him.

Mr. Barlow slumped in his chair, his face dark as thunder. "Son of a bitch. I knew it was too good to be true." He addressed Cole. "Can you take her place? We could put you in a wig and white greasepaint."

Cole shook his head. "Won't work. Pepper does things for Lilly she won't do for me."

"If you're open to suggestions, I have an idea," Lilly said. "Why don't you tell everyone The Albino Elephant is performing in Europe? Then, come spring, people will flock back to see what they missed."

Mr. Barlow took a long swig of bourbon, put his glass down hard on the table, and glared at her. "Jesus Christ. One way or another you manage to screw up every act you've ever been in. I'm starting to wonder if I should keep you on at all."

"If she goes, I go," Cole said. "And my father too."

"I'm not paying her until she's back to work," Mr. Barlow said.

"You just started paying me two months ago," Lilly said. "And not much, I might add, considering what the crowds have been."

"Now hold on, young lady," Mr. Barlow said. "You've been nothing but trouble since the day you arrived, and I'm not paying you until you're back on that bull."

"Yeah," Merrick said. "We can't have an albino

taking tickets and selling cotton candy. It'll scare the kiddies." Amused with himself, he grinned, a wad of chewing tobacco in one cheek.

"Shut up, Merrick," Cole said. "This doesn't concern you."

Merrick sneered at him. "We could put her back in the sideshow," he said. "Tell everyone she's giving birth to an alien."

"Absolutely not," Lilly said.

"She can help me and my father take care of the bulls," Cole said. "That's worth something at least."

"I'm still not paying her," Mr. Barlow said.

"Fine," Lilly said. "But if Pepper and I are still the main draw when I come back, I want benefits."

Mr. Barlow's eyebrows shot up and one edge of his mustache quivered. Lilly thought he was going to scream or get up and slap her. Then he exploded, laughing so hard his face and neck turned red. "Oh, Lilly," he said. "Oh dear. That's good. You're here telling me you can't work for a while, at the same time you're asking for the entire profits from one or more performances if you're the star?" He clutched his midriff, as if trying to contain himself. "That's priceless." Merrick laughed with him. Mr. Barlow leaned back in his chair and chuckled, then wiped his eyes. "I have to say, I haven't heard anything quite that funny in a while."

"It's only fair that part of my pay should depend on my drawing power," Lilly said.

"That's the way Ringling Brothers and Barnum and Bailey do it," Cole said.

With that, Mr. Barlow shot to his feet and stormed toward them, his eyes on fire. "You're lucky I don't get rid of the both of you right now, let alone pay you more," he yelled. "Do you have any idea how many circuses went out of business last year? No, you don't. And I don't want to talk to either of you until Lilly is ready to perform again. That's just what we need around here, another mouth to feed and my biggest draw off the bill!" He pointed at the exit. "Now get the hell out of my car!"

CHAPTER 26

Julia

Julia stood, stunned, staring at the hidden door inside the small room on the third floor of Blackwood Manor. She was too surprised to do anything. The door was smaller than normal, less than five feet tall, and the wallpaper on the top half along with the wainscoting on the bottom matched the rest of the wall perfectly. Even the hasp and padlock had been painted red to blend in. Why had someone gone to such great lengths to hide the door? Was it the entrance to the attic, or something else?

Then she reached for the padlock and her heart dropped. Where was the key?

She tried the keys on Mother's key ring. None worked. She yanked on the padlock, hoping it was broken or unlocked. It didn't budge. She pushed on the door with both hands to test its strength. It felt sound. She examined the back of the table, hoping to find the key taped there. No luck. She felt inside the table's velvet-lined drawer. Still no luck. Discouraged, she stood in the middle of the room and looked around. Maybe there was a loose piece of wainscoting or a hidden compartment somewhere. Then she glanced at the tapestry again, rolled up like a rug below the rod.

The key hung from a hook attached to the hanging rod, hidden behind one of the tapestry tabs.

"You've got to be kidding," she said to herself.

She took the key from the hook and tried it in the padlock. It fit, turned, and unlocked the clasp. With her heart hammering in her chest, she pulled the padlock from the hasp and opened the door. A gust of stale air brushed over her face, as if the house were exhaling after decades of holding its breath.

To her surprise, the opening behind the door was even smaller than the door itself, like an entrance made for children. The upper edge hung a foot lower than the top of the doorframe, and the bottom edge rose a foot from the floor. In stark contrast to the shiny wallpaper and glossy wainscoting on the outside of the door, rotted, wormy wood surrounded the opening on three sides, and the mortar below the warped threshold had cracked and fallen away, revealing pitted craters of filthy plaster. Black streaks of tar ran down the plaster like melted wax. The opening reminded Julia of abandoned houses, or hiding places for Jews in black and white WWII photos. She shivered. Had the hidden door been there the entire time she was growing up? Maybe there really was someone living behind the walls.

Weak light from the outer room fell across the grimy landing of the opening and what looked like a bottom step. She picked up the flashlight, turned it on, and shone it into the door. Her light revealed a cramped, narrow stairwell with worn wooden steps and a tangle of electrical wires running along the edge of the slanted ceiling like a black snake. Chunks of yellowed wallpaper hung from the stairwell like flaps of dried skin, revealing broken patches of lathe and plaster. It looked like a tight fit, and the space above the steps remained hidden in darkness.

She stood transfixed, her heart kicking in her

chest. Maybe she should wait and ask Fletcher to go up with her. It was going to be dark soon, and tomorrow, during daylight, they could go up together. Because what if she found the rats? What if one of the steps gave way and she broke her leg? What if one of the attic floorboards snapped around her ankle like a bear trap? No one would find her for days.

Then she remembered telling Claude about the rats in the attic. If she went missing, he would know where to look. Besides, she couldn't wait until tomorrow. She had to know what was behind the hidden door. *Curiosity killed the cat,* she thought, and stepped into the dank opening.

She made her way up the steep stairs one step at a time, testing each step as she went, cobwebs clinging to her arms and face. The air was close and musty, and plaster and dried paint crunched beneath her shoes. Up she went, moving slowly and shining the flashlight on every worn rung to check for rotted or cracked wood. Halfway to the top, she felt dizzy and stopped. She put a hand on the wall to steady herself, then realized she was holding her breath. She inhaled deeply a few times, then moved up the staircase again. Near the top, she pointed her flashlight toward the ceiling. The circle of light revealed wood planks and rough-hewn beams soaring above her like the upside-down bowels of an old ship.

The attic.

Finally, she reached the top step and cast the flashlight beam around the attic, which was even bigger than she'd imagined. And on that rainy day, it was dark up there, the far reaches of the vast space hanging in shadows. The dormer windows were few and far between and crusted up with watermarks and mold. It was so quiet she could hear the creak and sway of the house, and the rain filtering through the leaf-choked gutters. Except for narrow walkways snaking through cobweb- and dust-covered piles of normal attic things—old trunks and dressers, mirrors and wardrobes, empty picture frames and faded portraits, china sets and books, boxes and crates and another headless dummy—every inch of space was filled.

No wonder there were rats up here. It was a rodent paradise. But how would she ever find out where they were getting in, let alone go through all of this stuff for clues about her dead sister and whatever sins her parents had been hiding?

She sighed and started through a narrow walkway, testing the strength of the floor as she went. It squeaked and groaned, but seemed sound. Faded portraits and landscapes hung from rusty wires on the opposite wall at the far end of the attic, their frames skewed this way and that. She made her way toward them.

When she reached the paintings, she stopped in

her tracks. There was another door in the wall, a foot up from the floor.

"What in the world?" she said to herself.

This time, though, she didn't have to search for a key. It hung from a hook next to the door-frame. She unlocked the door, turned the knob, and the door creaked on its hinges and swung inward. She took a deep breath and stepped over the high threshold into another part of the attic. To her surprise, it was bare, except for an empty bookcase and two cane-back chairs.

And then she saw a third door.

CHAPTER 27
Lilly

Outside Lilly and Cole's sleeper car, the sun was blazing and the air was heavy. The land was flat as far as the eye could see, and the lot was covered in dry grass the color of hay. The roustabouts were raising the tent city, and the clatter of chutes, shouting, cursing, and the thunder of four-horse hitches filled the air. They were in Broken Arrow, Oklahoma, and if Lilly's estimates were right, it had been nearly two years since she and Pepper made their first appearance under the big top on these very grounds.

After her daughter, Phoebe Lillian Holt, was born, it didn't take long for word to travel that the Albino Queen & Her Elephant were back from Europe, and the crowds entering the big top doubled. Mr. Barlow was happy, and so was everyone else. The money coming in was better than ever, and that made up for everything. Four to five nights a week they performed at a new spot, and for the first time ever, Lilly was getting paid on a regular basis. She and Cole owned their own sleeper car, and Lilly finally convinced Glory to leave Merrick for good, retire from the freak show, and take care of Phoebe when Lilly and Cole were working.

Now, Lilly sat in the rectangle of sunlight coming in through the open window of the sleeper car and looked over at her twelve-month-old daughter napping in her cushioned crib.

In her deepest fears during pregnancy, Lilly worried her baby would be born with some kind of abnormality, either albinism or something else. She'd been lucky enough to fall in love and get married, but would she be fortunate enough to have a normal, healthy child too? Every day while waiting for the baby to arrive, she became more and more certain she'd only be allowed one of those things, not both. She never thought she'd be this happy, let alone content with this strange circus life that had been forced on her. Was it possible to be doubly blessed? Then

Phoebe was born with delicate blond curls covering her little head, perfectly normal pink baby skin, and cobalt blue eyes, like Cole's, shining like opals above her chubby cheeks. It felt like a miracle, almost too good to be true, and sometimes Lilly woke up in the middle of the night, panicked and terrified none of it was real.

After Phoebe was born, Cole bought a camera in a red case, and the walls of their car were filled with photos—Phoebe sitting on Pepper with Lilly, Phoebe having her face painted by clowns, Phoebe perched on Brutus the Texas Giant's shoulders, Phoebe sunbathing on a blanket with Cole. On her first birthday, Lilly made Phoebe a stuffed elephant out of yellow and pink calico print, with button eyes and blue yarn for a tail. It was Phoebe's favorite toy, and now, it lay beside her in her crib.

Lilly watched her daughter sleep, wishing she could skip this afternoon's performance. Today was going to be even hotter than yesterday, and she wanted to let Phoebe play in a cool bath. She didn't want to miss a second of her daughter's life, but knew she didn't have a choice. When Glory showed up to babysit in a few minutes, Lilly would go to the dressing tent and get ready to perform. After all, the show must go on.

Later that afternoon, while the animals and performers lined up behind the big top before the grand parade, the air seemed saturated with an eerie yellowish-green glow. The distant clouds grew dark and the wind picked up. The flags fluttered, the tents rocked and rolled, and the ropes stretched left and right. The monkeys whined and the hyenas howled, and the normally lethargic cats snarled and growled and paced back and forth inside their dens. The horses whinnied and danced restlessly in their hitches while the drivers held tight to their reins and tried talking them down. The handlers did their best to keep the animals under control, but it didn't help. Even Pepper couldn't stand still. Lilly told her to calm down but had to keep repositioning herself on her back every time she moved. Cole got down from JoJo, took him out of the lineup, and led him in circles to distract him. Hank tried to calm Flossie and Petunia by rubbing their legs and scratching their trunks. It was normal for the animals to get restless during bad weather, but Lilly had never seen them act like this.

"What do you think has them riled up?" she asked Hank.

"They sense a storm coming," he said. "Hearing them snarl and whine and bellow makes you feel kind of funny in the pit of the stomach, don't it?"

She nodded. "You mean a thunderstorm?"

He scanned the horizon. "At least that. But it smells like tornado weather to me."

Lilly drew in a sharp breath. "Do you really think it'll get that bad?"

"More than likely. When I first started out with a show in Hutchinson, Kansas, a twister just missed us. I won't ever forget the way that air smelled. We didn't have much warning, but we all saw the black-green cloud with its trailing funnel comin' at us."

"What did you do?"

"The roustabouts got busy grouping the loose equipment and lashing everything together with ropes and chains. We covered the animal wagons and dropped all canvas flat to the ground, striking all poles. A few seconds later, the twister was upon us, cuttin' a swath right through the center of the lot. We were lucky, though, because nobody got hurt and we didn't lose anything."

Lilly gripped Pepper's headpiece tighter. "Maybe I should go back to the car and check on Phoebe," she said.

"She'll be all right," he said. "If there's a storm, she's safer on the train than we are out here."

Lilly pressed her lips together and looked at the sky, worry knotting her gut.

Mr. Barlow appeared and walked up and down the line, shouting orders, his face dark and brooding. One of the lions reached through his cage and swatted at him with a clawed mitt. Mr. Barlow turned, outraged, and dragged his riding crop along the bars. The lion snarled and reached for him again. Mr. Barlow cussed and gave the cage another whack, then marched into the big top.

Cole brought JoJo back into line and climbed on.

"Your father thinks there might be a tornado," Lilly said to him.

Concern lined Cole's face, but before he could respond, Mr. Barlow's whistle sounded inside the tent and the parade began. While the band played the grand march, the big top leaned and twisted, the great canvas ceiling and walls billowing up and down and side to side like a giant handkerchief. The majority of the rubes were oblivious, applauding and spellbound by the clowns and zebras and elephants circling the hippodrome. But some looked up and frowned.

When Pepper and Lilly reached the halfway point on the other side of the hippodrome, a smattering of heavy raindrops drummed on the tent ceiling. At first, the sound was barely audible above the music, but then it began pouring. Sheets of rain beat on the canvas like a hundred galloping hooves. The light outside the entrance turned leaden and the canvas ceiling grew dark. Lilly glanced at Cole, struggling to push down the panic rising in her chest. He nodded once as if to tell her everything was okay, and she forced herself to keep smiling and waving. Then she saw something move near the bale rings and her heart stopped.

Three birds had flown into the tent and now they circled the center poles, frantically darting back and forth, searching for a way out. A bird in the big top meant death for a performer. And there were three of them. Lilly's smile faltered and she checked to see if anyone else had noticed. One of the female trapeze artists was staring up at the dreaded flying omens, along with the lion tamer and three tightrope walkers, all with ashen faces.

Nerves prickled along Lilly's skin and it was all she could do to keep her arm in the air. She glanced at Cole again and said his name. He didn't hear her.

Just then, lightning flashed outside the main entrance and lit up the canvas roof. A deafening clap of thunder startled the horses, then rolled over and over on top of itself until it felt like the entire earth was shaking. Lightning flickered again and again and again, and the musicians lost their tempo. Near the pit, Mr. Barlow motioned frantically for the band to keep playing, then raised his arm and moved his hand in small circles to signal the performers and animals to keep moving. The audience looked at one another with worried faces.

After a long, tense minute, lightning flashed again, this time not as brightly, and the following thunder sounded farther away. The band picked up the tempo and a collective feeling of relief seemed to fill the tent. The clowns waved to the kiddies, the acrobats tumbled and pranced in the parade, and the candy butchers sold peanuts and cotton candy up and down the bleachers. Lilly took a deep breath and relaxed a little. It seemed like the storm was moving away.

Then a great gust of wind hit the big top and the entire tent leaned to one side like a ship rolling on rough seas. Lilly grabbed Pepper's headpiece with both hands and Cole's face went dark. Women shrieked and gaped up at the ceiling with open mouths. Children started to cry and several of the horses reared, their nostrils flaring, their eyes spinning with terror. The wagon drivers yanked back on the horses' reins, and the performers and clowns slowed and stopped. Section by section the parade came to a lurching halt. Two zebras pulled away from their handlers and ran across the center ring toward the exit, with several clowns giving chase. The Bally girls ducked for cover beneath the animal wagons, ignoring the drivers' warnings that it wasn't safe.

Every instinct screamed at Lilly to get out of there, but there was nowhere to run. She and Cole and the elephants were stopped in the middle of the tent, sandwiched between the big cat wagons and the camels, halfway between any possible exits. The only possible escape would involve plowing through the center rings and yelling at everyone to get out of the way. In what seemed like slow motion, the big top shifted and fell back into place, and for a second, she loosened her grip on Pepper's headpiece. They were going to be all right. Then a sidewall suddenly lifted from the ground and the ceiling began folding in on itself, the canvas tugging and creasing and ripping. The trapeze artists' ladders shuddered and twisted. Poles pulled out of the dirt, and ropes vibrated and snapped.

"Tornado!" a man yelled.

The crowd jumped to their feet and fought to get down from the bleachers in one giant swell, dropping popcorn boxes and cotton candy, yelling and pushing and shoving one another out of the way. Parents grabbed children's hands and glanced up at the ceiling with panic-filled eyes, trying to watch their step at the same time. An old woman fell halfway down and her husband helped her up, struggling to keep his balance while being crowded from behind. Two boys jumped from the sides of the bleachers and dropped to the ground below. Several others followed suit. One woman tumbled and fell off the side, lay there for a moment, then got up and limped as fast as she could toward the exit.

Mr. Barlow ran into the center ring, red-faced and yelling, arms flapping as he ordered everyone to get the animals and wagons out of the tent. Hank and the other handlers rushed in with hooks and lead lines, and the wagon drivers turned the horses toward the back exit. The roustabouts scurried around gathering all movable equipment and gear, trying to lash everything together with ropes and chains.

"Get out of here!" Cole shouted at Lilly. "I'll be right behind you!"

He didn't need to tell her twice. She steered Pepper around a wagon toward the back exit, the coppery tang of fear in her throat. The rest of the performers headed that way too, and the escape route became an obstacle course full of camels and horses and giraffes and workers and clowns and acrobats and women in tutus.

Lilly and Pepper started and stopped what seemed like a hundred times, trying not to step on anyone. Then the back wall of the tent collapsed, and poles and ropes and great swathes of canvas fell sideways, covering the musicians and part of the bleachers still filled with panicked circusgoers. The band screeched to a halt with a clang of a cymbal and a squawk of a clarinet. The center poles of the big top leaned left and right, and the attached ropes stretched and pulled and snapped. Loud, vibrating pings and ripping sounds filled the air as the ceiling creaked and shifted above their heads, and several of the bale rings tore from the canvas.

Terror flooded the tent like a living, breathing thing.

With the back access damaged and the ceiling falling in, the only way out was through the main entrance. Everyone stampeded toward it. The tent exploded with screams and shouts, the sounds of bodies shoving past bodies, and people running off bleachers and stands. Broken ropes whipped in the air like frenzied snakes, and wooden poles and ladders splintered and crashed. Lilly turned Pepper around and urged her toward the entrance, then glanced over her shoulder to make sure Cole and the other elephants were following. They were farther back, trying to make their way through the chaotic throng of animals and people. When Lilly faced forward again, Mr. Barlow was blocking her way, a bull hook in his hands. Pepper stopped in her tracks and trumpeted loudly.

"What are you doing?" Lilly yelled. "Get out of the way!"

"You can't take her out there!" Mr. Barlow shouted.

"Are you out of your mind? We've got to get out of here!" Lilly urged Pepper forward, but Mr. Barlow refused let her pass, barring her way at every turn. Pepper trumpeted and reared, but not enough to make Lilly fall off.

Mr. Barlow raised the bull hook, his face threatening. "She's not leaving this tent!"

Terror and confusion twisted in Lilly's chest. Why was Mr. Barlow trying to stop Pepper from getting to safety? It didn't make sense. Pepper was his biggest draw and worth a lot of money. All around them, handlers and animals and rubes and performers stampeded out of the tent, a blur of human limbs, furry heads, tails, and hoofed feet. Llamas and horses and poodles and people zigzagged and bolted and jumped over one another, screaming and galloping and trying to escape. Women fell and shrieked. Children stumbled and vanished and parents yanked them up to carry them, flailing and crying, out of the big top.

If Lilly had to force Pepper to trample Mr. Barlow into the ground to escape, she was getting them out of there alive. She urged Pepper forward, but Pepper refused to run him over. Mr. Barlow raised the bull hook and struck Pepper in the chest, grunting with the effort. Pepper cried out in pain and Lilly shrieked in anger. She swung her leg over Pepper's head and put her feet together, ready to slide down Pepper's side and wrestle the bull hook away from Mr. Barlow. But before she could, Cole stopped JoJo beside them and told her to stay put. He jumped down from JoJo and grabbed the bull hook with both hands, his face contorted with fury. Mr. Barlow held on and they grappled with it above their heads, grimacing and pushing each other back and forth.

"Go on!" Cole shouted at Lilly "Take JoJo and get out of here!"

Lilly urged Pepper toward the exit, trying not to trample anyone, and yelled for JoJo to come too. When she glanced over her shoulder, she saw Cole yank the bull hook from Mr. Barlow's grip and throw it over the bleachers. But JoJo refused to leave Cole, no matter how many terrified animals and panicked rubes bumped into him, or how many times Lilly called his name. When she neared the exit, she looked back one more time. A draft horse knocked Mr. Barlow off his feet and Cole climbed back on JoJo. She watched for as long as she could, then leaned forward and flattened her body close to Pepper's head so the low doorframe wouldn't knock her off. At last, they were out of the big top.

Praying Phoebe was safe in the train and Cole and the rest of the elephants were behind her, she steered Pepper toward the other side of the midway. Wind and rain shrieked all around, beating against her skin like bullets, and the sounds of ripping canvas, snapping wood, and screaming people filled the air. She squinted against the rain and looked back at the big top just as the colossal tent lifted off the ground, the canvas twisting and turning like rags inside a washer. The last of the rubes scurried out of the rising entrance and ran left and right, their hands on their heads, their faces knotted with terror.

Ropes and stakes pulled out of the dirt and the wind tore the roof apart seam by seam, leaving the poles and rigging suspended in the air like a giant black web. The sidewalls were torn to shreds; then the entire tent rose in the air and suddenly vanished, as if plucked from the earth by a giant hand.

Several hundred yards away, a black, rotating funnel roared toward them—wood and trees and dirt swirling around it like twigs and grass being sucked into a whirlpool. Horror filled Lilly's mind, but she couldn't pull her eyes away. She felt the rumbling growl of the approaching twister in her stomach, and the wet, green musky smell of dirt and vegetation filled her nostrils. *This is it,* she thought. *I knew happiness was too good to last. I'm sorry, Phoebe. I hope you never forget how much I love you.* Then, as suddenly as it appeared, the funnel lifted off the earth and got smaller and smaller and higher and higher, hanging from the sky like an elephant's trunk before disappearing into a churning black cloud. When it was over, Lilly let out her breath and fell forward on Pepper, limp with relief.

Cole and JoJo stopped beside her. "Are you all right?"

She pushed herself up and nodded, too shaken to speak.

Within minutes, the wind died down and a yellow shaft of sunlight peeked over the horizon, as if God had flicked on a giant switch. Everyone stopped running and looked around with dazed, exhausted expressions, surveying the damage or searching for loved ones in the crowd. Some stood rooted to one spot, mumbling and staring, rivulets of blood running in their hair or down their arms and legs, their clothes ripped and torn. Shoeless children wandered aimlessly, crying and calling for their parents.

Debris littered the lot—popcorn boxes and ripped flags, soaked streamers and torn posters, soggy stuffed animals and overturned ticket booths, wet straw, boards, and rope. The freak-show banners had been torn from their moorings and now hung from their corners, sagging like giant tablecloths across puddles of mud. Dolly the World's Most Beautiful Fat Woman, Mabel the Four-Legged Woman, and Penelope the Singing Midget came out of the freak-show tent, eyes wide, mouths gaping. Behind the big-top area, the back lot had been stripped clean. The menagerie tent was gone, along with several animal cages and wagons. The ground was strewn with straw and shovels and rope and wood and bent metal.

The rubes and performers and handlers and roustabouts viewed the wreckage in shocked silence, amazed and stunned and relieved to be alive. Mr. Barlow stormed through the middle of it all and made his way toward Lilly and

413

Pepper, limping and wet, one sleeve torn from his red jacket. He gestured furiously, waving her away and yelling at her to get Pepper out of there. Lilly didn't understand why he was so angry. She had saved Pepper's life. Then, for the first time since escaping the big top, she looked down at the bull. At first, she couldn't comprehend what she was seeing. Then she realized why Mr. Barlow didn't want Pepper to leave the big top, and renewed dread filled her chest.

Wet paint ran off Pepper's head and back, trickling down her sides in white streams, her gray skin showing through in mottled blotches.

"Let's go," Lilly said to Pepper and Cole. "We have to get out of here."

But before they could turn and leave, a boy pointed at Pepper and shouted, "The Albino Elephant is fake!"

Several other rubes noticed and stared, slack-jawed.

"The damn thing is covered in paint!" another voice called out.

Mr. Barlow turned to face the rubes and held up his hands. "Hold on now," he said. "I can assure you The Albino Elephant is real. The white paint only enhanced the natural paleness of her skin."

Several men marched toward him, their hands in fists, their faces contorted in anger.

Lilly turned Pepper away and steered her toward

the train, trying to remind herself that she and Cole had just missed being killed by a tornado, and how lucky they were to be able to go home to their daughter. Right now that was all that mattered. But another storm was brewing in the distance and, this time, she didn't know if she'd be safe.

It took a full day to clean up after the tornado ripped the Barlow Brothers' big top from the earth, during which time the local police had to keep the rubes off the lot. Word had spread like wildfire that The Albino Elephant was fake and the locals wanted their money back. And after so many had nearly lost their lives during the tornado, they weren't above using their fists to get it. It took another half day for Mr. Barlow and Merrick to convince the sheriff that The Barlow Brothers' Circus wouldn't be back.

In the meantime, rumors spread among the performers, freaks, trainers, and roustabouts that The Barlow Brothers' Circus was finished. Between the exposure of the fake albino elephant and the loss of the big top and menagerie tent, there was no way Mr. Barlow could recoup and reopen. Not this season anyway. They were all out, all over. The blowdown had done them in.

When the circus train finally pulled out of town the next day, it traveled all night and half the day without stopping. No one knew where it was headed, and no one dared ask. If The Barlow

Brothers' Circus showed up at the previously scheduled stops without The Albino Princess and The Albino Elephant featured on the advance posters put up by the twenty-four-hour man, it would be a disaster.

When the train finally stopped, word spread throughout the cars that they were at a new spot on a rail lot outside of Nashville, Tennessee. Supposedly, Mr. Barlow had arranged for a new big top to be set up, and when the performers and workers looked out the train windows, they were relieved and surprised to see the flying squadron there. The cookhouse was up, the canvas man was laying out the lot, and hundreds of men were lugging rigging and pounding in stakes. The sideshow and dressing tents had been erected too, but patches of long grass and two rusty barrels occupied the center of the lot, where the big top should have been spread out, waiting to be raised.

After everyone was done with breakfast and the cookhouse had closed until lunch, the performers went back to the train to wait and see what happened next. A short time later, another train rolled in on a sideline between them and the train depot. When Lilly and Cole saw the other train pulling in next to their car, they got up from playing on the floor with Phoebe and looked out the window. It was the Rowe & Company Circus. They glanced at each other with alarm. Two circuses showing up on the same lot could only mean trouble.

"What do you think is going on?" Lilly said.

"I hate to say it," Cole said. "But they might be here to pick through our pieces."

"What does that mean?"

"Either we're shutting down after this spot and Mr. Barlow is selling off what he can to save himself, or—"

A knock on the door interrupted Cole mid-sentence. He left the window and went over to answer it. Hank entered, his face grim.

"Mr. Barlow wants the elephants off the train," he said.

"Why?" Cole said.

"He has a buyer."

A hard knot twisted in Lilly's chest. *No. Not the elephants.*

"Come give me a hand," Hank said. "And keep your mouth shut."

Lilly pulled on her shoes and scooped Phoebe off the floor, where she had been playing with her favorite doll and calico elephant. Phoebe started crying and reached for her toys. Lilly grabbed the elephant, gave it to her, and started toward the door, panic rising like a flood in her chest. Phoebe hugged the elephant beneath her chin and grinned, oblivious to her mother's distress.

"Stay here," Cole said to Lilly.

"I'll do no such thing," Lilly said. "I'm taking

the baby over to Glory and coming with you."

Cole studied her face, then went with his father out the door. There was nothing he could do to stop her, and he knew it. She followed him outside, then hurried along the train in the other direction until she reached the car Glory shared with Ruby, Rosy, and three other sideshow performers. Glory and Ruby sat in folding lawn chairs next to the tracks, smoking and soaking up the sun.

Sweating and out of breath, Lilly stopped and put Phoebe in Glory's lap. "Can you watch her for a little while?"

Glory nodded and held on to Phoebe, confusion wrinkling her brow. "Sure," she said. "But what's going on? Everything okay?"

"No," Lilly said. "Everything's not okay. Mr. Barlow has a buyer for the elephants." The words caught in her throat.

"Oh my God," Glory said. "All of them?"

"I don't know," Lilly said, her chin quivering. "But I need to find out."

"Do whatever you need to do. I'll take care of Phoebe."

"Thanks," Lilly said. She kissed her daughter on the head, whispered she'd be back soon, and hurried away.

By the time she got to the stock cars, a crowd of performers and roustabouts was already forming. She pushed her way through the gathering to see what was happening. The equestrian director and several handlers had lined the horses up next to the train, and Cole, Hank, and two handlers brought the elephants down the ramps, led them over to the row of horses, then stood holding their leg chains. Two men in suits and shiny shoes walked up and down the line inspecting the stock, one tall and thin, with dark hair and a walrus mustache, the other with a bald head and silver cane. Mr. Barlow and Merrick handed out hearty handshakes and strolled beside them, smiling. The local sheriff and the railroad officials were there too, along with a bunch of townies gawking from the other side of the tracks.

One of the acrobats asked the head of the Flying Zoppe Brothers if he thought they were shutting down.

The Flying Zoppe brother shook his head. "Mr. Barlow's selling off ring stock to pay for a new big top."

Shaking and nauseous, Lilly hurried over to the elephants and came to a stop next to Merrick and Mr. Barlow. Cole frowned at her and shook his head, cautioning her to keep quiet.

"You can't sell the bulls," she said to Mr. Barlow. "They're your biggest draw."

Mr. Barlow ignored her and kept smiling and nodding at the men in suits, who were inspecting the elephants up close.

"Mind your own business," Merrick said to her under his breath.

"They are my business," she said. "If they go to another circus, Cole and I go with them."

"He's only selling one," Merrick said.

The bald man pointed at JoJo with his cane. "We'll take the young one," he said.

Lilly went rigid. *No. Not JoJo. It will break Pepper's heart!*

"Sold," Mr. Barlow said. "You've made a fine choice, gentlemen. He's one of the smartest bulls we've ever had."

"That's not true," Lilly said in a loud voice. "He's been in the parade, but he's as dumb as they come. We can't teach him anything."

Mr. Barlow glared at her and Cole gave her a stern look.

"And you are?" the man with the walrus mustache asked Lilly.

"I work with these elephants," she said. "I'm sure you've heard of The Albino Princess and her Albino Elephant?"

The bald man knitted his brow and regarded Mr. Barlow. "You better not be trying to pull a fast one on us," he said.

"Of course not," Mr. Barlow said. "And to prove I'm an honest businessman, if this bull turns out to be a dud, I'll take him back and give you two others to replace him."

The bald man smiled and shook Mr. Barlow's hand. "It's a deal."

"You're making a mistake," Lilly said, trying

to keep her voice even. "JoJo won't mind anyone but me and my husband. And even then, he's the most stubborn bull I've ever seen."

"Don't listen to her," Mr. Barlow said. "She's just a bleeding heart who's too attached to the stock. She'd make a fuss no matter who I sold." He motioned his strongmen to move her away from him.

The strongmen grabbed Lilly, dragged her over with the rest of the spectators, and held her there. She struggled to get free, tears blurring her vision. "You can't take JoJo away from his mother!" she shouted. "You just can't!"

The man with the walrus mustache ordered his handlers to take JoJo and load him on their train, and the bald man counted out a stack of bills into Mr. Barlow's hand, his silver-tipped cane held beneath his arm. One of the Rowe & Company handlers took JoJo's front leg chain from Cole, yanking on it to get him moving. When JoJo refused, another man jabbed a bull hook into his shoulder.

"Hey!" Cole shouted. "There's no need for that!"

The man ignored him and jabbed JoJo harder. JoJo curled his trunk and bellowed in pain, then started walking. Following the handlers along the train in fits and starts, he stopped every few steps and glanced back at his mother. Every time he came to a halt, the handler jabbed him in the shoulder to get him moving again. Mr.

Barlow, Merrick, the sheriff, and the railroad officials followed, talking and oblivious to the drama that was unfolding.

Breathing hard, Lilly pushed her elbows into her sides, the world a blur through her tears. It was all she could do not to scream. There was no way to stop what was happening. Pepper trumpeted and called out to her son, lifting her front feet one at a time and getting more and more agitated. Cole talked to her and rubbed her legs and shoulders, trying to get her to calm down, but it was no use. Pepper knew her baby was being taken away. When the handlers steered JoJo around the caboose and out of sight, Pepper broke free and charged forward, ripping her leg chain from Cole's hands. Cole raced after her, but Pepper was running at full bore, a cloud of dust rising at her heels. It seemed like the entire earth quaked beneath her massive feet. The strongmen let Lilly go and she and the other Barlow Brothers' handlers gave chase.

By the time Lilly and the handlers reached the other side of the caboose, the Rowe & Company men were already trying to load JoJo on their train, shouting and cussing and jabbing him with bull hooks to move him up the ramp. Mr. Barlow, Merrick, the sheriff, and the railroad officials stood nearby and watched, indifferent. Pepper stampeded toward the train with her trunk held high, moving faster than Lilly thought possible. Cole couldn't keep up. A collective gasp erupted from the townies gathered near the tracks and they moved back, eyes wide. JoJo stopped halfway up the ramp, looked back at his mother, and trumpeted loudly. When Merrick saw Pepper running toward them, he took a cattle prod from one of the handlers and pushed it into JoJo's back leg. JoJo bellowed in pain and moved up the ramp.

Merrick made a move to hit JoJo with the cattle prod again, but before he could, Pepper reached him and knocked him to the ground with her trunk. A woman screamed and someone shouted for everyone to run. The Rowe & Company handlers kept their eyes on Pepper but continued to force JoJo into the boxcar, striking him faster and harder with every panicked blow. Pepper roared and sideswiped the handlers off the ramp, her trunk swinging like a baseball bat. The men fell in the dirt, scrambled to their feet, and moved away.

"Pepper, no!" Lilly shouted, still running toward her.

Cole stopped and grabbed her by the arm. "There's nothing you can do."

Lilly watched helplessly beside Cole, one trembling hand over her mouth. *Please, Pepper. Don't hurt them. They don't understand.*

One of the Rowe & Company handlers picked

up a bull hook, wielded it like a sword, and moved toward Pepper. She growled and charged at him, then stopped, her head held high as if daring him to come closer. He dropped the bull hook and retreated, his face suddenly drained of color. Pepper turned away, gently guided JoJo down the ramp with her trunk, and stepped backward to give him room to turn around.

Behind Pepper, Merrick got off the ground, picked up a bull hook with both hands, and swung it at her back leg, puncturing her thigh. He yanked it out and her skin ripped open. Pepper's head jerked up and she bellowed in pain. Merrick hammered the bull hook into her hide again and again and again, until blood gushed from the wounds and ran down her leg. Pepper spun around and swatted him to the ground with her trunk. He landed on his side and lay there crumpled and moaning, then turned over on his back. Pepper lowered her head and charged him. Merrick's eyes went wide with terror and he crawled backward in the dirt, trying to get away. Pepper reached him before he could get up and whacked him sideways with one foot. He rolled away in the dust and she followed, batting him back and forth with her front feet, her leg chain swinging through the air like a whip. Merrick screamed and begged for help, lifting his arms to protect himself, the wet crack of his breaking bones like snapping sticks. The townies recoiled in horror and scrambled away. Women shrieked, and the Rowe & Company handlers ran for safety.

"Pepper, stop!" Lilly cried. She started toward her again, but Cole held her back. "Let me go! I have to stop her! She'll listen to me!"

"You don't know that," Cole said. "There no telling what she'll do right now, even to you. Not when she's protecting JoJo."

"Pepper, please!" she shouted. "Don't!" She gave in and sank to her knees, her gorge rising in her throat. Cole was right, there was no stopping Pepper now. It was a mother's instinct to protect her young no matter what it took, and Lilly would have done the same thing if someone tried to take Phoebe. But Pepper was an animal, and she would be punished.

A few seconds later, Merrick stopped screaming. Blood covered one side of his face, and his head, arms, and legs flopped around like a rag doll. Pepper continued to bat him back and forth with her feet and trunk, tossing him around like a cat playing with a dead mouse. Gasps of horror rose from the crowd and a woman fainted. Cole knelt beside Lilly and she buried her face in his shoulder. She couldn't watch. Not because of what was happening to Merrick, but because she knew what Mr. Barlow and the others would do to Pepper for acting like a mother and an elephant.

Then a shot rang out and Lilly looked up. The sheriff was pointing a rifle at Pepper. Pepper took a step backward, away from Merrick, blood running from her shoulder. The sheriff fired three more times and bullets hit Pepper in the back and thigh. Pepper lifted her head and roared in agony, then turned, stumbled, and listed slightly to one side. The handlers slowly moved toward her with bull hooks and cattle prods, arms out, ready to run if she turned on them. Merrick lay still as a stone on the ground, his arms and legs twisted at odd angles, his head surrounded by a growing puddle of blood.

Lilly got to her feet and raced toward Pepper. "Stay away from her!" she shouted. The handlers stopped and watched with wary eyes. When she got closer to Pepper, Lilly slowed and put out a hand. "It's all right. Calm down, girl, you're okay."

Pepper's sad, amber eyes sought Lilly's, her impossibly long lashes splattered with droplets of blood. She sighed, a low rattling sound that was more of a moan, reached for Lilly's hand with her trunk, and pulled her closer. Lilly choked back a sob and leaned against Pepper, unable to speak around the burning lump in her throat. With a grave look on his face, Cole came over and picked up Pepper's leg chain. Behind her, the Rowe & Company handlers quickly prodded JoJo back up the ramp and into the boxcar, jabbing the cattle prod into his neck every time he tried to glance back at his mother.

"Chain that goddamned bull down!" Mr. Barlow ordered his handlers.

"Kill it!" one of the townies shouted.

"Kill it!" someone else yelled. "Kill the elephant!"

Other voices joined in, "Kill the elephant! Kill the elephant!"

Lilly shook her head, the world a blur though her tears. *No, no, no,* her mind screamed. *This can't be happening. It just can't.* She took a few steps away from Pepper, toward the Barlow Brothers' train. "Come," she managed. Pepper stood rooted to the ground, head hanging. "Please, Pepper. You've got to follow me."

Cole gave her leg chain a gentle tug. "Come on, girl," he said. "It's time to go."

The sheriff approached with his rifle, his finger on the trigger, ready to shoot again. Mr. Barlow followed, his sweat-covered face pale, motioning his handlers forward. The walrus-mustached man from Rowe & Company drew a pistol from the waist of his suit and moved toward Pepper, his mouth hard. Lilly turned toward them and held out her arms.

"Please," she said, choking back tears. "Don't shoot her. She was just trying to protect her baby. You can't punish a mother for acting like a mother, or an animal for acting like an animal."

Cole moved between Lilly and the men. "Let us take her back to the train," he said. "She's not going to hurt anyone else."

"The hell she won't," the sheriff said.

"Listen," Cole said. "I've worked with this bull my entire life. She doesn't have a mean bone in her body."

"She's got the taste a' blood now," one of the railroad officials said. "She's a murderer."

"That's right," the sheriff said.

Just then, Viktor stormed around the caboose of the Barlow Brothers' train. The townies gasped and looked at one another with confusion and fear. Some moved farther away. Viktor hurried over to Merrick's lifeless body and dropped to his knees, his giant shoulders slumped. He put a hand on Merrick's neck to feel for a pulse, listened to his chest, then threw back his head and howled, a low, guttural, awful-sounding cry that tore from his throat. Everyone froze, their mouths and eyes wide with shock. Several women held trembling fingers over their lips and started to cry while others twisted their faces in disgust. The mournful sound pierced Lilly's soul and she nearly cried out too, devastated for JoJo and Pepper. When it was over, Viktor staggered upright, scooped Merrick's broken, bloody body into his muscular arms, and trudged back to the Barlow Brothers' train.

"What the hell was that?" the sheriff said.

"Never mind that freak," the mustached man from Rowe & Company said. "What are we doing about this damn bull?" The men retrained their guns on Pepper.

"Now listen, boys," Mr. Barlow said. "You can't just kill a $20,000 elephant. If this bull needs to be shot, I'll be the one to do it. If nothing else, she'll keep my big cats fed for a week." He jerked his chin at Cole. "Put her back on the train."

"Now hold on," the sheriff said. "That elephant's gone rogue. You can't put it back in the circus."

"For Christ's sake, I'm not an idiot," Mr. Barlow said. "From here on out, that bull will be raising tents and hauling equipment. If she acts up, I'll put her down. My bull, my problem. Unless whoever finishes her off wants to pay me what she's worth."

Reluctantly, the men lowered their guns.

Lilly's shoulders sagged in relief. "Come on, girl," she said to Pepper. "Let's go."

Cole tugged on Pepper's leg chain again and, after what seemed like forever, she took a tentative step forward, then another. The sheriff and handlers moved back to give her room, still on high alert. Lilly walked backward beside Cole and urged Pepper to follow them toward the Barlow Brothers' train. Pepper took half a dozen more steps, then stopped and glanced back at JoJo standing in the open door of the stock car, his legs in chains. Lilly called Pepper's name, pleading with her to keep moving forward, and after a few long seconds, she did as she was told. The sheriff and the Rowe & Company man followed, guns at the ready. When they reached the Barlow Brothers' caboose, Pepper stopped and looked back at JoJo again. Tear tracks stained her cheeks. JoJo raised his trunk and bellowed.

"Shut that bloody door!" the bald man from Rowe & Company shouted. The handlers shoved JoJo backward into the car and pushed the door across its railings, slamming it shut with a final thud. Pepper flattened her ears and hung her head.

Lilly could barely see through her tears. "Come on, Pepper," she managed. "Come with me, sweet girl."

Pepper moaned, long and low, and trudged on, her wide feet dragging in the dust. Streaks of blood ran down her legs like circus stripes. By the time Cole, Lilly, and Pepper made their way to the other side of the Barlow Brothers' train, Flossie and Petunia, along with the horses, had been reloaded. Viktor had disappeared with Merrick's body, and Glory was making her way toward them with Phoebe in her arms, her brow furrowed. When they reached each other, Lilly took Phoebe and hugged Glory hard. Cole stopped to kiss his daughter. Behind them,

Pepper stopped too. Lilly's throat and nose were so swollen from crying she could hardly breathe. She drew away from Glory's embrace and searched her face.

"I'm sorry about Merrick," she managed.

"Me too," Cole said.

"It's all right," Glory said. She ran a hand under her nose. "From what I heard, the bastard had it coming."

Lilly didn't know what to say. Glory was right, Merrick had finally paid the ultimate price for being so cruel, but she would never say that out loud. Because even after Glory moved out of Merrick's car, she still cared about him. Whether it was blind love or gratitude for saving Viktor, Lilly had no idea. But she had to respect Glory's feelings, no matter how misguided she thought they were.

"I'm sorry about JoJo," Glory said. "And Pepper."

Lilly nodded, gave her another hug, and they started walking again. Pepper followed, lost in her misery. Lilly clasped Phoebe to her chest and kissed her soft forehead, her endless tears falling on her daughter's blond curls. Phoebe peeked over Lilly's shoulder and pointed at Pepper with a drool-covered finger.

"Pepa!" she said in a high, excited voice. She giggled and gazed at Lilly with bright, happy eyes.

Lilly tried to smile. "That's right, baby girl. That's Pepper."

"Why don't you take Phoebe back to our car," Cole said. "I can load Pepper."

Glory held out her arms. "Here," she said to Lilly. "I'll take her. You go with Pepper. She needs you."

"Are you sure?" Lilly said.

"Of course," Glory said. "Take as long as you need. Our little princess will be fine."

Lilly kissed Phoebe again and handed her to Glory. "Thank you."

"No problem," Glory said. She hugged Lilly again, then took Phoebe back to her car.

The rest of the Barlow Brothers' performers and workers gathered along the tracks to watch Pepper return. Dolly the World's Most Beautiful Fat Woman wept uncontrollably while Ruby and Rosy patted her wide shoulders, tears running down their rouged faces. The Flying Zoppe Brothers stood with the Bally girls and Mrs. Benini, all with somber faces. With a quivering chin, Natasha the trapeze artist held tight to Chloe the tightrope walker's hand. Aldo the Alligator Man wiped Dina the Living Half Girl's cheeks, and the midgets, Penelope and Pierre, had their arms around each other. There wasn't a dry eye in the lineup.

When Lilly and Cole loaded Pepper onto the train, Flossie and Petunia reached out to her with their trunks, swaying and making low, moaning noises. Pepper stopped briefly in front of JoJo's empty spot, her ears and trunk drooping, then made her way into her own. She went down on her knees in the straw and lay on her side, her eyes wet, her face streaked with tears. Cole fastened her leg chain to the wall and Lilly sat beside her, caressing her wrinkled cheek. Hank came into the stock car and knelt down to examine Pepper.

"Is she going to be all right?" Lilly said.

"I think so," Hank said. "If the bullets had hit anything vital, she'd be down by now."

Lilly got to her feet and kissed Pepper's forehead. "I'll be right back," she whispered. "Just hold on, girl."

She went with Cole over to the open stock car door. Everyone looked up at them expectantly.

"She's restrained," Cole said to Mr. Barlow and the sheriff.

"Good," the sheriff said. "Now you'd best pack up and leave. We don't need no murderin' elephant around these parts."

"Now hold on," Mr. Barlow said. "This is an important stop for us and we're scheduled for three shows. We're just picking up after nearly losing everything in a tornado, and on top of that, I lost my long-time business partner and the owner of the sideshow." He lowered his head and pinched the bridge of his nose as if struggling to hold himself together. After a long moment, he took a deep breath, sighed long and loud, and looked up. "If we don't do tomorrow's show, it could mean ruin. You're not going to kick a hardworking man when he's down, are you?" He clapped the sheriff on the shoulder. "These are hard times, my friend."

"You're right, these are hard times," the sheriff said. "And I was hired to keep the people in this county safe. I'm not going to lose my job over a damn elephant."

Mr. Barlow nodded as if he understood, then reached into his pocket, pulled out a money clip, and started counting out a stack of bills. "That bull won't appear in any of my shows," he said. "You have my word."

The sheriff scowled. "Are you trying to bribe me, Mr. Barlow?"

"Just want to say thank you for your service here today," Mr. Barlow said. "Your quick action saved a lot of lives and we're grateful for it." He held out the money.

The sheriff looked at the ground a moment, hiked up the belt of his pants, then took the bills and shoved them in his pocket. "I was planning on bringing the twins to the show tomorrow," he said. "They been looking forward to it for a week and the last thing I want to do is disappoint my girls."

"Perfectly understandable," Mr. Barlow said.

"And to show you how much I appreciate your support, there'll be free tickets for you and your family waiting at the ticket booth."

The sheriff wrinkled his brow. "Free tickets or not, I'm not going to be happy if I see an elephant with patched bullet holes in the ring."

"Of course not," Mr. Barlow said. "That elephant is a workhorse from now on, nothing more."

"You better be telling the truth, or I'll shut you down and run you out of town for good."

"I can assure you," Mr. Barlow said. "Taking that risk wouldn't be a good business move. And if there's one thing I pride myself on, it's being a smart businessman. I meant it when I said I'll kill that bull myself if necessary." He extended his hand.

The sheriff shook Mr. Barlow's hand, then left. Mr. Barlow moved closer to the stock car and fixed hard eyes on Lilly and Cole, eyes that said, *This is your fault.*

That night, Glory took care of Phoebe while Lilly and Cole slept in the stock car with Pepper. Hank had pulled the bullets out of Pepper's hide and, to ward off infection, applied a thick coating of zinc ointment to the wounds. Lilly lay next to Cole in the straw, awake and silently weeping, trying to grasp the nightmarish reality that JoJo was gone, Pepper had killed Merrick, and now, somehow, Pepper was going to pay for following her natural-born instincts. Just thinking about someone taking Phoebe made Lilly's heart cramp with panic and her stomach churn with fear. No wonder Pepper went wild. Lilly would have too. The difference between her and Pepper was that no one would shoot her for trying to save her baby.

She could only imagine the terror and grief Pepper must have felt when the Rowe & Company handlers took her son, and the pain she must be in now, not only from the her physical wounds, but from her shattered heart. How was she even breathing? At least Mr. Barlow didn't let the sheriff kill her. But what was going to happen to Pepper now? Was Mr. Barlow going to make her a workhorse like he said, or would he try to sell her? Or even worse, would he shoot her and feed her to the cats?

Then Lilly pictured JoJo, alone and afraid in the boxcar on the other train, and her tears started all over again. She knew that horrible, heavy ache of homesickness in his chest, that helplessness of being ripped from everything familiar, that all-consuming terror of imagining what was going to happen next. Was JoJo wondering why she and Cole and Pepper let strangers take him? Did he think they had gotten rid of him on purpose? The thought of JoJo feeling unloved and discarded was almost more than she could bear. She closed her flooding eyes and prayed for exhaustion to overtake her, to release her into sleep. Hours later, when it finally did, she slept in fits and starts, alternating between dreams of being locked in her old attic bedroom and riding Pepper in the grand parade.

The next morning, the stock car door slid open and sunshine cut like a knife through the gloomy interior, hay chafe and dust floating in the yellow light. Someone entered and Lilly looked toward the door, rubbing her swollen eyes and expecting to see Hank. When she saw Glory standing over her, she bolted upright, fear gripping her throat.

"Where's Phoebe?" she said.

"Still sleeping," Glory whispered. "Don't worry, she's fine. Penelope is with her."

Cole blinked and sat up, his face puffy with sleep. "What's going on?"

"What are you doing in here?" Lilly asked Glory. "And why are you whispering?"

Glory edged closer and knelt in the straw. "I came to warn you," she said. "Alana said a group of local officials paid a visit to Mr. Barlow last night. Seems the town leaders of the next eight stops on our route threatened to cancel if we have Pepper with us."

"But Mr. Barlow assured the sheriff she wasn't part of the show anymore," Lilly said. "He said she's a work animal now."

"That doesn't mean they believe him," Cole said.

"Cole's right," Glory said. "The rubes can't tell one bull from another. Mr. Barlow could put Pepper back in the ring and they'd never know the difference."

"Then that's what he should do," Lilly said. "She's not dangerous. She was protecting JoJo."

"You and I know that," Cole said. "But no one else will believe it."

"Mr. Barlow will never put Pepper back in the ring," Glory said. "It's too big a risk. If word got out, it'd mean certain ruin."

"Then what are you saying?" Lilly said. "What did you come to warn us about?"

"Penelope overheard Mr. Barlow and Viktor talking outside Mr. Barlow's car. Viktor wants Pepper to pay for killing Merrick, and Mr. Barlow said no one will book us with a rogue bull in the troupe, even if she's not in the show."

"And?" Lilly said. Her legs and arms started to vibrate.

Glory's eyes grew glassy. "Mr. Barlow said there's only one way to prove Pepper is no longer part of The Barlow Brothers' Circus."

Lilly's breath grew shallow and fast. "How?"

"They're going to . . ." Glory's chin trembled and she took Lilly's hand with cold, shaking fingers.

Lilly thought she would scream before Glory told her the rest. "They're going to what? Tell me!"

"They're going to kill her, Lilly. They're going to kill her, and they're going to do it in public."

"Oh my God. No!" Lilly cried. She put her hands over her mouth, certain she was going to be sick. Cole put an arm around her and she stared at Glory, tears burning her eyes. "How?"

"I don't know," Glory said.

"When?"

"As soon as they can get the word out. Probably tomorrow, after the afternoon performance."

Lilly shook her head. "No." She looked at Pepper lying on her side and watching them with sad, wet eyes. "No, I won't let them." She crawled over to Pepper and leaned against her, one arm around her front leg. Pepper let out a long, shuddering sigh, lifted her trunk, and draped it across Lilly's shoulder.

"I'm afraid there's nothing you can do," Cole said softly. "Mr. Barlow will have you arrested, or worse, if you try to stop him. I'm so sorry."

Lilly turned her head to look at him, her face soaked with tears. "Of course there's something I can do. I can get her out of here. And you can help me."

CHAPTER 28
Julia

In the shadow-filled attic of Blackwood Manor, Julia stood frozen, shining her flashlight at the third door on the other side of the second section of the vast space. At first glance, the door looked set in an outside wall, as if it might lead out to a balcony. But there were no balconies on that side of the house, or any other part of Blackwood Manor for that matter. Besides, unlike the rest of the walls, this wall was made of brick, not wood. She directed the flashlight at the nearest dormer. It looked like all the rest, with a moldy, watermarked window. But the placement seemed odd. It was too close to the brick wall. Which meant the wall might have been added later, and there could be more space on the other side of the door.

"My God," she said to herself. "How big is this attic?"

Shivering with anticipation, she started across the second section. Then she suddenly stopped, shoulders hunched, every sense on high alert. Maybe this part of the attic was walled off and empty because the floor was rotten. She cast the flashlight over the floorboards, looking for cracks or signs of decay. There were none. She pressed one foot into the plank in front of her. It felt firm. She took a deep breath, then carefully crept across the attic, testing each step until she reached the third door.

The door was padlocked.

"Shit," she whispered.

She swept the flashlight along the floor and wall to look for the key, scanning the brick and mortar for a hook or hiding place. She searched above the doorframe, her fingers blindly feeling the narrow lip, and came back with nothing but dust. She sighed heavily and tried to think. If she couldn't find the key, maybe she could break the door down. After all, it was her house, she could do whatever she wanted. She rammed her shoulder into it several times. The hasp and padlock rattled, but the door didn't budge. It was like trying to move the brick wall.

"Damn it all to hell and back!" she said.

She rubbed her shoulder and frowned at the door. Maybe she could bust it open with an ax. Maybe Fletcher could do it. Or maybe he was strong enough to break the lock. With that thought, she grabbed the padlock to examine it closer. It had been put back in the flange, but the shank had not been pushed into the body. The door had been unlocked the entire time.

Berating herself for not checking the padlock sooner, she removed it from the hasp and opened the door. Then she shined the flashlight inside and nearly sank to the floor in astonishment.

Her light revealed a cramped, narrow bedroom, complete with a dresser, armoire, and a rusted iron bed beneath a wallpapered nook. Paper flowers hung from the walls and ceilings, their faded petals droopy and gray. The bed looked recently slept in, with a head-shaped indent in the pillow and the red, dust-covered duvet pushed to one side. Across from the bed, cobwebs shrouded a white wicker table, a rocking chair, and a short bookcase. Next to the rocking chair, a dollhouse filled with dead bugs and miniature furniture sat on a wooden chest near three porcelain dolls in a wicker pram, their grimy faces cracked, their hair tangled beneath hoary nets of dirt and spider webs. One looked back at Julia with a drooping eyelid, frozen mid-wink.

Julia stood there, staring and too stunned to move. Why was there a bedroom hidden behind three locked doors in the attic of Blackwood Manor? Who in the world had slept there? And why?

Judging by the toys, it was a child. A little girl.

Icy shivers crawled up the back of Julia's neck. How could anyone do this? How could anyone lock a child in an attic bedroom? And why? It was unimaginable and creepy as hell. Then she noticed the cloth-bound Bible on the nightstand and the cross on the wall, and she knew. Mother had something to do with this.

"Dear God," she whispered.

The words in her father's journal flashed in her mind:

We have buried our firstborn. May she rest in peace. God speed her soul to heaven. And may God help us for what we have done.

A sickening knot of disgust and anger twisted in Julia's gut. Her father's entry said they buried their *firstborn,* not their newborn. It could have been an older child. A child old enough to play with dolls and make paper flowers. Old enough to read. *It could have been my sister,* Julia thought. Her knees went weak. What in the world had her parents done? Had they kept their own child locked in this room? Had she died right here in this little bed? And why had they kept her hidden? Was she sick? Deformed? Illegitimate?

Another memory came to Julia and she put a hand over her stomach, suddenly nauseous. Mother always said bad things would happen if she didn't behave. Is that what happened to her sister? Had Mother locked her up for misbehaving? Who would do such a thing? She shook her head. No, that couldn't have been it. It had to be something else. Mother was strict, but she wasn't that strict. Was she? And Father wouldn't have gone along with it. Then she had another thought. Maybe that was why her father drank, to bury his guilt.

Overcome with the feeling that she didn't know her parents at all, Julia started to tremble. She had wanted answers about her unhappy childhood, and now she was finding them. All this time, Mother had blamed her for Father's drinking and death, but something else had been going on inside Blackwood Manor, something that seemed straight out of a nightmare. And now, no matter how awful it was, Julia was going to get to the bottom of it. Whether she wanted to or not, there was no going back now.

She steeled herself and entered the room, casting the flashlight into dark corners. The fusty smell of old wood and warm dust filled the air, stronger and more concentrated than in the rest of the attic, along with an underlying rancid odor that reminded her of finding dead mice in Big Al's Diner. She crept over to the bed, moving slowly out of fear or astonishment she wasn't sure, and tried the lamp on the bedside table. The knob clicked, but nothing happened. She shined the flashlight up and down the bedcovers. Brown and yellow blotches stained the wrinkled sheet and pillowcase, overlapping at different points in varying degrees of light and dark.

She went into the dormer and tried to look out. Black patches of mildew mottled the glass, but she could make out the hulking barn through the rain, the gray scudding clouds above its gabled roof. She imagined a little girl, her sister, standing where she stood, looking out and wondering what else lay beyond this grimy window. Goose bumps rose on her arms. The longer she was in the room, the more nauseous she felt. Pain and despair fell around her like a weight.

Something clunked behind her. She spun around and swept the flashlight around the bedroom, her heart racing. Maybe there weren't rats in the attic after all. Maybe it was her sister all along, making the noises in the ceilings and walls. The hairs on the back of her neck stood up.

"Hello?" she said.

The only sounds were the creak and sway of the house, and the rain filtering through the leaf-choked gutters.

"Is someone there?"

Nothing.

Shaking harder now, she slowly got down on her knees and looked under the bed. The flashlight beam jittered over cobwebs and dust, but no living thing looked back. She stood, took a deep breath, and tried to slow her thundering heart.

"You're being ridiculous," she whispered.

"There's no one up here but you." *Unless your sister is surviving on rats.*

She pushed the image away and swept the flashlight around the room again. Nothing moved. She gritted her teeth and edged close to the armoire. The door was open a crack. She opened it all the way and shined the flashlight inside. Moth-eaten dresses and yellowed blouses hung from the clothes bar, and several pairs of little girl's shoes lined the bottom. But they weren't toddler shoes. They looked big enough for a seven- or eight-year-old. *My God, how long was she up here? All her life? Or only after she had grown old enough to misbehave?*

What looked like a white dress lay crumpled in the bottom corner of the armoire. She reached in to pick it up, then let out a screech and jumped back. A small skeleton lay on top of the dress, its dusty brown spine curled against the inside wall. She stared at the armoire, breathing hard and trying to pull herself together. If the skeleton belonged to a child, she didn't know what she would do. Scream? Throw up? Call the police? She held her breath and peered in again. The flashlight beam illuminated tiny brown ribs, an elongated skull, sharp teeth, and a segmented tail. It looked like a cat. She exhaled and straightened. Thank God it wasn't a child, but finding the remains of a cat was still upsetting. Had the poor thing been left alone up here to starve? Who would do such an awful thing?

The same people who locked a little girl in this attic, her mind screamed. *Your parents.*

She pictured a little girl reading in the rocking chair, or having a tea party at the wicker table with her dolls. She could see her in the little bed, curled up with her beloved cat, trying to understand why she felt so lost and unloved. Suddenly, a profound sense of loneliness and misery overwhelmed her, as if every emotion absorbed by the bedroom walls had been released all at once. Either that, or her sister's ghost was in the room with her.

It was more than she could take. Overcome by the feeling that she was stuck in a nightmare or horror movie, she rushed out of the room, shut the door, and made her way across the divided attic. After going through the second door, she scurried through the maze of dusty books and boxes and shelves toward the hidden staircase, panic growing in her mind. What if the little door at the bottom of the steps was closed and locked? What if she was stuck up there forever? The idea was absurd, but when she saw the dim light glowing through the opening in the floor that led to the stairway, a flood of relief washed through her. The door at the bottom of the steps was open. With one hand against the gritty wall for support and the other gripping the flashlight, she went down the steps, which somehow seemed steeper and narrower than before. At the bottom, she closed and locked the door, fully aware there was no reason to lock it, at the same time a small, frightened part of her imagined her sister still living in the attic, sneaking out the door in the middle of the night. And after all those years alone up there, she had to be insane. It was a crazy, ridiculous notion, but then again, she never thought she'd find a hidden bedroom in the attic of her childhood home. Without bothering to roll down the tapestry or return the claw-foot table to its original place, she left the little room and hurried downstairs to the first floor.

In her father's den, she picked up his journal off the desk and flipped to the first page with trembling fingers. The entry marking the death of her sister was 1940—Julia had been two years old. She sank into the chair, her mind racing and her insides churning. While her sister had been locked in the attic, she'd been downstairs playing with toys, laughing, and taking naps, oblivious to the horrors being committed a few floors up. There were no rats in the walls of Blackwood Manor. Just a little girl hidden in the attic.

It was horrible and inconceivable and unreal.

CHAPTER 29
Lilly

At half past midnight the day after Pepper killed Merrick, Lilly and Cole crept out of their sleeper car, suitcases in hand, Phoebe sound asleep in a cloth sling against Cole's chest, unaware her parents were leading her into an uncertain future. The night was still and humid, and a half-moon cast a bluish glow over the train and ground and trees, emitting just enough light for them to see where they were going. Cole had a lantern in his backpack but didn't dare use it until they were far enough away not to be caught.

Earlier, they had talked for hours about what saving Pepper would mean for the three of them and decided that, despite the risks of starting over with nothing but their clothes and a little money, they wouldn't be able to live with themselves if they stood by and did nothing. Cole hoped they'd find a new circus willing to take them in, along with a free, albeit "rogue," bull. Because where else would an albino, a lifelong circus performer, and an elephant have any sort of chance at starting over? If that plan didn't work, he wasn't sure what they would do. But Lilly insisted they try.

After the decision was made, they asked Hank over to their car to say good-bye. He agreed they had to save Pepper and wanted to go with them, but Cole refused in case they got caught. Hank understood and made them promise to find a way to let him know where they landed, and if they were safe. He took Phoebe in his lap and kissed her cheeks until she got tired and wanted her mother. Lilly hugged him and Cole promised they'd see each other again, and if a spot for an experienced bull man opened up in their next digs, he'd send word. By the time Hank left, they were all in tears.

Now, Lilly followed Cole along the train, fear and adrenaline roaring through her veins, a fine sheen of nervous sweat on her forehead. She felt like she was about to jump out of her skin. If they got caught or escaped, who knew what would happen. When they reached the elephant car, Cole stopped, shoulders hunched, and held up a hand. Lilly came to a halt behind him and waited while he slowly slid open the stock car door, cringing with every metal rasp and scrape. When it was finally open all the way, Cole acted as a lookout and she climbed inside, crept across the aisle, and crouched beside Pepper, praying she'd be able to get the brokenhearted, injured bull up and out of the car without too much noise. Pepper lay on her side in the straw, streaks of dried tears on her wrinkled face. Lilly ran a gentle hand down her giant ear and Pepper opened her eyes and lifted her head. Her long trunk unfurled like a fern leaf and reached for Lilly's arm.

"Up," Lilly whispered. "Get up, girl."

Pepper groaned and struggled to her feet. Flossie and Petunia craned their necks to see what was going on, snuffling and snorting when they saw Lilly. She went over and rubbed their trunks, whispering that they should go back to sleep. The elephants sighed, low and rumbling, and put their trunks back down. Lilly unlocked the chain around Pepper's leg, wrapped it around Pepper's ankle, and secured it in place. Then she started toward the door, hoping the great beast would be willing and able to get out of the car without using the ramp. Otherwise, it would take too long and make too much noise. Pepper followed her out of the stall and Lilly climbed out of the stock car.

In the open doorway, Pepper hesitated, no doubt confused and in pain. Lilly quietly begged her to come down, rubbing her plate-sized feet and telling her it would be okay. Pepper swayed back and forth, unsure. Cole watched with a worried face, and Lilly felt panic rising in her chest. If they had to use the ramp, they'd get caught for sure. Then, at last, Pepper stepped out of the car, her great gray heft shuddering when her front foot hit the ground. She grumbled deep in her throat, but kept coming, her rear end high in the air, her front feet on the ground. For a heart-stopping second, Lilly thought she might fall out of the door. If she got hurt, they'd be done for. Then, finally, Pepper managed to pull one of her back legs out and bring the other one down too, and Lilly could breathe again.

Once Pepper was free of the car and standing on all fours, Cole slowly slid the door shut and they started walking toward the end of the train. Pepper lumbered behind Lilly, stopping when she stopped, slowing when she slowed. Together, they took a wide berth around Mr. Barlow's car and the caboose, then followed the tracks away from The Barlow Brothers' Circus. The only things Lilly could hear were the blood rushing through her veins and the anxious thud of her heart. She turned every once in a while to make sure Pepper was still behind them. In the weak moonlight, the bull's silhouette swayed side to side, the dark wings of her ears slowly fanning forward and back, her mighty legs plodding along the tracks like the limbs of a prehistoric creature.

When Lilly felt sure they had escaped undiscovered, she unclenched her jaw and her heartbeat slowed. She hooked her arm through Cole's and leaned against his shoulder as they walked along the railroad ties, nearly limp with relief. Phoebe was still sound asleep in the sling, her little blond head bobbing against Cole's chest in time with his strides. Neither Lilly nor Cole spoke, each lost in their own thoughts and fears about the future. The only thing they knew for sure was they were headed west, toward a town named Waverly, where rumor had it The Sparks World Circus was being cannibalized by Ringling. If the three of them didn't get picked up by Ringling, at least they'd have better luck finding a new circus with the remnants of Sparks World than they would on their own. Lilly had already imagined a new act with Pepper, one that included Cole and Phoebe, and now she rehearsed it in her mind to calm her nerves.

Then she saw the silhouette of someone on the tracks, and she came to a halt. Cole took another step, then stopped too. The person was quite large, with an unusually big head and broad shoulders, and he was coming toward them.

It was Viktor.

Cole pulled Lilly off the tracks toward a line of trees.

"Come," Lilly said to Pepper as loud as she dared. Pepper followed, crashing through the dry brush like a tank.

"Stop right there!" Viktor shouted. "That damn bull isn't getting off that easy!" He turned on a flashlight and shined it in their direction. Lill and Cole froze and she grabbed his arm, her blood running cold. Viktor had a gun.

CHAPTER 30
Julia

The morning after finding the hidden staircase up to the attic, Julia pulled herself out of bed and looked out the window. To her surprise, the sun was out and Claude had already piled the broken branches and sticks from the ice storm in the side yard. She glanced at the clock on her bedside table. It was already nine-thirty. How in the world had she slept so long? Then the memory of finding the attic bedroom hit her and she sat down hard on her bed. Her mind felt like she had lived a thousand years and, for some reason, her body ached like it too. Either that, or she was coming down with something. No, that wasn't it. After learning she had a sister, finding the hidden bedroom, and speculating nonstop about what her parents had done, it was no wonder she wanted to sleep. It was too much to digest all at once, and she wanted it to go away. And yet, she had to know the truth. There was no other choice.

She got dressed, made her way down to the kitchen, and stood at the sink, staring out the window. How in the world she was going to fit all the pieces together? Why was her sister locked in the attic? And for how long? What happened to her? Did her parents have something to do with her death? Where was she buried? Was there a birth certificate? A death certificate? Was it possible the albino woman, Lilly, had something to do with this, or was she a separate issue altogether? Could the little girl have been Lilly's child, an illegitimate baby shamefully hidden away when Mother found out about the affair?

There were probably more clues in the attic, but it would take months to go through everything, and Julia couldn't wait that long. Besides, she wouldn't know where to start. Her parents wouldn't have wanted anyone to know they were hiding a child in the attic, so there probably wasn't anyone to question. But someone, somewhere, had to know something. Then it hit her. There was one person who had been here through everything.

Claude.

She put on boots and a jacket, went out the back door, and marched over to the barn. Claude was at the desk in the office doing paperwork. He glanced up when she came in.

"Morning," he said, then looked down at his work again.

"Morning," she said. She waited on the other side of the desk, her hands in her jacket pockets to keep them from shaking. She wasn't sure if she was worried he'd tell her the truth, or worried he'd refuse to talk again.

"I see you cleaned up the yard," she said.

He kept his eyes on the papers. "Almost," he said. "There's still a few branches lying around, but most of it's ready to be burned."

"I can do that."

"Suit yourself." He penciled numbers into a ledger, concentrating.

She bit her lip, unsure how to begin. If he didn't help her, she wouldn't know what to do next. "I know you're busy," she said. "But can you come over to the house for a minute?"

"What for?"

"I need you to see something."

He turned the ledger page and wrote down more numbers. "What is it? I've got to finish these accounts."

"I'm not sure," she said. "That's why I need you to take a look."

He finally looked up at her, his forehead furrowed. "Why don't you ask Fletcher? He'll be here in a few minutes."

She shook her head. "Fletcher can't help me with this. And I don't have anyone else to ask. I found something in the house, something horrible and shocking . . . and . . . and if I don't figure out what my parents . . ." Her voice caught in her throat and she pressed her fingers against her lips for a moment, trying to stop the sudden flow of tears. When she could speak again, she said, "I just want to know the truth."

He leaned back in his chair and studied her face, as if sizing her up or judging her motives. Anger hardened his features, but she held his gaze, refusing to look away. If he read the determination in her eyes, so be it. She needed him to tell her what he knew.

After what seemed like forever, he sat forward, took off his cap, and scrubbed a hand over his graying hair. He set the cap on the desk and clasped his hands together against his mouth, thinking. Then he looked her in the eye. She thought he was going to refuse to help again, but his brow relaxed and his unyielding eyes softened. Defiance turned into something that looked like sadness, or maybe it was regret.

"You found a way into the attic," he said. It wasn't a question.

Her legs went watery. "Mm-hm," she managed.

"And the hidden bedroom."

She nodded, pulled a stool away from the wall, and sat down before she fell. "What do you know about it?"

He scratched the back of his neck and frowned, hesitant to go on. When he finally spoke, his voice was tight, as if the words were hard to say. "Your parents had another child."

She nodded again.

"She wasn't . . . she wasn't . . . normal."

Julia swallowed. "What do you mean? Was she deformed or something?"

He stood and made his way around the desk, then headed toward the door. She thought he was going to leave and she got to her feet, ready to beg him to stay. But he stopped and stared out the window next to the door. She sat back down, studying his profile. He looked troubled.

"It's what people did back then," he said. His voice sounded different, sad almost. Or maybe it was weary. "I suppose it was better than being put in an institution somewhere."

"I don't know," she said. "Maybe if she had gotten help—"

"It wasn't my business."

She wanted to ask why a child being locked in an attic wasn't his business, but she refrained. If she made him mad, he might clam up again. "What was wrong with her?"

"I'm not sure. Some sort of skin condition, I think, but your father said she had other problems."

Julia stiffened. Skin condition? What kind of skin condition? Albinism? Her mind reeled. Was it possible Lilly was her sister, not her father's mistress? Is that why her father went to the circus all the time? But if her sister was locked in the attic, how and when did she get out?

How did she end up joining the circus? It didn't seem possible.

"Did you ever see her?"

Claude pressed his lips together and shook his head. He was lying again. She could tell.

"Was she an albino?" she said.

"I don't know. Your father didn't say much about her. He and Mrs. Blackwood were—"

"Ashamed?"

He turned to look at her. "I was going to say private. Mr. and Mrs. Blackwood were very private people. And I can't be sure, but their decision might have had something to do with Mrs. Blackwood's religious beliefs."

"In what way?"

He shrugged. "It's just the feeling I got."

"What was her name?"

"I don't know."

"Was it Lilly?"

"I'm not sure."

"What happened to her?"

He shrugged again and went back to his desk.

"Is she dead?" Julia pressed.

He sat down and shuffled through the papers. "Listen, that's all I know. Like I said, your father didn't talk about her much. I think it was too hard for him." He put his cap back on and picked up a pencil, his face guarded again. "Now, if you don't mind, I've got work to do."

Julia dug her fingernails into her palms,

struggling to stay calm. He wasn't telling her everything, and she had no idea why. They were talking about *her* house, *her* parents, *her* sister. She had a right to know what happened. Frustration and anger built up like steam inside her head. She got up, snatched the papers from his desk, and held them out of his reach.

"I don't believe you," she said. "If my parents didn't want anyone to know about my sister, why would my father tell you she was up in the attic? He must have trusted you. With all of it."

He frowned. "I don't know. It was a long time ago. Maybe he needed to get it off his chest."

"Did you go to the police? Did you try to get her out of there?"

He shook his head.

"Why not?"

"By the time your father told me, it was . . ." He shifted in his chair.

"It was what?"

"It was too late."

"Too late for what?"

He clenched his jaw, his temples working in and out. "You're asking questions I don't have the answers to."

It was all she could do not to throw the papers at him. "I don't understand why you're lying," she said. "My parents are dead. So who are you protecting?"

"I'm not protecting anyone."

"Did my sister die up there? Did she escape? I need to know what happened!"

"I told you, I don't know anything else. I made it my business not to know."

She dropped the papers on the desk, sadness and disgust welling up in her eyes. Several of them slid into his lap, but he made no move to retrieve them. She went to door and glared back at him. "Then you're just as guilty as my parents," she said, and walked out.

CHAPTER 31

Lilly

"I can't take this much longer," Lilly said to Cole. "What is Mr. Barlow going to do to us for stealing Pepper?"

They were sitting on the sofa, locked inside their sleeper car on the rail lot where Pepper killed Merrick, roustabouts and strongmen guarding the windows and doors. It had been nearly fifteen hours since Viktor forced them back to the train by gunpoint, and she couldn't stop thinking about the three birds in the big top during the tornado. Three birds, three deaths. Merrick was dead, so who was next? Her and Cole?

"I don't know," Cole said. "If he was going to call the cops and have us arrested, he would have done it by now. Knowing him, he's coming up with his own punishment."

Lilly hugged her daughter to her chest and kissed the top of her head, tears burning her eyes. "If something happens to us, who will take care of Phoebe?"

Cole put an arm around her. "Try not to worry. I'll talk to Mr. Barlow. Maybe he'll let us work without pay for a few years, or I can take the punishment for both of us. Whatever happens, you're not going to be separated from our little girl, I promise."

Lilly closed her eyes and buried her nose into Phoebe's silky hair. What had they done? Not only had they failed to save Pepper, but they had put their daughter's future in danger too.

Just then, the pounding chug of an approaching locomotive thudded outside. A short train passed by the windows of their car, and iron brakes caught and screeched, caught and screeched. Cole got up and pushed aside the curtain to look out. "My God," he said in a quiet voice.

"What is it?" Lilly set Phoebe on the sofa and went to the window.

On the other side of a second set of tracks, a crowd of townies had gathered around the train depot. Men, women, and children filled every available spot, perched on top of lone boxcars, sitting inside open car doors, standing on water tower stairs and overturned barrels. The adults jostled one another for prime viewing space while children held balloons and ate popcorn and cotton candy, or played tag in front of the platform. A half-dozen men set up cameras.

"That bastard got the word out all right," Cole said. "He must have made an announcement during this afternoon's show."

"Do you think he sold tickets?" Lilly said.

"No, it's a publicity stunt."

Lilly buried her face in her hands. "Poor Pepper."

Cole pulled her to him and they both grew quiet.

When Lilly could speak around the lump in her throat, she looked up and said, "How do you think he's going to do it?"

Cole jerked his chin toward the window to indicate the locomotive that had just pulled in. "With that."

Lilly drew away from him and looked out. The locomotive sat on the tracks several hundred feet away, situated halfway between the Barlow Brothers' train and the depot. Only one railcar sat behind the engine—a derrick car mounted with an industrial crane used for lifting railway carriages on and off the tracks.

"I don't understand," Lilly said. "How—"

Before she could finish her question, keys rattled in their door. The handle turned and Viktor walked in with Mr. Barlow's men.

"Let's go," he snarled at Cole and Lilly.

"Where?" Cole said.

"Mr. Barlow wants you to witness the execution," he said.

"How can you go along with this?" Lilly cried. "Pepper was only trying to protect JoJo! Even Glory understands that!"

"Merrick saved my life," Viktor said. "That bull killed him."

"Do you really think Merrick took you out of that asylum because he cared?" she said. "He did it to make money off you, the same way he made money off me."

"Shut up and let's go," Viktor said.

"No," Lilly said. "I can't. I won't."

"I'll go," Cole said. "Let her stay here with Phoebe."

With that, one of Mr. Barlow's men rushed Cole and wrestled his arm behind his back. On the sofa, Phoebe began to wail.

"What the hell?" Cole said. He grimaced and struggled to get away.

"Mr. Barlow wants you both there," Viktor said.

The other man made a move to grab Lilly.

"Leave her alone!" Cole shouted.

Lilly moved away from the strongman and

put up her hands. "All right, all right. I'll come," she said. "There's no need for force." She whisked Phoebe off the sofa and held her close. "Shhh, sweet baby. Mommy's right here."

"I said I'd cooperate," Cole said. "Now let me go."

The man released Cole but stayed beside him, ready to grab him again if necessary. Cole rubbed his arm and gazed at Lilly, silently warning her to go along with whatever they said. Lilly stared back, terror and grief twisting in her chest.

Together they followed Viktor out of the sleeper car and along the train, trailed by Mr. Barlow's men. A thousand horrible thoughts raced through Lilly's mind, and her legs and arms felt like rubber.

"Let me leave Phoebe with Glory," Lilly said to Viktor. "She doesn't need to see this."

Viktor said nothing, but stopped farther along the train outside Glory's car. Glory took Phoebe with tears in her eyes and hugged Lilly and Cole, refusing to look at her brother. "Everything's going to be okay," she whispered in Lilly's ear. "Don't worry."

Lilly nodded and kissed Phoebe's soft cheek, her eyes flooding, then followed Viktor around to the other side of the train. They stopped across from the crowded depot next to a group of railroad officials, important-looking men in suits and shiny shoes, and the sheriff who shot Pepper. The townies who hadn't seen Viktor yet pointed and stared at him, and numerous children ran frightened and crying to their mothers. Several hundred yards away, a trio of railroad men used a steam shovel to dig a giant grave in an empty lot. Lilly clung to Cole, trembling in the grip of impending doom.

With everyone in place, Mr. Barlow promenaded out from behind the derrick car, smiling in his top hat and red jacket. He faced the audience and lifted his hands and chin, as if getting ready to announce an act inside the big top, then waved an arm to one side to draw everyone's attention to his left. A group of animal handlers brought Pepper out of the Barlow Brothers' train, whacking her with bull hooks and cattle prods. Pepper lifted her trunk and bellowed with each strike before hurrying forward. Streaks of blood ran down her sides and legs. When she reached the derrick, the handlers chained her back leg to the tracks and moved away.

Every beat of Lilly's heart felt like an explosion beneath her ribcage. She couldn't believe what she was seeing. Mr. Barlow was going to execute Pepper, and in front of all these people. People who had come to see her killed. And humans called animals bloodthirsty.

Pepper swayed back and forth next to the

tracks, shaking and trembling. She knew something bad was going to happen. Then she saw Lilly and lifted her trunk. She trumpeted and reached out in desperation, her wide ears fanning back and forth. Lilly swallowed a sob and started toward her. She had to get to Pepper, to comfort her and apologize for not doing more to save her. If Pepper was going to die, she deserved to know she was loved. Viktor caught Lilly and yanked her back.

Cole tore Viktor's hand from her arm. "Don't touch her," he snarled.

"Tell her to stay put," Viktor said.

Cole pulled Lilly close. "I'm sorry," he said. "I know you want to help, but there's nothing you can do."

She sagged against him. He was right, and the fact that Pepper might think she and Cole had something to do with her execution felt like a knife in her heart.

A roustabout threw a heavy chain around Pepper's neck, fastened it like a noose, and fitted the end through a steel ring on the derrick cable. Mr. Barlow signaled the derrick operator and the crowd grew quiet.

"Oh my God," Lilly cried. "You can't do this! You can't do this!"

"Shut up," Viktor growled.

The derrick operator pulled a handle back, the winch squealed, and the chain rattled and

467

constricted around Pepper's neck. Lilly's knees went weak and the blood drained from her face. The chain pulled tighter and tighter, slowly lifting Pepper's front feet off the ground. Pepper struggled and bellowed and threw her head back and forth, her eyes wide with terror. Bile rose in the back of Lilly's throat and, for a second, she thought she was going to pass out. Then there was a gruesome ripping sound and Pepper screamed. The audience gasped. The derrick operator lowered Pepper onto the tracks, and the chain loosened around her neck. Two roustabouts ran over and undid the chain around her back leg, but her ankle was already torn open.

A rush of adrenaline surged through Lilly and she yanked herself from Cole's arms and ran toward Pepper.

"Lilly, no!" Cole shouted. He chased after her, but Viktor grabbed him and held him back.

When Lilly reached the terrified bull, she slowed. Pepper was panicking, moving back and forth and side to side, shaking her head and trying to get loose of the chain. The roustabouts and handlers stayed clear.

"It's all right, Pepper," Lilly said, holding out a hand. "I'm going to help you. It's okay."

At first, Pepper didn't respond. Then she noticed Lilly and stopped struggling. A deep, mournful sound rumbled in her throat.

Out of the corner of her eye, Lilly saw Mr. Barlow storming toward them. She moved closer to Pepper. "Come on, girl," she said. "Pick me up."

Pepper limped forward, wrapped her trunk around Lilly, and lifted her onto her head. Lilly moved to Pepper's back, grabbed the derrick cable, and tried undoing the chain from the steel ring. If she could get Pepper free of the noose, or even if she couldn't, she was going stay put until Mr. Barlow agreed not to follow through with the execution. He wouldn't kill Pepper while Lilly was on top of her, not in public anyway. After that, she had no idea what would happen. But she had to try something. She pulled down on the steel ring, struggling to loosen the cable and release the chain. It was too tight.

"What the hell do you think you're doing?" Mr. Barlow yelled up at her. "Get down from there!" Behind him, a group of roustabouts were closing in. Cole had gotten away from Viktor and was running toward her, Viktor on his heels.

Mr. Barlow signaled the derrick operator again, despite the fact that Lilly was standing on top of the bull. The winch powered up, the operator pulled the handle, and the cable tightened. Lilly lost her balance and fell to her knees. She nearly slipped off Pepper's back, but held on to the chain around her neck. Women gasped and pulled their children into their skirts while men craned their necks to get a better look. Cole ran over to the derrick car, scrambled up the side, grabbed the operator by the shirt, and hauled him out of the cab. Then he climbed into the driver's seat, pushed the handle forward, and the cable went loose. Lilly stood and struggled to undo the chain again. Viktor climbed up the derrick car, seized Cole by the collar, and punched him hard in the face. Cole listed to one side, seemingly out cold, then straightened and rammed a fist into Viktor's steam-shovel jaw. Unfazed, Viktor punched Cole again, harder this time, then dragged him out of the operator's seat and took his place. Four roustabouts latched on to Cole's legs, yanked him down from the car, and held him to the ground. Cole thrashed and cussed, frantically fighting to get away. One of Mr. Barlow's strongmen kicked him in the head and he went limp, his face turned to one side.

In the derrick operator's seat, Viktor pushed the levers and moved the handle, and the crane swung to the left, jerking Pepper in the same direction. Lilly tumbled sideways and straddled Pepper's neck, hanging on for dear life. When the crane slowly swung back again, she scrambled to her feet, reached for the steel ring, and tried to pull down on the chain at the same time. Viktor jostled the handle forward and to the right, and the crane lowered and swung to the other side. The cable loosened and Lilly yanked down on the steel ring and struggled to undo the chain. A whooshing noise sounded above her head and she looked up. The boom of the crane dropped down and over, then switched direction and headed straight at her. Before she could react, it slammed into her stomach, cracked her ribcage, and knocked her off Pepper's back. In what seemed like slow motion, she flew through the air, her lungs empty and useless, her arms and hair out like the limbs of a falling doll.

She struck a railroad switch several yards away, the metal sign smashing into her lower spine, the sound of splintering bones exploding in her brain. She screamed and hit the ground with a thud, her body rigid with agony. Somewhere in the back of her mind, she heard the crowd gasp. The world swam in and out of focus, blurred behind a bloody film of tears. She closed her eyes, panting and trying to hold on to consciousness. Her torso burned as if someone had set her on fire.

After what seemed like forever, the dizziness passed and she opened her eyes. On her side in the dirt, she was facing the circus train, and her legs and arms felt bent at odd angles. Several railroad officials and the sheriff rushed toward her. Behind them, Mr. Barlow's strongmen dragged Cole away.

She gritted her teeth and tried to sit up. Her arms worked, but she couldn't push herself off the ground. The pain in her middle was like nothing she had ever felt before, every breath like a hundred twisting blades in her spine. She tried to roll over, but no matter how hard she struggled, she couldn't move. She looked down at her stomach. A gore-streaked bar stuck out of her lower abdomen, and blood oozed from the wound. Oddly, she felt no pain. She touched the area around the metal bar and sticky blood coated her fingers. *Once that's out, I'll be fine,* she thought.

A cluster of boots and shoes appeared and the sheriff knelt beside her, his face lined with alarm. "Don't move," he said. "You're going to be okay."

Behind her, the derrick crane powered up again. The winch squealed and the chain rattled.

"No . . ." she said, reaching for the sheriff with a bloody hand. "Don't . . . don't let . . . them kill Pepper."

"Just hold on and we'll get help," the sheriff said. He stood and shouted, "Someone get an ambulance!"

Behind Lilly, the crane creaked, the cable whined, and the crowd laughed and clapped. Pepper bellowed several times, then let out shriek after agonized shriek. Lilly put her hands over her ears, but the sounds of Pepper struggling found its way through her trembling hands and ripped into her brain. She sobbed and gagged, her breath growing shallow and fast. Iron and steel creaked in protest against the heavy weight of Pepper's writhing body until, little by little, the cable stopped squeaking and the crowd grew quiet. Lilly's arms went limp and her vision started closing in, like a dark curtain drawing in around her. The world spun out of control and a feeling of utter doom swallowed her. *This must be what it feels like to die,* she thought. *But I can't . . . Phoebe needs me. . . .* Then she felt like she was falling and the world went black.

CHAPTER 32

Julia

After questioning Claude about the hidden bedroom and her sister, Julia trudged back to the manor, her mind reeling. She had spent her entire life feeling sorry for herself because of Mother's coldness and Father's distance, thinking something had to be wrong with her to make her unworthy of their love. And even though she knew deep in her heart her father's car accident wasn't her fault, she'd always blamed herself for that too. Sure, he was the one who chose to drink and drive, but she was the one who had skipped church to go swimming. The burden she carried was real.

Now she realized she was the lucky one. She had been able to live a relatively normal life and leave Blackwood Manor, unlike her sister who had been kept prisoner because of the way she looked. Sadly, it came as no surprise that Mother was ashamed of her firstborn. Because despite her pious ways in private, outward appearances had always mattered most to her, hence the fancy dresses and furs when she went out in public, and the happy family charade for the outside world. But locking up a child was unimaginable. It was monstrous and cruel and disgusting. And Father had been in on it. No wonder he drank. Was that why he needed God's forgiveness, or was it something else?

When Julia got back to the house, she rolled up every shade, yanked aside every heavy drape, and opened every window. Fresh air and sunshine would never flush Blackwood Manor of its horrible secrets and lies, but airing out the house felt like something she needed to do. If only she could open windows in her head and air out her mind. Unfortunately, the image of a little girl in the attic bedroom had burned itself into her brain for all eternity. After grabbing a box of matches from a kitchen cupboard, she put on a heavy coat, boots, and gloves, and went back outside to burn the pile of fallen branches from the ice storm. Physical labor always helped her think, and she needed to figure out what to do next.

Her father always burned leaves in the fall, and she could still picture him sitting on a stump in the side yard, chain-smoking cigarettes and swigging whiskey from a silver flask. He looked like a man condemned to hell on earth, and it had filled her heart with fear to see him there, his shoulders slumped like something bad had happened. Now she knew why he looked that way. Terrible secrets, like poison, eat away at you from the inside.

At the burning spot, the mound of downed branches and sticks from the storm was as big as a car. Along with a base of old leaves from last fall, it would create quite a fire. Julia walked the perimeter of the lawn, picking up stray branches to add to the pile.

On her first turn around the yard, she stopped by the garden shed and looked up at Blackwood Manor. Unlike the front and back of the house, which had eight attic dormers, this side of the house had only four. None of them would have been in the hidden bedroom, but she couldn't help imagining a pale little girl looking out one of the moldy windows, alone and wondering why she couldn't go outside. The thought of it twisted and burned inside her chest as surely as an arrow piercing her heart would have caused her agony. Even if she gutted the manor and redid the inside, how could she live there, knowing the pain and suffering an innocent child had suffered behind its walls?

She threw a handful of sticks on the pile and went into the garden shed. The stack of old newspapers in a wooden crate was still there, and a tin of lantern oil high on a shelf. Back out at the burning spot, she stuffed crumpled newspaper between the bottom branches of the mound, poured lantern oil over the sticks and old leaves, then lit the paper and stepped back. The fire caught immediately and spread, filling the quiet afternoon with the sound of snapping fingers. The orange and blue flames crackled and spit and rose quickly toward the sky.

She stared at the fire, mesmerized and watching the flames blacken the branches and devour the leaves. The fire grew higher and warmed her face and hands. If anyone had seen her standing there, they would have no clue of the chaos swirling inside her head. How was it possible for parents to lock up their own child? How could they live with themselves, knowing their daughter was being held prisoner, unable to breathe fresh air and feel the sun on her skin while they were free do as they pleased? Did they hide her in the attic as soon as she was born? Did they tell everyone she was stillborn? A memory flickered in her mind—someone saying how happy they were to see Julia had grown up healthy and strong after Mother spent her entire pregnancy in bed. Who was it? She couldn't remember. Were they worried because they'd been told Mother lost her first baby? Was there a birth certificate in the house with the name of Mother's doctor? Was Lilly her sister? What happened to her? Was she dead? Did her parents need forgiveness for locking her up, or something else? Did she die in the attic, or did she escape and join the circus? Was it possible the circus was still in business? How did Lilly's camera get in Father's desk, not to mention her hairbrush and jewelry? Hundreds of questions boggled Julia's mind and made her sick to her stomach all at the same time.

She blinked and stepped back, the skin on her face burning as though she'd been out in the sun too long, and panic suddenly tightened her chest. While she'd been in a trance, the fire had grown taller and wider and hotter. It singed the lower branches of a nearby tree and inched into the yard, blackening and destroying the brown grass like water eroding a sand beach. She looked around for something to put out the errant flames. Her father used to use a shovel and pitchfork to keep the fire in check, but she realized too late that she had neither. She looked over at the barn to see if Claude was watching. Maybe he could help. She didn't see him anywhere.

Desperate, she stomped the burning ground to put out the spreading flames. But the intense heat burned her skin and throat, forcing her back. She held her breath and kept trying, but couldn't get close for more than a second or two. Then the huge pile shifted and started to collapse, and embers and sparks flew through the air. She jumped out of the way and looked around the yard for something to put out the inferno—a shovel, a hose, a bucket of rainwater. She saw nothing. She had to get Claude. She started toward the barn, running and yelling for help, then glanced over her shoulder at the fire. A flash of red caught her eye and she stopped in her tracks to look back at the house.

Flames engulfed a set of curtains in an open window.

Father's den.

For a second, horror paralyzed her. Then she came to her senses and ran into the house. She grabbed the braided rug in front of the kitchen sink and raced toward the den. The fire had already destroyed the curtains and was crawling across the ceiling, the dry wood bursting into orange and yellow flames. Smoke filled the room and piles of old papers and books blackened and curled and burned next to the fiery window. She held her breath and beat the rug against the books and papers, but no sooner had she put one blaze out, when another started. Smoke burned her eyes and bits and pieces of burning ceiling fell on her pants and jacket. Coughing and squinting, she tried beating back the flames with the rug, but they were spreading too fast.

Claude suddenly appeared beside her, a fire extinguisher in his hands. "Get out of the way!" he yelled.

She backed up, hacking and gagging, the back of her hand over her mouth. Claude pulled the fire extinguisher pin and aimed the hose at the flames. For a brief moment, Julia thought the fire was going out. Then the extinguisher quit working. Claude frantically turned the knob, shook the cylinder, and hit it with his hand, but it didn't help. The wall above the window buckled, the frame caved in, and burning timbers dropped to the floor. With more air to feed it, the fire flared higher. More papers caught fire and a section of burning ceiling fell to the floor in a thunderous crash, throwing up more flames and sparks. Claude grabbed Julia's arm and steered her toward the door.

"We need to get out of here!" he shouted.

In the hall, smoke filled the ceiling and slithered toward the other rooms. Claude and Julia hurried into the kitchen and out the back door. When they were far enough away, she stopped to look back, her face covered in soot and sweat, one trembling hand over her mouth. Fire and smoke poured out of the den windows, and flames licked up the siding toward the second story. Julia's legs went weak. What had she done?

The ruins of Blackwood Manor lay in a smoking pile of black timbers and smoldering ashes, two charred chimneys and numerous sections of burnt walls standing amongst the rubble. By the time the fire trucks had arrived, the flames had fully engulfed half the house. There was nothing Julia and Claude could do but watch.

When the roof caved in, Julia fell to her knees on the ground. Claude stood silently beside her, his face a curious mixture of shock and relief. The firemen rushed toward the burning building with their hoses, and the second and third floors collapsed in a thunderous, fiery heap. Julia trembled and stared as they struggled to put out the flames, tears streaming down her soot-covered face. She felt disconnected; as if it were happening to someone else, or it would end soon, like a nightmare or practical joke. Someone or something would wake her and she'd find out it was all a dream, she was sure of it.

Then a fireman brought over two blankets and

wrapped one around her shoulders, and she realized that, indeed, this was happening to her. Somehow, she had started a fire in Blackwood Manor and now it was being destroyed, along with its horrible, hidden secrets. The fireman offered a blanket to Claude, but he shook his head.

The fireman knelt next to Julia and said, "Are you all right, miss?"

She managed a nod.

"Were you inside when the fire started?" the fireman said.

She shook her head.

He looked at Claude. "What about you?"

"I was in the barn," he said.

The fireman put a hand under Julia's arm. "Come on," he said. "Let's get you off this wet ground. It's cold out here."

Julia let him help her up and stood on shaky legs.

"Are you sure you're not hurt?" the fireman said. "The ambulance is on its way. Maybe someone should take a look at you."

She swallowed and tried to find her voice. When she did, it was raspy and weak. "I'm fine."

"All right," the fireman said. "If you say so. But don't hesitate to ask for help if you need it." He gave her a quick nod and went back to the trucks to help the others.

After a few minutes, Fletcher sped into the barn

driveway and barreled over the lawn toward Julia and Claude. When he reached them, he slammed on his brakes and jumped out of his truck, his face pale, his eyes wide.

"What happened?" he said. "Are you guys okay?"

"We're all right," Claude said. He nodded once at Julia. "But she needs to sit down in your truck."

"Come on," Fletcher said to Julia. "You're white as a sheet." He took her arm and led her over to his truck. Claude followed and opened the passenger side door.

In what felt like a trance, she climbed in and sat with the blanket around her shoulders, her teeth chattering. Fletcher got in the driver's side and turned on the heater while Claude stood in the open passenger door.

"What the hell happened?" Fletcher said again.

"It's my fault," Julia and Claude said at the same time.

She turned and gaped at Claude. Why was he taking the blame? She was the one who opened the house windows and started a fire in the side yard. She was the one who hadn't been paying attention and let the flames get out of hand. Then another thought crossed her mind. Maybe she had been hoping it would happen. Maybe the horrible truth about her parents and the cruelty committed inside Blackwood Manor was too much to face. No, it didn't make sense. She needed answers and now she might never find them. And she wanted justice, for herself and her sister. Now she had no proof her sister ever existed. Everything was gone.

"It's my fault," Claude said with more conviction.

Julia shook her head. "What are you talking about? I was the one who left the windows open. I was the one burning branches and not—"

"I knew about your sister," Claude said.

"I know," she said. "You told me that."

Claude straightened his shoulders and stared at her, as if steeling himself for what he had to say next. Julia bit down on her lip and waited, her knees quivering with apprehension.

"There's more," he said.

"I know that too," she said.

He blew out a hard breath. "You positive you want to know the truth?"

She nodded.

"Okay. Then if you're feeling up to it, I want to show you something."

She started climbing out of the truck.

Fletcher put a gentle hand on her arm. "What are you doing?" he said. "I don't think you should leave. You might be going into shock, and the police will have questions about the fire."

She gave him a weak smile and got out of the

truck. "I'll be fine. This is something I need to do."

Fletcher frowned. "What the hell is going on around here? Can't this wait?"

"We're not going far," Claude said to him. "When the police arrive tell them the fire was an accident and we'll be right back. Do you have a flashlight?"

Fletcher sighed loudly and shook his head, clearly frustrated and confused. There was no arguing with Claude and he knew it. He swore under his breath, got out, and rummaged around behind his seat. He pulled out a flashlight, came around the front of the truck, and handed it to Julia, worry written on his face. "Julia, please," he said. "You can do this later."

"No," she said. "I can't. I have to do it now. I'll explain everything when we come back." She took off the blanket and looked at Claude, gripping the flashlight with both hands. "Lead the way."

Claude turned and started toward the woods.

In the backyard behind the still-burning remains of Blackwood Manor, Julia followed Claude to the far edge of the lawn, through a narrow space between clipped hedges. Together they crossed a swath of dead weeds and icy puddles, then entered the woods and ducked between gangly saplings and pine trees. There was no need for the flashlight yet, but Julia was glad they had it just in case. When they followed what looked like an animal path deeper into the forest, a memory played around the edges of her mind.

As a child, she wasn't allowed to leave the yard or go into the woods. But at age fourteen, she had ventured into the dark interior to smoke her first cigarette, curious why the kids in school and her father found them so appealing. After the first puffs made her cough and nearly throw up, she put the cigarette out, waited for the dizziness to pass, and started back the way she came. The sun was setting, the sky between the overhead foliage had turned purple, and within minutes she was lost, imagining her father finding her body, her arms and face gnawed by wild animals. She stumbled through the brush in a panic, Mother's warning that bad things would happen when you misbehaved playing over and over in her mind. When, at last, she found her way out, she burst through the hedgerow into the yard, her face covered in scratches and tears, and vowed never to go into the woods again.

And yet, as she followed Claude on the winding path between tree roots and boulders, it seemed as though there was something else she should remember, something more than sneaking a cigarette, more than disobeying her parents, more than the fear of getting lost and eaten by wild animals.

High-skirted evergreens and branches rustled overhead, and the charred smell of the burning house filtered in through the woods. Where sunlight barely broke through to the musty forest floor, patches of snow and ice remained here and there among the scrubs and bushes. Damage from the ice storm disfigured the larger trees, their high limbs splintered and hanging, or broken and scattered on the ground. Claude cleared debris from the trail several times, and they had to climb over an old fallen oak in their path. The farther into the woods she and Claude went, the more the old fear of getting lost returned. The shattered trees and the death-like stink of smoke reminded her of a war zone or postapocalyptic wasteland, mirroring her frame of mind. Her entire world had been turned upside down and destroyed, and she had no idea where she was going.

But there was no turning back now. She had to know the truth. Besides, Claude seemed to know the way. Near what looked like the end of the path, he pushed aside the boughs of a tall spruce, held them back, and waited while she stepped through. On the other side of the spruce, hawthorn and juniper encircled a clearing full of tussocky, snow-covered grass, leaves and brambles, and moldering logs encased in ice.

In the center of the clearing, an iron fence surrounded a single headstone.

Julia stopped in her tracks and another memory came to her, vague and blurry—her father carrying her into the woods, the two of them planting flowers inside a fence, then picking dandelions and laying them beside a square, gray stone. A hollow draft of dread moved through her bones.

"Who is this?" she said.

Claude said nothing and continued over to the fence. He kicked aside wet leaves and broken branches in front of the gate, lifted the clasp and opened it. The metal hinges screeched in the quiet forest and a rustle sounded nearby as some small creature scurried away. Claude gazed at her, waiting, his eyes tired, his face worn. She swallowed, stepped warily through the gate, and read the simple stone. Above a carved cross, it read:

BELOVED DAUGHTER

Julia blinked back tears and moved closer, trembling fingers over her mouth. Claude followed and stood beside her.

"How did you know she was here?" Julia said.

"I helped your father bury her."

She drew in a sharp breath. A million questions raced through her mind, but she had to be careful and not push too hard. She needed Claude to tell her everything. "What happened to her?"

"I've never told anyone about this. And I've had to live with it all these years."

"Live with what?"

"I was working late that night because a buyer was coming early the next morning and I had to get the horses ready."

She looked at him. "What night?"

"The night I saw your mother, I mean Mrs. Blackwood, take the girl out of the house."

The hairs on the back of Julia's neck stood up. *The girl.* The feeling that she was about to learn a horrible truth fell over her like an icy shroud. "So my sister got out of the attic. And you knew about her all along. How long was she up there?"

He held up a hand. "Please. Just hear me out. I need to get through this."

She clenched her jaw and waited.

"It was nearly midnight," he said. "Mr. Blackwood was out of town, and I was having a quick smoke out on the other side of the barn. Next thing I know, I see Mrs. Blackwood leading the girl across the north pasture into the woods." He paused to brush a tangle of dead leaves from the top of the gravestone.

"Then what happened?"

"I had no idea what they were up to and I didn't know what to do. Of course, looking back, I should have done something. But at the time . . ." He scrubbed a hand over his forehead.

"After a while, I saw Mrs. Blackwood come out of the woods alone."

Goose bumps broke out on Julia's arms. *What on earth had Mother done?*

"The next day Mr. Blackwood told me his daughter passed," he continued. "I swear that was the first time he mentioned her to me. Up until then, I thought she was stillborn like they said." His eyes grew glassy.

"Oh my God," Julia breathed. She gaped at the tombstone and ground. Was this where her sister died after being locked up in the attic? Were they standing on the very spot she was murdered? She put a hand on her chest. It felt like the air was being pulled from her lungs.

"After he told me she was dead, I didn't know what to do. I kept thinking I should have done something, anything to stop Mrs. Blackwood from doing whatever she'd done. I called in sick for two days because I couldn't face them. I didn't know if I should call the police or . . ." He hesitated as if searching for the right words, then looked at her with desperate eyes. "You have to understand, I had a wife and son to take care of and jobs were scarce back then. And God help me, I told myself there was nothing I could do at that point. What was done was done. Losing my job wasn't going to bring that little girl back. So I went back to work and kept my mouth shut. That's when Mr. Blackstone started drinking."

The ground seemed to tilt beneath Julia's feet. "Are you saying my mother . . . my mother . . ." She couldn't finish.

He shook his head. "No, no. That's not what I'm saying. I've had a lot of years to mull this over, and I think I figured out what happened. A circus was leasing land on the other side of the tree line, over past the north pasture. After they pulled out the next day, that's when Mr. Blackstone told me his daughter was gone."

She gaped at Claude, a confusing mixture of relief and disgust and adrenaline rushing through her. Relief because Mother wasn't a murderer, disgust and adrenaline because she knew what was coming next. "Are you saying my mother gave my sister to the circus?"

He shook his head again. "No, I think she *sold* her to the circus."

Julia's heartbeat picked up speed. She was right. Lilly was her sister, not her father's mistress. That was why he saved the circus posters and tickets. That was why he clipped those articles. Still, she couldn't believe what she was hearing. Questions popped into her head faster than she could process them.

"But why? To get rid of her? It's not like they needed the money."

"I'm not entirely sure. But you have to remember it was the early thirties, during the Depression. The Blackwoods were struggling like everyone else, not horribly by any means, but they were still struggling."

"I don't care! That's no excuse for—"

"Just hear me out, will you?"

She bit her lip, sorrow and anger like a growing mass inside her chest. No wonder her father and mother needed God's forgiveness. She thought she might scream before Claude told her the rest.

"About a week after the girl disappeared," he said, "the Blackwoods bought Blue Venture, the horse that came in second at that year's Belmont Stakes and Kentucky Derby. After that, this farm really started raking in money. The Blackwoods hired a trainer, won a few races, then put Blue Venture up for stud. That horse saved Blackwood Farm. And buying him was Mrs. Blackwood's idea."

"Are you telling me my mother used the money to buy a horse?"

"I believe so."

Julia closed her eyes for a moment to let it sink in. How could anyone be so heartless? Keeping your daughter locked in the attic was horrific enough, but selling her to the circus was disgusting and sick. She looked at Claude.

"How old was my sister when Mother sold her?"

"Must have been about nine or ten, I'm not completely sure."

"Jesus," she said. "She locked her daughter in the attic for ten years, then sold her to a circus? What kind of monster was my mother anyway?"

Claude looked away, a dark shadow passing over his face. He scrubbed a hand over his forehead again and sighed loudly, as if he wanted to be anywhere but there. Then he gazed at her with troubled eyes. "There's something else."

She steeled herself. She wasn't sure she could take much more. "What?"

"I'm sorry to be the one to tell you this, but Mrs. Blackwood wasn't your mother. This is your mother, right here in this grave."

Julia's knees went weak. "What . . . what do you mean?" She shook her head. "No, that's . . . that's not possible. You must be confused."

"I'm not confused. Somehow, your mother ended up back on the farm with your grandparents. And you were with her."

"My grandparents?" At first, Julia didn't know who he was talking about, then it hit her and she dropped the flashlight and sank to the ground. My God. The people she thought were her parents were really her grandparents. And Lilly was her mother, not her sister. Her mind reeled with a thousand questions, but she could barely string two thoughts together. "But how . . . why . . ." She struggled to find the right words. "Why on earth would she ever come back here?"

He shrugged.

She stared at the gravestone, dizzy and light-headed. "How did she die?"

"Mr. Blackwood said it was pneumonia."

"Did you believe him?"

"I had no reason not to."

"How old was I?"

"I'm not sure. Just a baby."

"But how . . . ?" She paused, suddenly nauseous. All those stories "Mother" had told about being on bed rest while pregnant, about how happy they were when she was born healthy. They were lies. Nothing but lies. And what about her memories? What about "Mother" singing lullabies and tucking her in at night? Were they real or just a figment of her imagination?

"So my parents . . . I mean, my grand-parents . . . told everyone I was theirs?"

He nodded.

"How did they explain that?"

"There wasn't much need to explain anything. After Mrs. Blackwood sold your mother to the circus and Mr. Blackwood started drinking, things got pretty bad. The farm was prospering, but their lives were a mess. They stopped seeing friends, turned down invitations to social events, and the only people who came by the barn were clients. It was easy for them to tell everyone the doctor put Mrs. Blackwood on bed rest while she was 'expecting' and she wasn't up to visitors, especially after the story about your 'sister' being stillborn. And after you were 'born,' they said you were too fragile to come out of the house and no one was allowed to come by until you got stronger. They put a sign on the front door telling people to go to the barn and ask for me. I was ordered to call the house and let them know who it was, and they turned nearly everyone away, or your grandfather came over to the barn. I believe you were a toddler the first time I saw you outside."

She buried her face in her hands. Of course her grandparents had to lie, otherwise they would have been forced to admit what they'd done to their daughter. All this time, she had been blamed for her "father's" drinking and death. All this time, she wondered why she was unworthy of her "parents'" love. With a strange mixture of shock and relief, she realized everything she'd believed about herself and her "parents" was a lie. On one hand, she was thankful to know the truth. On the other, between burning down Blackwood Manor and the bombshell that Lilly was her mother, it was almost more than she could bear.

She took slow, deep breaths and tried to pull herself together. She scrubbed the tears from her face and touched the grave marker, the dead cold of stone biting through her skin. This was her mother. The mother she never knew. A woman—an albino—who had been locked in an attic as a child and sold to the circus. It was incredible and wretched and heartbreaking all at the same time. And yet it answered so many questions. Except one. How could her parents—her grandparents—have been so cruel? Somewhere in the back of her mind, she wondered what her life would have been like if her biological mother hadn't died. But trying to imagine a woman she'd never met as her mother was too overwhelming for her muddled brain right now. And trying to imagine growing up in a circus was impossible. She wouldn't even know where to start.

"So her name was Lilly?" she said.

"Yes."

"And my father?"

"Mr. Blackwood said he was dead, killed in some type of accident."

Julia pushed herself up on shaking legs. "And you helped bury my mother?"

"Yes."

"You helped take the body into the woods?"

"Yes."

"Where was she?"

"What do you mean?"

"Where was Lilly when she died?"

He rubbed the back of his neck, then looked at her with tortured eyes. "In the attic."

CHAPTER 33
Lilly

A yellow shaft of morning light penetrated the darkness, waking Lilly from a fitful sleep. She blinked and opened her eyes. A headache pounded at the back of her skull and her mind was slow and foggy. She felt like she'd been in a fight, every muscle aching and sore. She had no idea where she was, but she was lying on a bed. The sheet beneath her was cold and wet, and the was air filled with the stench of urine and the metallic odor of blood. A square of sunshine landed on a brick wall across the way, forming a silhouette of what looked like a narrow window covered with curly branches. She squinted, trying to figure out what she was seeing. Then a feathery shadow trembled at the bottom of the silhouette, like leaves on a branch. It was a bird. On a sill.

She drew in a sharp breath. It all seemed so familiar and strange at the same time, like something she had seen in a recurring dream. She looked up. Flowered wallpaper covered the arched ceiling above the bed—the same wallpaper her father had hung in her nook a hundred years ago. Her heart skipped a beat, then pounded hard in her chest. She turned her head and glanced around the room.

There was her dollhouse and her bookshelf full of books.

There was her tea set, complete with a lace doily, silver serving tray, and china cups.

There were her model farm animals, lined up on a shelf above her bookcase, all facing the same way.

She pressed the heels of her palms against her flooding eyes.

Was it all a dream? Had seeing the circus out her dormer window given her nightmares?

No. It was real. Merrick, Glory, the elephants, Cole.

Phoebe.

She put her hands to her chest. *I'm a woman now. A mother. It was real. All of it.* Panic exploded in her mind. *Where is my baby? And how did I get back in this room?* Then she realized she was wearing a hospital gown and could feel tight bandages around her middle. She remembered trying to save Pepper, being knocked by the crane to the ground, and someone saying they were taking her to a hospital. The image of Pepper hanging from the derrick cable flashed in her mind and a hot rush of grief ripped through her insides.

Pepper was dead.

She had to get out of here. She had to find

Cole and Phoebe. She had to make Mr. Barlow pay for what he had done. She tried to sit up but couldn't. Her stomach and back screamed in pain, and her lungs rattled and wheezed. She opened her mouth to scream for help but started coughing instead. She covered her mouth and tried to stop, but couldn't. Every bark sent a jolt of agony through her middle and she felt like she was being ripped in half. Beads of sweat broke out on her forehead. When she could finally take a breath without hacking, dark blotches of blood splattered the palm of her hand, and a warm, coppery taste filled her mouth. She touched her forehead with shaking fingers. She was burning with fever.

A key rattled in the door lock, the handle turned, and a woman entered the room.

It was Momma.

Using every ounce of strength she had, Lilly pushed herself up on her elbows, her heart thundering in her chest. Momma looked exactly the same, except for a sprinkle of gray hairs throughout her perfectly coiffed head and the crepey, pinched skin around her eyes and mouth. She was tanned and slender, with rosy cheeks and shining eyes, with the self-assured poise of a woman who had lived a happy and guilt-free life. The sight of her burned like acid in Lilly's gut. Momma approached with the familiar key ring attached to her apron, her face void of emotion.

"You're awake," she said.

"Where's my daughter?" Lilly said. Her voice was raspy and weak, and her throat felt like she had swallowed shredded glass. She started coughing again and had to force words out. "What . . . am I . . . doing here?"

"Your daughter is safe," Momma said.

Lilly clenched her jaw and tried to catch her breath. "Where is she?"

"Downstairs with her father."

Lilly gasped. "Cole?"

Momma shook her head. "No, she's downstairs with *your* father. Your husband, or whatever he was, is dead."

For a terrifying second, Lilly thought her heart stopped. A sudden falling sensation swept over her and she shook her head. "No," she said. "You're lying."

Momma frowned. "I never lie. Mr. Barlow said your husband was a thief and a coward, and instead of facing the consequences of his actions, he jumped from the train and died at the bottom of a river trestle."

"No!" she cried. "That's not true. Cole would never do that! If he's dead, Mr. Barlow had him thrown him off the train!"

Momma shrugged. "Who knows. I don't believe a word you circus people say anyway."

Lilly fell back on the pillow and buried her face in her hands, her mouth twisting in anguish.

No. Not Cole. I need him. Phoebe needs him! An image of his face flashed in her mind, and the black manacle of grief tightened around her heart and locked eternally into place with a solid, final thud. She sobbed and started coughing again, her shoulders convulsing. What was she going to do without her husband and best friend? How would she and Phoebe ever get out of here without him? She felt like she was going to die right there and then.

No. She had to pull herself together, for Phoebe's sake. She clenched her jaw and forced herself to breathe normally, then turned to look at Momma, her mind and body quaking with sorrow and fear.

"How did I get here?" she said. "How long have I been—"

"Since yesterday morning. Your father and I drove all the way to Nashville to get you. The doctors weren't sure you'd make the trip back."

"But why—"

"Mr. Barlow called us. Didn't surprise me when he said you'd been nothing but trouble since the day he met you. Don't try denying it. He told me everything. He's done with you and didn't want to get stuck with your hospital bills and taking care of your daughter. Your father insisted the least we could do was bring you back here. And once I realized the little girl was normal, I knew somebody had to look after her."

The icy fingers of fear clutched Lilly's throat. She glared at Momma. "Bring her to me."

Momma shook her head. "It's for the best."

Lilly pushed herself up on trembling arms. There was no way in hell she was going to let Momma raise Phoebe. She'd kill her before she'd let that happen. She had to get out of this room. She had to get her baby girl and leave this house. She struggled to get out of bed, but her legs wouldn't move. With growing horror, she realized she couldn't feel them. She squeezed her knees and pounded on her thighs, but they were lifeless and limp. She couldn't feel a thing. Tears blurred her vision and panic tore at her chest.

"You're paralyzed from the waist down," Momma said. "The doctors said it'd likely be the case if you survived."

Lilly sagged back on the pillow, trying to maintain her last shreds of sanity. If she couldn't get out of bed, she'd never get out of this room. She'd never get Phoebe back. *How could this be happening?* "Please," she cried. "I'm begging you. I have to see my little girl."

"I don't think that's a good idea."

"What are you talking about? She's my daughter! She needs me!"

"You're in no shape to be a mother. I always say God works in mysterious ways and every-thing happens for a reason. And finally, after

501

everything you put us through, your father and I are getting the daughter we deserve. She's taken to us like a fish to water, as she should. We're her grandparents, after all."

Terror and rage burned beneath Lilly's ribcage. "You're nothing to her!" she cried. "She's mine!" She coughed again, and a sharp pain ripped through her middle, like a thousand daggers stabbing her sinew and muscle and veins. She sobbed and retched, growing weaker and dizzier with every passing second. "I won't let you have her. Please. You have to bring her to me!"

"I'm sorry, but what's done is done." Momma went to the door, her keys clanking on her hip. Then she turned to look at Lilly, her fingers on the door handle. "If I were you, I'd stop begging for things you can't have and start making peace with God. Lord knows you've committed your fair share of sins." Then she walked out and locked the door.

Lilly wasn't sure how much time had passed since she woke up to find herself back in the attic of Blackwood Manor, but the window silhouette slowly made its way along the brick wall as morning turned to afternoon, then evening, night, and morning again. A deep but fragile sleep kept her mind from further torture, but it only protected her for short periods. Every few hours, she startled awake, coughing and instantly assaulted with the knowledge that Cole was dead, Momma had taken Phoebe, and she was trapped in the attic again. Every time she opened her eyes and remembered where she was and why, a sudden avalanche of grief and anger threatened to crush her. But she had to hold on for her daughter.

In between periods of exhausted oblivion, she used every ounce of strength she had left to try moving her legs, willing her brain to make them work. If she could get out of bed, she could hit Momma over the head, escape, and get Phoebe back. She tried lifting her thighs with her hands and a brutal twist of pain ripped through her middle. Beads of sweat dripped from her face. After every attempt, she fell back on the bed, drained and delirious with despair. She was still burning with fever, her lips were parched, her sheets were soiled and rank, and she was growing weaker by the hour.

"Please, God," she whispered. "Please. If you're there, I need you now more than ever."

But it was no use. Her legs were dead and lifeless.

No one brought her water or food, and she was beginning to think Momma was going to let her starve. How was it possible that her lungs still drew in air and her shattered heart was still beating? Agony nearly swallowed her.

A few hours after the sun came up, a key rattled

in the lock and the door opened. Phoebe toddled into the room, one finger in her cupid-bow mouth, her tiny brow creased with uncertainty. Lilly cried out and reached for her with trembling hands.

"Come here, baby girl," she said, tears flooding her eyes.

When Phoebe saw Lilly, her face lit up and she waddled over to the bed on chubby legs. Using what little strength she had left, Lilly lifted her up, ignoring the horrific pain in her stomach and back, and settled her on a clean section of blanket between her and the wall. She kissed her forehead and cheeks and mouth, drinking in the warm, sweet smell of baby skin and wispy hair. Phoebe looked healthy, clean, and well-fed. At least her parents were taking good care of her.

"I missed you so much," Lilly said to her. "And I love you more than anything in the world. Did you miss me, sweet pea?"

Phoebe grinned and Lilly pushed a stray lock of hair behind her small pink ear. Without looking, she knew her father was watching from the doorway.

"Aren't you worried about getting caught?" she said.

"Your mother is taking a nap."

"She's not my mother," Lilly said. She looked over at him. "And you're not my father."

He was carrying a tray, with food and a jug of water. Gray hair covered his head, and his tanned face resembled cracked leather. He looked like he had aged ten years since the day he came into The Albino Medium tent. Still, the remnants of a younger, handsomer man lingered in his strong jawline and rainwater blue eyes. He moved closer and set the tray on her bedside table.

"I'm sorry," he said in a miserable voice. "For everything."

"It's too late for that."

"I still need to say it."

He poured water into a mug and held it out to her. She struggled to sit up and he held the mug to her lips. She took a sip and nearly choked, sputtering and holding a hand to her mouth. Phoebe watched with worried eyes. When she stopped coughing, Lilly took a few more sips, then lay back down again, too weak to hold herself up any longer. Her father picked up half a sandwich from the tray and held it out to her.

She shook her head. "Not now." Phoebe snuggled in the crook of Lilly's arm and put her head on her shoulder. Lilly stroked her soft cheek and, keeping her eyes on her daughter, said to her father, "I just want to know one thing. Why did you let her do it?"

"I was out of town, remember? I didn't know you were gone until I came back. By then, it was too late."

505

"I'm not talking about selling me to the circus. I want to know why you let her lock me up in the first place. There was nothing wrong with me. My skin was different, that's all." She turned to see his reaction.

He leaned against the wall near the foot of her bed, pain and something that looked like shame lining his face. "I had no choice."

"Everyone has a choice."

"You don't understand. Your mother and I had been praying for you for years."

Tears blurred her vision. "Stop lying to me. I want the truth. You owe me that."

"It is the truth. Coralline was desperate to be a mother. And after her eighth miscarriage, she said she would have sold her soul to the devil to have a baby. We both know how hard it was for her to say that. When she found out she was four months along with you, she knew her prayers had finally been answered."

"Until she saw me."

He took a deep breath and sighed, his shoulders sagging as if telling the truth was the hardest thing he had ever done. It crossed her mind to point out that his suffering was nothing compared to what she had been through, was still going through, but she kept quiet. She was too exhausted to have that discussion. The only thing she needed to know was why. She gazed at Phoebe, who had fallen asleep next to her.

"It wasn't that simple," he said. "Your mother went into labor in the middle of a terrible storm. Roads were flooded, bridges had been washed out, and she was beside herself because we couldn't get to the hospital and the doctor couldn't come to us. She gave birth alone in our bedroom, refusing any help from me. Her labor went on all day and into the night, and when she stopped screaming I thought I'd lost her. All I could hear was you, wailing on the other side of the locked door. I was getting ready to break it down when she finally let me in and collapsed on the bed next to your bassinet. Her nightgown and the sheets were covered in blood, and she was white as a ghost. I thought she was dying. Then she looked at me with bloodshot eyes and said, "We have to get rid of it."

Lilly's lip trembled. "Is that supposed to make me feel better?"

"You don't understand. She thought she was being punished."

"For what?"

"For saying she'd make a deal with the devil."

"So she locked me in the attic."

He shook his head. "No, I did."

For a second, Lilly stopped breathing. She couldn't believe what she was hearing. All this time, she had blamed Momma for everything. All this time, she thought her mother hated her and her father was a spineless coward. "Why?" she managed.

"She wanted me to take you into the woods and leave you there."

Lilly bit her bottom lip and closed her eyes. What little strength she had left seemed to slip away. Her mother never meant to lock her away, she wanted her dead. She was beyond cold and cruel, she was willing to murder her own baby. And now she had stolen Phoebe. When Lilly found her voice, it was weak and rattling. "Because she thought I was a monster. And she was ashamed of me."

"No, because she thought she was being tested by God. She had made a deal with the devil and you terrified her, not because you were a monster, but because you were perfect. You were without a blemish or a spot, like the sacrificial lamb." He stepped closer. "Don't you see? I locked you in the attic to save you. By the time she discovered you were still alive, you were four months old. I warned her to leave you alone or I'd tell everyone the truth. We said you were stillborn. There was a funeral and . . ." He stopped and pressed his fingers into his temple, his brow creased.

Tears spilled down Lilly's cheeks. "Why didn't you do what she wanted? Why didn't you take me into the woods and leave me there?"

"Because what she was saying was crazy. I

508

thought she'd lost her mind and would come around after she got over the shock."

"But she didn't. So you left me in the attic."

He nodded.

"Why didn't you come looking for me after she sold me to the circus?"

"She said you ran away."

"And you believed her."

"At first I was afraid she'd done something . . ." He hesitated, then went on. "I kept asking her how you got out and found your way downstairs. She said you knocked her down and ran. She had bruises on her arm and scratches on her cheek."

"She was lying."

"I realized that when I saw a circus poster in Pennsylvania with your picture on it. I—"

"You knew where I was then," she said. "All this time."

"Yes."

"You didn't want to know if I was all right? If I was happy?"

He sighed. "Of course, I did. That's why I came to see you in the medium tent."

"That was six years after I disappeared. What took you so long?"

He shook his head. "You're wrong. I went to a show at least once a year. You never knew I was there, but I saw you in the freak show. I saw you on the white elephant." A sad smile played around his lips. "You looked so beautiful . . . and happy."

Lilly put her hands over her face. She had been happy. Finally. But then the tornado took the big top and Mr. Barlow sold JoJo and . . .

She couldn't think of anything else to say. She could barely string two thoughts together. The longer they talked, the weaker she grew.

"You must hate me," her father said.

She took her hands from her face and shook her head, weeping openly now. "I loved you, and Momma too, because I didn't know any better. But when I saw myself in a mirror for the first time and realized there was no reason to lock me up, I hated you both. For a long time. Now, you're not important enough to hate."

"I'm sorry," he said again. "For everything. I still love you. I never stopped, not for one minute."

On watery arms, she pushed herself up again, trying not to disturb Phoebe. "If you still love me, take me to the hospital. Give me back my daughter. Please. You can't let Momma take her. She's all I have."

He clenched his jaw, his temples pulsing in and out. "And then what, Lilly? What do you think the police would do if they found out we locked you up? What do you think would happen if they found out your mother sold you to a circus sideshow?"

"I won't tell them," she croaked. Her voice was giving out. She fell back on the pillow, breathing hard. "You have to give me a fighting chance. You owe me that much."

He moved closer, slowly shaking his head. "I hope you'll forgive me someday, but right now, the only thing I can do is promise to give your daughter the life you never had. If something happened to me and your mother, who would take care of her?" He reached over Lilly and lifted Phoebe from the bed. Lilly tried to hold on, but she was too weak. Her father pulled away and stood over her, Phoebe asleep in his arms, tears shining in his eyes. "You wouldn't want her sent to an orphanage, would you?" Before Lilly could say anything else, he walked out of the room and locked the door behind him.

Lilly threw her head back and screamed until she tasted blood.

CHAPTER 34
Julia

Spring had appeared by the time Julia's new house was finished—a modest cottage with a porch swing and windows overlooking the main barn and pasture. The daffodils were up, the apple trees were covered in white and pink blossoms, and the lilac trees were budding. Robins bounced along the muddy grass, and sparrows lined the fences and barn roof.

On her way across the lawn to the new barn construction site, Julia turned her face toward the sun, hopeful about the future for the first time in her life. But there were still so many things that needed to be done. The new barn was being built where Blackwood Manor once stood, the new fences needed to be put up, and the electricity was being turned on today. And she was thinking about getting a dog or two, maybe a yellow lab and a chocolate one too.

It was relief in the end, to have the manor gone. Now that she knew the truth, she wanted nothing more than to put the past behind her and start over. Living in the manor would have felt like living in a mausoleum, every little thing a reminder of the hurt and fear she felt as a child, of the guilt she felt when her "father" was drinking, and mostly, of the suffering her mother, Lilly, had endured. It would have seemed wrong to live there, not to mention too hard to live in a place that had witnessed such overwhelming sadness and cruelty. Besides, going through everything would have taken forever—reading all her father's papers, selling off the antiques, clearing out the attic. More importantly, making a loving home in the same house her mother had been kept prisoner and died in would have been impossible. Now the house and everything in it was gone, destroyed and purified by fire.

Although she tried not to, she thought about her grandparents a lot. When she told Fletcher what had happened, he said people who were cold and aggressive were not happy people. They treated others the way they did because they were unhappy within themselves. She wasn't sure if she believed him, but she appreciated his efforts to help. After all, she had been unhappy most of her life, and she always tried hard, maybe too hard, to be kind to others. She had heard the saying that those who hurt others had been hurt themselves. But she didn't believe that either. She had been hurt and knew how awful it felt, so she tried not to hurt anyone. Maybe some people never learned.

It was hard to feel sympathy for her grand-father, who let such horrible things happen under his own roof, then drank himself to death trying to forget what he had done to his daughter. It was even harder to find sympathy for her grandmother, who had gotten rid of one child and raised another without love. She supposed her grandmother didn't know how to love. That she was born flawed. It was the only explanation that made sense.

She supposed it was only natural to think often of Lilly. But her heart ached imagining the nightmare she endured, and the life they could have had together if things had turned out differently. She wished she had the picture of herself as a baby on her mother's lap, smiling and holding the calico elephant, but it was destroyed in the fire. Claude had no idea how long Lilly survived in the attic after her accident, but a heavy, nauseous feeling came over Julia when she realized it could have been weeks or months or even years. And she had been eating and sleeping and playing all that time, with no clue her mother was living in misery right upstairs. She wondered too what kind of mother Lilly would have been after being treated so cruelly by her parents. She liked to imagine her as a loving, affectionate woman who, like Julia, had learned to be gentle and kind as a result of what others had done to her.

While waiting for the new house to be built, she stayed in an inn on the interstate and went to the barn every day to work with Claude, Fletcher, and the horses. Bonnie Blue's foal, Samantha, was growing fast and strong, as was her best friend Molly, the filly Fletcher had brought home. Julia planned to keep them both on the farm for the rest of their lives. And after doing research on the racing industry, she made the decision that no more Blackwood Farm horses would be sold into racing.

When she wasn't at the farm, she was at the library doing research on The Barlow Brothers' Circus and Lilly. Along with the same clippings she had read in her grandfather's den, she found an article about two circus performers who had tried to steal an elephant. One was her mother, Lilly, and the other was a performer named Cole Holt. They were husband and wife. She also found a horrifying article about the execution of an elephant named Pepper, the same elephant her parents had been trying to steal, and another article about Lilly being injured while trying to save her. But she found no record of what happened to her father, Cole, and he remained a mystery. After reading about Lilly trying to save Pepper, she tried to think of a way to honor her mother's courage, and the solution came to her a few weeks ago.

Now, as she reached the new barn, Fletcher pulled in with a horse trailer. She went over to the driveway and waited, trying to ignore the nerves fluttering in her stomach. He got out of the truck and shut the door, grinning like a schoolboy.

"Do you have them?" she said.

"Sure do," Fletcher said. "And there's more where these came from."

He went around the back of the trailer and she followed. He unlocked the ramp, let it down, and reached for her hand. She smiled and took it, and he pulled her up the ramp. Together, they peered into the trailer.

A dozen fuzzy heads looked up at them, and several soft muzzles reached over the trailer door. Foals of all ages and colors—bays and palominos, chestnuts and paints, and one skinny runt the color of cinnamon—stood, wobbly-legged, in the straw.

Julia's eyes grew moist. "They're beautiful."

"And they're alive because of you," Fletcher said.

She grinned and he pulled her to him. Thinking it was a congratulatory hug, she laughed. But then he lowered his mouth to hers and kissed her, hard on the lips. At first she moved away, surprised; then she kissed him back. It was a short kiss, but they both recognized the affection behind it. When they drew apart, they reached in to pet the foals at the same time and smiled.

Julia's heart swelled with pride and love and

something that felt like joy. For the first time that she could remember, she felt elation. This was the beginning of a new future, and she could think of no better way to live her life than to save these helpless creatures. She and Fletcher and Claude would rescue nurse mare foals and other horses in Lilly's memory. They would care for them and train them until they were old enough to be adopted into loving homes. In the meantime, the horses would be free to run in the fields, to play and jump and sleep on the grass, and chase away the ghosts of Blackwood Manor.

AUTHOR'S NOTE

During the writing of *The Life She Was Given*, I relied on the following books: *American Sideshow* by Marc Hartzman; *Shocked and Amazed: On & Off the Midway* by James Taylor; *Step Right This Way: The Photographs of Edward J. Kelty;* and *Carney Folk: The World's Weirdest Sideshow Acts* by Francine Hornberger.

A Reading Group Guide

THE LIFE SHE WAS GIVEN

Ellen Marie Wiseman

ABOUT THIS GUIDE

The suggested questions are included to enhance your group's reading of Ellen Marie Wiseman's *The Life She Was Given.*

Discussion Questions

1. In the beginning of the book, Lilly has never stepped foot outside the attic of Blackwood Manor. Yet she dreams of escaping and exploring the outside world. What effect do you think being locked up for the first ten years of her life had on her? Do you think it's possible for a child in that situation to develop normally? When Momma finally lets her out, Lilly is frightened and wants to return to the attic. Why do you think she feels that way?

2. Julia was brought up believing bad things would happen if she didn't behave. What effect do you think that belief had on her relationships with other people? Do you think she was a people-pleaser? Why or why not? How do you think she changed over the course of the novel? What were the most important events that facilitated those changes?

3. Momma is strict, cold, and physically abusive. But even after she sells Lilly to the circus sideshow, Lilly still loves and misses her. Do you think that's realistic? Why or why not?

4. Julia can't help but study the interactions between mothers and daughters. She is drawn to watching people who clearly love each other, especially parents and their children whose faces light up with affection and recognition of their unconditional love. She wonders what that feels like. How do you think that fascination with parental love affected her decisions concerning the horses at Blackwood Farm? What events revealed how she felt about them?

5. How much of a role do you think religion played in Momma's decision to keep Lilly locked in the attic? How much of a role do

you think shame played? Have you ever heard stories of parents hiding their mentally or physically handicapped children in an attic or back bedroom? Do you think that still happens today?

6. Before she knows the truth, Julia briefly wonders if Lilly would have been better off if she had "gotten help." What do you think would have happened to Lilly if she had been sent away instead of locked in the attic? Considering the time period of the story, would she have been better off or worse? Why?

7. How long did it take for you to figure out what was "wrong" with Lilly? Were you surprised when you learned the truth? What do you think the real reason was behind Momma's decision to sell Lilly to the sideshow? Was it money, or something else?

8. When Momma takes Lilly out of the house the first time, she gives her a jacket despite the fact that she's selling her to the circus and it's a warm summer night. Why do you think she does it? What do you think it means, if anything? What do you think would have happened to Lilly if she had been able to get away from Momma that night? Would she have survived? How?

9. Why do you think Julia was so determined to take good care of the horses and the farm? Why do you think she wanted to prove herself to Claude?

10. Lilly feels like she has a lot in common with the circus animals. Why do you think that is? What does she have in common with Pepper? What about JoJo? Is there a difference between what she has in common with each of them?

11. Both Momma and Merrick used fear to keep Lilly from trying to escape. In what ways did they use it similarly? In what ways did they use it differently?

12. Claude knew the truth about Lilly all along. Why do you think he kept it a secret? Do you agree with his reasoning? What would you have done if you saw Momma taking Lilly into the woods, then coming back without her? What do you think made Claude change his mind about telling Julia the truth? How did you feel about him in the beginning of the book? How did you feel about him at the end?

13. Lilly goes from being locked in an attic to performing in front of thousands of people. What fears did she need to conquer to make that transition? What other changes did

she make to survive in the circus? What aspects of her earlier life do you think were hardest for her to overcome?

14. In the 1870s, P. T. Barnum was one of the first showmen to take a collection of oddities and human marvels on the road with his circus. Back then, the sideshow created quite a sensation and became a popular form of entertainment. In the heyday of the sideshow, human curiosities were respected as the bread and butter of the circus, and revered all over the world. The freaks were royalty, not victims or monsters. Certainly there was exploitation, as in the case of Daisy and Violet Hilton, Siamese twins who were kept in a cage, beaten, and passed down in their aunt's estate like a piece of old jewelry. But for the most part, the sideshow provided the opportunity for people who couldn't make a living in the traditional ways to stand on their own two feet, instead of slowly dying in institutions. Eventually the appeal of sideshows declined because of various factors, including increased medical knowledge, political correctness, and the belief that disease and abnormalities should evoke pity rather than wonder. Have you ever been to a sideshow? How did it make you feel? What do you think of people brave enough

to expose their vulnerabilities to the world? If you were born with an anomaly or deformity, would you be willing to let people stare at you to make a living?

15. What did you think of Lilly's father when you first met him? How did your perception of him change over the course of the book? What could he have done differently? He attends the circus once a year to see Lilly, but she never knows he's there. How did you feel when he showed up in her tent? Were you surprised by his confession at the end of the story?

16. Pepper is based on a real elephant, Mary, who was hanged by the neck from a railcar-mounted industrial crane in 1916 for killing an inexperienced trainer after he prodded her behind the ear with a hook when she reached down to nibble on a watermelon rind. The first attempt to hang Mary resulted in a snapped chain, causing Mary to fall and break her hip as dozens of children fled in terror. The gravely wounded elephant died during a second attempt at execution and was buried beside the tracks. A veterinarian examined Mary after the hanging and determined she had a severely infected tooth in the precise spot where the trainer had prodded her. When Pepper kills Merrick

for trying to take JoJo, Lilly is devastated because she knows Pepper is going to be punished. She hates the fact that people get mad at animals for acting like animals. Her worst fears come true when the crowd wants Pepper killed and Mr. Barlow makes the decision to execute her. Do you think animals should be killed for injuring or killing humans? Does it depend on the circumstance, for instance, if an animal is being caged, forced to perform, or a human threatens the animal's young or encroaches on its territory? Do you think it's okay to kill an animal based solely on its potential to be dangerous?

17. What do you think Lilly's life would have been like if Momma had never sold her to the circus? How long do you think she would have lived in the attic? Do you think she would have eventually escaped? How? What would you have done if you were in that situation?

18. Besides honoring Lilly, why do you think Julia started the horse rescue? What do you think Julia's life was like after she discovered the truth about her family?

Books are produced in the United States using U.S.-based materials

Books are printed using a revolutionary new process called THINKtech™ that lowers energy usage by 70% and increases overall quality

Books are durable and flexible because of smythe-sewing

Paper is sourced using environmentally responsible foresting methods and the paper is acid-free

Center Point Large Print
600 Brooks Road / PO Box 1
Thorndike, ME 04986-0001 USA

(207) 568-3717

US & Canada:
1 800 929-9108
www.centerpointlargeprint.com